THE BOOK OF LOST TALES
Part I

THE HISTORY OF MIDDLE-EARTH

I
THE BOOK OF LOST TALES, PART ONE

II
THE BOOK OF LOST TALES, PART TWO
(in preparation)

III
THE LAYS OF BELERIAND
(in preparation)

J. R. R. TOLKIEN

THE
BOOK OF LOST TALES

PART I

Edited by Christopher Tolkien

HOUGHTON MIFFLIN COMPANY
BOSTON

First American edition 1984

Copyright © 1983 by Frank Richard Williamson and Christopher Reuel Tolkien
as Executors of the Estate of J. R. R. Tolkien

Library of Congress Cataloging in Publication Data

Tolkien, J. R. R. (John Ronald Reuel), 1892–1973.
The book of lost tales.

(The History of Middle-earth ; 1-   )
Includes index.
1. Tolkien, Christopher. II. Title. III. Series
Tolkien, J. R. R. (John Ronald Reuel), 1892–1973.
History of Middle-earth ; 1.
PR6039.032B6   1984   823′.912   83-12782
ISBN 0-395-35439-0 (v. 1)

Printed in the United States of America

S 10 9 8 7 6 5 4 3 2 1

CONTENTS

FOREWORD

The Book of Lost Tales, written between sixty and seventy years ago, was the first substantial work of imaginative literature by J. R. R. Tolkien, and the first emergence in narrative of the Valar, of the Children of Ilúvatar, Elves and Men, of the Dwarves and the Orcs, and of the lands in which their history is set, Valinor beyond the western ocean, and Middle-earth, the 'Great Lands' between the seas of east and west. Some fifty-seven years after my father ceased to work on the *Lost Tales*, *The Silmarillion*,* profoundly transformed from its distant forerunner, was published; and six years have passed since then. This Foreword seems a suitable opportunity to remark on some aspects of both works.

The Silmarillion is commonly said to be a 'difficult' book, needing explanation and guidance on how to 'approach' it; and in this it is contrasted to *The Lord of the Rings*. In Chapter 7 of his book *The Road to Middle-earth* Professor T. A. Shippey accepts that this is so ('*The Silmarillion* could never be anything but hard to read', p. 201), and expounds his view of why it should be. A complex discussion is not treated justly when it is extracted, but in his view the reasons are essentially two (p. 185). In the first place, there is in *The Silmarillion* no 'mediation' of the kind provided by the hobbits (so, in *The Hobbit*, 'Bilbo acts as the link between modern times and the archaic world of dwarves and dragons'). My father was himself well aware that the absence of hobbits would be felt as a lack, were 'The Silmarillion' to be published – and not only by readers with a particular liking for them. In a letter written in 1956 (*The Letters of J. R. R. Tolkien*, p. 238), soon after the publication of *The Lord of the Rings*, he said:

> I do not think it would have the appeal of the L.R. – no hobbits! Full of mythology, and elvishness, and all that 'heigh stile' (as Chaucer might say), which has been so little to the taste of many reviewers.

In 'The Silmarillion' the draught is pure and unmixed; and the reader is worlds away from such 'mediation', such a deliberate collison (far more than a matter of styles) as that produced in the meeting between King Théoden and Pippin and Merry in the ruins of Isengard:

> 'Farewell, my hobbits! May we meet again in my house! There you shall sit beside me and tell me all that your hearts desire: the deeds of

* When the name is printed in italics, I refer to the work as published; when in inverted commas, to the work in a more general way, in any or all of its forms.

your grandsires, as far as you can reckon them . . .'

The hobbits bowed low. 'So that is the King of Rohan!' said Pippin in an undertone. 'A fine old fellow. Very polite.'

In the second place,

Where *The Silmarillion* differs from Tolkien's earlier works is in its refusal to accept novelistic convention. Most novels (including *The Hobbit* and *The Lord of the Rings*) pick a character to put in the foreground, like Frodo and Bilbo, and then tell the story as it happens to him. The novelist of course is inventing the story, and so retains omniscience: he can explain, or show, what is 'really' happening and contrast it with the limited perception of his character.

There is, then, and very evidently, a question of literary 'taste' (or literary 'habituation') involved; and also a question of literary 'disappointment' – the '(mistaken) disappointment in those who wanted a second *Lord of the Rings*' to which Professor Shippey refers. This has even produced a sense of outrage – in one case formulated to me in the words 'It's like *the Old Testament*!': a dire condemnation against which, clearly, there can be no appeal (though this reader cannot have got very far before being overcome by the comparison). Of course, 'The Silmarillion' was intended to move the heart and the imagination, directly, and without peculiar effort or the possession of unusual faculties; but its mode is inherent, and it may be doubted whether any 'approach' to it can greatly aid those who find it unapproachable.

There is a third consideration (which Professor Shippey does not indeed advance in the same context):

One quality which [*The Lord of the Rings*] has in abundance is the Beowulfian 'impression of depth', created just as in the old epic by songs and digressions like Aragorn's lay of Tinúviel, Sam Gamgee's allusions to the Silmaril and the Iron Crown, Elrond's account of Celebrimbor, and dozens more. This, however, is a quality of *The Lord of the Rings*, not of the inset stories. To tell these in their own right and expect them to retain the charm they got from their larger setting would be a terrible error, an error to which Tolkien would be more sensitive than any man alive. As he wrote in a revealing letter dated 20 September 1963:

I am doubtful myself about the undertaking [to write *The Silmarillion*]. Part of the attraction of The L.R. is, I think, due to the glimpses of a large history in the background: an attraction like that of viewing far off an unvisited island, or seeing the towers of a distant city gleaming in a sunlit mist. To go there is to destroy the magic, unless new unattainable vistas are again revealed. (*Letters*, p. 333)

To go there is to destroy the magic. As for the revealing of 'new un-attainable vistas', the problem there – as Tolkien must have thought many times – was that in *The Lord of the Rings* Middle-earth was already old, with a vast weight of history behind it. *The Silmarillion*, though, in its longer form, was bound to begin at the beginning. How could 'depth' be created when you had nothing to reach further back to?

The letter quoted here certainly shows that my father felt this, or perhaps rather one should say, at times felt this, to be a problem. Nor was it a new thought: while he was writing *The Lord of the Rings*, in 1945, he said in a letter to me (*Letters*, p. 110):

A story must be told or there'll be no story, yet it is the untold stories that are most moving. I think you are moved by *Celebrimbor* because it conveys a sudden sense of endless *untold* stories: mountains seen far away, never to be climbed, distant trees (like Niggle's) never to be approached – or if so only to become 'near trees' . . .

This matter is perfectly illustrated for me by Gimli's song in Moria, where great names out of the ancient world appear utterly remote:

> The world was fair, the mountains tall
> In Elder Days before the fall
> Of mighty kings in Nargothrond
> And Gondolin, who now beyond
> The Western Seas have passed away . . .

'I like that!' said Sam. 'I should like to learn it. *In Moria, in Khazad-dûm.* But it makes the darkness seem heavier, thinking of all those lamps.' By his enthusiastic 'I like that!' Sam not only 'mediates' (and engagingly 'Gamgifies') the 'high', the mighty kings of Nargothrond and Gondolin, Durin on his carven throne, but places them at once at an even remoter distance, a magical distance that it might well seem (*at that moment*) destructive to traverse.

Professor Shippey says that 'to tell [the stories that are only alluded to in *The Lord of the Rings*] in their own right and expect them to retain the charm they got from their larger setting would be a terrible error'. The 'error' presumably lies in the holding of such an expectation, if the stories were told, not in the telling of the stories at all; and it is apparent that Professor Shippey sees my father as wondering, in 1963, whether he should or should not put pen to paper, for he expands the words of the letter, 'I am doubtful myself about the undertaking', to mean 'the undertaking to write *The Silmarillion*'. But when my father said this he was not – most emphatically not – referring to the work itself, which was in any case already written, and much of it many times over (the allusions in *The Lord of the Rings* are not illusory): what was in question for him, as he said earlier in this same letter, was its *presentation*, in a publication, *after* the appearance of *The Lord of the Rings*, when, as he thought, the right time to make it known was already gone.

> I am afraid all the same that the presentation will need a lot of work, and I work so slowly. The legends have to be worked over (they were written at different times, some many years ago) and made consistent; and they have to be integrated with The L.R.; and they have to be given some progressive shape. No simple device, like a journey and a quest, is available.
>
> I am doubtful myself about the undertaking . . .

When after his death the question arose of publishing 'The Silmarillion' in some form, I attached no importance to this doubt. The effect that 'the glimpses of a large history in the background' have in *The Lord of the Rings* is incontestable and of the utmost importance, but I did not think that the 'glimpses' used there with such art should preclude all further knowledge of the 'large history'.

The literary 'impression of depth . . . created by songs and digressions' cannot be made a criterion by which a work in a wholly different mode is measured: this would be to treat the history of the Elder Days as of value primarily or even solely in the artistic use made of it in *The Lord of the Rings*. Nor should the device of a backward movement in imagined time to dimly apprehended events, whose attraction lies in their very dimness, be understood mechanically, as if a fuller account of the mighty kings of Nargothrond and Gondolin would imply a dangerously near approach to the bottom of the well, while an account of the Creation would signify the striking of the bottom and a definitive running-out of 'depth' – 'nothing to reach further back to'.

This, surely, is not how things work, or at least not how they need work. 'Depth' in this sense implies a relation between different temporal layers or levels within the same world. Provided that the reader has a place, a point of vantage, *in the imagined time* from which to look back, the extreme oldness of the extremely old can be made apparent and made to be felt continuously. And the very fact that *The Lord of the Rings* establishes such a powerful sense of a real time-structure (far more powerful than can be done by mere chronological assertion, tables of dates) provides this necessary vantage-point. To read *The Silmarillion* one must place oneself imaginatively at the time of the ending of the Third Age – within Middle-earth, looking back: at the temporal point of Sam Gamgee's 'I like that!' – adding, 'I should like to know more about it'. Moreover the compendious or epitomising form and manner of *The Silmarillion*, with its suggestion of ages of poetry and 'lore' behind it, strongly evokes a sense of 'untold tales', even in the telling of them; 'distance' is never lost. There is no narrative urgency, the pressure and fear of the immediate and unknown event. We do not actually see the Silmarils as we see the Ring. The maker of 'The Silmarillion', as he himself said of the author of *Beowulf*, 'was telling of things already old and weighted with regret, and he expended his art in making keen that touch upon the heart which sorrows have that are both poignant and remote'.

As has now been fully recorded, my father greatly desired to publish 'The Silmarillion' together with *The Lord of the Rings*. I say nothing of its practicability at the time, nor do I make any guesses at the subsequent fate of such a much longer combined work, quadrilogy or tetralogy, or at the different courses that my father might then have taken – for the further development of 'The Silmarillion' itself, the history of the Elder Days, would have been arrested. But by its posthumous publication nearly a quarter of a century later the natural order of presentation of the whole 'Matter of Middle-earth' was inverted; and it is certainly debatable whether it was wise to publish in 1977 a version of the primary 'legendarium' standing on its own and claiming, as it were, to be self-explanatory. The published work has no 'framework', no suggestion of what it is and how (within the imagined world) it came to be. This I now think to have been an error.

The letter of 1963 quoted above shows my father pondering the mode in which the legends of the Elder Days might be presented. The original mode, that of *The Book of Lost Tales*, in which a Man, Eriol, comes after a great voyage over the ocean to the island where the Elves dwell and learns their history from their own lips, had (by degrees) fallen away. When my father died in 1973 'The Silmarillion' was in a characteristic state of disarray: the earlier parts much revised or largely rewritten, the concluding parts still as he had left them some twenty years before; but in the latest writing there is no trace or suggestion of any 'device' or 'framework' in which it was to be set. I think that in the end he concluded that nothing would serve, and no more would be said beyond an explanation of how (within the imagined world) it came to be recorded.

In the original edition of *The Lord of the Rings* Bilbo gave to Frodo at Rivendell as his parting gift 'some books of lore that he had made at various times, written in his spidery hand, and labelled on their red backs: *Translations from the Elvish, by B.B.*' In the second edition (1966) 'some books' was changed to 'three books', and in the *Note on the Shire Records* added to the Prologue in that edition my father said that the content of 'the three large volumes bound in red leather' was preserved in that copy of the Red Book of Westmarch which was made in Gondor by the King's Writer Findegil in the year 172 of the Fourth Age; and also that

> These three volumes were found to be a work of great skill and learning in which ... [Bilbo] had used all the sources available to him in Rivendell, both living and written. But since they were little used by Frodo, being almost entirely concerned with the Elder Days, no more is said of them here.

In *The Complete Guide to Middle-earth* Robert Foster says: '*Quenta Silmarillion* was no doubt one of Bilbo's *Translations from the Elvish* preserved in the Red Book of Westmarch.' So also I have assumed: the 'books of lore' that Bilbo gave to Frodo provided in the end the solution: they were 'The Silmarillion'. But apart from the evidence cited here, there is, so far as I know, no other statement on this matter anywhere in my father's writings; and (wrongly, as I think now) I was reluctant to step into the breach and make definite what I only surmised.

The choice before me, in respect of 'The Silmarillion', was threefold. I could withhold it indefinitely from publication, on the ground that the work was incomplete and incoherent between its parts. I could accept the nature of the work as it stood, and, to quote my Foreword to the book, 'attempt to present the diversity of the materials – to show "The Silmarillion" as in truth a continuing and evolving creation extending over more than half a century'; and that, as I have said in *Unfinished Tales* (p. 1), would have entailed 'a complex of divergent texts interlinked by commentary' – a far larger undertaking than those words suggest. In the event, I chose the third course, 'to work out a single text, selecting and arranging in such a way as seemed to me to produce the most coherent and internally self-consistent narrative'. Having come, at length, to that decision, all the editorial labour of myself and of Guy Kay who assisted me was directed to the end that my father had stated in the letter of 1963: 'The legends have to be worked over . . . and made consistent; and they have to be integrated with the L.R.' Since the object was to present 'The Silmarillion' as 'a completed and cohesive entity' (though that could not in the nature of the case be entirely successful), it followed that there would be in the published book no exposition of the complexities of its history.

Whatever may be thought of this matter, the result, which I by no means foresaw, has been to add a further dimension of obscurity to 'The Silmarillion', in that uncertainty about the age of the work, whether it is to be regarded as 'early' or 'late' or in what proportions, and about the degree of editorial intrusion and manipulation (or even invention), is a stumbling-block and a source of much misapprehension. Professor Randel Helms, in *Tolkien and the Silmarils* (p. 93), has stated the question thus:

Anyone interested, as I am, in the growth of *The Silmarillion* will want to study *Unfinished Tales*, not only for its intrinsic value but also because its relationship to the former provides what will become a classic example of a long-standing problem in literary criticism: what, really, *is* a literary work? Is it what the author intended (or may have intended) it to be, or is it what a later editor makes of it? The problem becomes especially intense for the practising critic when, as happened with *The Silmarillion*, a writer dies before finishing his work and leaves more than one version of some of its parts, which then find publication elsewhere. Which version will the critic approach as the 'real' story?

But he also says: 'Christopher Tolkien has helped us in this instance by honestly pointing out that *The Silmarillion* in the shape that we have it is the invention of the son not the father'; and this is a serious misapprehension to which my words have given rise.

Again, Professor Shippey, while accepting (p. 169) my assurance that a 'very high proportion' of the 1937 'Silmarillion' text remained into the published version, is nonetheless elsewhere clearly reluctant to see it as other than a 'late' work, even the latest work of its author. And in an article entitled 'The Text of *The Hobbit*: Putting Tolkien's Notes in Order' (English Studies in Canada, VII, 2, Summer 1981) Constance B. Hieatt concludes that 'it is very clear indeed that we shall never be able to see the progressive steps of authorial thinking behind *The Silmarillion*'.

But beyond the difficulties and the obscurities, what is certain and very evident is that for the begetter of Middle-earth and Valinor there was a deep coherence and vital interrelation between all its times, places, and beings, whatever the literary modes, and however protean some parts of the conception might seem when viewed over a long lifetime. He himself understood very well that many who read *The Lord of the Rings* with enjoyment would never wish to regard Middle-earth as more than the mise-en-scène of the story, and would delight in the sensation of 'depth' without wishing to explore the deep places. But the 'depth' is not of course an illusion, like a line of imitation book-backs with no books inside them; and Quenya and Sindarin are comprehensive structures. There are explorations to be conducted in this world with perfect right quite irrespective of literary-critical considerations; and it is proper to attempt to comprehend its structure in its largest extent, from the myth of its Creation. Every person, every feature of the imagined world that seemed significant to its author is then worthy of attention in its own right, Manwë or Fëanor no less than Gandalf or Galadriel, the Silmarils no less than the Rings; the Great Music, the divine hierarchies, the abodes of the Valar, the fates of the Children of Ilúvatar, are essential elements in the perception of the whole. Such enquiries are in no way illegitimate in principle; they arise from an acceptance of the imagined world as an object of contemplation or study valid as many other objects of contemplation or study in the all too unimaginary world. It was in this opinion and in the knowledge that others shared it that I made the collection called *Unfinished Tales*.

But the author's vision of his own vision underwent a continual slow shifting, shedding and enlarging: only in *The Hobbit* and *The Lord of the Rings* did parts of it emerge to become fixed in print, in his own lifetime. The study of Middle-earth and Valinor is thus complex; for the object of the study was not stable, but exists, as it were 'longitudinally' in time (the author's lifetime), and not only 'transversely' in time, as a printed book that undergoes no essential further change. By the publication of 'The Silmarillion' the 'longitudinal' was cut 'transversely', and a kind of finality imposed.

★

This rather rambling discussion is an attempt to explain my primary motives in offering *The Book of Lost Tales* for publication. It is the first step in presenting the 'longitudinal' view of Middle-earth and Valinor: when the huge geographical expansion, swelling out from the centre and (as it were) thrusting Beleriand into the west, was far off in the future; when there were no 'Elder Days' ending in the drowning of Beleriand, for there were as yet no other Ages of the World; when the Elves were still 'fairies', and even Rúmil the learned Noldo was far removed from the magisterial 'loremasters' of my father's later years. In *The Book of Lost Tales* the princes of the Noldor have scarcely emerged, nor the Grey-elves of Beleriand; Beren is an Elf, not a Man, and his captor, the ultimate precursor of Sauron in that rôle, is a monstrous cat inhabited by a fiend; the Dwarves are an evil people; and the historical relations of Quenya and Sindarin were quite differently conceived. These are a few especially notable features, but such a list could be greatly prolonged. On the other hand, there was already a firm underlying structure that would endure. Moreover in the history of the history of Middle-earth the development was seldom by outright rejection − far more often it was by subtle transformation in stages, so that the growth of the legends (the process, for instance, by which the Nargothrond story made contact with that of Beren and Lúthien, a contact not even hinted at in the *Lost Tales*, though both elements were present) can seem like the growth of legends among peoples, the product of many minds and generations.

The Book of Lost Tales was begun by my father in 1916−17 during the First War, when he was 25 years old, and left incomplete several years later. It is the starting-point, at least in fully-formed narrative, of the history of Valinor and Middle-earth; but before the *Tales* were complete he turned to the composition of long poems, the *Lay of Leithian* in rhyming couplets (the story of Beren and Lúthien), and *The Children of Húrin* in alliterative verse. The prose form of the 'mythology' began again from a new starting-point* in a quite brief synopsis, or 'Sketch' as he called it, written in 1926 and expressly intended to provide the necessary background of knowledge for the understanding of the alliterative poem. The further written development of the prose form proceeded from that 'Sketch' in a direct line to the version of 'The Silmarillion' which was nearing completion towards the end of 1937, when my father broke off to send it as it stood to Allen and Unwin in November of that year; but there were also important side-branches and subordinate texts composed in the 1930s, as the *Annals of Valinor* and the *Annals of Beleriand* (fragments of which are extant also in the Old English translations made by Ælfwine (Eriol)), the cosmological account called *Ambarkanta*, the

---

* Only in the case of *The Music of the Ainur* was there a direct development, manuscript to manuscript, from *The Book of Lost Tales* to the later forms; for *The Music of the Ainur* became separated off and continued as an independent work.

Shape of the World, by Rúmil, and the *Lhammas* or 'Account of Tongues', by Pengolod of Gondolin. Thereafter the history of the First Age was laid aside for many years, until *The Lord of the Rings* was completed, but in the years preceding its actual publication my father returned to 'The Silmarillion' and associated works with great vigour.

This edition of the *Lost Tales* in two parts is to be, as I hope, the beginning of a series that will carry the history further through these later writings, in verse and prose; and in this hope I have applied to this present book an 'overriding' title intended to cover also those that may follow it, though I fear that 'The History of Middle-earth' may turn out to have been over-ambitious. In any case this title does not imply a 'History' in the conventional sense: my intention is to give complete or largely complete texts, so that the books will be more like a series of editions. I do not set myself as a primary object the unravelling of many single and separate threads, but rather the making available of works that can and should be read as wholes.

The tracing of this long evolution is to me of deep interest, and I hope that it may prove so to others who have a taste for this kind of enquiry: whether the major transformations of plot or cosmological theory, or such a detail as the premonitory appearance of Legolas Greenleaf the keen-sighted in the tale of *The Fall of Gondolin*. But these old manuscripts are by no means of interest only for the study of origins. Much is to be found there that my father never (so far as one can tell) expressly rejected, and it is to be remembered that 'The Silmarillion', from the 1926 'Sketch' onwards, was written as an abridgement or epitome, giving the substance of much longer works (whether existing in fact, or not) in a smaller compass. The highly archaic manner devised for his purpose was no fustian: it had range and great vigour, peculiarly apt to convey the magical and eerie nature of the early Elves, but as readily turned to the sarcastic, sneering Melko or the affairs of Ulmo and Ossë. These last approach at times a comic conception, and are delivered in a rapid and lively language that did not survive in the gravity of my father's later 'Silmarillion' prose (so Ossë 'fares about in a foam of business' as he anchors the islands to the sea-bed, the cliffs of Tol Eressëa new-filled with the first sea-birds 'are full of a chattering and a smell of fish, and great conclaves are held upon its ledges', and when the Shoreland Elves are at last drawn over the sea to Valinor Ulmo marvellously 'fares at the rear in his fishy car and trumpets loudly for the discomfiture of Ossë').

The *Lost Tales* never reached or even approached a form in which my father could have considered their publication before he abandoned them; they were experimental and provisional, and the tattered notebooks in which they were written were bundled away and left unlooked at as the years passed. To present them in a printed book has raised many thorny editorial problems. In the first place, the manuscripts are intrinsically very difficult: partly because much of the text was written rapidly in pencil and is now in places extremely hard to read, requiring a magnifying glass and much patience, not always rewarded. But also in some of the *Tales* my father erased the original pencilled text and wrote a revised version over it in ink – and since at this period he used bound notebooks rather than loose sheets, he was liable to find himself short of space: so detached portions of tales were written in the middle of other tales, and in places a fearsome textual jigsaw puzzle was produced.

Secondly, the *Lost Tales* were not all written progressively one after the other in the sequence of the narrative; and (inevitably) my father began a new arrangement and revision of the *Tales* while the work was still in progress. *The Fall of Gondolin* was the first of the tales told to Eriol to be composed, and the *Tale of Tinúviel* the second, but the events of those tales take place towards the end of the history; on the other hand the extant texts are later revisions. In some cases nothing earlier than the revised form can now be read; in some both forms are extant for all, or a part, of their length; in some there is only a preliminary draft; and in some there is no formed narrative at all, but only notes and projections. After much experimentation I have found that no method of presentation is feasible but to set out the *Tales* in the sequence of the narrative.

And finally, as the writing of the *Tales* progressed, relations were changed, new conceptions entered, and the development of the languages *pari passu* with the narrative led to continual revision of names.

An edition that takes account of such complexities, as this does, rather than attempt to smooth them artificially away, is liable to be an intricate and crabbed thing, in which the reader is never left alone for a moment. I have attempted to make the *Tales* themselves accessible and uncluttered while providing a fairly full account, for those who want it, of the actual textual evidences. To achieve this I have drastically reduced the quantity of annotation to the texts in these ways: the many changes made to names are all recorded, but they are lumped together at the end of each tale, not recorded individually at each occurrence (the places where the names occur can be found from the Index); almost all annotation concerned with content is taken up into, or boiled down into, a commentary or short essay following each tale; and almost all linguistic comment (primarily the etymology of names) is collected in an Appendix on Names at the end of the book, where will be found a great deal of information relating to the earliest stages of the 'Elvish' languages. In this way the numbered notes are very largely restricted to variants and divergences found in other texts, and the reader who does not wish to trouble with these can read the *Tales* knowing that that is almost all that he is missing.

The commentaries are limited in their scope, being mostly concerned to discuss the implications of what is said within the context of the *Tales* themselves, and to compare them with the published *Silmarillion*. I have eschewed parallels, sources, influences; and have mostly avoided the complexities of the development between the *Lost Tales* and the published work (since to indicate these even cursorily would, I think, be distracting), treating the matter in a simplified way, as between two fixed points. I do not suppose for one moment that my analyses will prove either altogether just or altogether accurate, and there must be clues to the solution of puzzling features in the *Tales* which I have failed to observe. There is also included a short glossary of words occurring in the *Tales* and poems that are obsolete, archaic, or rare.

The texts are given in a form very close to that of the original manuscripts. Only the most minor and obvious slips have been silently corrected; where sentences fall awkwardly, or where there is a lack of grammatical cohesion, as is sometimes the case in the parts of the *Tales* that never got beyond a first rapid draft, I have let them stand. I have allowed myself greater freedom in providing punctuation, for my father when writing at speed often punctuated erratically or not at all; and I have gone further than he did in consistency of capitalisation. I have adopted, though hesitantly, a consistent system of accentuation for Elvish names. My father wrote, for instance: *Palûrien, Palúrien, Palurien*; *Ōnen, Onen*; *Kôr, Kor*. I have used the acute accent for macron, circumflex, and acute (and occasional grave) accents of the original texts, but the circumflex on monosyllables – thus *Palúrien, Ónen, Kôr*: the same system, at least to the eye, as in later Sindarin.

Lastly, the division of this edition into two parts is entirely due to the length of the *Tales*. The edition is conceived as a whole, and I hope that the second part will appear within a year of the first; but each part has its own Index and Appendix on Names. The second part contains what are in many respects the most interesting of the *Tales*: *Tinúviel, Turambar* (Túrin), *The Fall of Gondolin*, and the *Tale of the Nauglafring* (the Necklace of the Dwarves); outlines for the *Tale of Eärendel* and the conclusion of the work; and *Ælfwine of England*.

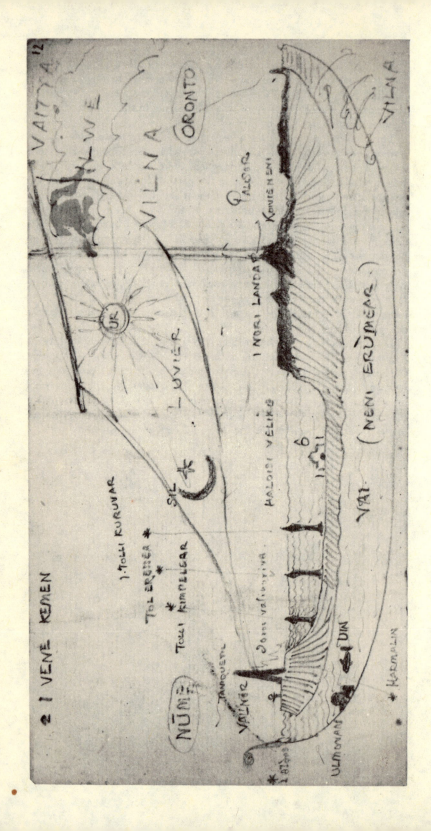

I

THE COTTAGE OF LOST PLAY

On the cover of one of the now very battered 'High School Exercise Books' in which some of the *Lost Tales* were composed my father wrote: *The Cottage of Lost Play, which introduceth [the] Book of Lost Tales*; and on the cover is also written, in my mother's hand, her initials, E.M.T., and a date, Feb. 12th 1917. In this book the tale was written out by my mother; and it is a fair copy of a very rough pencilled manuscript of my father's on loose sheets, which were placed inside the cover. Thus the date of the actual composition of this tale could have been, but probably was not, earlier than the winter of 1916–17. The fair copy follows the original text precisely; some further changes, mostly slight (other than in the matter of names), were then made to the fair copy. The text follows here in its final form.

Now it happened on a certain time that a traveller from far countries, a man of great curiosity, was by desire of strange lands and the ways and dwellings of unaccustomed folk brought in a ship as far west even as the Lonely Island, Tol Eressëa in the fairy speech, but which the Gnomes[1] call Dor Faidwen, the Land of Release, and a great tale hangs thereto.

Now one day after much journeying he came as the lights of evening were being kindled in many a window to the feet of a hill in a broad and woody plain. He was now near the centre of this great island and for many days had wandered its roads, stopping each night at what dwelling of folk he might chance upon, were it hamlet or good town, about the hour of eve at the kindling of candles. Now at that time the desire of new sights is least, even in one whose heart is that of an explorer; and then even such a son of Eärendel as was this wayfarer turns his thoughts rather to supper and to rest and the telling of tales before the time of bed and sleep is come.

Now as he stood at the foot of the little hill there came a faint breeze and then a flight of rooks above his head in the clear even light. The sun had some time sunk beyond the boughs of the elms that stood as far as eye could look about the plain, and some time had its last gold faded through the leaves and slipped across the glades to sleep beneath the roots and dream till dawn.

Now these rooks gave voice of home-coming above him, and with

a swift turn came to their dwelling in the tops of some high elms at
the summit of this hill. Then thought Eriol (for thus did the people
of the island after call him, and its purport is 'One who dreams alone',
but of his former names the story nowhere tells): 'The hour of rest
is at hand, and though I know not even the name of this fair-seeming
town upon a little hill here I will seek rest and lodging and go no
further till the morrow, nor go even then perchance, for the place
seems fair and its breezes of a good savour. To me it has the air of
holding many secrets of old and wonderful and beautiful things in
its treasuries and noble places and in the hearts of those that dwell
within its walls.'

Now Eriol was coming from the south and a straight road ran
before him bordered at one side with a great wall of grey stone topped
with many flowers, or in places overhung with great dark yews.
Through them as he climbed the road he could see the first stars shine
forth, even as he afterwards sang in the song which he made to that
fair city.

Now was he at the summit of the hill amidst its houses, and step-
ping as if by chance he turned aside down a winding lane, till, a
little down the western slope of the hill, his eye was arrested by a
tiny dwelling whose many small windows were curtained snugly,
yet only so that a most warm and delicious light, as of hearts content
within, looked forth. Then his heart yearned for kind company,
and the desire for wayfaring died in him – and impelled by a great
longing he turned aside at this cottage door, and knocking asked one
who came and opened what might be the name of this house and who
dwelt therein. And it was said to him that this was Mar Vanwa
Tyaliéva, or the Cottage of Lost Play, and at that name he wondered
greatly. There dwelt within, 'twas said, Lindo and Vairë who had
built it many years ago, and with them were no few of their folk
and friends and children. And at this he wondered more than before,
seeing the size of the cottage; but he that opened to him, perceiving
his mind, said: 'Small is the dwelling, but smaller still are they that
dwell here – for all who enter must be very small indeed, or of their
own good wish become as very little folk even as they stand upon the
threshold.'

Then said Eriol that he would dearly desire to come therein and
seek of Vairë and Lindo a night's guest-kindliness, if so they would,
and if he might of his own good wish become small enough there
upon the threshold. Then said the other, 'Enter', and Eriol stepped
in, and behold, it seemed a house of great spaciousness and very
great delight, and the lord of it, Lindo, and his wife, Vairë, came

forth to greet him; and his heart was more glad within him than it
had yet been in all his wanderings, albeit since his landing in the
Lonely Isle his joy had been great enough.

And when Vairë had spoken the words of welcome, and Lindo
had asked of him his name and whence he came and whither he
might be seeking, and he had named himself the Stranger and said
that he came from the Great Lands,[2] and that he was seeking whither-
so his desire for travel led him, then was the evening meal set out
in the great hall and Eriol bidden thereto. Now in this hall despite
the summertide were three great fires – one at the far end and one
on either side of the table, and save for their light as Eriol entered
all was in a warm gloom. But at that moment many folk came in
bearing candles of all sizes and many shapes in sticks of strange
pattern: many were of carven wood and others of beaten metal,
and these were set at hazard about the centre table and upon those
at the sides.

At that same moment a great gong sounded far off in the house
with a sweet noise, and a sound followed as of the laughter of many
voices mingled with a great pattering of feet. Then Vairë said to
Eriol, seeing his face filled with a happy wonderment: 'That is the
voice of Tombo, the Gong of the Children, which stands outside the
Hall of Play Regained, and it rings once to summon them to this hall
at the times for eating and drinking, and three times to summon
them to the Room of the Log Fire for the telling of tales,' and added
Lindo: 'If at his ringing once there be laughter in the corridors and
a sound of feet, then do the walls shake with mirth and stamping at
the three strokes in an evening. And the sounding of the three strokes
is the happiest moment in the day of Littleheart the Gong-warden,
as he himself declares who has known happiness enough of old;
and ancient indeed is he beyond count in spite of his merriness of
soul. He sailed in Wingilot with Eärendel in that last voyage wherein
they sought for Kôr. It was the ringing of this Gong on the Shadowy
Seas that awoke the Sleeper in the Tower of Pearl that stands far
out to west in the Twilit Isles.'

To these words did Eriol's mind so lean, for it seemed to him
that a new world and very fair was opening to him, that he heard
naught else till he was bidden by Vairë to be seated. Then he looked
up, and lo, the hall and all its benches and chairs were filled with
children of every aspect, kind, and size, while sprinkled among them
were folk of all manners and ages. In one thing only were all alike,
that a look of great happiness lit with a merry expectation of further
mirth and joy lay on every face. The soft light of candles too was

upon them all; it shone on bright tresses and gleamed about dark hair, or here and there set a pale fire in locks gone grey. Even as he gazed all arose and with one voice sang the song of the Bringing in of the Meats. Then was the food brought in and set before them, and thereafter the bearers and those that served and those that waited, host and hostess, children and guest, sat down: but Lindo first blessed both food and company. As they ate Eriol fell into speech with Lindo and his wife, telling them tales of his old days and of his adventures, especially those he had encountered upon the journey that had brought him to the Lonely Isle, and asking in return many things concerning the fair land, and most of all of that fair city wherein he now found himself.

Lindo said to him: 'Know then that today, or more like 'twas yesterday, you crossed the borders of that region that is called Alalminórë or the "Land of Elms", which the Gnomes call Gar Lossion, or the "Place of Flowers". Now this region is accounted the centre of the island, and its fairest realm; but above all the towns and villages of Alalminórë is held Koromas, or as some call it, Kortirion, and this city is the one wherein you now find yourself. Both because it stands at the heart of the island, and from the height of its mighty tower, do those that speak of it with love call it the Citadel of the Island, or of the World itself. More reason is there thereto than even great love, for all the island looks to the dwellers here for wisdom and leadership, for song and lore; and here in a great *korin* of elms dwells Meril-i-Turinqi. (Now a *korin* is a great circular hedge, be it of stone or of thorn or even of trees, that encloses a green sward.) Meril comes of the blood of Inwë, whom the Gnomes call Inwithiel, he that was King of all the Eldar when they dwelt in Kôr. That was in the days before hearing the lament of the world Inwë led them forth to the lands of Men: but those great and sad things and how the Eldar came to this fair and lonely island, maybe I will tell them another time.

'But after many days Ingil son of Inwë, seeing this place to be very fair, rested here and about him gathered most of the fairest and the wisest, most of the merriest and the kindest, of all the Eldar.[3] Here among those many came my father Valwë who went with Noldorin to find the Gnomes, and the father of Vairë my wife, Tulkastor. He was of Aulë's kindred, but had dwelt long with the Shoreland Pipers, the Solosimpi, and so came among the earliest to the island.

'Then Ingil built the great tower[4] and called the town Koromas, or "the Resting of the Exiles of Kôr", but by reason of that tower it is now mostly called Kortirion.'

Now about this time they drew nigh the end of the meal; then did Lindo fill his cup and after him Vairë and all those in the hall, but to Eriol he said: 'Now this which we put into our cups is *limpë*, the drink of the Eldar both young and old, and drinking, our hearts keep youth and our mouths grow full of song, but this drink I may not administer: Turinqi only may give it to those not of the Eldar race, and those that drink must dwell always with the Eldar of the Island until such time as they fare forth to find the lost families of the kindred.' Then he filled Eriol's cup, but filled it with golden wine from ancient casks of the Gnomes; and then all rose and drank 'to the Faring Forth and the Rekindling of the Magic Sun'. Then sounded the Gong of the Children thrice, and a glad clamour arose in the hall, and some swung back big oaken doors at the hall's end – at that end which had no hearth. Then many seized those candles that were set in tall wooden sticks and held them aloft while others laughed and chattered, but all made a lane midmost of the company down which went Lindo and Vairë and Eriol, and as they passed the doors the throng followed them.

Eriol saw now that they were in a short broad corridor whose walls half-way up were arrassed; and on those tapestries were many stories pictured whereof he knew not at that time the purport. Above the tapestries it seemed there were paintings, but he could not see for gloom, for the candle-bearers were behind, and before him the only light came from an open door through which poured a red glow as of a big fire. 'That,' said Vairë, 'is the Tale-fire blazing in the Room of Logs; there does it burn all through the year, for 'tis a magic fire, and greatly aids the teller in his tale – but thither we now go,' and Eriol said that that seemed better to him than aught else.

Then all that company came laughing and talking into the room whence came the red glow. A fair room it was as might be felt even by the fire-flicker which danced upon the walls and low ceiling, while deep shadows lay in the nooks and corners. Round the great hearth was a multitude of soft rugs and yielding cushions strewn; and a little to one side was a deep chair with carven arms and feet. And so it was that Eriol felt at that time and at all others whereon he entered there at the hour of tale-telling, that whatso the number of the folk and children the room felt ever just great enough but not large, small enough but not overthronged.

Then all sat them down where they would, old and young, but Lindo in the deep chair and Vairë upon a cushion at his feet, and Eriol rejoicing in the red blaze for all that it was summer stretched nigh the hearthstone.

Then said Lindo: 'Of what shall the tales be tonight? Shall they be of the Great Lands, and of the dwellings of Men; of the Valar and Valinor; of the West and its mysteries, of the East and its glory, of the South and its untrodden wilds, of the North and its power and strength; or of this island and its folk; or of the old days of Kôr where our folk once dwelt? For that this night we entertain a guest, a man of great and excellent travel, a son meseems of Eärendel, shall it be of voyaging, of beating about in a boat, of winds and the sea?'[5]

But to this questioning some answered one thing and some another, till Eriol said: 'I pray you, if it be to the mind of the others, for this time tell me of this island, and of all this island most eagerly would I learn of this goodly house and this fair company of maids and boys, for of all houses this seems to me the most lovely and of all gatherings the sweetest I have gazed upon.'

Then said Vairë: 'Know then that aforetime, in the days of[6] Inwë (and farther back it is hard to go in the history of the Eldar), there was a place of fair gardens in Valinor beside a silver sea. Now this place was near the confines of the realm but not far from Kôr, yet by reason of its distance from the sun-tree Lindelos there was a light there as of summer evening, save only when the silver lamps were kindled on the hill at dusk, and then little lights of white would dance and quiver on the paths, chasing black shadow-dapples under the trees. This was a time of joy to the children, for it was mostly at this hour that a new comrade would come down the lane called Olórë Mallë or the Path of Dreams. It has been said to me, though the truth I know not, that that lane ran by devious routes to the homes of Men, but that way we never trod when we fared thither ourselves. It was a lane of deep banks and great overhanging hedges, beyond which stood many tall trees wherein a perpetual whisper seemed to live; but not seldom great glow-worms crept about its grassy borders.

'Now in this place of gardens a high gate of lattice-work that shone golden in the dusk opened upon the lane of dreams, and from there led winding paths of high box to the fairest of all the gardens, and amidmost of the garden stood a white cottage. Of what it was built, nor when, no one knew, nor now knows, but it was said to me that it shone with a pale light, as it was of pearl, and its roof was a thatch, but a thatch of gold.

'Now on one side of the cot stood a thicket of white lilac and at the other end a mighty yew, from whose shoots the children fashioned bows or clambered by his branches upon the roof. But in the lilacs every bird that ever sang sweetly gathered and sang. Now the walls of the cottage were bent with age and its many small lattice windows were twisted into strange shapes. No one, 'tis said, dwelt in the cottage, which was however guarded secretly and jealously by the Eldar so that no harm came nigh it, and that yet might the children playing therein in freedom know of no guardianship. This was the Cottage of the Children, or of the Play of Sleep, and not of Lost Play, as has wrongly been said in song among Men – for no play was lost then, and here alas only and now is the Cottage of Lost Play.

'These too were the earliest children – the children of the fathers of the fathers of Men that came there; and for pity the Eldar sought to guide all who came down that lane into the cottage and the garden, lest they strayed into Kôr and became enamoured of the glory of Valinor; for then would they either stay there for ever, and great grief fall on their parents, or would they wander back and long for ever vainly, and become strange and wild among the children of Men. Nay, some even who wandered on to the edge of the rocks of Eldamar and there strayed, dazzled by the fair shells and the fishes of many colours, the blue pools and the silver foam, they drew back to the cottage, alluring them gently with the odour of many flowers. Yet even so there were a few who heard on that beach the sweet piping of the Solosimpi afar off and who played not with the other children but climbed to the upper windows and gazed out, straining to see the far glimpses of the sea and the magic shores beyond the shadows and the trees.

'Now for the most part the children did not often go into the house, but danced and played in the garden, gathering flowers or chasing the golden bees and butterflies with embroidered wings that the Eldar set within the garden for their joy. And many children have there become comrades, who after met and loved in the lands of Men, but of such things perchance Men know more than I can tell you. Yet some there were who, as I have told, heard the Solosimpi piping afar off, or others who straying again beyond the garden caught a sound of the singing of the Telelli on the hill, and even some who reaching Kôr afterwards returned home, and their minds and hearts were full of wonder. Of the misty aftermemories of these, of their broken tales and snatches of song, came many strange legends that delighted Men for long, and still do, it may be; for of such were the poets of the Great Lands.[7]

'Now when the fairies left Kôr that lane was blocked for ever with great impassable rocks, and there stands of a surety the cottage empty and the garden bare to this day, and will do until long after the Faring Forth, when if all goes well the roads through Arvalin to Valinor shall be thronged with the sons and daughters of Men. But seeing that no children came there for refreshment and delight, sorrow and greyness spread amongst them and Men ceased almost to believe in, or think of, the beauty of the Eldar and the glory of the Valar, till one came from the Great Lands and besought us to relieve the darkness.

'Now there is alas no safe way for children from the Great Lands hither, but Meril-i-Turinqi hearkened to his boon and chose Lindo my husband to devise some plan of good. Now Lindo and I, Vairë, had taken under our care the children – the remainder of those who found Kôr and remained with the Eldar for ever: and so here we builded of good magic this Cottage of Lost Play: and here old tales, old songs, and elfin music are treasured and rehearsed. Ever and anon our children fare forth again to find the Great Lands, and go about among the lonely children and whisper to them at dusk in early bed by night-light and candle-flame, or comfort those that weep. Some I am told listen to the complaints of those that are punished or chidden, and hear their tales and feign to take their part, and this seems to me a quaint and merry service.

'Yet all whom we send return not and that is great grief to us, for it is by no means out of small love that the Eldar held children from Kôr, but rather of thought for the homes of Men; yet in the Great Lands, as you know well, there are fair places and lovely regions of much allurement, wherefore it is only for the great necessity that we adventure any of the children that are with us. Yet the most come back hither and tell us many stories and many sad things of their journeys – and now I have told most of what is to tell of the Cottage of Lost Play.'

Then Eriol said: 'Now these are tidings sad and yet good to hear, and I remember me of certain words that my father spake in my early boyhood. It had long, said he, been a tradition in our kindred that one of our father's fathers would speak of a fair house and magic gardens, of a wondrous town, and of a music full of all beauty and longing – and these things he said he had seen and heard as a child, though how and where was not told. Now all his life was he restless, as if a longing half-expressed for unknown things dwelt within him; and 'tis said that he died among rocks on a lonely coast on a night of storm – and moreover that most of his children and their children since have been of a restless mind – and methinks I know now the truth of the matter.'

And Vairë said that 'twas like to be that one of his kindred had found the rocks of Eldamar in those old days.

NOTES

1 *Gnomes*: the Second Kindred, the *Noldoli* (later *Noldor*). For the use
 of the word *Gnomes* see p. 43; and for the linguistic distinction made
 here see pp. 50–1.
2 The 'Great Lands' are the lands East of the Great Sea. The term
 'Middle-earth' is never used in the *Lost Tales*, and in fact does not
 appear until writings of the 1930s.
3 In both MSS the words 'of all the Eldar' are followed by: 'for of
 most noble there were none, seeing that to be of the blood of the
 Eldar is equal and sufficient'; but this was struck out in the second
 MS.
4 The original reading was 'the great Tirion', changed to 'the great
 tower'.
5 This sentence, from 'a son meseems . . .', replaced in the original MS
 an earlier reading: 'shall it be of Eärendel the wanderer, who alone of
 the sons of Men has had great traffic with the Valar and Elves, who
 alone of their kindred has seen beyond Taniquetil, even he who sails
 for ever in the firmament?'
6 The original reading was 'before the days of', changed to 'in the first
 days of', and then to the reading given.
7 This last phrase was an addition to the second MS.

Changes made to names in
The Cottage of Lost Play

The names were at this time in a very fluid state, reflecting in part the
rapid development of the languages that was then taking place. Changes
were made to the original text, and further changes, at different times, to
the second text, but it seems unnecessary in the following notes to go
into the detail of when and where the changes were made. The names
are given in the order of their occurrence in the tale. The signs ⟩ and ⟨
are used to mean 'changed to' and 'changed from'.

Dor Faidwen The Gnomish name of Tol Eressëa was changed many
 times: *Gar Eglos* ⟩ *Dor Edloth* ⟩ *Dor Usgwen* ⟩ *Dor Uswen* ⟩ *Dor
 Faidwen*.
Mar Vanwa Tyaliéva In the original text a space was left for the Elvish
 name, subsequently filled in as *Mar Vanwa Taliéva*.
Great Lands Throughout the tale *Great Lands* is an emendation of
 Outer Lands, when the latter was given a different meaning (lands
 West of the Great Sea).
Wingilot ⟨ *Wingelot*.
Gar Lossion ⟨ *Losgar*.

Koromas ⟨ *Kormas*.

Meril-i-Turinqi The first text has only *Turinqi*, with in one place a
   space left for a personal name.

Inwë ⟨ *Ing* at each occurrence.

Inwithiel ⟨ *Gim Githil*, which was in turn ⟨ *Githil*.

Ingil ⟨ *Ingilmo*.

Valwë ⟨ *Manwë*. It seems possible that *Manwë* as the name of Vairë's
   father was a mere slip.

Noldorin The original reading was *Noldorin whom the Gnomes name
   Goldriel*; *Goldriel* was changed to *Golthadriel*, and then the reference
   to the Gnomish name was struck out, leaving only *Noldorin*.

Tulkastor ⟨ *Tulkassë* ⟨ *Turenbor*.

Solosimpi ⟨ *Solosimpë* at each occurrence.

Lindelos ⟨ *Lindeloksë* ⟨ *Lindeloktë Singing Cluster* (*Glingol*).

Telelli ⟨ *Telellë*.

Arvalin ⟨ *Harmalin* ⟨ *Harwalin*.

Commentary on
The Cottage of Lost Play

The story of Eriol the mariner was central to my father's original conception of the mythology. In those days, as he recounted long after in a
letter to his friend Milton Waldman,* the primary intention of his work
was to satisfy his desire for a specifically and recognizably *English* literature of 'faerie':

> I was from early days grieved by the poverty of my own beloved
> country: it had no stories of its own (bound up with its tongue and soil),
> not of the quality that I sought, and found (as an ingredient) in legends
> of other lands. There was Greek, and Celtic, and Romance, Germanic,
> Scandinavian, and Finnish (which greatly affected me); but nothing
> English, save impoverished chap-book stuff.

In his earliest writings the mythology was anchored in the ancient legen-
dary history of England; and more than that, it was peculiarly associated
with certain places in England.

   Eriol, himself close kin of famous figures in the legends of North-western
Europe, came at last on a voyage westward over the ocean to Tol Eressëa,
the Lonely Isle, where Elves dwelt; and from them he learned 'The Lost
Tales of Elfinesse'. But his rôle was at first to be more important in the
structure of the work than (what it afterwards became) simply that of a
man of later days who came to 'the land of the Fairies' and there acquired

---

* *The Letters of J. R. R. Tolkien*, ed. Humphrey Carpenter, 1981, p. 144.
The letter was almost certainly written in 1951.

lost or hidden knowledge, which he afterwards reported in his own tongue: at first, Eriol was to be an important element in the fairy-history itself – the witness of the ruin of Elvish Tol Eressëa. The element of ancient English history or 'historical legend' was at first not merely a framework, isolated from the great tales that afterwards constituted 'The Silmarillion', but an integral part of their ending. The elucidation of all this (so far as elucidation is possible) must necessarily be postponed to the end of the *Tales*; but here something at least must be said of the history of Eriol up to the time of his coming to Tol Eressëa, and of the original significance of the Lonely Isle.

The 'Eriol-story' is in fact among the knottiest and most obscure matters in the whole history of Middle-earth and Aman. My father abandoned the writing of the *Lost Tales* before he reached their end, and when he abandoned them he had also abandoned his original ideas for their conclusion. Those ideas can indeed be discerned from his notes; but the notes were for the most part pencilled at furious speed, the writing now rubbed and faint and in places after long study scarcely decipherable, on little slips of paper, disordered and dateless, or in a little notebook in which, during the years when he was composing the *Lost Tales*, he jotted down thoughts and suggestions (see p. 171). The common form of these notes on the 'Eriol' or 'English' element is that of short outlines, in which salient narrative features, often without clear connection between them, are set down in the manner of a list; and they vary constantly among themselves.

In what must be, at any rate, among the very earliest of these outlines, found in this little pocket-book, and headed 'Story of Eriol's Life', the mariner who came to Tol Eressëa is brought into relation with the tradition of the invasion of Britain by Hengest and Horsa in the fifth century A.D. This was a matter to which my father gave much time and thought; he lectured on it at Oxford and developed certain original theories, especially in connection with the appearance of Hengest in *Beowulf*.*

From these jottings we learn that Eriol's original name was *Ottor*, but that he called himself *Wǽfre* (an Old English word meaning 'restless, wandering') and lived a life on the waters. His father was named *Eoh* (a word of the Old English poetic vocabulary meaning 'horse'); and Eoh was slain by his brother *Beorn* (in Old English 'warrior', but originally meaning 'bear', as does the cognate word *björn* in Old Norse; cf. Beorn the shape-changer in *The Hobbit*). Eoh and Beorn were the sons of *Heden* 'the leather and fur clad', and Heden (like many heroes of Northern legend) traced his ancestry to the god Wóden. In other notes there are other connections and combinations, and since none of this story was written as a coherent narrative these names are only of significance as showing the direction of my father's thought at that time.

Ottor Wǽfre settled on the island of Heligoland in the North Sea, and

* J. R. R. Tolkien, *Finn and Hengest*, ed. Alan Bliss, 1982.

he wedded a woman named *Cwén* (Old English: 'woman', 'wife'); they had two sons named 'after his father' *Hengest* and *Horsa* 'to avenge Eoh' (*hengest* is another Old English word for 'horse').

Then sea-longing gripped Ottor Wǽfre: he was a son of *Eärendel*, born under his beam. If a beam from Eärendel fall on a child new-born he becomes 'a child of Eärendel' and a wanderer. (So also in *The Cottage of Lost Play* Eriol is called both by the author and by Lindo a 'son of Eärendel'.) After the death of Cwén Ottor left his young children. Hengest and Horsa avenged Eoh and became great chieftains; but Ottor Wǽfre set out to seek, and find, Tol Eressëa, here called in Old English *se uncúþa holm*, 'the unknown island'.

Various things are told in these notes about Eriol's sojourn in Tol Eressëa which do not appear in *The Book of Lost Tales*, but of these I need here only refer to the statements that 'Eriol adopted the name of *Angol*' and that he was named by the Gnomes (the later Noldor, see below p. 43) *Angol* 'after the regions of his home'. This certainly refers to the ancient homeland of the 'English' before their migration across the North Sea to Britain: Old English *Angel, Angul*, modern German *Angeln*, the region of the Danish peninsula between the Flensburg fjord and the river Schlei, south of the modern Danish frontier. From the west coast of the peninsula it is no very great distance to the island of Heligoland.

In another place *Angol* is given as the Gnomish equivalent of *Eriollo*, which names are said to be those of 'the region of the northern part of the Great Lands, "between the seas", whence Eriol came'. (On these names see further under *Eriol* in the Appendix on Names.)

It is not to be thought that these notes represent in all respects the story of Eriol as my father conceived it when he wrote *The Cottage of Lost Play* – in any case, it is said expressly there that *Eriol* means 'One who dreams alone', and that 'of his former names the story nowhere tells' (p. 14). But what is important is that (according to the view that I have formed of the earliest conceptions, apparently the best explanation of the very difficult evidence) this was still the leading idea when it was written: *Eriol came to Tol Eressëa from the lands to the East of the North Sea*. He belongs to the period preceding the Anglo-Saxon invasions of Britain (as my father, for his purposes, wished to represent it).

Later, his name changed to *Ælfwine* ('Elf-friend'), the mariner became an Englishman of the 'Anglo-Saxon period' of English history, who sailed west over sea to Tol Eressëa – he sailed from England out into the Atlantic Ocean; and from this later conception comes the very remarkable story of *Ælfwine of England*, which will be given at the end of the *Lost Tales*. But in the earliest conception he was not an Englishman of England: England in the sense of the land of the English did not yet exist; for the cardinal fact (made quite explicit in extant notes) of this conception is that *the Elvish isle to which Eriol came was England* – that is to say, Tol Eressëa would become England, the land of the English, at the end of the story. Koromas or Kortirion, the town in the centre of Tol Eressëf to which Eriol comes in *The Cottage of Lost Play*, would become in after days Warwick (and the elements *Kor-* and *War-* were etymologically connected);* Alalminórë, the Land of Elms, would be Warwickshire; and Tavrobel, where Eriol sojourned for a while in Tol Eressëa, would afterwards be the Staffordshire village of Great Haywood.

None of this is explicit in the written *Tales*, and is only found in notes independent of them; but it seems certain that it was still present when *The Cottage of Lost Play* was written (and indeed, as I shall try to show later, underlies all the *Tales*). The fair copy that my mother made of it was dated February 1917. From 1913 until her marriage in March 1916 she lived in Warwick and my father visited her there from Oxford; after their marriage she lived for a while at Great Haywood (east of Stafford), since it was near the camp where my father was stationed, and after his return from France he was at Great Haywood in the winter of 1916–17. Thus the identification of Tol Eressëan Tavrobel with Great Haywood cannot be earlier than 1916, and the fair copy of *The Cottage of Lost Play* (and quite possibly the original composition of it) was actually done there.

In November 1915 my father wrote a poem entitled *Kortirion among the Trees* which was dedicated to Warwick.† To the first fair copy of the poem there is appended a prose introduction, as follows:

Now on a time the fairies dwelt in the Lonely Isle after the great wars with Melko and the ruin of Gondolin; and they builded a fair city amidmost of that island, and it was girt with trees. Now this city they called Kortirion, both in memory of their ancient dwelling of Kôr in Valinor, and because this city stood also upon a hill and had a great tower tall and grey that Ingil son of Inwë their lord let raise.

Very beautiful was Kortirion and the fairies loved it, and it became rich in song and poesy and the light of laughter; but on a time the great Faring Forth was made, and the fairies had rekindled once more the Magic Sun of Valinor but for the treason and faint hearts of Men. But so it is that the Magic Sun is dead and the Lonely Isle drawn back unto the confines of the Great Lands, and the fairies are scattered through all the wide unfriendly pathways of the world; and now Men dwell even on this faded isle, and care nought or know nought of its ancient days. Yet still there be some of the Eldar and the Noldoli‡ of old who linger in the island, and their songs are heard about the shores of the land that once was the fairest dwelling of the immortal folk.

* The great tower or *tirion* that Ingil son of Inwe built (p. 16) and the great tower of Warwick Castle are not identified, but at least it is certain that Koromas had a great tower because Warwick has one.

† This poem is given, in three different texts, on pp. 33–43. – A poem written at Étaples in the Pas de Calais in June 1916 and entitled 'The Lonely Isle' is explicitly addressed to England. See *Letters*, p. 437, note 4 to letter 43.

‡ For the distinction between *Eldar* and *Noldoli* see pp. 50–1.

And it seems to the fairies and it seems to me who know that town and have often trodden its disfigured ways that autumn and the falling of the leaf is the season of the year when maybe here or there a heart among Men may be open, and an eye perceive how is the world's estate fallen from the laughter and the loveliness of old. Think on Kortirion and be sad – yet is there not hope?

Both here and in *The Cottage of Lost Play* there are allusions to events still in the future when Eriol came to Tol Eressëa; and though the full exposition and discussion of them must wait until the end of the *Tales* it needs to be explained here that 'the Faring Forth' was a great expedition made from Tol Eressëa for the rescue of the Elves who were still wandering in the Great Lands – cf. Lindo's words (p. 17): 'until such time as they fare forth to find the lost families of the kindred'. At that time Tol Eressëa was uprooted, by the aid of Ulmo, from the sea-bottom and dragged near to the western shores of the Great Lands. In the battle that followed the Elves were defeated, and fled into hiding in Tol Eressëa; Men entered the isle, and the fading of the Elves began. The subsequent history of Tol Eressëa is the history of England; and Warwick is 'disfigured Kortirion', itself a memory of ancient Kôr (the later Tirion upon Túna, city of the Elves in Aman; in the *Lost Tales* the name Kôr is used both of the city and the hill).

Inwë, referred to in *The Cottage of Lost Play* as 'King of all the Eldar when they dwelt in Kôr', is the forerunner of Ingwë King of the Vanyar Elves in *The Silmarillion*. In a story told later to Eriol in Tol Eressëa Inwë reappears as one of the three Elves who went first to Valinor after the Awakening, as was Ingwë in *The Silmarillion*; his kindred and descendants were the *Inwir*, of whom came Meril-i-Turinqi, the Lady of Tol Eressëa (see p. 50). Lindo's references to Inwë's hearing 'the lament of the world' (i.e. of the Great Lands) and to his leading the Eldar forth to the lands of Men (p. 16) are the germ of the story of the coming of the Hosts of the West to the assault on Thangorodrim: 'The host of the Valar prepared for battle; and beneath their white banners marched the Vanyar, the people of Ingwë . . .' (*The Silmarillion*, p. 251). Later in the *Tales* it is said to Eriol by Meril-i-Turinqi that 'Inwë was the eldest of the Elves, and had lived yet in majesty had he not perished in that march into the world; but Ingil his son went long ago back to Valinor and is with Manwë'. In *The Silmarillion*, on the other hand, it is said of Ingwë that 'he entered into Valinor [in the beginning of the days of the Elves] and sits at the feet of the Powers, and all Elves revere his name; but he came never back, nor looked again upon Middle-earth' (p. 53).

Lindo's words about the sojourn of Ingil in Tol Eressëa 'after many days', and the interpretation of the name of his town Koromas as 'the Resting of the Exiles of Kôr', refer to the return of the Eldar from the Great Lands after the war on Melko (Melkor, Morgoth) for the deliverance of the enslaved Noldoli. His words about his father Valwë 'who went with

Noldorin to find the Gnomes' refer to an element in this story of the expedition from Kôr.*

It is important to see, then, that (if my general interpretation is correct) in *The Cottage of Lost Play* Eriol comes to Tol Eressëa *in the time after* the Fall of Gondolin and the march of the Elves of Kôr into the Great Lands for the defeat of Melko, when the Elves who had taken part in it had returned over the sea to dwell in Tol Eressëa; but *before the time* of the 'Faring Forth' and the removal of Tol Eressëa to the geographical position of England. This latter element was soon lost in its entirety from the developing mythology.

Of the 'Cottage' itself it must be said at once that very little light can be cast on it from other writings of my father's; for the entire conception of the Children who went to Valinor was to be abandoned almost without further trace. Later in the *Lost Tales*, however, there are again references to Olóre Mallë. After the description of the Hiding of Valinor, it is told that at the bidding of Manwë (who looked on the event with sorrow) the Valar Oromë and Lórien devised strange paths from the Great Lands to Valinor, and the way of Lórien's devising was Olórë Mallë, the Path of Dreams; by this road, when 'Men were yet but new-wakened on the earth', 'the children of the fathers of the fathers of Men' came to Valinor in their sleep (pp. 211, 213). There are two further mentions in tales to be given in Part II: the teller of the *Tale of Tinúviel* (a child of Mar Vanwa Tyaliéva) says that she saw Tinúviel and her mother with her own eyes 'when journeying by the Way of Dreams in long past days', and the teller of the *Tale of Turambar* says that he 'trod Olórë Mallë in the days before the fall of Gondolin'.

There is also a poem on the subject of the Cottage of Lost Play, which has many of the details of the description in the prose text. This poem, according to my father's notes, was composed at 59 St John's Street, Oxford, his undergraduate lodgings, on 27–28 April 1915 (when he was 23). It exists (as is constantly the case with the poems) in several versions, each modified in detail from the preceding one, and the end of the poem was twice entirely rewritten. I give it here first in the earliest form, with changes made to this in notes at the foot of the page, and then in the final version, the date of which cannot be certainly determined. I suspect that it was very much later – and may indeed have been one of the revisions made to old poems when the collection *The Adventures of Tom Bombadil* (1962) was being prepared, though it is not mentioned in my father's correspondence on that subject.

The original title was: *You and Me | and the Cottage of Lost Play* (with

* A little light on Lindo's references to the ringing of the Gong on the Shadowy Seas and the Sleeper in the Tower of Pearl will be shed when the story of Eärendel is reached at the end of the *Tales*.

an Old English rendering *Þæt húsincel ǽrran gamenes*), which was changed to *Mar Vanwa Tyaliéva, The Cottage of Lost Play*; in the final version it is *The Little House of Lost Play: Mar Vanwa Tyaliéva.* The verse-lines are indented as in the original texts.

You & Me
and the Cottage of Lost Play

You and me – we know that land
   And often have been there
In the long old days, old nursery days,
   A dark child and a fair.
5   Was it down the paths of firelight dreams
   In winter cold and white,
Or in the blue-spun twilit hours
   Of little early tucked-up beds
   In drowsy summer night,
10   That You and I got lost in Sleep
   And met each other there –
Your dark hair on your white nightgown,
   And mine was tangled fair?

We wandered shyly hand in hand,
15   Or rollicked in the fairy sand
And gathered pearls and shells in pails,
   While all about the nightingales
   Were singing in the trees.
We dug for silver with our spades
20   By little inland sparkling seas,
Then ran ashore through sleepy glades
   And down a warm and winding lane
   We never never found again
   Between high whispering trees.

25   The air was neither night or day,
   But faintly dark with softest light,
When first there glimmered into sight
   The Cottage of Lost Play.
'Twas builded very very old
30   White, and thatched with straws of gold,
   And pierced with peeping lattices
   That looked toward the sea;

1 You and I
3 In the long old days, the shining days,
15 in the golden sand
23 That now we cannot find again
25 night nor day
29 New-built it was, yet very old,

And our own children's garden-plots
Were there – our own forgetmenots,
    Red daisies, cress and mustard,
      And blue nemophilë.
O! all the borders trimmed with box
Were full of favourite flowers – of phlox,
Of larkspur, pinks, and hollyhocks
      Beneath a red may-tree:
And all the paths were full of shapes,
Of tumbling happy white-clad shapes,
      And with them You and Me.
And some had silver watering-cans
      And watered all their gowns,
Or sprayed each other; some laid plans
    To build them houses, fairy towns,
      Or dwellings in the trees;
And some were clambering on the roof;
      Some crooning lonely and aloof;
And some were dancing fairy-rings
    And weaving pearly daisy-strings,
      Or chasing golden bees;
But here and there a little pair
    With rosy cheeks and tangled hair
      Debated quaint old childish things – *
      And we were one of these.

35, 40, 45, 50, 55 (margin line numbers)

37 And all the borders
43 That laughed with You and Me.
47 little towns
56 Debated ancient childish things

Lines 58–65 (p. 30) were subsequently rewritten:

    But why it was there came a time
    When we could take the road no more,
      Though long we looked, and high would climb,
      Or gaze from many a seaward shore
    To find the path between sea and sky
      To those old gardens of delight;
    And how it goes now in that land,
      If there the house and gardens stand,
      Still filled with children clad in white –
      We know not, You and I.

* This seems to echo the lines of Francis Thompson's poem *Daisy*:

    Two children did we stray and talk
    Wise, idle, childish things.

My father acquired the Works of Francis Thompson in 1913 and 1914.

And why it was Tomorrow came
    And with his grey hand led us back;
60   And why we never found the same
    Old cottage, or the magic track
    That leads between a silver sea
And those old shores and gardens fair
Where all things are, that ever were –
65   We know not, You and Me.

This is the final version of the poem:

The Little House of Lost Play
Mar Vanwa Tyaliéva

We knew that land once, You and I,
    and once we wandered there
in the long days now long gone by,
    a dark child and a fair.
5   Was it on the paths of firelight thought
    in winter cold and white,
or in the blue-spun twilit hours
of little early tucked-up beds
    in drowsy summer night,
10   that you and I in Sleep went down
    to meet each other there,
your dark hair on your white nightgown
    and mine was tangled fair?

We wandered shyly hand in hand,
15   small footprints in the golden sand,
and gathered pearls and shells in pails,
while all about the nightingales
    were singing in the trees.
We dug for silver with our spades,
20   and caught the sparkle of the seas,
then ran ashore to greenlit glades,
and found the warm and winding lane
that now we cannot find again,
    between tall whispering trees.

25   The air was neither night nor day,
an ever-eve of gloaming light,
when first there glimmered into sight
    the Little House of Play.
New-built it was, yet very old,

62   That leads between the sea and sky
63   To those old shores
65   We know not, You and I.

30 white, and thatched with straws of gold,
  and pierced with peeping lattices
   that looked toward the sea;
 and our own children's garden-plots
 were there: our own forgetmenots,
35 red daisies, cress and mustard,
  and radishes for tea.
 There all the borders, trimmed with box,
 were filled with favourite flowers, with phlox,
 with lupins, pinks, and hollyhocks,
40 beneath a red may-tree;
 and all the gardens full of folk
 that their own little language spoke,
  but not to You and Me.

 For some had silver watering-cans
45 and watered all their gowns,
 or sprayed each other; some laid plans
 to build their houses, little towns
  and dwellings in the trees.
 And some were clambering on the roof;
50 some crooning lonely and aloof;
 some dancing round the fairy-rings
 all garlanded in daisy-strings,
  while some upon their knees
 before a little white-robed king
55 crowned with marigold would sing
  their rhymes of long ago.
 But side by side a little pair
 with heads together, mingled hair,
  went walking to and fro
60 still hand in hand; and what they said,
 ere Waking far apart them led,
  that only we now know.

It is notable that the poem was called *The Cottage*, or *The Little House of Lost Play*, whereas what is described is the Cottage of the Children in Valinor, near the city of Kôr; but this, according to Vairë (p. 19), 'the Cottage of the Play of Sleep', was 'not of Lost Play, as has wrongly been said in song among Men'.

 I shall not attempt any analysis or offer any elucidation of the ideas embodied in the 'Cottages of the Children'. The reader, however he interprets them, will in any case not need to be assisted in his perception of the personal and particular emotions in which all was still anchored.

 As I have said, the conception of the coming of mortal children in sleep to the gardens of Valinor was soon to be abandoned in its entirety, and in the developed mythology there would be no place for it – still less for the idea that in some possible future day 'the roads through Arvalin to Valinor shall be thronged with the sons and daughters of Men'.

Likewise, all the 'elfin' diminutiveness soon disappeared. The idea of the Cottage of the Children was already in being in 1915, as the poem *You and Me* shows; and it was in the same year, indeed on the same days of April, that *Goblin Feet* (or *Cumaþ þá Nihtielfas*) was written, concerning which my father said in 1971: 'I wish the unhappy little thing, representing all that I came (so soon after) to fervently dislike, could be buried for ever.'* Yet it is to be observed that in early notes Elves and Men are said to have been 'of a size' in former days, and the smallness (and filminess and transparency) of the 'fairies' is an aspect of their 'fading', and directly related to the domination of Men in the Great Lands. To this matter I shall return later. In this connection, the diminutiveness of the Cottage is very strange, since it seems to be a diminutiveness peculiar to itself: Eriol, who has travelled for many days through Tol Eressëa, is astonished that the dwelling can hold so many, and he is told that all who enter it must be, or must become, very small. But Tol Eressëa is an island inhabited by Elves.

I give now three texts of the poem *Kortirion among the Trees* (later *The Trees of Kortirion*). The very earliest workings (November 1915) of this poem are extant,† and there are many subsequent texts. The prose introduction to the early form has been cited on pp. 25–6. A major revision was made in 1937, and another much later; by this time it was almost a different poem. Since my father sent it to Rayner Unwin in February 1962 as a possible candidate for inclusion in *The Adventures of Tom Bombadil*, it seems virtually certain that the final version dates from that time.‡

I give the poem first in its pre-1937 form, when only slight changes had yet been made. In one of the earliest copies it bears a title in Old English: *Cor Tirion þǽra béama on middes*, and is 'dedicated to Warwick'; but in another the second title is in Elvish (the second word is not perfectly legible): *Narquelion la . . tu y aldalin Kortirionwen* (i.e. 'Autumn (among) the trees of Kortirion').

---

* He had been asked for his permission to include the poem in an anthology, as it had been several times previously. See Humphrey Carpenter, *Biography*, p. 74, where (a part only) of the poem is printed, and also his bibliography *ibid.* (year 1915).

† According to my father's notes, the original composition dates from November 21–28, 1915, and was written in Warwick on 'a week's leave from camp'. This is not precisely accurate, since letters to my mother survive that were written from the camp on November 25 and 26, in the second of which he says that he has 'written out a pencil copy of "Kortirion"'.

‡ In his letter my father said: '*The Trees* is too long and too ambitious, and even if considered good enough would probably upset the boat.'

Kortirion among the Trees

The First Verses

O fading town upon a little hill,
　　Old memory is waning in thine ancient gates,
The robe gone gray, thine old heart almost still;
　　The castle only, frowning, ever waits
5　　And ponders how among the towering elms
The Gliding Water leaves these inland realms
　　And slips between long meadows to the western sea –
Still bearing downward over murmurous falls
　　One year and then another to the sea;
10　And slowly thither have a many gone
Since first the fairies built Kortirion.

O spiry town upon a windy hill
　　With sudden-winding alleys shady-walled
(Where even now the peacocks pace a stately drill,
15　　Majestic, sapphirine, and emerald),
Behold thy girdle of a wide champain
Sunlit, and watered with a silver rain,
　　And richly wooded with a thousand whispering trees
That cast long shadows in many a bygone noon,
20　　And murmured many centuries in the breeze.
Thou art the city of the Land of Elms,
Alalminórë in the Faery Realms.

　　Sing of thy trees, old, old Kortirion!
　　Thine oaks, and maples with their tassels on,
25　　Thy singing poplars; and the splendid yews
　　That crown thine agéd walls and muse
　　　　Of sombre grandeur all the day –
　　Until the twinkle of the early stars
　　Is tangled palely in their sable bars;
30　　Until the seven lampads of the Silver Bear
　　Swing slowly in their shrouded hair
　　　　And diadem the fallen day.
　　O tower and citadel of the world!
　　When bannered summer is unfurled
35　　Most full of music are thine elms –
　　A gathered sound that overwhelms
　　　　The voices of all other trees.
　　Sing then of elms, belov'd Kortirion,
　　How summer crowds their full sails on,
40　　Like clothéd masts of verdurous ships,
　　A fleet of galleons that proudly slips
　　　　Across long sunlit seas.

The Second Verses

    Thou art the inmost province of the fading isle
     Where linger yet the Lonely Companies.
45   Still, undespairing, do they sometimes slowly file
     Along thy paths with plaintive harmonies:
    The holy fairies and immortal elves
    That dance among the trees and sing themselves
    A wistful song of things that were, and could be yet.
50   They pass and vanish in a sudden breeze,
     A wave of bowing grass - and we forget
    Their tender voices like wind-shaken bells
    Of flowers, their gleaming hair like golden asphodels.

    Spring still hath joy: thy spring is ever fair
55   Among the trees; but drowsy summer by thy streams
    Already stoops to hear the secret player
     Pipe out beyond the tangle of her forest dreams
    The long thin tune that still do sing
    The elvish harebells nodding in a jacinth ring
60   Upon the castle walls;
    Already stoops to listen to the clear cold spell
     Come up her sunny aisles and perfumed halls:
    A sad and haunting magic note,
     A strand of silver glass remote.

65   Then all thy trees, old town upon a windy bent,
    Do loose a long sad whisper and lament;
    For going are the rich-hued hours, th'enchanted nights
    When flitting ghost-moths dance like satellites
     Round tapers in the moveless air;
70   And doomed already are the radiant dawns,
    The fingered sunlight dripping on long lawns;
    The odour and the slumbrous noise of meads,
    When all the sorrel, flowers, and pluméd weeds
     Go down before the scyther's share.
75   Strange sad October robes her dewy furze
    In netted sheen of gold-shot gossamers,
    And then the wide-umbraged elm begins to fail;
    Her mourning multitudes of leaves go pale
     Seeing afar the icy shears
80   Of Winter, and his blue-tipped spears
    Marching unconquerable upon the sun
    Of bright All-Hallows. Then their hour is done,
    And wanly borne on wings of amber pale
    They beat the wide airs of the fading vale
85   And fly like birds across the misty meres.

The Third Verses

Yet is this season dearest to my heart,
   Most fitting to the little faded town
With sense of splendid pomps that now depart
   In mellow sounds of sadness echoing down
90   The paths of stranded mists. O! gentle time
When the late mornings are bejewelled with rime,
   And the blue shadows gather on the distant woods.
The fairies know thy early crystal dusk
   And put in secret on their twilit hoods
95   Of grey and filmy purple, and long bands
Of frosted starlight sewn by silver hands.

They know the season of the brilliant night,
   When naked elms entwine in cloudy lace
The Pleiades, and long-armed poplars bar the light
100   Of golden-rondured moons with glorious face.
O fading fairies and most lonely elves
Then sing ye, sing ye to yourselves
   A woven song of stars and gleaming leaves;
Then whirl ye with the sapphire-wingéd winds;
105   Then do ye pipe and call with heart that grieves
To sombre men: 'Remember what is gone –
The magic sun that lit Kortirion!'

Now are thy trees, old, old Kortirion,
   Seen rising up through pallid mists and wan,
110   Like vessels floating vague and long afar
Down opal seas beyond the shadowy bar
   Of cloudy ports forlorn:
They leave behind for ever havens throng'd
Wherein their crews a while held feasting long
115   And gorgeous ease, who now like windy ghosts
Are wafted by slow airs to empty coasts;
   There are they sadly glimmering borne
   Across the plumbless ocean of oblivion.
Bare are thy trees become, Kortirion,
120   And all their summer glory swiftly gone.
The seven lampads of the Silver Bear
Are waxen to a wondrous flare
   That flames above the fallen year.
Though cold thy windy squares and empty streets;
125   Though elves dance seldom in thy pale retreats
(Save on some rare and moonlit night,
   A flash, a whispering glint of white),
   Yet would I never need depart from here.

The Last Verse

130

I need not know the desert or red palaces
     Where dwells the sun, the great seas or the magic isles,
The pinewoods piled on mountain-terraces;
     And calling faintly down the windy miles
Touches my heart no distant bell that rings
In populous cities of the Earthly Kings.

135

     Here do I find a haunting ever-near content
Set midmost of the Land of withered Elms
(Alalminórë of the Faery Realms);
     Here circling slowly in a sweet lament
Linger the holy fairies and immortal elves

140

Singing a song of faded longing to themselves.

★

I give next the text of the poem as my father rewrote it in 1937, in the later of slightly variant forms.

Kortirion among the Trees

I

O fading town upon an inland hill,
     Old shadows linger in thine ancient gate,
Thy robe is grey, thine old heart now is still;
     Thy towers silent in the mist await

5

Their crumbling end, while through the storeyed elms
The Gliding Water leaves these inland realms,
     And slips between long meadows to the Sea,
Still bearing downward over murmurous falls
     One day and then another to the Sea;

10

And slowly thither many years have gone,
Since first the Elves here built Kortirion.

O climbing town upon thy windy hill
     With winding streets, and alleys shady-walled
Where now untamed the peacocks pace in drill

15

     Majestic, sapphirine, and emerald;
Amid the girdle of this sleeping land,
Where silver falls the rain and gleaming stand
     The whispering host of old deep-rooted trees
That cast long shadows in many a bygone noon,

20

     And murmured many centuries in the breeze;
Thou art the city of the Land of Elms,
Alalminórë in the Faery Realms.

Sing of thy trees, Kortirion, again:
The beech on hill, the willow in the fen,
25   The rainy poplars, and the frowning yews
Within thine agéd courts that muse
    In sombre splendour all the day;
Until the twinkle of the early stars
Comes glinting through their sable bars,
30   And the white moon climbing up the sky
Looks down upon the ghosts of trees that die
    Slowly and silently from day to day.
O Lonely Isle, here was thy citadel,
Ere bannered summer from his fortress fell.
35   Then full of music were thine elms:
Green was their armour, green their helms,
    The Lords and Kings of all thy trees.
Sing, then, of elms, renowned Kortirion,
That under summer crowds their full sail on,
40   And shrouded stand like masts of verdurous ships,
A fleet of galleons that proudly slips
    Across long sunlit seas.

II

Thou art the inmost province of the fading isle,
  Where linger yet the Lonely Companies;
45   Still, undespairing, here they slowly file
  Along thy paths with solemn harmonies:
The holy people of an elder day,
Immortal Elves, that singing fair and fey
  Of vanished things that were, and could be yet,
50   Pass like a wind among the rustling trees,
  A wave of bowing grass, and we forget
Their tender voices like wind-shaken bells
Of flowers, their gleaming hair like golden asphodels.

Once Spring was here with joy, and all was fair
  Among the trees; but Summer drowsing by the stream
55   Heard trembling in her heart the secret player
  Pipe, out beyond the tangle of her forest dream,
The long-drawn tune that elvish voices made
Foreseeing Winter through the leafy glade;
60   The late flowers nodding on the ruined walls
Then stooping heard afar that haunting flute
  Beyond the sunny aisles and tree-propped halls;
For thin and clear and cold the note,
As strand of silver glass remote.

65 Then all thy trees, Kortirion, were bent,
    And shook with sudden whispering lament:
    For passing were the days, and doomed the nights
    When flitting ghost-moths danced as satellites
        Round tapers in the moveless air;
70 And doomed already were the radiant dawns,
    The fingered sunlight drawn across the lawns;
    The odour and the slumbrous noise of meads,
    Where all the sorrel, flowers, and pluméd weeds
        Go down before the scyther's share.
75 When cool October robed her dewy furze
    In netted sheen of gold-shot gossamers,
    Then the wide-umbraged elms began to fail;
    Their mourning multitude of leaves grew pale,
        Seeing afar the icy spears
80 Of Winter marching blue behind the sun
    Of bright All-Hallows. Then their hour was done,
    And wanly borne on wings of amber pale
    They beat the wide airs of the fading vale,
    And flew like birds across the misty meres.

III

85 This is the season dearest to the heart,
        And time most fitting to the ancient town,
    With waning musics sweet that slow depart
        Winding with echoed sadness faintly down
    The paths of stranded mist. O gentle time,
90 When the late mornings are begemmed with rime,
        And early shadows fold the distant woods!
    The Elves go silent by, their shining hair
        They cloak in twilight under secret hoods
    Of grey, and filmy purple, and long bands
95 Of frosted starlight sewn by silver hands.

    And oft they dance beneath the roofless sky,
        When naked elms entwine in branching lace
    The Seven Stars, and through the boughs the eye
        Stares golden-beaming in the round moon's face.
100 O holy Elves and fair immortal Folk,
    You sing then ancient songs that once awoke
        Under primeval stars before the Dawn;
    You whirl then dancing with the eddying wind,
        As once you danced upon the shimmering lawn
105 In Elvenhome, before we were, before
    You crossed wide seas unto this mortal shore.

Now are thy trees, old grey Kortirion,
Through pallid mists seen rising tall and wan,
Like vessels floating vague, and drifting far
110 Down opal seas beyond the shadowy bar
    Of cloudy ports forlorn;
Leaving behind for ever havens loud,
Wherein their crews a while held feasting proud
And lordly ease, they now like windy ghosts
115 Are wafted by slow airs to windy coasts,
    And glimmering sadly down the tide are borne.
Bare are thy trees become, Kortirion;
The rotted raiment from their bones is gone.
The seven candles of the Silver Wain,
120 Like lighted tapers in a darkened fane,
    Now flare above the fallen year.
Though court and street now cold and empty lie,
And Elves dance seldom neath the barren sky,
Yet under the white moon there is a sound
125 Of buried music still beneath the ground.
    When winter comes, I would meet winter here.

I would not seek the desert, or red palaces
    Where reigns the sun, nor sail to magic isles,
Nor climb the hoary mountains' stony terraces;
130   And tolling faintly over windy miles
To my heart calls no distant bell that rings
In crowded cities of the Earthly Kings.
    For here is heartsease still, and deep content,
Though sadness haunt the Land of withered Elms
135 (Alalminórë in the Faery Realms);
    And making music still in sweet lament
The Elves here holy and immortal dwell,
And on the stones and trees there lies a spell.

★

I give lastly the final poem, in the second of two slightly different versions;
composed (as I believe) nearly half a century after the first.

The Trees of Kortirion

I

Alalminórë

O ancient city on a leaguered hill!
    Old shadows linger in your broken gate,

Your stones are grey, your old halls now are still,
      Your towers silent in the mist await
5   Their crumbling end, while through the storeyed elms
The River Gliding leaves these inland realms
      And slips between long meadows to the Sea,
Still bearing down by weir and murmuring fall
      One day and then another to the Sea;
10   And slowly thither many days have gone
Since first the Edain built Kortirion.

Kortirion! Upon your island hill
      With winding streets, and alleys shadow-walled
Where even now the peacocks pace in drill
15   Majestic, sapphirine and emerald,
Once long ago amid this sleeping land
Of silver rain, where still year-laden stand
      In unforgetful earth the rooted trees
That cast long shadows in the bygone noon,
20   And whispered in the swiftly passing breeze,
Once long ago, Queen of the Land of Elms,
High City were you of the Inland Realms.

Your trees in summer you remember still:
The willow by the spring, the beech on hill;
25   The rainy poplars, and the frowning yews
Within your aged courts that muse
      In sombre splendour all the day,
Until the firstling star comes glimmering,
And flittermice go by on silent wing;
30   Until the white moon slowly climbing sees
In shadow-fields the sleep-enchanted trees
      Night-mantled all in silver-grey.
Alalminor! Here was your citadel,
Ere bannered summer from his fortress fell;
35   About you stood arrayed your host of elms:
Green was their armour, tall and green their helms,
      High lords and captains of the trees.
But summer wanes. Behold, Kortirion!
The elms their full sail now have crowded on
40   Ready to the winds, like masts amid the vale
Of mighty ships too soon, too soon, to sail
      To other days beyond these sunlit seas.

II

*Narquelion**

 Alalminórë! Green heart of this Isle
  Where linger yet the Faithful Companies!
45 Still undespairing here they slowly file
  Down lonely paths with solemn harmonies:
 The Fair, the first-born in an elder day,
 Immortal Elves, who singing on their way
  Of bliss of old and grief, though men forget,
50 Pass like a wind among the rustling trees,
  A wave of bowing grass, and men forget
 Their voices calling from a time we do not know,
 Their gleaming hair like sunlight long ago.

 A wind in the grass! The turning of the year.
55 A shiver in the reeds beside the stream,
 A whisper in the trees – afar they hear,
  Piercing the heart of summer's tangled dream,
 Chill music that a herald piper plays
 Foreseeing winter and the leafless days.
60 The late flowers trembling on the ruined walls
 Already stoop to hear that elven-flute.
  Through the wood's sunny aisles and tree-propped halls
 Winding amid the green with clear cold note
 Like a thin strand of silver glass remote.

65 The high-tide ebbs, the year will soon be spent;
 And all your trees, Kortirion, lament.
 At morn the whetstone rang upon the blade,
 At eve the grass and golden flowers were laid
  To wither, and the meadows bare.
70 Now dimmed already comes the tardier dawn,
 Paler the sunlight fingers creep across the lawn.
 The days are passing. Gone like moths the nights
 When white wings fluttering danced like satellites
  Round tapers in the windless air.
75 Lammas is gone. The Harvest-moon has waned.
 Summer is dying that so briefly reigned.
 Now the proud elms at last begin to quail,
 Their leaves uncounted tremble and grow pale,
  Seeing afar the icy spears

* With the name *Narquelion* (which appears also in the title in Elvish of the original poem, see p. 32) cf. *Narquelië* 'Sun-fading', name of the tenth month in Quenya (*The Lord of the Rings*, Appendix D).

80   Of winter march to battle with the sun.
            When bright All-Hallows fades, their day is done,
            And borne on wings of amber wan they fly
            In heedless winds beneath the sullen sky,
                And fall like dying birds upon the meres.

                                III

                             *Hrívion**

85   Alas! Kortirion, Queen of Elms, alas!
                This season best befits your ancient town
            With echoing voices sad that slowly pass,
                Winding with waning music faintly down
            The paths of stranded mist. O fading time,
90   When morning rises late all hoar with rime,
                And early shadows veil the distant woods!
            Unseen the Elves go by, their shining hair
                They cloak in twilight under secret hoods
            Of grey, their dusk-blue mantles gird with bands
95   Of frosted starlight sewn by silver hands.

            At night they dance beneath the roofless sky,
                When naked elms entwine in branching lace
            The Seven Stars, and through the boughs the eye
                Stares down cold-gleaming in the high moon's face.
100   O Elder Kindred, fair immortal folk!
            You sing now ancient songs that once awoke
                Under primeval stars before the Dawn;
            You dance like shimmering shadows in the wind,
                As once you danced upon the shining lawn
105   Of Elvenhome, before we were, before
            You crossed wide seas unto this mortal shore.

            Now are your trees, old grey Kortirion,
            Through pallid mists seen rising tall and wan,
            Like vessels vague that slowly drift afar
110   Out, out to empty seas beyond the bar
                Of cloudy ports forlorn;
            Leaving behind for ever havens loud,
            Wherein their crews a while held feasting proud
            In lordly ease, they now like windy ghosts
115   Are wafted by cold airs to friendless coasts,
                And silent down the tide are borne.
            Bare has your realm become, Kortirion,

            * Cf. *hrívë* 'winter', *The Lord of the Rings*, Appendix D.

Stripped of its raiment, and its splendour gone.
Like lighted tapers in a darkened fane
120 The funeral candles of the Silver Wain
    Now flare above the fallen year.
Winter is come. Beneath the barren sky
The Elves are silent. But they do not die!
Here waiting they endure the winter fell
125 And silence. Here I too will dwell;
    Kortirion, I will meet the winter here.

IV

*Mettanyë**

I would not find the burning domes and sands
    Where reigns the sun, nor dare the deadly snows,
Nor seek in mountains dark the hidden lands
130   Of men long lost to whom no pathway goes;
I heed no call of clamant bell that rings
Iron-tongued in the towers of earthly kings.
    Here on the stones and trees there lies a spell
Of unforgotten loss, of memory more blest
135   Than mortal wealth. Here undefeated dwell
The Folk Immortal under withered elms,
Alalminórë once in ancient realms.

★

I conclude this commentary with a note on my father's use of the word
Gnomes for the *Noldor*, who in the *Lost Tales* are called *Noldoli*. He con-
tinued to use it for many years, and it still appeared in earlier editions of
The Hobbit.†

In a draft for the final paragraph of Appendix F to *The Lord of the
Rings* he wrote:

I have sometimes (not in this book) used 'Gnomes' for *Noldor* and
'Gnomish' for *Noldorin*. This I did, for whatever Paracelsus may have
thought (if indeed he invented the name) to some 'Gnome' will still

---

* *Mettanyë* contains *metta* 'ending', as in *Ambar-metta*, the ending of the
world (*The Return of the King*, VI.5).

† In Chapter 3, *A Short Rest*, 'swords of the High Elves of the West'
replaced 'swords of the elves that are now called Gnomes'; and in Chapter
8, *Flies and Spiders*, the phrase 'There the Light-elves and the Deep-elves
and the Sea-elves went and lived for ages' replaced 'There the Light-elves
and the Deep-elves (or Gnomes) and the Sea-elves lived for ages'.

suggest knowledge.* Now the High-elven name of this people, Noldor, signifies Those who Know; for of the three kindreds of the Eldar from their beginning the Noldor were ever distinguished both by their knowledge of things that are and were in this world, and by their desire to know more. Yet they in no way resembled the Gnomes either of learned theory or popular fancy; and I have now abandoned this rendering as too misleading. For the Noldor belonged to a race high and beautiful, the elder Children of the world, who now are gone. Tall they were, fair-skinned and grey-eyed, and their locks were dark, save in the golden house of Finrod . . .

In the last paragraph of Appendix F *as published* the reference to 'Gnomes' was removed, and replaced by a passage explaining the use of the word *Elves* to translate *Quendi* and *Eldar* despite the diminishing of the English word. This passage – referring to the Quendi as a whole – continues however with the same words as in the draft: 'They were a race high and beautiful, and among them the Eldar were as kings, who now are gone: the People of the Great Journey, the People of the Stars. They were tall, fair of skin and grey-eyed, though their locks were dark, save in the golden house of Finrod . . .' Thus these words describing characters of face and hair were actually written of the Noldor only, and *not* of all the Eldar: indeed the Vanyar had golden hair, and it was from Finarfin's Vanyarin mother Indis that he, and Finrod Felagund and Galadriel his children, had their golden hair that marked them out among the princes of the Noldor. But I am unable to determine how this extraordinary perversion of meaning arose.†

* Two words are in question: (1) Greek *gnōmē* 'thought, intelligence' (and in the plural 'maxims, sayings', whence the English word *gnome*, a maxim or aphorism, and adjective *gnomic*); and (2) the word *gnome* used by the 16th-century writer Paracelsus as a synonym of *pygmaeus*. Paracelsus 'says that the beings so called have the earth as their element . . . through which they move unobstructed as fish do through water, or birds and land animals through air' (*Oxford English Dictionary* s.v. *Gnome²*). The *O.E.D.* suggests that whether Paracelsus invented the word himself or not it was intended to mean 'earth-dweller', and discounts any connection with the other word *Gnome*. (This note is repeated from that in *The Letters of J. R. R. Tolkien*, p. 449; see the letter (no. 239) to which it refers.)

† The name *Finrod* in the passage at the end of Appendix F is now in error: Finarfin was Finrod, and Finrod was Inglor, until the second edition of *The Lord of the Rings*, and in this instance the change was overlooked.

II
THE MUSIC OF THE AINUR

In another notebook identical to that in which *The Cottage of Lost Play* was written out by my mother, there is a text in ink in my father's hand (and all the other texts of the *Lost Tales* are in his hand, save for a fair copy of *The Fall of Gondolin**) entitled: *Link between Cottage of Lost Play and (Tale 2) Music of Ainur*. This follows on directly from Vairë's last words to Eriol on p. 20, and in turn links on directly to *The Music of the Ainur* (in a third notebook identical to the other two). The only indication of date for the *Link* and the *Music* (which were, I think, written at the same time) is a letter of my father's of July 1964 (*Letters* p. 345), in which he said that while in Oxford 'employed on the staff of the then still incomplete great Dictionary' he 'wrote a cosmogonical myth, "The Music of the Ainur"'. He took up the post on the Oxford Dictionary in November 1918 and relinquished it in the spring of 1920 (*Biography* pp. 99, 102). If his recollection was correct, and there is no evidence to set against it, some two years or more elapsed between *The Cottage of Lost Play* and *The Music of the Ainur*.

The *Link* between the two exists in only one version, for the text in ink was written over a draft in pencil that was wholly erased. In this case I follow the *Link* with a brief commentary, before giving *The Music of the Ainur*.

'But,' said Eriol, 'still are there many things that remain dark to me. Indeed I would fain know who be these Valar; are they the Gods?'

'So be they,' said Lindo, 'though concerning them Men tell many strange and garbled tales that are far from the truth, and many strange names they call them that you will not hear here'; but Vairë said: 'Nay then, Lindo, be not drawn into more tale-telling tonight, for the hour of rest is at hand, and for all his eagerness our guest is way-worn. Send now for the candles of sleep, and more tales to his head's filling and his heart's satisfying the wanderer shall have on the morrow.' But to Eriol she said: 'Think not that you must leave our house tomorrow of need; for none do so – nay, all may remain while a tale remains to tell which they desire to hear.'

Then said Eriol that all desire of faring abroad had left his heart

---

* The actual title of this tale is *Tuor and the Exiles of Gondolin*, but my father referred to it as *The Fall of Gondolin* and I do likewise.

and that to be a guest there a while seemed to him fairest of all things. Thereupon came in those that bore the candles of sleep, and each of that company took one, and two of the folk of the house bade Eriol follow them. One of these was the door-ward who had opened to his knocking before. He was old in appearance and grey of locks, and few of that folk were so; but the other had a weather-worn face and blue eyes of great merriment, and was very slender and small, nor might one say if he were fifty or ten thousand. Now that was Ilverin or Littleheart. These two guided him down the corridor of broidered stories to a great stair of oak, and up this he followed them. It wound up and round until it brought them to a passage lit by small pendent lamps of coloured glass, whose swaying cast a spatter of bright hues upon the floors and hangings.

In this passage the guides turned round a sudden corner, then going down a few dark steps flung open a door before him. Now bowing they wished him good sleep, and said Littleheart: 'dreams of fair winds and good voyages in the great seas', and then they left him; and he found that he stood in a chamber that was small, and had a bed of fairest linen and deep pillows set nigh the window – and here the night seemed warm and fragrant, although he had but now come from rejoicing in the blaze of the Tale-fire logs. Here was all the furniture of dark wood, and as his great candle flickered its soft rays worked a magic with the room, till it seemed to him that sleep was the best of all delights, but that fair chamber the best of all for sleep. Ere he laid him down however Eriol opened the window and scent of flowers gusted in therethrough, and a glimpse he caught of a shadow-filled garden that was full of trees, but its spaces were barred with silver lights and black shadows by reason of the moon; yet his window seemed very high indeed above those lawns below, and a nightingale sang suddenly in a tree nearby.

Then slept Eriol, and through his dreams there came a music thinner and more pure than any he heard before, and it was full of longing. Indeed it was as if pipes of silver or flutes of shape most slender-delicate uttered crystal notes and threadlike harmonies be-neath the moon upon the lawns; and Eriol longed in his sleep for he knew not what.

When he awoke the sun was rising and there was no music save that of a myriad of birds about his window. The light struck through the panes and shivered into merry glints, and that room with its fragrance and its pleasant draperies seemed even sweeter than before; but Eriol arose, and robing himself in fair garments laid ready for him that he might shed his raiment stained with travel went forth and strayed about the passages of the house, until he chanced upon a little stairway, and going down this he came to a porch and a sunny court. Therein was a lattice-gate that opened to his hand and led into that garden whose lawns were spread beneath the window of his room. There he wandered breathing the airs and watching the sun rise above the strange roofs of that town, when behold the aged door-ward was before him, coming along a lane of hazel-bushes. He saw not Eriol, for he held his head as ever bent towards the earth, and muttered swiftly to himself; but Eriol spake bidding him good morrow, and thereat he started.

Then said he: 'Your pardon, sir! I marked you not, for I was listening to the birds. Indeed sir you find me in a sour temper; for lo! here I have a black-winged rogue fat with impudence who singeth songs before unknown to me, and in a tongue that is strange! It irks me sir, it irks me, for methought at least I knew the simple speeches of all birds. I have a mind to send him down to Mandos for his pertness!' At this Eriol laughed heartily, but said the door-ward: 'Nay sir, may Tevildo Prince of Cats harry him for daring to perch in a garden that is in the care of Rúmil. Know you that the Noldoli grow old astounding slow, and yet have I grey hairs in the study of all the tongues of the Valar and of Eldar. Long ere the fall of Gondolin, good sir, I lightened my thraldom under Melko in learning the speech of all monsters and goblins – have I not conned even the speeches of beasts, disdaining not the thin voices of the voles and mice? – have I not cadged a stupid tune or two to hum of the speechless beetles? Nay, I have worried at whiles even over the tongues of Men, but Melko take them! they shift and change, change and shift, and when you have them are but a hard stuff whereof to labour songs or tales. Wherefore is it that this morn I felt as Ómar the Vala who knows all tongues, as I hearkened to the blending of the voices of the birds comprehending each, recognising each well-loved tune, when *tiripti lirilla* here comes a bird, an imp of Melko – but I weary you sir, with babbling of songs and words.'

'Nay, not so,' quoth Eriol, 'but I beg of you be not disheartened by one fat imp of an ousel. If my eyes deceive not, for a good age of years you have cared for this garden. Then must you know store of songs and tongues sufficient to comfort the heart of the greatest of all sages, if indeed this be the first voice that you have heard therein, and lacked its interpretation. Is it not said that the birds of every district, nay almost of every nest, speak unalike?'

''Tis said so, and said truly,' quoth Rúmil, 'and all the songs of Tol Eressëa are to be heard at times within this garden.'

'More than heart-content am I,' said Eriol, 'to have learned that one fair tongue which the Eldar speak about this isle of Tol Eressëa – but I marvelled to hear you speak as if there were many speeches of the Eldar: are there so?'

'Aye,' said Rúmil, 'for there is that tongue to which the Noldoli cling yet – and aforetime the Teleri, the Solosimpi, and the Inwir had all their differences. Yet these were slighter and are now merged in that tongue of the island Elves which you have learnt. Still are there the lost bands too that dwell wandering sadly in the Great Lands, and maybe they speak very strangely now, for it was ages gone that that march was made from Kôr, and as I hold 'twas but the long wandering of the Noldoli about the Earth and the black ages of their thraldom while their kin dwelt yet in Valinor that caused the deep sundering of their speech. Akin nonetheless be assuredly Gnome-speech and Elfin of the Eldar, as my lore teacheth me – but lo! I weary you again. Never have I found another ear yet in the world that grew not tired ere long of such discourse. "Tongues and speeches," they will say, "one is enough for me" – and thus said Littleheart the Gong-warden once upon a time: "Gnome-speech," said he, "is enough for me – did not that one Eärendel and Tuor and Bronweg my father (that mincingly ye miscall Voronwë) speak it and no other?" Yet he had to learn the Elfin in the end, or be doomed either to silence or to leave Mar Vanwa Tyaliéva – and neither fate would his heart suffer. Lo! now he is chirping Eldar like a lady of the Inwir, even Meril-i-Turinqi our queen herself – Manwë care for her. But even these be not all – there is beside the secret tongue in which the Eldar wrote many poesies and books of wisdom and histories of old and earliest things, and yet speak not. This tongue do only the Valar use in their high counsels, and not many of the Eldar of these days may read it or solve its characters. Much of it I learnt in Kôr, a lifetime gone, of the goodness of Aulë, and thereby I know many matters: very many matters.'

'Then,' quoth Eriol, 'maybe you can tell me of things that I greatly desire to know since the words by the Tale-fire yester-eve. Who be the Valar – Manwë, Aulë, and the ones ye name – and wherefore came ye Eldar from that home of loveliness in Valinor?'

Now came those two to a green arbour and the sun was up and warm, and the birds sang mightily, but the lawns were spread with gold. Then Rúmil sat upon a seat there of carven stone grown with moss, and said he: 'Very mighty are the things that you ask, and their true answer delves beyond the uttermost confines of the wastes of time, whither even the sight of Rúmil the aged of the Noldoli may not see; and all the tales of the Valar and the Elves are so knit together that one may scarce expound any one without needing to set forth the whole of their great history.'

'Yet', said Eriol, 'tell me, Rúmil, I beg, some of what you know even of the first beginnings, that I may begin to understand those things that are told me in this isle.'

But Rúmil said: 'Ilúvatar was the first beginning, and beyond that no wisdom of the Valar or of Eldar or of Men can go.'

'Who was Ilúvatar?' said Eriol. 'Was he of the Gods?'

'Nay,' said Rúmil, 'that he was not, for he made them. Ilúvatar is the Lord for Always who dwells beyond the world; who made it and is not of it or in it, but loves it.'

'This have I never heard elsewhere,' said Eriol.

'That may be,' said Rúmil, 'for 'tis early days in the world of Men as yet, nor is the Music of the Ainur much spoken of.'

'Tell me,' said Eriol, 'for I long to learn, what was the Music of the Ainur?'

Commentary on the Link between The Cottage of Lost Play and The Music of the Ainur

Thus it was that the *Ainulindalë* was first to be heard by mortal ears, as Eriol sat in a sunlit garden in Tol Eressëa. Even after Eriol (or Ælfwine) had fallen away, Rúmil remained, the great Noldorin sage of Tirion 'who first achieved fitting signs for the recording of speech and song' (*The Silmarillion* p. 63), and *The Music of the Ainur* continued to be ascribed to him, though invested with the gravity of a remote time he moved far away from the garrulous and whimsical philologist of Kortirion. It is to be noted that in this account Rúmil had been a slave under Melko.

Here the Exile of the Noldor from Valinor appears, for it is to this that Rúmil's words about the march from Kôr undoubtedly refer, rather than to Inwë's 'march into the world' (pp. 16, 26); and something is said also of the languages, and of those who spoke them.

In this link-passage Rúmil asserts:

(1) that the *Teleri*, *Solosimpi*, and *Inwir* had linguistic differences in the past;

(2) but that these dialects are now merged in the 'tongue of the island Elves';

(3) that the tongue of the *Noldoli* (Gnomes) was deeply sundered through their departure into the Great Lands and their captivity under Melko;

(4) that those Noldoli who now dwell in Tol Eressëa have learnt the tongue of the island Elves; but others remain in the Great Lands. (When Rúmil spoke of 'the lost bands that dwell wandering sadly in the Great

Lands' who 'maybe speak very strangely now' he seems to have been referring to remnants of the Noldorin exiles from Kôr who had not come to Tol Eressëa (as he himself had done), rather than to Elves who never went to Valinor.)*

In the *Lost Tales* the name given to the Sea-elves afterwards called the *Teleri* – the third of the three 'tribes' – is *Solosimpi* ('Shoreland Pipers'). It must now be explained that, confusingly enough, the first of the tribes, that led by King Inwë, were called the *Teleri* (the *Vanyar* of *The Silmaril-lion*). Who then were the *Inwir*? Eriol was told later by Meril-i-Turinqi (p. 115) that the Teleri were those that followed Inwë, 'but his kindred and descendants are that royal folk the Inwir of whose blood I am.' The Inwir were then a 'royal' clan *within the Teleri*; and the relation between the old conception and that of *The Silmarillion* can be shown thus:

	Lost Tales					*The Silmarillion*
I	Teleri	..	..	..	..	Vanyar
	(including Inwir)					
II	Noldoli	..	..	..	..	Noldor
	(Gnomes)					
III	Solosimpi	..	..	..	..	Teleri

In this link-passage Rúmil seems to say that the 'Eldar' are distinct from the 'Gnomes' – 'akin nonetheless be assuredly Gnome-speech and Elfin of the Eldar'; and 'Eldar' and 'Noldoli' are opposed in the prose preamble to *Kortirion among the Trees* (p. 25). Elsewhere 'Elfin', as a language, is used in opposition to 'Gnomish', and 'Eldar' is used of a word of form in contradistinction to 'Gnomish'. It is in fact made quite explicit in the *Lost Tales* that the Gnomes were themselves Eldar – for instance, 'the Noldoli, who were the sages of the Eldar' (p. 58); but on the other hand we read that after the Flight of the Noldoli from Valinor Aulë 'gave still his love to those few faithful Gnomes who remained still about his halls, yet did he name them thereafter "Eldar"' (p. 176). This is not so purely contradictory as appears at first sight. It seems that (on the one hand) the opposition of 'Eldar' or 'Elfin' to 'Gnomish' arose because Gnomish had become a language apart; and while the Gnomes were certainly themselves Eldar, their language was not. But (on the other hand) the Gnomes had long ago left Kôr, and thus came to be seen as not 'Koreldar', and therefore not 'Eldar'. The word *Eldar* had thus narrowed its meaning, but might at any moment be expanded again to the older sense in which the Noldoli were 'Eldar'.

If this is so, the narrowed sense of *Eldar* reflects the situation in after days in Tol Eressëa; and indeed, in the tales that follow, where the

---

* On the other hand it is possible that by 'the lost bands' he did in fact mean the Elves who were lost on the journey from the Waters of Awakening (see p. 118); i.e. the implication is: 'if the sundering of the speech of the Noldoli from that of the Eldar who remained in Valinor is very deep, how much more so must be the speech of those who never crossed the sea'.

narrative is concerned with the time before the rebellion of the Noldoli
and their departure from Valinor, they are firmly 'Eldar'. *After* the
rebellion, in the passage cited above, Aulë would not call the Noldoli
who remained in Valinor by that name – and, by implication, he would
not call those who had departed 'Eldar'.

The same ambiguity is present in the words *Elves* and *Elfin*. Rúmil
here calls the language of the Eldar 'Elfin' in opposition to 'Gnomish';
the teller of the *Tale of Tinúviel* says: 'This is my tale, and 'tis a tale of
the Gnomes, wherefore I beg that thou fill not Eriol's ear with thy Elfin
names', and in the same passage 'Elves' are specifically opposed to
'Gnomes'. But, again, in the tales that follow in this book, *Elves* and
Eldar and *Eldalië* are used interchangeably of the Three Kindreds (see
for instance the account of the debate of the Valar concerning the summoning of the Elves to Valinor, pp. 116–18). And finally, an apparently
similar variation is seen in the word 'fairy'; thus Tol Eressëa is the name
'in the fairy speech', while 'the Gnomes call it Dor Faidwen' (p. 13), but
on the other hand Gilfanon, a Gnome, is called 'one of the oldest of the
fairies' (p. 175).

It will be seen from Rúmil's remarks that the 'deep sundering' of the
speech of the Elves into two branches was at this time given an historical
basis wholly different from that which afterwards caused the division.
Here, Rúmil ascribes it to 'the long wandering of the Noldoli about the
Earth and the black ages of their thraldom while their kin dwelt yet in
Valinor' – in later terms, 'the Exile of the Noldor'. In *The Silmarillion*
(see especially pp. 113, 129) the Noldor brought the Valinórean tongue to
Middle-earth but abandoned it (save among themselves), and adopted
instead the language of Beleriand, *Sindarin* of the Grey-elves, who had
never been to Valinor: Quenya and Sindarin were of common origin,
but their 'deep sundering' had been brought about through vast ages of
separation. In the *Lost Tales*, on the other hand, the Noldor still brought
the Elvish speech of Valinor to the Great Lands, but they retained it,
and there it itself changed and became wholly different. In other words,
in the original conception the 'second tongue' only split off from the
parent speech through the departure of the Gnomes from Valinor into the
Great Lands; whereas afterwards the 'second tongue' separated from the
'first tongue' near the very beginning of Elvish existence in the world.
Nonetheless, Gnomish *is* Sindarin, in the sense that Gnomish is *the actual
language* that ultimately, as the whole conception evolved, became that
of the Grey-elves of Beleriand.

With Rúmil's remarks about the secret tongue which the Valar use and
in which the Eldar once wrote poetry and books of wisdom, but few of
them now know it, cf. the following note found in the little *Lost Tales*
pocket-book referred to on p. 23:

The Gods understood the language of the Elves but used it not among
themselves. The wiser of the Elves learned much of the speech of the

Gods and long treasured that knowledge among both Teleri and Noldoli, but by the time of the coming to Tol Eressëa none knew it save the Inwir, and now that knowledge is dead save in Meril's house.

Some new persons appear in this passage. Ómar the Vala 'who knows all tongues' did not survive the *Lost Tales*; a little more is heard of him subsequently, but he is a divinity without much substance. Tuor and Bronweg appear from the tale of *The Fall of Gondolin*, which was already written; *Bronweg* is the Gnomish form of *Voronwë*, that same Voronwë who accompanied Tuor from Vinyamar to Gondolin in the later legend. Tevildo Prince of Cats was a demonic servant of Melko and the remote forerunner of Sauron; he is a principal actor in the original story of Beren and Tinúviel, which was also already written (the *Tale of Tinúviel*).

Littleheart the Gong-warden, son of Bronweg, now receives an Elvish name, *Ilverin* (an emendation from *Elwenildo*).

The Music of the Ainur

The original hastily pencilled and much emended draft text of *The Music of the Ainur* is still extant, on loose sheets placed inside the cover of the notebook that contains a fuller and much more finished text written in ink. This second version was however closely based on the first, and changed it chiefly by additions. The text given here is the second, but some passages where the two differ notably are annotated (few of the differences between the two texts are in my opinion of much significance). It will be seen from passages of the first draft given in the notes that the plural was originally *Ainu*, not *Ainur*, and that *Ilúvatar* was originally *Ilu* (but *Ilúvatar* also occurs in the draft).

Then said Rúmil:

'Hear now things that have not been heard among Men, and the Elves speak seldom of them; yet did Manwë Súlimo, Lord of Elves and Men, whisper them to the fathers of my father in the deeps of time.[1] Behold, Ilúvatar dwelt alone. Before all things he sang into being the Ainur first, and greatest is their power and glory of all his creatures within the world and without. Thereafter he fashioned them dwellings in the void, and dwelt among them, teaching them all manner of things, and the greatest of these was music.

Now he would speak propounding to them themes of song and joyous hymn, revealing many of the great and wonderful things that he devised ever in his mind and heart, and now they would make music unto him, and the voices of their instruments rise in splendour about his throne.

Upon a time Ilúvatar propounded a mighty design of his heart to the Ainur, unfolding a history whose vastness and majesty had never been equalled by aught that he had related before, and the glory of its beginning and the splendour of its end amazed the Ainur, so that they bowed before Ilúvatar and were speechless.

Then said Ilúvatar: "The story that I have laid before you, and that great region of beauty that I have described unto you as the place where all that history might be unfolded and enacted, is related only as it were in outline. I have not filled all the empty spaces, neither have I recounted to you all the adornments and things of loveliness and delicacy whereof my mind is full. It is my desire now that ye make a great and glorious music and a singing of this theme; and (seeing that I have taught you much and set brightly the Secret Fire within you)[2] that ye exercise your minds and powers in adorning the theme to your own thoughts and devising. But I will sit and hearken and be glad that through you I have made much beauty to come to Song."

Then the harpists, and the lutanists, the flautists and pipers, the organs and the countless choirs of the Ainur began to fashion the theme of Ilúvatar into great music; and a sound arose of mighty melodies changing and interchanging, mingling and dissolving amid the thunder of harmonies greater than the roar of the great seas, till the places of the dwelling of Ilúvatar and the regions of the Ainur were filled to overflowing with music, and the echo of music, and the echo of the echoes of music which flowed even into the dark and empty spaces far off. Never was there before, nor has there been since, such a music of immeasurable vastness of splendour; though it is said that a mightier far shall be woven before the seat of Ilúvatar by the choirs of both Ainur and the sons of Men after the Great End. Then shall Ilúvatar's mightiest themes be played aright; for then Ainur and Men will know his mind and heart as well as may be, and all his intent.

But now Ilúvatar sat and hearkened, and for a great while it seemed very good to him, for the flaws in that music were few, and it seemed to him the Ainur had learnt much and well. But as the great theme progressed it came into the heart of Melko to interweave matters of his own vain imagining that were not fitting to that great theme of Ilúvatar. Now Melko had among the Ainur been given some of the greatest gifts of power and wisdom and knowledge by Ilúvatar; and he fared often alone into the dark places and the voids seeking the Secret Fire that giveth Life and Reality (for he had a very hot desire to bring things into being of his own); yet he found it not, for it dwelleth with Ilúvatar, and that he knew not till afterward.[3]

There had he nonetheless fallen to thinking deep cunning thoughts of his own, all of which he showed not even to Ilúvatar. Some of these devisings and imaginings he now wove into his music, and straightway harshness and discordancy rose about him, and many of those that played nigh him grew despondent and their music feeble, and their thoughts unfinished and unclear, while many others fell to attuning their music to his rather than to the great theme wherein they began.

In this way the mischief of Melko spread darkening the music, for those thoughts of his came from the outer blackness whither Ilúvatar had not yet turned the light of his face; and because his secret thoughts had no kinship with the beauty of Ilúvatar's design its harmonies were broken and destroyed. Yet sat Ilúvatar and hearkened till the music reached a depth of gloom and ugliness unimaginable; then did he smile sadly and raised his left hand, and immediately, though none clearly knew how, a new theme began among the clash, like and yet unlike the first, and it gathered power and sweetness. But the discord and noise that Melko had aroused started into uproar against it, and there was a war of sounds, and a clangour arose in which little could be distinguished.

Then Ilúvatar raised his right hand, and he no longer smiled but wept; and behold a third theme, and it was in no way like the others, grew amid the turmoil, till at the last it seemed there were two musics progressing at one time about the feet of Ilúvatar, and these were utterly at variance. One was very great and deep and beautiful, but it was mingled with an unquenchable sorrow, while the other was now grown to unity and a system of its own, but was loud and vain and arrogant, braying triumphantly against the other as it thought to drown it, yet ever, as it essayed to clash most fearsomely, finding itself but in some manner supplementing or harmonising with its rival.

At the midmost of this echoing struggle, whereat the halls of Ilúvatar shook and a tremor ran through the dark places, Ilúvatar raised up both his hands, and in one unfathomed chord, deeper then the firmament, more glorious than the sun, and piercing as the light of Ilúvatar's glance, that music crashed and ceased.

Then said Ilúvatar: "Mighty are the Ainur, and glorious, and among them is Melko the most powerful in knowledge; but that he may know, and all the Ainur, that I am Ilúvatar, those things that ye have sung and played, lo! I have caused to be — not in the musics that ye make in the heavenly regions, as a joy to me and a play unto yourselves, alone, but rather to have shape and reality even as have ye Ainur, whom I have made to share in the reality of Ilúvatar myself. Maybe I shall love these things that come of my song even as I love the Ainur who are of my thought,[4] and maybe more. Thou Melko shalt see that no theme can be played save it come in the end of Ilúvatar's self, nor can any alter the music in Ilúvatar's despite. He that attempts this finds himself in the end but aiding me in devising a thing of still greater grandeur and more complex wonder: – for lo! through Melko have terror as fire, and sorrow like dark waters, wrath like thunder, and evil as far from my light as the depths of the uttermost of the dark places, come into the design that I laid before you. Through him has pain and misery been made in the clash of overwhelming musics; and with confusion of sound have cruelty, and ravening, and darkness, loathly mire and all putrescence of thought or thing, foul mists and violent flame, cold without mercy, been born, and death without hope. Yet is this through him and not by him; and he shall see, and ye all likewise, and even shall those beings, who must now dwell among his evil and endure through Melko misery and sorrow, terror and wickedness, declare in the end that it redoundeth only to my great glory, and doth but make the theme more worth the hearing, Life more worth the living, and the World so much the more wonderful and marvellous, that of all the deeds of Ilúvatar it shall be called his mightiest and his loveliest."

Then the Ainur feared and comprehended not all that was said, and Melko was filled with shame and the anger of shame; but Ilúvatar seeing their amaze arose in glory and went forth from his dwellings, past those fair regions he had fashioned for the Ainur, out into the dark places; and he bade the Ainur follow him.

Now when they reached the midmost void they beheld a sight of surpassing beauty and wonder where before had been emptiness; but Ilúvatar said: "Behold your choiring and your music! Even as ye played so of my will your music took shape, and lo! even now the world unfolds and its history begins as did my theme in your hands. Each one herein will find contained within the design that is mine the adornments and embellishments that he himself devised; nay, even Melko will discover those things there which he thought to contrive of his own heart, out of harmony with my mind, and he will find them but a part of the whole and tributary to its glory. One thing only have I added, the fire that giveth Life and Reality" – and behold, the Secret Fire burnt at the heart of the world.

Then the Ainur marvelled to see how the world was globed amid the void and yet separated from it; and they rejoiced to see light, and found it was both white and golden, and they laughed for the pleasure of colours, and for the great roaring of the ocean they were filled with longing. Their hearts were glad because of air and the winds, and the matters whereof the Earth was made – iron and stone and silver and gold and many substances: but of all these water was held the fairest and most goodly and most greatly praised. Indeed there liveth still in water a deeper echo of the Music of the Ainur than in any substance else that is in the world, and at this latest day many of the Sons of Men will hearken unsatedly to the voice of the Sea and long for they know not what.

Know then that water was for the most part the dream and invention of Ulmo, an Ainu whom Ilúvatar had instructed deeper than all others in the depths of music; while the air and winds and the ethers of the firmament had Manwë Súlimo devised, greatest and most noble of the Ainur. The earth and most of its goodly substances did Aulë contrive, whom Ilúvatar had taught many things of wisdom scarce less than Melko, yet was there much therein that was nought of his.[5]

Now Ilúvatar spake to Ulmo and said: "Seest thou not how Melko hath bethought him of biting colds without moderation, yet hath not destroyed the beauty of thy crystal waters nor of all thy limpid pools. Even where he has thought to conquer utterly, behold snow has been made, and frost has wrought his exquisite works; ice has reared his castles in grandeur."

Again said Ilúvatar: "Melko hath devised undue heats, and fires without restraint, and yet hath not dried up thy desire nor utterly quelled the music of thy seas. Rather behold now the height and glory of the clouds and the magic that dwells in mist and vapours; listen to the whisper of rains upon the earth."

Then said Ulmo: "Yea truly is water fairer now than was my best devising before. Snow is of a loveliness beyond my most secret thoughts, and if there is little music therein, yet rain is beautiful indeed and hath a music that filleth my heart, so glad am I that my ears have found it, though its sadness is among the saddest of all things. Lo! I will go seek Súlimo of the air and winds, that he and I play melodies for ever and ever to thy glory and rejoicing."

Now Ulmo and Manwë have been great friends and allies in almost all matters since then.[6]

Now even as Ilúvatar spake to Ulmo, the Ainur beheld how the

world unfolded, and that history which Ilúvatar had propounded to
them as a great music was already being carried out. It is of their
gathered memories of the speech of Ilúvatar and the knowledge,
incomplete it may be, that each has of their music, that the Ainur
know so much of the future that few things are unforeseen by them –
yet are there some that be hidden even from these.[7] So the Ainur
gazed; until long before the coming of Men – nay, who does not
know that it was countless ages before even the Eldar arose and sang
their first song and made the first of all the gems, and were seen by
both Ilúvatar and the Ainur to be of exceeding loveliness – there grew
a contention among them, so enamoured did they become of the
glory of the world as they gazed upon it, and so enthralled by the
history enacted therein to which the beauty of the world was but the
background and the scene.

Now this was the end, that some abode still with Ilúvatar beyond
the world – and these were mostly those who had been engrossed in
their playing with thoughts of Ilúvatar's plan and design, and cared
only to set it forth without aught of their own devising to adorn it;
but some others, and among them many of the most beautiful and
wisest of the Ainur, craved leave of Ilúvatar to dwell within the world.
For said they: "We would have the guarding of those fair things of
our dreams, which of thy might have now attained to reality and
surpassing beauty; and we would instruct both Eldar and Men in
their wonder and uses whenso the times come that those appear upon
Earth by your intent, first the Eldar and at length the fathers of the
fathers of Men." And Melko feigned that he desired to control the
violence of the heats and turmoils he had set in the Earth, but of a
truth purposed deep in his heart to usurp the power of the other
Ainur and make war upon Eldar and Men, for he was wroth at those
great gifts which Ilúvatar had purposed to give to these races.[8]

Now Eldar and Men were of Ilúvatar's devising only, nor, for
they comprehended not fully when Ilúvatar first propounded their
being, did any of the Ainur dare in their music to add anything to
their fashion; and these races are for that reason named rightly the
Children of Ilúvatar. This maybe is the cause wherefore many others
of the Ainur, beside Melko, have ever been for meddling with both
Elves and Men, be it of good or evil intent; yet seeing that Ilúvatar
made the Eldar most like in nature if not in power and stature to
the Ainur, while to Men he gave strange gifts, their dealings have
been chiefly with the Elves.[9]

Knowing all their hearts, still did Ilúvatar grant the desire of the
Ainur, nor is it said he was grieved thereat. So entered these great

ones into the world, and these are they whom we now call the Valar (or the Vali, it matters not).[10] They dwelt in Valinor, or in the firmament; and some on earth or in the deeps of the Sea. There Melko ruled both fires and the cruellest frost, both the uttermost colds and the deepest furnaces beneath the hills of flame; and whatso is violent or excessive, sudden or cruel, in the world is laid to his charge, and for the most part with justice. But Ulmo dwells in the outer ocean and controls the flowing of all waters and the courses of rivers, the replenishment of springs and the distilling of rains and dews throughout the world. At the bottom of the sea he bethinks him of music deep and strange yet full ever of a sorrow: and therein he has aid from Manwë Súlimo.

The Solosimpi, what time the Elves came and dwelt in Kôr, learnt much of him, whence cometh the wistful allurement of their piping and their love to dwell ever by the shore. Salmar there was with him, and Ossë and Ónen to whom he gave the control of the waves and lesser seas, and many another.

But Aulë dwelt in Valinor and fashioned many things; tools and instruments he devised and was busied as much in the making of webs as in the beating of metals; tillage too and husbandry was his delight as much as tongues and alphabets, or broideries and painting. Of him did the Noldoli, who were the sages of the Eldar and thirsted ever after new lore and fresh knowledge, learn uncounted wealth of crafts, and magics and sciences unfathomed. From his teaching, whereto the Eldar brought ever their own great beauty of mind and heart and imagining, did they attain to the invention and making of gems; and these were not in the world before the Eldar, and the finest of all gems were Silmarilli, and they are lost.

Yet was the greatest and chief of those four great ones Manwë Súlimo; and he dwelt in Valinor and sate in a glorious abode upon a throne of wonder on the topmost pinnacle of Taniquetil that towers up upon the world's edge. Hawks flew ever to and fro about that abode, whose eyes could see to the deeps of the sea or penetrate the most hidden caverns and profoundest darkness of the world. These brought him news from everywhere of everything, and little escaped him – yet did some matters lie hid even from the Lord of the Gods. With him was Varda the Beautiful, and she became his spouse and is Queen of the Stars, and their children were Fionwë-Úrion and Erinti most lovely. About them dwell a great host of fair spirits, and their happiness is great; and men love Manwë even more than mighty Ulmo, for he hath never of intent done ill to them nor is he so fain of honour or so jealous of his power as that ancient one

of Vai. The Teleri whom Inwë ruled were especially beloved of
him, and got of him poesy and song; for if Ulmo hath a power of
musics and of voices of instruments Manwë hath a splendour of
poesy and song beyond compare.

Lo, Manwë Súlimo clad in sapphires, ruler of the airs and wind,
is held lord of Gods and Elves and Men, and the greatest bulwark
against the evil of Melko.'[11]

Then said Rúmil again:

'Lo! After the departure of these Ainur and their vassalage all
was quiet for a great age while Ilúvatar watched. Then on a sudden
he said: "Behold I love the world, and it is a hall of play for Eldar
and Men who are my beloved. But when the Eldar come they will
be the fairest and the most lovely of all things by far; and deeper in
the knowledge of beauty, and happier than Men. But to Men I will
give a new gift, and a greater." Therefore he devised that Men
should have a free virtue whereby within the limits of the powers
and substances and chances of the world they might fashion and
design their life beyond even the original Music of the Ainur that
is as fate to all things else. This he did that of their operations everything should in shape and deed be completed, and the world fulfilled
unto the last and smallest.[12] Lo! Even we Eldar have found to our
sorrow that Men have a strange power for good or ill and for turning
things despite Gods and Fairies to their mood in the world; so that
we say: "Fate may not conquer the Children of Men, but yet are
they strangely blind, whereas their joy should be great."

Now Ilúvatar knew that Men set amid the turmoils of the Ainur
would not be ever of a mind to use that gift in harmony with his
intent, but thereto he said: "These too in their time shall find that
all they have done, even the ugliest of deeds or works, redounds at
the end only to my glory, and is tributary to the beauty of my world."
Yet the Ainur say that the thought of Men is at times a grief even to
Ilúvatar; wherefore if the giving of that gift of freedom was their
envy and amazement, the patience of Ilúvatar at its misuse is a
matter of the greatest marvelling to both Gods and Fairies. It is
however of one with this gift of power that the Children of Men
dwell only a short time in the world alive, yet do not perish utterly
for ever, whereas the Eldar dwell till the Great End[13] unless they be
slain or waste in grief (for to both of these deaths are they subject),
nor doth eld subdue their strength, except it may be in ten thousand
centuries; and dying they are reborn in their children, so that their
number minishes not, nor grows. Yet while the Sons of Men will

after the passing of things of a certainty join in the Second Music of the Ainur, what Ilúvatar has devised for the Eldar beyond the world's end he has not revealed even to the Valar, and Melko has not discovered it.'

NOTES

1   This opening sentence is lacking in the draft.
2   The reference to the setting of the Secret Fire within the Ainur is lacking in the draft.
3   This passage, from 'Now Melko had among the Ainur . . .', is developed from one much briefer in the draft: 'Melko had among the Ainu fared most often alone into the dark places and the voids [added afterwards: seeking the secret fires].'
4   The words 'my song' and 'my thought' were in the text as written in reversed positions, and were emended afterwards in pencil to the reading given. At the beginning of the text occurs the phrase: 'Before all things he sang into being the Ainur first.' Cf. the opening of the Ainulindalë in The Silmarillion: 'The Ainur . . . that were the offspring of his thought.'
5   There is no reference here in the draft to Manwë or Aulë.
6   This sentence concerning the friendship and alliance of Manwë and Ulmo is lacking in the draft.
7   This passage was quite different in the draft text:
    And even as Ilu was speaking to Ulmo the Ainu beheld how the great history which Ilu had propounded to them to their amazement and whereto all his glory was but the hall of its enactment – how it was unfolding in myriad complexities even as had been the music they played about the feet of Ilu, how beauty was whelmed in uproar and tumult and again new beauty arose therefrom, how the earth changed and stars went out and stars were kindled, and the air swept about the firmament, and the sun and moon were loosened on their courses and had life.
8   This sentence concerning Melko is lacking in the draft.
9   In the draft this paragraph reads:
    Now Eldar and Men were of Ilu's devising alone, nor had any of the Ainu nor even Melko aught to do with their fashioning, though in truth his music of old and his deeds in the world mightily affected their history thereafter. For this reason maybe, Melko and many of the Ainu out of good or evil mind would ever be for meddling with them, but seeing that Ilu had made the Eldar too alike in nature if not in stature to the Ainu their dealings have been chiefly with Men.
    The conclusion of this passage seems to be the only place where the second text is in direct contradiction of the draft.

10   The draft has: 'and these are they whom ye and we now call the Valur and Valir.'

11   The entire passage following the mention of the Solosimpi and 'their love to dwell ever by the shore' is lacking in the draft.

12   For this passage the draft has:

> "... but to Men I will appoint a task and give a great gift." And he devised that they should have free will and the power of fashioning and designing beyond the original music of the Ainu, that by reason of their operations all things shall in shape and deed be fulfilled, and the world that comes of the music of the Ainu be completed unto the last and smallest.

13   'whereas the Eldar dwell for ever' draft text.

Changes made to names in
The Music of the Ainur

Ainur   Always *Ainu* in the draft text.

Ilúvatar   Usually *Ilu* in the draft text, but also *Ilúvatar*.

Ulmo   In the draft text Ulmo is thus named but also *Linqil* (corrected to *Ulmo*).

Solosimpi < *Solosimpë*.

Valar or Vali   Draft text *Valur and Valir* (these appear to be masculine and feminine forms).

Ónen < *Ówen*.

Vai < *Ulmonan*.

Commentary on
The Music of the Ainur

A linking passage continues the text of *The Music of the Ainur* and leads into the story of *The Building of Valinor* without any break in the narrative; but I postpone this link until the next chapter. The actual written text is likewise continuous between the two tales, and there is no suggestion or indication that the composition of *The Building of Valinor* did not follow that of *The Music of the Ainur*.

In later years the Creation myth was revised and rewritten over and over again; but it is notable that in this case only and in contrast to the development of the rest of the mythology there is a direct tradition, manuscript to manuscript, from the earliest draft to the final version: each text is directly based on the one preceding.* Moreover, and most

---

* For compariso. with the published text in *The Silmarillion* it should be noted that some of the matter of the early version does not appear in the *Ainulindalë* itself but at the end of Chapter 1, *Of the Beginning of Days* (pp. 39–42).

remarkably, the earliest version, written when my father was 27 or 28 and embedded still in the context of the Cottage of Lost Play, was so evolved in its conception that it underwent little change of an essential kind. There were indeed very many changes, which can be followed stage by stage through the successive texts, and much new matter came in; but the fall of the original sentences can continually be recognized in the last version of the *Ainulindalë*, written more than thirty years later, and even many phrases survived.

It will be seen that the great theme that Ilúvatar propounded to the Ainur was originally made somewhat more explicit ('The story that I have laid before you,' p. 53), and that the words of Ilúvatar to the Ainur at the end of the Music contained a long declaration of what Melko had brought about, of what he had introduced into the world's history (p. 55). But by far the most important difference is that in the early form the Ainur's first sight of the World was in its actuality ('even now the world unfolds and its history begins', p. 55), not as a Vision that was taken away from them and only given existence in the words of Ilúvatar: *Eä! Let these things Be!* (*The Silmarillion* p. 20).

Yet when all differences have been observed, they are much less remarkable than the solidity and completeness with which the myth of the Creation emerged at its first beginning.

In this 'Tale', also, many specific features of less general import make their appearance; and many of them were to survive. Manwë, called 'lord of Gods and Elves and Men', is surnamed *Súlimo*, 'ruler of the airs and wind'; he is clad in sapphires, and hawks of penetrating sight fly from his dwelling on Taniquetil (*The Silmarillion* p. 40); he loves especially the Teleri (the later Vanyar), and from him they received their gifts of poetry and song; and his spouse is Varda, Queen of the Stars.

Manwë, Melko, Ulmo, and Aulë are marked out as 'the four great ones'; ultimately the great Valar, the *Aratar*, came to be numbered nine, but there was much shifting in the membership of the hierarchy before this was reached. The characteristic concerns of Aulë, and his particular association with the Noldoli, emerge here as they were to remain, though there is attributed to him a delight in 'tongues and alphabets', whereas in *The Silmarillion* (p. 39), while this is not denied, it seems to be implied that this was rather the peculiar endowment and skill of the Noldorin Elves; later in the *Lost Tales* (p. 141) it is said that Aulë himself 'aided by the Gnomes contrived alphabets and scripts'. Ulmo, specially associated with the Solosimpi (the later Teleri), is here presented as more 'fain of his honour and jealous of his power' than Manwë; and he dwells in Vai. Vai is an emendation of Ulmonan; but this is not simply a replacement of one name by another: Ulmonan was the name of Ulmo's halls, which were in Vai, the Outer Ocean. The significance of Vai, an important element in the original cosmology, will emerge in the next chapter.

Other divine beings now appear. Manwë and Varda have offspring, Fionwë-Úrion and Erinti. Erinti later became Ilmarë 'handmaid of Varda'

(*The Silmarillion* p. 30), but nothing was ever told of her (see p. 202). Fionwë, his name long afterwards changed to Eönwë, endured to become the Herald of Manwë, when the idea of 'the Children of the Valar' was abandoned. Beings subordinate to Ulmo, Salmar, Ossë, and Ónen (later Uinen) appear; though these all survived in the pantheon, the conception of Maiar did not emerge for many years, and Ossë was long numbered among the Valar. The Valar are here referred to as 'Gods' (indeed when Eriol asked 'are they the Gods?' Lindo replied that they were, p. 45), and this usage survived until far on in the development of the mythology.

The idea of Elvish rebirth in their own children is here formally stated, and the different fates of Elves and Men. In this connection, the following curious matter may be mentioned. Early in the text just given (p. 53) occurs the sentence: 'It is said that a mightier [music] far shall be woven before the seat of Ilúvatar by the choirs of both Ainur *and the sons of Men* after the Great End'; and in the concluding sentence of the text: 'Yet while *the sons of Men* will after the passing of things of a certainty join in the Second Music of the Ainur, what Ilúvatar has devised for the Eldar beyond the world's end he has not revealed even to the Valar, and Melko has not discovered it.' Now in the first revision of the *Ainulindalë* (which dates from the 1930s) the first of these sentences was changed to read: '. . . by the choirs of the Ainur *and the Children of Ilúvatar* after the end of days'; whereas the second remained, in this essential, unchanged. This remained the case right through to the final version. It is possible that the change in the first passage was unintentional, the substitution of another common phrase, and that this was never subsequently picked up. However, in the published work (pp. 15, 42) I left the two passages as they stand.

III
THE COMING OF THE VALAR
AND THE BUILDING OF VALINOR

As I have already noticed, the next tale is linked to *The Music of the Ainur* without narrative break; and it has no title in the text. It is contained in three separate books (the *Lost Tales* were written in the most bewildering fashion, with sections from different tales interleaved with each other); and on the cover of the book that has the opening section, following on *The Music of the Ainur*, is written: 'containeth also the Coming of the Valar and beginneth the Building of Valinor'. The text is in ink, written over an erased pencil manuscript.

Then when Rúmil finished and fell silent Eriol said after a pause: 'Great are these tidings and very new and strange in my ears, yet doth it seem that most whereof you have yet told happened outside this world, whereas if I know now wherefrom comes its life and motion and the ultimate devising of its history, I would still hear many things of the earliest deeds within its borders; of the labours of the Valar I would know, and the great beings of most ancient days. Whereof, tell me, are the Sun or the Moon or the Stars, and how came their courses and their stations? Nay more – whence are the continents of the earth, the Outer Lands, the great seas, and the Magic Isles? Even of the Eldar and their arising and of the coming of Men I would listen to your tales of wisdom and wonder.'

Then answered Rúmil: 'Nay, but your questions are nigh as long and wordy as my tales – and the thirst of your curiosity would dry a well deeper than even my lore, an I let you drink and come again unstinted to your liking. Indeed you know not what you ask nor the length and complexity of the stories you would hear. Behold, the sun is well above the roofs and this is no hour of the day for the telling of tales. Rather is it time already, and something more, for the breaking of the fast.' With these words Rúmil went down that lane of hazels, and passing a space of sunlight entered the house at great speed, for all that he looked ever before his toes as he went.

But Eriol sat musing in that arbour, pondering what he had heard, and many questions came into his mind that he desired to ask, until he forgot that he fasted still. But now comes Littleheart and another bearing covers and fair linen, and they say to him: 'It is the words of

Rúmil the Sage that you are fainting in the Arbour of the Thrushes for hunger and for weariness of his garrulous tongue – and thinking that very like to be, we are come to aid thee.'

Then Eriol thanked them, and breaking his fast spent the remainder of that fair day hidden in the quiet alleys of that garden deep in thought; nor did he have lack of pleasance, for although it seemed enclosed within great stone walls covered with fruit-trees or with climbing plants whose golden and red blossoms shone beneath the sun, yet were the nooks and corners of the garden, its coppices and lawns, its shady ways and flowering fields, without end, and exploration discovered always something new. Nonetheless even greater was his joy when that night again the toast was drunk to the 'Rekindling of the Magic Sun' and the candles held aloft and the throng went once more to the room where the Tale-fire burnt.

There said Lindo: 'Is it to be tales, as of custom, again this night, or shall it be musics and the singing of songs?' And the most said songs and music, and thereat skilled ones arose who sang old melodies or maybe roused dead minstrelsy of Valinor to life amid the flicker of that firelit room. Some too spake poesies concerning Kôr, and Eldamar, short snatches of the wealth of old; but soon the song and music died down and there was a quiet, while those there thought of the departed beauty and longed eagerly for the Rekindling of the Magic Sun.

Now at length spake Eriol to Lindo, saying: 'One Rúmil the doorward, and, methought, a great sage, did this morning in the garden relate to me the beginning of the world and the coming of the Valar. Now fain would I hear of Valinor!'

Then said Rúmil, for he sat upon a stool in a deep-shadowed nook: 'Then with the leave of Lindo and of Vairë I will begin the tale, else will you go on asking for ever; and may the company have pardon if they hear old tales again.' But Vairë said that those words concerning the oldest things were far from stale yet in the ears of the Eldar.

Then said Rúmil:

'Behold, Manwë Súlimo and Varda the Beautiful arose. Varda it was who at the playing of the Music had thought much of light that was of white and silver, and of stars. Those twain gathered now wings of power to themselves and fared swiftly through the three airs. Vaitya is that which is wrapped dark and sluggish about the world and without it, but Ilwë is blue and clear and flows among the stars, and last came they to Vilna that is grey and therein may the birds fly safely.

With them came many of those lesser Vali who loved them and

had played nigh them and attuned their music to theirs, and these are the Mánir and the Súruli, the sylphs of the airs and of the winds.

Now swiftly as they fared Melko was there before them, having rushed headlong flaming through the airs in the impetuosity of his speed, and there was a tumult of the sea where he had dived and the mountains above him spouted flames and the earth gaped and rocked; but Manwë beholding this was wroth.

Thereafter came Ulmo and Aulë, and with Ulmo were none, save Salmar only who was after known as Noldorin, for good though the heart of that mighty one he thought ever deep thoughts alone, and was silent and aloof and haughty even to the Ainur; but with Aulë was that great lady Palúrien whose delights were richness and fruits of the earth, for which reason has she long been called Yavanna among the Eldar. About them fared a great host who are the sprites of trees and woods, of dale and forest and mountain-side, or those that sing amid the grass at morning and chant among the standing corn at eve. These are the Nermir and the Tavari, Nandini and Orossi, brownies, fays, pixies, leprawns, and what else are they not called, for their number is very great: yet must they not be confused with the Eldar, for they were born before the world and are older than its oldest, and are not of it, but laugh at it much, for had they not somewhat to do with its making, so that it is for the most part a play for them; but the Eldar are of the world and love it with a great and burning love, and are wistful in all their happiness for that reason.

Now behind those greatest chieftains came Falman-Ossë of the waves of the sea and Ónen his consort, and with them the troops of the Oarni and Falmaríni and the long-tressed Wingildi, and these are the spirits of the foam and the surf of ocean. Now Ossë was a vassal and subordinate to Ulmo, and was so for fear and reverence and not for love. Behind him there came Tulkas Poldórëa rejoicing in his strength, and those brethren the Fánturi, Fantur of Dreams who is Lórien Olofántur, and Fantur of Death who is Vefántur Mandos, and those twain also who are named Tári for they are ladies of great worship, queens of the Valar. The one was the spouse of Mandos, and is known to all as Fui Nienna by reason of her glooms, and she is fain of mourning and tears. Many other names has she that are spoken seldom and all are grievous, for she is Núri who sighs and Heskil who breedeth winter, and all must bow before her as Qalmë-Tári the mistress of death. But lo, the other was the spouse of Oromë the hunter who is named Aldaron king of forests, who shouts for joy upon mountain-tops and is nigh as lusty as that perpetual youth Tulkas. Oromë is the son of Aulë and Palúrien, and that Tári who is his wife is known to all as Vána the fair and loveth mirth and youth and beauty, and is happiest of all beings, for she is Tuilérë or as the Valar said Vána Tuivána who bringeth spring, and all sing her praises as Tári-Laisi mistress of life.

Yet even when all these had crossed the confines of the world and Vilna was in uproar with their passing, there came still hurrying late Makar and his fierce sister Meássë; and it had been better had they not found the world but remained for ever with the Ainur beyond Vaitya and the stars, for both were spirits of quarrelsome mood, and with some other lesser ones who came now with them had been the first and chief to join in the discords of Melko and to aid in the spreading of his music.

Last of all came Ómar who is called Amillo, youngest of the great Valar, and he sang songs as he came.

Then when all these great spirits were gathered together within the confines of the world Manwë spake to them, saying: "Lo now! How may the Valar abide in this fair place or be happy and rejoice in its goodness, if Melko be suffered to destroy it, and make fire and turmoil, so that we have not where to sit in peace, nor may the earth blossom or the designs of Ilúvatar come to being?"

Then all the Valar were angered with Melko, and Makar alone spoke against Manwë; but the rest chose certain of their number to seek out the wrongdoer, and these were Mandos and Tulkas, Mandos for that of his dread aspect was Melko more in fear than of aught else save it were the strength of Tulkas' arm, and Tulkas was the other.

Now those two sought him out and constrained him to come before Manwë, and Tulkas whose heart misliked the crooked guile of Melko gave him a blow with his fist, and he abode that then but did not forget. Yet did he speak the Gods fair, and said how he did scant harm, revelling only a while in the newness of the world; nor, said he, would he ever seek to do aught against the lordship of Manwë or the dignity of those chiefs Aulë and Ulmo, nor indeed to the hurt of any beside. Rather was it his counsel that each of the Valar should now depart and dwell amid those things that he loved upon Earth, nor should any seek to extend his sway beyond its just boundaries. In this there was some covert reflection upon Manwë and Ulmo, but of the Gods some took his words in faith and would use his advice, but others distrusted; and in the midst of their debate Ulmo arose and went to the Outermost Seas that were set beyond the Outer Lands. He loved not high words nor concourse of folk, and in those deep waters moveless and empty he purposed to dwell, leaving the governance of the Great and lesser seas to Ossë and Ónen his vassals. Yet ever of his magic deep in his outermost sea-halls of Ulmonan he controlled the faint stirrings of the Shadowy Seas, and ruled the lakes and springs and rivers of the world.

Now this was the manner of the Earth in those days, nor has it since changed save by the labours of the Valar of old. Mightiest of regions are the Great Lands where Men do dwell and wander now, and the Lost Elves sing and dance upon the hills; but beyond their westernmost limits lie the Great Seas, and in that vast water of the West are many smaller lands and isles, ere the lonely seas are found whose waves whisper about the Magic Isles. Farther even than this, and few are the boats of mortal men that have dared so far, are set the Shadowy Seas whereon there float the Twilit Isles and the Tower of Pearl rises pale upon their most western cape; but as yet it was not built, and the Shadowy Seas stretched dark away till their uttermost shore in Eruman.

Now the Twilit Isles are reckoned the first of the Outer Lands, which are these and Eruman and Valinor. Eruman or Arvalin is to the southward, but the Shadowy Seas run even to the edges of Eldamar to the north; yet must ships sail farther to reach these silver strands, for beyond Eruman stand the Mountains of Valinor in a great ring curving westward, and the Shadowy Seas to north of Eruman bend a vast bay inward, so that waves beat even upon the feet of the great cliffs and the Mountains stand beside the sea. There is Taniquetil glorious to behold, loftiest of all mountains, clad in purest snow, and he looks from the bay's head southward across Eruman and northward across the Bay of Faëry; indeed all the Shadowy Seas, even the sails of ships upon the sunlit waters of the great ocean and the throngs about westward havens in the lands of Men could afterward be seen therefrom, albeit that distance is counted out in unimagined leagues. But as yet the Sun had not risen and the Mountains of Valinor had not been raised, and the vale of Valinor lay wide and cold. Beyond Valinor I have never seen or heard, save that of a surety there are the dark waters of the Outer Seas, that have no tides, and they are very cool and thin, that no boat can sail upon their bosom or fish swim within their depths, save the enchanted fish of Ulmo and his magic car.

Thither is he now gone, but the Gods hold council concerning the words of Melko. It was the rede of Aulë and of his wife Palúrien, for they were the most grieved by the mischief of Melko's turmoils and trusted his promises not at all, that the Gods should not separate as

he bid, lest he take it into his heart perchance to attack them singly
or do hurt to their possessions. "Is he not," said they, "more powerful
than any one of us save Manwë only? Rather let us build a dwelling
wherein we may abide in joy together, faring only at need to the
care and survey of our goods and fiefs. There even such as be of
other mind may dwell at times, and find rest and pleasance after
labours in the world." Now Aulë's mind and fingers itched already
to be making things, and he urged this matter the more for that;
and to most of the Gods it seemed a good counsel, and they fared
about the world seeking a place to dwell in. Those were the days of
Gloaming (Lomendánar), for light there was, silver and golden, but
it was not gathered together but flowed and quivered in uneven
streams about the airs, or at times fell gently to the earth in glittering
rain and ran like water on the ground; and at that time Varda in her
playing had set but a few stars within the sky.

In this dimness the Gods stalked North and South and could see
little; indeed in the deepest of these regions they found great cold
and solitude and the rule of Melko already fortified in strength; but
Melko and his servants were delving in the North, fashioning the
grim halls of Utumna, for he had no thought to dwell amongst the
others, howso he might feign peace and friendship for the time.

Now because of the darkness Aulë suaded Melko to build two
towers to the North and South, for he purposed to set upon them
mighty lamps one upon each. These did Aulë himself fashion of gold
and silver, and the pillars were raised by Melko and were very tall,
and shone like pale blue crystal; and when Aulë smote them with
his hand they rang like metal. They sprang up through the lower air
even to Ilwë and the stars, and Melko said they were of an imperish-
able substance of great strength that he had devised; and he lied,
for he knew that they were of ice. That one of the North he named
Ringil and of the South Helkar, and the lamps were made ready and
set upon them, being filled with gathered light, silver to the North
and golden to the South. This light had Manwë and Varda gathered
lavishly from the sky, that the Gods might the better explore the
regions of the world, and choose the fairest for their home.

Now in that flaming light did they fare East and West, and East
was a waste of tumbled lands and West great seas of darkness, for
indeed they were gathered now upon those Twilit Isles and stood
there gazing westward, when lo! the lamps to North and South
flickered and fell, and as they fell the waters rose about the isles.
Now these things they did not then understand, but it so happened
that the blaze of those lights had melted the treacherous ice of the

pillars of Melko, Ringil and Helkar, and great floods of water had poured from them into the Shadowy Seas. So great was their thaw that whereas those seas were at first of no great size but clear and warm, now were they black and wide and vapours lay upon them and deep shades, for the great cold rivers that poured into them. Thus were the mighty lamps unseated from on high and the clangour of their fall shook the stars, and some of their light was spilled again into the air, but much flowed upon the earth and made fires and deserts for its great volume ere it gathered into lakes and pools.

Then was the time of first night and it was very long; but the Valar were sorely wroth at the treachery of Melko and were like to be whelmed in the shadowy seas that now arose and sucked about their feet, covering many of the islands in their waves.

Then Ossë, for Ulmo was not there, gathered to him the Oarni, and putting forth their might they dragged that island whereon stood the Valar westward from the waters till they came to Eruman, whose high shores held the angry flood – and that was the first tide.

Then said Manwë: "Now will we make a dwelling speedily and a bulwark against evil." So they fared over Arvalin and saw a wide open space beyond, reaching for unknown leagues even to the Outer Seas. There, said Aulë, would be a place well suited to great building and to a fashioning of realms of delight; wherefore the Valar and all their folk first gathered the most mighty rocks and stones from Arvalin and reared therewith huge mountains between it and that plain which now they name Valinor, or the land of the Gods. Aulë indeed it was himself who laboured for seven ages at Manwë's bidding in the piling of Taniquetil, and the world rumbled in the gloom and Melko heard the noises of their labour. By reason of their great masonry is Erumáni now very broad and bare and of a marvellous level, for they removed all the stone and rock that was there; but the Mountains of Valinor are rugged and of impregnable height. Seeing at length that these towered mightily between Valinor and the world the Gods drew breath; but Aulë and Tulkas fared abroad with many of their folk and brought back all they might of marbles and good stones, of iron and gold and silver and bronze and all manner of substances. These they heaped amid the plain, and straightway Aulë began to labour mightily.

At last he says: "It is ill working in this gloom, and 'twas an evil deed of Melko's that brought to ruin those fair lamps." But Varda answering said: "Still is there much light remaining both in the airs and that which floweth spilled upon the earth", and she wished to gather new store and set a beacon on Taniquetil. But Manwë suffered not more radiance to be gleaned from heaven, for that the dark was already that of night, but at his asking Ulmo rose from his deeps and fared to the blazing lakes and the pools of brilliance. Therefrom he drew rivers of light into vast vessels, pouring back waters in their place, and with these he got him back to Valinor. There was all the light poured into two great cauldrons that Aulë fashioned in the gloom against his return, and those are called Kulullin and Silindrin.

Now in the midmost vale they digged two great pits, and those are leagues asunder yet nigh together beside the vastness of that plain. In the one did Ulmo set seven rocks of gold brought from the most silent deeps of the sea, and a fragment was cast thereafter of the lamp that had burned awhile upon Helkar in the South. Then was the pit covered with rich earths that Palúrien devised, and Vána came who loveth life and sunlight and at whose song the flowers arise and open, and the murmur of her maidens round her was like to the merry noise of folk that stir abroad for the first time on a bright morning. There sang she the song of spring upon the mound, and danced about it, and watered it with great streams of that golden light that Ulmo had brought from the spilled lakes – yet was Kulullin almost o'erflowing at the end.

But in the other pit they cast three huge pearls that Ossë found in the Great Sea, and a small star Varda cast after them, and they covered it with foams and white mists and thereafter sprinkled lightly earth upon it, but Lórien who loveth twilights and flittering shadows, and sweet scents borne upon evening winds, who is the lord of dreams and imaginings, sat nigh and whispered swift noiseless words, while his sprites played half-heard tunes beside him like music stealing out into the dark from distant dwellings; and the Gods poured upon that place rivers of the white radiance and silver light which Silindrin held even to the brim – and after their pouring was Silindrin yet well nigh full.

Then came Palúrien, even Kémi the Earth-lady, wife of Aulë, mother of the lord of forests, and she wove spells about those two places, deep enchantments of life and growth and putting forth of leaf, blossoming and yielding of fruit – but she mingled no word of fading in her song. There having sung she brooded for a great while, and the Valar sat in a circle about, and the plain of Valinor was dark. Then after a time there came at last a bright gleam of gold amid the gloom, and a cry of joy and praise was sent up by the Valar and all their companies. Behold from that place that had been watered from Kulullin rose a slender shoot, and from its bark pale gold effulgence poured; yet did that plant grow apace so that in seven hours there was a tree of mighty stature, and all the Valar and their folk might sit beneath its branches. Of a great shapeliness and goodly growth was that stock, and nought was there to break its smooth rind, which glowed faintly with a yellow light, for a vast height above the earth. Then did fair boughs thrust overhead in all directions, and golden buds swelled from all the twigs and lesser branches, and from these burst leaves of a rich green whose edges shone. Already was the light that that tree gave wide and fair, but as the Valar gazed it put forth blossom in exceeding great profusion, so that all its boughs were hidden by long swaying clusters of gold flowers like a myriad hanging lamps of flame, and light spilled from the tips of these and splashed upon the ground with a sweet noise.

Then did the Gods praise Vána and Palúrien and rejoice in the light, saying to them: "Lo, this is a very fair tree indeed, and must have a name unto itself," and Kémi said: "Let it be called Laurelin, for the brightness of its blossom and the music of its dew," but Vána would call it Lindeloksë, and both names remain.

Now was it twelve hours since Lindeloksë had first sprouted, and at that hour did a glint of silver pierce the yellow blaze, and behold the Valar saw a shoot arise in that place whereto the pools of Silindrin had been poured. It had a bark of tender white that gleamed like pearls and it grew even as swiftly as had Laurelin, and as it grew the glory of Laurelin abated and its blossom shone less, till that tree glowed only gently as in sleep: but, behold, the other waxed now to a stature even as lofty as Laurelin, and its stock was yet more shapely and more slender, and its rind like silk, but its boughs above were thicker and more tangled and its twigs denser, and they put forth masses of bluish green leaves like spearheads.

Then did the Valar stare in wonder, but Palúrien said: "Not yet has this tree ceased its growing", and behold as she spake it blossomed, and its blossoms did not hang in clusters but were like separate flowers growing each on fine stems that swung together, and were as silver and pearls and glittering stars and burnt with a white light; and it seemed as if the tree's heart throbbed, and its radiance wavered thereto waxing and waning. Light like liquid silver distilled from its bole and dripped to earth, and it shed a very great illumination about the plain, yet was that not as wide as the light of the tree of gold, and by reason also of its great leaves and of the throb of its inward life it cast a continual flutter of shadows among the pools of its brightness, very clear and black; whereat Lórien could not contain his joy, and even Mandos smiled. But Lórien said: "Lo! I will give this tree a name and call it Silpion", and that has ever been its name since. Then Palúrien arose and said to the Gods: "Gather ye now all the light that drips in liquid shape from this fair tree and store it in Silindrin, and let it fare thence but very sparingly. Behold, this tree, when the twelve hours of its fullest light are past, will wane again, and thereat will Laurelin blaze forth once more; but that it may not be exhausted water it ever gently from the cauldron of Kulullin at the hour when Silpion grows dim, but to Silpion do ye in the same manner, pouring back the gathered light from deep Silindrin at every waning of the tree of gold. Light is the sap of these trees and their sap is light!"

And in these words did she signify that albeit these trees must needs be watered with light to have sap and live, yet of their growth and being did they ever make light in great abundance still over and beyond that which their roots sucked in; but the Gods hearkened to her bidding, and Vána caused one of her own maidens, even Urwen, to care ever for this task of watering Laurelin, while Lórien bade Silmo, a youth he loved, to be ever mindful of the refreshing of Silpion. Wherefore is it said that at either watering of the trees there was a wondrous gloaming of gold and silver and mingled lights great beauty ere one tree quite faded or the other came to its full glory.

Now because of the bright trees had Aulë light in plenty for his works, and he set about many tasks, and Tulkas aided him much, and Palúrien mother of magic was at his side. First upon Taniquetil was a great abode raised up for Manwë and a watchtower set. Thence did he speed his darting hawks and receive them on his return, and thither fared often in later days Sorontur King of Eagles whom Manwë gave much might and wisdom.

That house was builded of marbles white and blue and stood amid the fields of snow, and its roofs were made of a web of that blue air called *ilwë* that is above the white and grey. This web did Aulë and his wife contrive, but Varda spangled it with stars, and Manwë dwelt thereunder; but in the plain in the full radiance of the trees was a cluster of dwellings built like a fair and smiling town, and that town was named Valmar. No metal and no stone, nor any wood of mighty trees was spared to their raising. Their roofs were of gold and their floors silver and their doors of polished bronze; they were lifted with spells and their stones were bound with magic. Separate from these and bordering upon the open vale was a great court, and this was Aulë's house, and it was filled with magic webs woven of the light of Laurelin and the sheen of Silpion and the glint of stars; but others there were made of threads of gold and silver and

iron and bronze beaten to the thinness of a spider's filament, and all
were woven with beauty to stories of the musics of the Ainur,
picturing those things that were and shall be, or such as have only
been in the glory of the mind of Ilúvatar.

In this court were some of all the trees that after grew upon the
earth, and a pool of blue water lay among them. There fruits fell
throughout the day, thudding richly to the earth upon the grass of
its margin, and were gathered by Palúrien's maids for her feasting
and her lord's.

Ossë too had a great house, and dwelt therein whenso a conclave
of the Valar was held or did he grow weary of the noise of the waves
upon his seas. Ónen and the Oarni brought thousands of pearls for
its building, and its floors were of sea-water, and its tapestries like
the glint of the silver skins of fishes, and it was roofed with foam.
Ulmo dwelt not in Valmar and fared back after its building to the
Outer Seas, and did he have need ever of sojourn in Valinor he would
go as guest to the halls of Manwë; – but this was not often. Lórien
too dwelt far away, and his hall was great and dimly lit and had wide
gardens. The place of his dwelling he called Murmuran, which Aulë
made of mists gathered beyond Arvalin upon the Shadowy Seas.
'Twas set in the South by the feet of the Mountains of Valinor upon
the confines of the realm, but its gardens wandered marvellously
about, winding nigh to the feet of Silpion whose shining lit them
strangely. They were full of labyrinths and mazes, for Palúrien had
given Lórien great wealth of yewtrees and cedars, and of pines that
exuded drowsy odours in the dusk; and these hung over deep pools.
Glowworms crept about their borders and Varda had set stars within
their depths for the pleasure of Lórien, but his sprites sang wonderfully in these gardens and the scent of nightflowers and the songs of
sleepy nightingales filled them with great loveliness. There too grew
the poppies glowing redly in the dusk, and those the Gods called
fumellar the flowers of sleep – and Lórien used them much in his
enchantments. Amidmost of those pleasances was set within a ring
of shadowy cypress towering high that deep vat Silindrin. There it
lay in a bed of pearls, and its surface unbroken was shot with silver
flickerings, and the shadows of the trees lay on it, and the Mountains
of Valinor could see their faces mirrored there. Lórien gazing upon
it saw many visions of mystery pass across its face, and that he
suffered never to be stirred from its sleep save when Silmo came
noiselessly with a silver urn to draw a draught of its shimmering
cools, and fared softly thence to water the roots of Silpion ere the
tree of gold grew hot.

Otherwise was the mind of Tulkas, and he dwelt amidmost of Valmar. Most youthful is he and strong of limb and lusty, and for that is he named Poldórëa who loveth games and twanging of bows and boxing, wrestling, running, and leaping, and songs that go with a swing and a toss of a well-filled cup. Nonetheless is he no wrangler or striker of blows unprovoked as is Makar, albeit there are none of Valar or Úvanimor (who are monsters, giants, and ogres) that do not fear the sinews of his arm and the buffet of his iron-clad fist, when he has cause for wrath. His was a house of mirth and revelry; and it sprang high into the air with many storeys, and had a tower of bronze and pillars of copper in a wide arcade. In its court men played and rivalled one another in doughty feats, and there at times would that fair maiden Nessa wife of Tulkas bear goblets of the goodliest wine and cooling drinks among the players. But most she loved to retire unto a place of fair lawns whose turf Oromë her brother had culled from the richest of all his forest glades, and Palúrien had planted it with spells that it was always green and smooth. There danced she among her maidens as long as Laurelin was in bloom, for is she not greater in the dance than Vána herself?

In Valmar too dwelt Noldorin known long ago as Salmar, playing now upon his harps and lyres, now sitting beneath Laurelin and raising sweet music with an instrument of the bow. There sang Amillo joyously to his playing, Amillo who is named Ómar, whose voice is the best of all voices, who knoweth all songs in all speeches; but whiles if he sang not to his brother's harp then would he be trilling in the gardens of Oromë when after a time Nielíqui, little maiden, danced about its woods.

Now Oromë had a vast domain and it was beloved by him, and no less by Palúrien his mother. Behold, the groves of trees they planted upon the plain of Valinor and even upon the foothills of the mountains have no compare on Earth. Beasts revelled there, deer among the trees, and herds of kine among its spaces and wide grass-lands; bison there were, and horses roaming unharnessed, but these strayed never into the gardens of the Gods, yet were they in peace and had no fear, for beasts of prey dwelt not among them, nor did Oromë fare to hunting in Valinor. Much indeed as he loves those realms yet is he very often in the world without; more often even than Ossë and as often as Palúrien, and then does he become the greatest of all huntsmen. But in Valmar his halls are wide and low, and skins and fells of great richness and price are strewn there without end upon the floor or hung upon the walls, and spears and bows and knives thereto. In the midst of each room and hall a living tree grows and holds up the roof, and its bole is hung with trophies and with antlers. Here is all Oromë's folk in green and brown and there is a noise of boisterous mirth, and the lord of forests makes lusty cheer; but Vána his wife so often as she may steals thence. Far away from the echoing courts of that house lie her gardens, fenced stoutly from the wilder lands with whitethorn of great size that blossoms like everlasting snow. Its innermost solitude is walled with roses, and this is the place best beloved of that fair lady of the Spring. Amidmost of this place of odorous air did Aulë set long ago that cauldron, gold Kulullin, filled ever with the radiance of Laurelin like shining water, and thereof he contrived a fountain so that all the garden was full of the health and happiness of its pure light. Birds sang there all the year with the full throat of spring, and flowers grew in a riot of blossom and of glorious life. Yet was none ever of that splendour spilled from the vat of gold save when Vána's maidens led by Urwen left that garden at the waxing of Silpion to water the roots of the tree of flame; but by the fountain it was always light with the amber light of day, as bees made busy about the roses, and there trod Vána lissomly while larks sang above her golden head.

So fair were these abodes and so great the brilliance of the trees of Valinor that Vefántur and Fui his wife of tears might not endure to stay there long, but fared away far to the northward of those regions, where beneath the roots of the most cold and northerly of the Mountains of Valinor, that rise here again almost to their height nigh Arvalin, they begged Aulë to delve them a hall. Wherefore, that all the Gods might be housed to their liking, he did so, and they and all their shadowy folk aided him. Very vast were those caverns that they made stretching even down under the Shadowy Seas, and they are full of gloom and filled with echoes, and all that deep abode is known to Gods and Elves as Mandos. There in a sable hall sat Vefántur, and he called that hall with his own name Vê. It was lit only with a single vessel placed in the centre, wherein there lay some gleaming drops of the pale dew of Silpion: it was draped with dark vapours and its floors and columns were of jet. Thither in after days fared the Elves of all the clans who were by illhap slain with weapons or did die of grief for those that were slain — and only so might the Eldar die, and then it was only for a while. There Mandos spake their doom, and there they waited in the darkness, dreaming of their past deeds, until such time as he appointed when they might again be born into their children, and go forth to laugh and sing again. To Vê Fui came not much, for she laboured rather at the distilling of salt humours whereof are tears, and black clouds she wove and floated up that they were caught in the winds and went about the world, and their lightless webs settled ever and anon upon those that dwelt therein. Now these tissues were despairs and hopeless mourning, sorrows and blind grief. The hall that she loved best was one yet wider and more dark than Vê, and she too named it with her own name, calling it Fui. Therein before her black chair burnt a brazier with a single flickering coal, and the roof was of bats' wings, and the pillars that upheld it and the walls about were made of basalt. Thither came the sons of Men to hear their doom, and thither are they brought by all the multitude of ills that Melko's evil music set within the world. Slaughters and fires, hungers and mishaps, diseases and blows dealt in the dark, cruelty and bitter cold and anguish and their own folly bring them here; and Fui reads their hearts. Some then she keeps in Mandos beneath the mountains and some she drives forth beyond the hills and Melko seizes them and bears them to Angamandi, or the Hells of Iron, where they have evil days. Some too, and these are the many, she sends aboard the black ship Mornië, who lieth ever and anon in a dark harbour of the North awaiting those times when the sad pomp winds to the beach down slow rugged paths from Mandos.

Then, when she is laden, of her own accord she spreads her sable sails and before a slow wind coasts down those shores. Then do all aboard as they come South cast looks of utter longing and regret to that low place amid the hills where Valinor may just be glimpsed upon the far off plain; and that opening is nigh Taniquetil where is the strand of Eldamar. No more do they ever see of that bright place, but borne away dwell after on the wide plains of Arvalin. There do they wander in the dusk, camping as they may, yet are they not utterly without song, and they can see the stars, and wait in patience till the Great End come.

Few are they and happy indeed for whom at a season doth Nornorë the herald of the Gods set out. Then ride they with him in chariots or upon good horses down into the vale of Valinor and feast in the halls of Valmar, dwelling in the houses of the Gods until the Great End come. Far away are they from the black mountains of the North or the misty plains of Arvalin, and music and fair light is theirs, and joy.

And lo! Now have I recounted the manner of the dwellings of all the great Gods which Aulë of his craftsmanship raised in Valinor, but Makar and his fierce sister Meássë built them a dwelling of themselves, aided only by their own folk, and a grim hall it was.

Upon the confines of the Outer Lands did it stand, nor was it

very far from Mandos. Of iron was it made, and unadorned. There
fought the vassals of Makar clad in armour, and a clash there was
and a shouting and a braying of trumps, but Meássë fared among the
warriors and egged them to more blows, or revived the fainting with
strong wine that they might battle still; and her arms were reddened
to the elbow dabbling in that welter. None of the Gods fared ever
there, save Tulkas, and did they seek to visit Mandos they went
thither by circuitous paths to avoid passing nigh to that clamorous
hall; but Tulkas would at times wrestle there with Makar or deal
sledge-blows among the fighters, and this he did that he might not
grow soft in his fair living, for he loved not that company nor in
sooth did they love him and his great unangered strength. Now the
battle of the courts of Makar was waged unceasingly save when men
gathered in the halls for feasting, or at those times when Makar and
Meássë were far abroad hunting together in the black mountains
wolves and bears. But that house was full of weapons of battle in
great array, and shields of great size and brightness of polish were
on the walls. It was lit with torches, and fierce songs of victory, of
sack and harrying, were there sung, and the torches' red light was
reflected in the blades of naked swords. There sit often Makar and
his sister listening to the songs, and Makar has a huge bill across his
knees and Meássë holds a spear. But in those days ere the closing
of Valinor did these twain fare mostly about the Earth and were often
far from the land, for they loved the unbridled turmoils which
Melko roused throughout the world.

Therefore is Valinor now built, and there is great peace there, and
the Gods in joy, for those quarrelsome spirits dwell not much among
them, and Melko comes not nigh.'

Then said a child among the company, a great drinker-in of both
tales and poesies: 'And would that he had never come there since,
and would that I might have seen that land still gleaming new as
Aulë left it.' Now she had heard Rúmil tell his tale before and was
much in thought of it, but to the most of the company it was new,
even as it was to Eriol, and they sat amazed. Then said Eriol: 'Very
mighty and glorious are the Valar, and I would fain hear yet more
of those oldest days, did I not see the glimmer of the Candles of
Sleep that fare now hither'; but another child spoke from a cushion
nigh Lindo's chair and said: 'Nay, 'tis in the halls of Makar I would
fain be, and get perchance a sword or knife to wear; yet in Valmar
methinks 'twould be good to be a guest of Oromë', and Lindo laughing said: ''Twould be good indeed,' and thereat he arose, and the
tale-telling was over for that night.

NOTES

Changes made to names in
The Coming of the Valar and the Building of Valinor

Ónen < *Ówen* (at the first occurrence only; subsequently *Ónen* is the name as first written).

Eruman and *Arvalin* The names of this region were originally written *Habbanan* and *Harmalin*, but were emended throughout the tale (except in two cases where *Habbanan* was overlooked) to *Eruman* (once *Erumáni*, p. 70) and *Arvalin*. (In the last three occurrences *Habbanan* > *Arvalin*, whereas in the earlier ones *Habbanan* > *Eruman*; but the difference is presumably without significance, since the names *Habbanan* / *Harmalin* and later *Eruman* / *Arvalin* were interchangeable.) In *The Cottage of Lost Play* the changes were *Harwalin* > *Harmalin* > *Arvalin* (p. 22).

Lomendánar < *Lome Danar*.

Silindrin < *Telimpë* (*Silindrin*) (at the first occurrence only; subsequently *Silindrin* is the name as first written).

Lindeloksë < *Lindelótë* (cf. p. 22).

Commentary on
The Coming of the Valar and the Building of Valinor

The abundant instruction provided by Rúmil on this occasion is best discussed in sections, and I begin with:

(i) The Coming of the Valar and their encounter with Melko
(pp. 65–7)

The description of the entry of the Valar into the world was not retained, though the account of them in this passage is the ultimate origin of that in the *Valaquenta* (*The Silmarillion* pp. 25–9): not, however, by continuous manuscript progression. The passage is of much interest, for here appear all at once many figures of the mythology who were to endure, beside others who were not. It is remarkable how many of the names of the Valar in the earliest writings were never afterwards displaced or reshaped: *Yavanna, Tulkas, Lórien, Nienna, Oromë, Aldaron, Vána, Nessa*, first appearing in this tale, and *Manwë, Súlimo, Varda, Ulmo, Aulë, Mandos, Ossë, Salmar*, who have appeared previously. Some were retained in a modified form: *Melkor* for *Melko*, *Uinen* (which appears already later in the *Lost Tales*) for *Ónen*, *Fëanturi* for *Fánturi*; while yet others, as Yavanna *Palúrien* and Tulkas *Poldórëa*, survived long in the 'Silmarillion' tradition before being displaced by *Kementári* (but cf. *Kémi* 'Earth-lady' in this tale) and *Astaldo*. But some of these early Valar had disappeared by the next stage or phase after the *Lost Tales*: Ómar-Amillo, and the barbaric war-gods Makar and Meássë.

Here appear also certain relations that survived to the latest form. Thus Lórien and Mandos were from the beginning 'brethren', each with his special association, of 'dreams' and 'death'; and Nienna stood from the beginning in a close relationship with them, here as 'the spouse of Mandos', though afterwards as the sister of the Fëanturi. The original conception of Nienna was indeed darker and more fearful, a death-goddess in close association with Mandos, than it afterwards became. Ossë's uncertain relations with Ulmo are seen to go back to the beginnings; but Ulmo's haughtiness and aloofness subsequently disappeared, at least as a feature of his divine 'character' explicitly described. Vána was already the spouse of Oromë, but Oromë was the son of Aulë and (Yavanna) Palúrien; in the later evolution of the myths Vána sank down in relation to Nienna, whereas Oromë rose, becoming finally one of the great Valar, the *Aratar*.

Particularly interesting is the passage concerning the host of lesser spirits who accompanied Aulë and Palúrien, from which one sees how old is the conception of the Eldar as quite dissimilar in essential nature from 'brownies, fays, pixies, leprawns', since the Eldar are 'of the world' and bound to it, whereas those others are beings from before the world's making. In the later work there is no trace of any such explanation of the 'pixie' element in the world's population: the Maiar are little referred to, and certainly not said to include such beings as 'sing amid the grass at morning and chant among the standing corn at eve'.*

Salmar, companion of Ulmo, who has appeared in *The Music of the Ainur* (p. 58), is now identified with Noldorin, who was mentioned by Vairë in *The Cottage of Lost Play* (p. 16); such of his story as can be discerned will appear later. Subsequent writings say nothing of him save that he came with Ulmo and made his horns (*The Silmarillion* p. 40).

In the later development of this narrative there is no mention of Tulkas (or Mandos!) going off to round up Melkor at the very outset of the history of the Valar in Arda. In *The Silmarillion* we learn rather of the great war between the Valar and Melkor 'before Arda was full-shaped', and how it was the coming of Tulkas from 'the far heaven' that routed him, so that he fled from Arda and 'brooded in the outer darkness'.

---

* Cf. *The Silmarillion* p. 30: 'With the Valar came other spirits whose being also began before the world, of the same order as the Valar but of less degree. These are the Maiar, the people of the Valar, and their servants and helpers. Their number is not known to the Elves, and few have names in any of the tongues of the Children of Ilúvatar.' An earlier version of this passage reads: 'Many lesser spirits they [the Valar] brought in their train, both great and small, and some of these Men have confused with the Eldar or Elves; but wrongly, for they were before the world, but Elves and Men awoke first in the world after the coming of the Valar.'

(ii) The earliest conception of the Western Lands, and the Oceans

In *The Cottage of Lost Play* the expression 'Outer Lands' was used of the lands to the east of the Great Sea, later Middle-earth; this was then changed to 'Great Lands' (p. 21). The 'Outer Lands' are now defined as

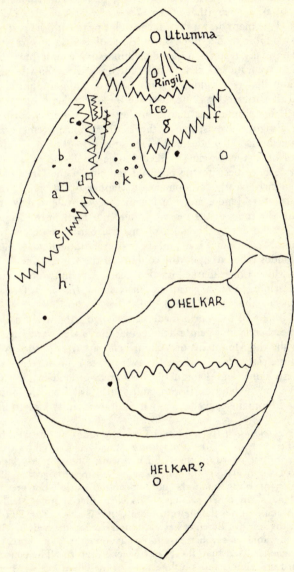

The earliest map

the Twilit Isles, Eruman (or Arvalin), and Valinor (p. 68). A curious usage, which often appears in the *Lost Tales*, is the equation of 'the world' with the Great Lands, or with the whole surface of the earth west of the Outer Lands; so the mountains 'towered mightily between Valinor and the world' (p. 70), and King Inwë heard 'the lament of the world' (p. 16).

It is convenient to reproduce here a map (p. 81), which actually appears in the text of a later tale (that of *The Theft of Melko and the Darkening of Valinor*). This map, drawn on a manuscript page with the text written round it, is no more than a quick scribble, in soft pencil, now rubbed and faded, and in many features difficult or impossible to interpret. The re-drawing is as accurate as I can make it, the only feature lost being some indecipherable letters (beginning with M) preceding the word *Ice*. I have added the letters *a*, *b*, *c*, etc. to make the discussion easier to follow.

Utumna (later Utumno) is placed in the extreme North, north of the lamp-pillar Ringil; the position of the southern pillar seems from this map to have been still undecided. The square marked *a* is obviously Valmar, and I take the two dots marked *b* to be the Two Trees, which are stated later to have been to the north of the city of the Gods. The dot marked *c* is fairly clearly the domain of Mandos (cf. p. 76, where it is said that Vefántur Mandos and Fui Nienna begged Aulë to delve them a hall 'beneath the roots of the most cold and northerly of the Mountains of Valinor');* the dot to the south of this can hardly represent the hall of Makar and Meássë, since it is said (p. 77-8) that though it was not very far from Mandos it stood 'upon the confines of the Outer Lands'.

The area which I have marked *h* is Eruman / Arvalin (which ultimately came to be named Avathar), earlier *Habbanan* / *Harmalin* (*Harwalin*), which are simple alternatives (see p. 79).

Later, in a map of the world made in the 1930s, the western shore of the Great Sea bends in a gentle and regular curve westward from north to south, while the Mountains of Valinor bend in virtually the reverse of the same curve eastward,)(; where the two curves come together at their midpoints are Túna, and Taniquetil. Two areas of land in the shape of elongated Vs thus extend northward and southward from the midpoint, between the Mountains and the Sea, which draw steadily away from each

---

* In *The Silmarillion* (p. 28) the halls of Mandos stood 'westward in Valinor'. The final text of the *Valaquenta* actually has 'northward', but I changed this to 'westward' in the published work (and similarly 'north' to 'west' on p. 52) on the basis of the statement in the same passage that Nienna's halls are 'west of West, upon the borders of the world', but are near to those of Mandos. In other passages it is clear that Mandos' halls were conceived as standing on the shores of the Outer Sea; cf. *The Silmarillion* p. 186: 'For the spirit of Beren at her bidding tarried in the halls of Mandos, until Lúthien came to say her last farewell upon the dim shores of the Outer Sea, whence Men that die set out never to return'. The conceptions of 'northward in Valinor' and 'on the shores of the Outer Sea' are not how-ever contradictory, and I regret this piece of unwarranted editorial meddling.

other; and these are named Eruman (to the northward) and Arvalin (to the southward).

In the little primitive map the line of the mountains is already thus, and it is described in the text as 'a great ring curving westward' (the curve is westward if the extremities are considered rather than the central portion) But the curve of the coast is different. Unhappily the little map is here very obscure, for there are several lines (marked *j*) extending north-wards from Kôr (marked *d*), and it is impossible to make out whether marks on them are directions for erasure or whether they represent parallel mountain-chains. But I think that in fact these lines merely represent variant ideas for the curve of the Mountains of Valinor in the north; and I have little doubt that at this time my father had no conception of a region of 'waste' north of Kôr and east of the mountains. This inter-pretation of the map agrees well with what is said in the tale (p. 68): 'the Shadowy Seas to north of Eruman bend a vast bay inwards, so that waves beat even upon the feet of the great cliffs, and the Mountains stand beside the sea', and 'Taniquetil looks from the bay's head southward across Eruman and northward across the Bay of Faëry'. On this view the name *Eruman* (later *Araman*), at first an alternative to *Arvalin*, was taken over for the northern waste when the plan of the coastal regions became more symmetrical.

It is said in the tale (p. 68) that 'in that vast water of the West are many smaller lands and isles, ere the lonely seas are found whose waves whisper about the Magic Isles'. The little circles on the map (marked *k*) are evidently a schematic representation of these archipelagoes (of the Magic Isles more will be told later). The Shadowy Seas, as will emerge more clearly later, were a region of the Great Sea west of Tol Eressëa. The other letters on the map refer to features that have not yet entered the narrative.

In this tale we meet the important cosmological idea of the Three Airs, Vaitya, Ilwë, and Vilna, and of the Outer Ocean, tideless, cold, and 'thin'. It has been said in *The Music of the Ainur* (p. 58) that Ulmo dwells in the Outer Ocean and that he gave to Ossë and Ónen 'control of the waves and lesser seas'; he is there called 'the ancient one of Vai' (emended from Ulmonan). It is now seen that *Ulmonan* is the name of his halls in the Outer Ocean, and also that the 'lesser seas' controlled by Ossë and Ónen include the Great Sea (p. 68).

There exists a very early and very remarkable drawing, in which the world is seen in section, and is presented as a huge 'Viking' ship, with mast arising from the highest point of the Great Lands, single sail on which are the Sun and Moon, sailropes fastened to Taniquetil and to a great mountain in the extreme East, and curved prow (the black marks on the sail are an ink-blot). This drawing was done fairly rapidly in soft pencil on a small sheet; and it is closely associated with the cosmology of the *Lost Tales*.

I give here a list of the names and words written on the drawing with,

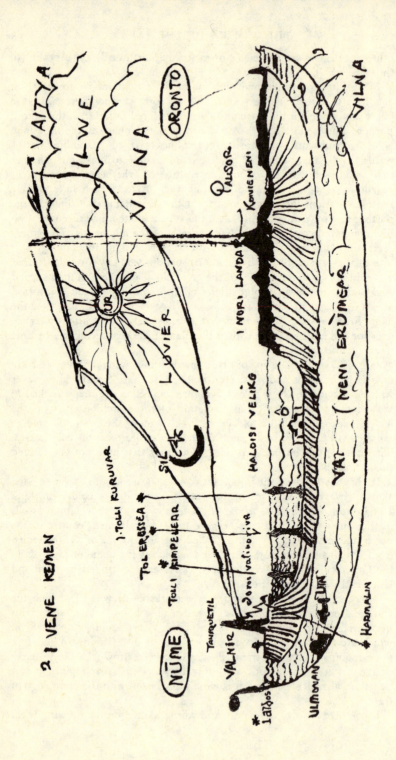

so far as possible, their meanings (but without any etymological detail, for which see the Appendix on Names, where names and words occurring only on this drawing are given separate entries).

I Vene Kemen   This is clearly the title of the drawing; it might mean 'The Shape of the Earth' or 'The Vessel of the Earth' (see the Appendix on Names, entry *Glorvent*).

Nūme   'West'.

Valinor; *Taniquetil*   (The vast height of Taniquetil, even granting the formalisation of this drawing, is noteworthy: it is described in the tale as being so high that 'the throngs about westward havens in the lands of Men could be seen therefrom' (p. 68). Its fantastic height is conveyed in my father's painting, dating from 1927–8 (*Pictures by J. R. R. Tolkien*, no. 31).)

Harmalin   Earlier name of *Arvalin* (see p. 79).

i aldas   'The Trees' (standing to the west of Taniquetil).

Toros valinoriva   *Toros* is obscure, but in any case the first letter of the first word, if it is a T, is a very uncharacteristic one. The reference seems to be to the Mountains of Valinor.

Tolli Kimpelear   These must be the Twilit Isles, but I have found no other occurrence of *Kimpelear* or anything similar.

Tol Eressëa   'The Lonely Isle'.

I Tolli Kuruvar   'The Magic Isles'.

Haloisi Velike   'The Great Sea'.

Ô   'The Sea'. (What is the structure at the sea-bottom shown below the name *Ô*? It must surely be the dwelling of Ossë beneath the Great Sea that is referred to in the next tale (p. 106).)

I Nori Landar   Probably means 'The Great Lands'.

Koivienéni   The precursor of *Cuiviénen*, the Waters of Awakening.

Palisor   The land where the Elves awoke.

Sil   'Moon'.

Ûr   'Sun'.

Luvier   'Clouds'.

Oronto   'East'.

Vaitya, *Ilwë*, and *Vilna* appear in the three layers described in the tale (p. 65), and *Vilna* reappears in the bottom right-hand corner of the drawing. There is nothing said in the *Lost Tales* to explain this last feature, nor is it at all evident what is represented by the curled lines in the same place (see p. 86).

Ulmonan   The halls of Ulmo.

Uin   The Great Whale, who appears later in the *Tales*.

Vai   The Outer Ocean.

Neni Erùmear   'Outermost Waters'=*Vai*.

It is seen from the drawing that the world floats in and upon Vai. This is indeed how Ulmo himself describes it to the Valar in a later tale (p. 214):

> Lo, there is but one Ocean, and that is Vai, for those that Ossë esteemeth
> as oceans are but seas, waters that lie in the hollows of the rock . . . In
> this vast water floateth the wide Earth upheld by the word of Ilúvatar . . .

In the same passage Ulmo speaks of the islands in the seas, and says that
('save some few that swim still unfettered') they 'stand now like pinnacles
from their weedy depths', as is also well seen in the drawing.

It might seem a plausible idea that there was some connection (physical
as well as etymological) between *Vai* and *Vaitya*, the outermost of the
Three Airs, 'wrapped dark and sluggish about the world and without it'
(at a later point in the *Tales*, p. 181, there is a reference to 'the dark
and tenuous realm of Vaitya that is outside all'). In the next 'phase' of
the mythical cosmology (dating from the 1930s, and very clearly and fully
documented and illustrated in a work called *Ambarkanta*, The Shape of
the World) the whole world is contained within *Vaiya*, a word meaning
'fold, envelope'; Vaiya 'is more like to sea below the Earth and more
like to air above the Earth' (which chimes with the description of the
waters of Vai (p. 68) as very 'thin', so that no boat can sail on them nor
fish swim in them, save the enchanted fish of Ulmo and his car); and in
Vaiya below the Earth dwells Ulmo. Thus Vaiya is partly a development
of Vaitya and partly of Vai.

Now since in the earliest word-list of the Qenya tongue (see the
Appendix on Names) both *Vaitya* ('the outermost air beyond the world')
and *Vai* ('the outer ocean') are derived from a root *vaya-* 'enfold', and
since Vaitya in the present tale is said to be 'wrapped about the world
and without it', one might think that Vaitya-Vai already in the early
cosmology was a continuous enfolding substance, and that the later
cosmology, in this point, only makes explicit what was present but un-
expressed in the *Lost Tales*. But there is certainly no actual suggestion of
this idea in any early writing; and when we look again at the drawing it
seems untenable. For Vai is obviously *not* continuous with Vaitya; and
if the appearance of Vilna in the bottom of the drawing is taken to mean
that the Earth, *and* the ocean Vai in and on which it floats, were contained
within the Three Airs, of which we see the reappearance of the innermost
(Vilna) below the earth and Vai, then the suggestion that Vaitya–Vai were
continuous is still more emphatically confounded.

There remains the baffling question of the representation of the world
as a ship. In only one place is there a suggestion that my father conceived
the world in such a way: the passage that I have cited above, in which
Ulmo addresses the Valar on the subject of Vai, concludes:

> O Valar, ye know not all wonders, and many secret things are there
> *beneath the Earth's dark keel*, even where I have my mighty halls of
> Ulmonan, that ye have never dreamed on.

But in the drawing Ulmonan is not beneath the ship's keel, it is within the ship's hull; and I am inclined to think that Ulmo's words 'beneath the Earth's dark keel' refer to the shape of the Earth itself, which is certainly ship-like. Moreover, close examination of the original drawing strongly suggests to me that the mast and sail, and still more clearly the curved prow, *were added afterwards*. Can it be that the shape of the Earth and of Vai as he had drawn them – with the appearance of a ship's hull – prompted my father to add mast, sail, and prow as a *jeu d'esprit*, without deeper significance? That seems uncharacteristic and unlikely, but I have no other explanation to offer.*

(iii) The Lamps (pp. 69–70)

In this part of the narrative the tale differs remarkably from the later versions. Here there is no mention of the dwelling of the Valar on the Isle of Almaren after the making of the Lamps (*The Silmarillion* p. 35), nor of course of the return of Melko from 'outside' – because here Melko not only did not leave the world after entering it, but actually himself made the pillars of the Lamps. In this story, though Melko was distrusted by some, his guileful co-operation (even to the extent of contributing names for the pillars) was accepted, whereas in the later story his hostility and malice were known and manifest to the Valar, even though they did not know of his return to Arda and the building of Utumno until too late. In the present tale there is a trickiness, a low cunning, in Melko's behaviour that could not survive (yet the story of his deceitful making of the pillars out of ice survived into the versions of the 1930s).

Later, it was the Lamps themselves that were named (ultimately, after intervening forms had been devised and discarded, *Illuin* the northern Lamp and *Ormal* the southern). In *The Silmarillion* Ringil (containing *ring* 'cold') survived only as the name of Fingolfin's sword, but Helcar is that of the Inland Sea which 'stood where aforetime the roots of the mountain of Illuin had been' (p. 49). In the present tale Helkar was the name of the southern, not the northern, pillar. Now *helkar* meant 'utter cold' (see the Appendix on Names), which shows that Helkar was originally in the extreme south (as it is in one of the two positions given for it on the little map, p. 81), just as Ringil was in the extreme north. In the tale there is no mention of the formation of Inland Seas at the fall of the Lamps; this idea appeared later, but it seems virtually certain that it arose from the story of the melting pillars of ice.

There is no later reference to the building of the Mountains of Valinor from great rocks gathered in Eruman / Arvalin, so that the region became flat and stoneless.

* If this is so, and if *I Vene Kemen* means 'The Earth-Ship', then this title must have been added to the drawing at the same time as the mast, sail, and prow. – In the little notebook referred to on p. 23 there is an isolated note: 'Map of the Ship of the World.'

(iv) The Two Trees (pp. 71–3)

This earliest account of the uprising of the Two Trees illuminates some elements of later versions more concentrated in expression. The enduring feature that the ground beneath Silpion (Telperion) was 'dappled with the shadows of his fluttering leaves' (*The Silmarillion* p. 38) is seen to have had its origin in the 'throbbing of the tree's heart'. The conception of light as a liquid substance that 'splashed upon the ground', that ran in rivers and was poured in cauldrons, though not lost in the published work (pp. 38–9), is here more strongly and physically expressed. Some features were never changed, as the clustered flowers of Laurelin and the shining edges of its leaves.

On the other hand there are notable differences between this and the later accounts: above all perhaps that Laurelin was in origin the Eldar Tree. The Two Trees had here periods of twelve hours, not as later seven;* and the preparations of the Valar for the birth of the Trees, with all their detail of physical 'magic', were afterwards abandoned. The two great 'cauldrons' Kulullin and Silindrin survived in the 'great vats like shining lakes' in which Varda hoarded 'the dews of Telperion and the rain that fell from Laurelin' (*ibid.* p. 39), though the names disappeared, as did the need to 'water' the Trees with the light gathered in the vats or cauldrons – or at any rate it is not mentioned later. Urwen ('Sun-maiden') was the forebear of Arien, Maia of the Sun; and Tilion, steersman of the Moon in *The Silmarillion*, who 'lay in dreams by the pools of Estë [Lórien's wife], in Telperion's flickering beams', perhaps owes something to the figure of Silmo, whom Lórien loved.

As I noted earlier, 'in the later evolution of the myths Vána sank down in relation to Nienna', and here it is Vána and (Yavanna) Palúrien who are the midwives of the birth of the Trees, not as afterwards Yavanna and Nienna.

As regards the names of the Trees, *Silpion* was for long the name of the White Tree; *Telperion* did not appear till long after, and even then *Silpion* was retained and is mentioned in *The Silmarillion* (p. 38) as one of its names. *Laurelin* goes back to the beginning and was never changed, but its other name in the *Lost Tales*, *Lindeloksë* and other similar forms, was not retained.

(v) The Dwellings of the Valar (pp. 73 ff.)

This account of the mansions of the Valar was very largely lost in the subsequent versions. In the published work nothing is told of Manwë's dwelling, save the bare fact that his halls were 'above the everlasting snow, upon Oiolossë, the uttermost tower of Taniquetil' (p. 26). Here

---

* Palúrien's words (p. 73) 'This tree, *when the twelve hours of its fullest light are past*, will wane again' seem to imply a longer space than twelve hours; but probably the period of waning was not allowed for. In an annotated list of names to the tale of *The Fall of Gondolin* it is said that Silpion lit all Valinor with silver light 'for half the twenty-four hours'.

now appears Sorontur King of Eagles, a visitor to Manwë's halls (cf. *The Silmarillion* p. 110: 'For Manwë to whom all birds are dear, and to whom they bring news upon Taniquetil from Middle-earth, had sent forth the race of Eagles'); he had in fact appeared already in the tale of *The Fall of Gondolin*, as 'Thorndor [the Gnomish name] King of Eagles whom the Eldar name Ramandur', Ramandur being subsequently emended to Sorontur.

Of Valmar and the dwellings of the Valar in the city scarcely anything survived in later writing, and there remain only phrases here and there (the 'golden streets' and 'silver domes' of Valmar, 'Valmar of many bells') to suggest the solidity of the original description, where Tulkas' house of many storeys had a tower of bronze and Oromë's halls were upheld by living trees with trophies and antlers hung upon their trunks. This is not to say that all such imagining was definitively abandoned: as I have said in the Foreword, the *Lost Tales* were followed by a version so compressed as to be no more than a résumé (as was its purpose), and the later development of the mythology proceeded from that – a process of re-expansion. Many things never referred to again after the *Lost Tales* may have continued to exist in a state of suspension, as it were. Valmar certainly remained a city, with gates, streets, and dwellings. But in the context of the later work one could hardly conceive of the tempestuous Ossë being possessed of a house in Valmar, even if its floor were of seawater and its roof of foam; and of course the hall of Makar and Meássë (where the life described owes something to the myths of the Unending Battle in ancient Scandinavia) disappeared with the disappearance of those divinities – a 'Melko-faction' in Valinor that was bound to prove an embarrassment.

Several features of the original descriptions endured: the rarity of Ulmo's visits to Valmar (cf. *The Silmarillion* p. 40), the frequency with which Palúrien and Oromë visit 'the world without' (*ibid.* pp. 29, 41, 47), the association of the gardens of Lórien with Silpion and of the gardens of Vána with Laurelin (*ibid.* p. 99); and much that is said here of the divine 'characters' can be seen to have remained, even if differently expressed. Here also appears Nessa, already as the wife of Tulkas and the sister of Oromë, excelling in the dance; and Ómar-Amillo is now named the brother of Noldorin-Salmar. It appears elsewhere (see p. 93) that Nielíqui was the daughter of Oromë and Vána.

(vi) The Gods of Death and the Fates of Elves and Men
(pp. 76–7)

This section of the tale contains its most surprising and difficult elements. Mandos and his wife Nienna appear in the account of the coming of the Valar into the world at the beginning of the tale (p. 66), where they are named 'Fantur of Death, Vefántur Mandos' and 'Fui Nienna', 'mistress of death'. In the present passage it is said that Vefántur named his dwelling Vê by his own name, whereas afterwards (*The Silmarillion* p. 28) he was called by the name of his dwelling; but in the early writing there is a distinction between the region (Mandos) and the halls (Vê and Fui) within the region. There is here no trace of Mandos as the 'Doomsman of the Valar', who 'pronounces his dooms and his judgements only at the bidding of Manwë', one of the most notable aspects of the later conception of this Vala; nor, since Nienna is the wife of Mandos, has Vairë the Weaver, his wife in the later story, appeared, with her tapestries that portray 'all things that have ever been in Time' and clothe the halls of Mandos 'that ever widen as the ages pass' – in the *Lost Tales* the name Vairë is given to an Elf of Tol Eressëa. Tapestries 'picturing those things that were and shall be' are found here in the halls of Aulë (p. 74).

Most important in the passage concerning Mandos is the clear statement about the fate of Elves who die: that they wait in the halls of Mandos until Vefántur decrees their release, to be reborn in their own children. This latter idea has already appeared in the tale of *The Music of the Ainur* (p. 59), and it remained my father's unchanged conception of Elvish 'immortality' for many years; indeed the idea that the Elves might die only from the wounds of weapons or from grief was never changed – it also has appeared in *The Music of the Ainur* (*ibid.*): 'the Eldar dwell till the Great End unless they be slain or waste in grief', a passage that survived with little alteration in *The Silmarillion* (p. 42).

With the account of Fui Nienna, however, we come upon ideas in deep contradiction to the central thought of the later mythology (and in this passage, also, there is a strain of another kind of mythic conception, in the 'conceits' of 'the distilling of salt humours whereof are tears', and the black clouds woven by Nienna which settle on the world as 'despairs and hopeless mourning, sorrows and blind grief'). Here we learn that Nienna is the judge of Men in her halls named *Fui* after her own name; and some she keeps in the region of Mandos (where is her hall), while the greater number board the black ship Mornië – which does no more than ferry these dead down the coast to Arvalin, where they wander in the dusk until the end of the world. But yet others are driven forth to be seized by Melko and taken to endure 'evil days' in Angamandi (in what sense are they dead, or mortal?); and (most extraordinary of all) there are a very few who go to dwell among the Gods in Valinor. We are far away here from the Gift of Ilúvatar, whereby Men are not bound to the world, but leave it, none know where;* and this is the true meaning of Death (for

---

* Cf. *The Silmarillion* p. 104: 'Some say that they [Men] too go to the halls of Mandos; but their place of waiting there is not that of the Elves, and Mandos under Ilúvatar alone save Manwë knows whither they go after the time of recollection in those silent halls beside the Outer Sea.' Also *ibid.* p. 186: 'For the spirit of Beren at her bidding tarried in the halls of Mandos, unwilling to leave the world, until Lúthien came to say her last farewell upon the dim shores of the Outer Sea, whence Men that die set out never to return.'

the death of the Elves is a 'seeming death', *The Silmarillion* p. 42): the final and inescapable exit.

But a little illumination, if of a very misty kind, can be shed on the idea of Men, after death, wandering in the dusk of Arvalin, where they 'camp as they may' and 'wait in patience till the Great End'. I must refer here to the details of the changed names of this region, which have been given on p. 79. It is clear from the early word-lists or dictionaries of the two languages (for which see the Appendix on Names) that the meaning of *Harwalin* and *Arvalin* (and probably *Habbanan* also) was 'nigh Valinor' or 'nigh the Valar'. From the Gnomish dictionary it emerges that the meaning of *Eruman* was 'beyond the abode of the Mánir' (i.e. south of Taniquetil, where dwelt Manwë's spirits of the air), and this dictionary also makes it clear that the word *Mánir* was related to Gnomish *manos*, defined as 'a spirit that has gone to the Valar or to Erumáni', and *mani* 'good, holy'. The significance of these etymological connections is very unclear.

But there is also a very early poem on the subject of this region. This, according to my father's notes, was written at Brocton Camp, Staffordshire, in December 1915 or at Étaples in June 1916; and it is entitled *Habbanan beneath the Stars*. In one of the three texts (in which there are no variants) there is a title in Old English: *þā gebletsode* ['blessed'] *felda under þām steorrum*, and in two of them *Habbanan* in the title was emended to *Eruman*; in the third *Eruman* stood from the first. The poem is preceded by a short prose preamble.

Habbanan beneath the Stars

Now Habbanan is that region where one draws nigh to the places that are not of Men. There is the air very sweet and the sky very great by reason of the broadness of the Earth.

> In Habbanan beneath the skies
> Where all roads end however long
> There is a sound of faint guitars
> And distant echoes of a song,
> For there men gather into rings
> Round their red fires while one voice sings –
> And all about is night.

★

> Not night as ours, unhappy folk,
> Where nigh the Earth in hazy bars,
> A mist about the springing of the stars,
> There trails a thin and wandering smoke
> Obscuring with its veil half-seen
> The great abysmal still Serene.

★

A globe of dark glass faceted with light
Wherein the splendid winds have dusky flight;
Untrodden spaces of an odorous plain
That watches for the moon that long has lain
And caught the meteors' fiery rain –
Such there is night.

There on a sudden did my heart perceive
That they who sang about the Eve,
Who answered the bright-shining stars
With gleaming music of their strange guitars,
These were His wandering happy sons
Encamped upon those aëry leas
Where God's unsullied garment runs
In glory down His mighty knees.

A final evidence comes from the early Qenya word-list. The original layer of entries in this list dates (as I believe, see the Appendix on Names) from 1915, and among these original entries, under a root *mana* (from which *Manwë* is derived), is given a word *manimo* which means a soul who is in *manimuine* 'Purgatory'.

This poem, and this entry in the word-list, offer a rare and very suggestive glimpse of the mythic conception in its earliest phase; for here ideas that are drawn from Christian theology are explicitly present. It is disconcerting to perceive that they are still present in this tale. For in the tale there is an account of the fates of dead Men after judgement in the black hall of Fui Nienna. Some ('and these are the many') are ferried by the death-ship to (Habbanan) Eruman, where they wander in the dusk and wait in patience till the Great End; some are seized by Melko and tormented in Angamandi 'the Hells of Iron'; and some few go to dwell with the Gods in Valinor. Taken with the poem and the evidence of the early 'dictionaries', can this be other than a reflection of Purgatory, Hell, and Heaven?

This becomes all the more extraordinary if we refer to the concluding passage of the tale of *The Music of the Ainur* (p. 59), where Ilúvatar said: 'To Men I will give a new gift and a greater', the gift that they might 'fashion and design their life beyond even the original Music of the Ainur that is as fate to all things else', and where it is said that 'it is one with this gift of power that the Children of Men dwell only for a short time in the world alive, yet do not perish utterly for ever . . .' In the final form given in *The Silmarillion* pp. 41–2 this passage was not very greatly changed. The early version does not, it is true, have the sentences:

But the sons of Men die indeed, and leave the world; wherefore they are called the Guests, or the Strangers. Death is their fate, the gift of Ilúvatar, which as Time wears even the Powers shall envy.

Even so, it seems clear that this central idea, the Gift of Death, was already present.

This matter I must leave, as a conundrum that I cannot solve. The most obvious explanation of the conflict of ideas within these tales would be to suppose *The Music of the Ainur* later than *The Coming of the Valar and the Building of Valinor*; but as I have said (p. 61) all the appearances are to the contrary.

Lastly may be noticed the characteristic linguistic irony whereby *Eruman* ultimately became *Araman*. For *Arvalin* meant simply 'near Valinor', and it was the other name *Eruman* that had associations with spirits of the dead; but *Araman* almost certainly simply means 'beside Aman'. And yet the same element *man-* 'good' remains, for *Aman* was derived from it ('the Unmarred State').

Two minor matters in the conclusion of the tale remain to be noticed. Here Nornorë is the Herald of the Gods; afterwards this was Fionwë (later Eonwë), see p. 63. And in the reference to 'that low place amid the hills where Valinor may just be glimpsed', near to Taniquetil, we have the first mention of the gap in the Mountains of Valinor where was the hill of the city of the Elves.

On blank pages near the end of the text of this tale my father wrote a list of secondary names of the Valar (as Manwë *Súlimo*, etc.). Some of these names appear in the text of the *Tales*; those that do not are given in the Appendix on Names under the primary names. It emerges from this list that Ómar-Amillo is the twin of Salmar-Noldorin (they are named as brothers in the tale, p. 75); that Nielíqui (p. 75) is the daughter of Oromë and Vána; and that Melko has a son ('by Ulbandi') called Kosomot: this, it will emerge later, was Gothmog Lord of Balrogs, whom Ecthelion slew in Gondolin.

IV
THE CHAINING OF MELKO

Following the end of Rúmil's tale of *The Coming of the Valar and the Building of Valinor* there is a long interlude before the next one, though the manuscript continues without even interrupting the paragraph. But on the cover of the notebook *The Chaining of Melko* is given as a separate title, and I have adopted this. The text continues in ink over an erased pencil manuscript.

That night Eriol heard again in his sleep the music that had so moved him on the first night; and the next morning he went again into the gardens early. There he met Vairë, and she called him *Eriol*: 'that was the first making and uttering of that name'. Eriol told Vairë of the 'dream-musics' he had heard, and she said that it was no dream-music, but rather the flute of Timpinen, 'whom those Gnomes Rúmil and Littleheart and others of my house call Tinfang'. She told him that the children called him Tinfang Warble; and that he played and danced in summer dusks for joy of the first stars: 'at every note a new one sparkles forth and glisters. The Noldoli say that they come out too soon if Tinfang Warble plays, and they love him, and the children will watch often from the windows lest he tread the shadowy lawns unseen.' She told Eriol that he was 'shier than a fawn – swift to hide and dart away as any vole: a footstep on a twig and he is away, and his fluting will come mocking from afar'.

'And a marvel of wizardry liveth in that fluting,' said Eriol, 'if that it be indeed which I have heard now for two nights here.'

'There be none,' said Vairë, 'not even of the Solosimpi, who can rival him therein, albeit those same pipers claim him as their kin; yet 'tis said everywhere that this quaint spirit is neither wholly of the Valar nor of the Eldar, but is half a fay of the woods and dells, one of the great companies of the children of Palúrien, and half a Gnome or a Shoreland Piper.[1] Howso that be he is a wondrous wise and strange creature, and he fared hither away with the Eldar long ago, marching nor resting among them but going always ahead piping strangely or whiles sitting aloof. Now does he play about the gardens of the land; but Alalminórë he loves the best, and this garden best of all. Ever and again we miss his piping for long months, and we say: "Tinfang Warble has gone heart-breaking in the Great Lands, and many a one in those far regions will hear his piping in the dusk outside tonight." But on a sudden will his flute be heard again at an hour of gentle gloaming, or will he play beneath a goodly moon and the stars go bright and blue.'

'Aye,' said Eriol, 'and the hearts of those that hear him go beating with a quickened longing. Meseemed 'twas my desire to open the window and leap forth, so sweet was the air that came to me from without, nor might I drink deep enough, but as I listened I wished to follow I know not whom, I know not whither, out into the magic of the world beneath the stars.'

'Then of a sooth 'twas Timpinen who played to you,' said Vairë, 'and honoured are you, for this garden has been empty of his melody many a night. Now, however, for such is the eeriness of that sprite, you will ever love the evenings of summer and the nights of stars, and their magic will cause your heart to ache unquenchably.'

'But have you not all heard him many times and often, that dwell here,' said Eriol, 'yet do not seem to me like those who live with a longing that is half understood and may not be fulfilled.'

'Nor do we so, for we have *limpë*,' said she, '*limpë* that alone can cure, and a draught of it giveth a heart to fathom all music and song.'

'Then,' said Eriol, 'would I might drain a goblet of that good drink'; but Vairë told him that that might only be if he sought out Meril the queen.

Of this converse of Eriol and Vairë upon the lawn that fair day-tide came it that Eriol set out not many days thereafter – and Tinfang Warble had played to him many times by dusk, by starry light and moongleam, till his heart was full. In that was Littleheart his guide, and he sought the dwellings of Meril-i-Turinqui in her *korin* of elms.

Now the house of that fair lady was in that very city, for at the foot of the great tower which Ingil had built was a wide grove of the most ancient and beautiful elms that all that Land of Elms possessed. High to heaven they rose in three lessening storeys of bright foliage, and the sunlight that filtered through was very cool – a golden green. Amidst of these was a great green sward of grass smooth as a web of stuffs, and about it those trees stood in a circle, so that shades were heavy at its edge but the gaze of the sun fell all day on its middle. There stood a beautiful house, and it was builded all of white and of a whiteness that shone, but its roof was so o'ergrown with mosses and with houseleek and many curious clinging plants that of what it was once fashioned might not be seen for the glorious maze of colours, golds and red-russets, scarlets and greens.

Innumerable birds chattered in its eaves; and some sang upon the housetops, while doves and pigeons circled in flights about the *korin*'s borders or swooped to settle and sun upon the sward. Now all that dwelling was footed in flowers. Blossomy clusters were about it, ropes and tangles, spikes and tassels all in bloom, flowers in panicles and umbels or with great wide faces gazing at the sun. There did they loose upon the faintly stirring airs their several odours blended to a great fragrance of exceeding marvellous enchantment, but their hues and colours were scattered and gathered seemingly as chance and the happiness of their growth directed them. All day long there went a hum of bees among those flowers: bees fared about the roof and all the scented beds and ways; even about the cool porches of the house. Now Littleheart and Eriol climbed the hill and it was late afternoon, and the sun shone brazen upon the western side of Ingil's tower. Soon came they to a mighty wall of hewn stone blocks, and this leaned outward, but grasses grew atop of it, and harebells, and yellow daisies.

A wicket they found in the wall, and beyond was a glade beneath the elms, and there ran a pathway bordered of one side with bushes while of the other flowed a little running water whispering over a brown bed of leafy mould. This led even to the sward's edge, and coming thither said Littleheart pointing to that white house: 'Behold the dwelling of Meril-i-Turinqui, and as I have no errand with so great a lady I will get me back again.' Then Eriol went over the sunny lawn alone until he was nigh shoulder-high in the tall flowers that grew before the porches of the door; and as he drew near a sound of music came to him, and a fair lady amid many maidens stepped forth as it were to meet him. Then said she smiling: 'Welcome, O mariner of many seas — wherefore do you seek the pleasure of my quiet gardens and their gentle noise, when the salt breezes of the sea and the snuff of winds and a swaying boat should rather be your joy?'

For a while Eriol might say nought thereto, being tongue-tied by the beauty of that lady and the loveliness of that place of flowers; yet at length he muttered that he had known sea enough, but of this most gracious land he might never be sated. 'Nay,' said she, 'on a day of autumn will come the winds and a driven gull, maybe, will wail overhead, and lo! you will be filled with desire, remembering the black coasts of your home.'[2] 'Nay, lady,' said Eriol, and now he spoke with eager voice, 'nay, not so, for the spirit that flutes upon twilit lawns has filled my heart with music, and I thirst for a draught of *limpë*!'

Then straightway did the smiling face of Meril grow grave, and bidding her maidens depart she prayed Eriol follow her to a space nigh to the house, and this was of cool grass but not very short. Fruit-trees grew there, and about the roots of one, an apple-tree of great girth and age, the soil was piled so that there was now a broad seat around its bole, soft and grass-covered. There sat Meril and she gazed upon Eriol and said: 'Know you then what it is that you ask?' and he said: 'I know nought save that I desire to know the soul of every song and of all music and to dwell always in fellowship and kinship with this wondrous people of the Eldar of the Isle, and to be free of unquenchable longing even till the Faring Forth, even till the Great End!'

But Meril said: 'Fellowship is possible, maybe, but kinship not so, for Man is Man and Elda Elda, and what Ilúvatar has made unalike may not become alike while the world remains. Even didst thou dwell here till the Great End and for the health of *limpë* found no death, yet then must thou die and leave us, for Man must die once. And hearken, O Eriol, think not to escape unquenchable longing with a draught of *limpë* – for only wouldst thou thus exchange desires, replacing thy old ones with new and deeper and more keen. Desire unsatisfied dwells in the hearts of both those races that are called the Children of Ilúvatar, but with the Eldar most, for their hearts are filled with a vision of beauty in great glory.' 'Yet, O Queen,' said Eriol thereto, 'let me but taste of this drink and become an agelong fellow of your people: O queen of the Eldalië, that I may be as the happy children of Mar Vanwa Tyaliéva.' 'Nay, not yet can I do that,' said Meril, 'for 'tis a graver matter far to give this drink to one who has known life and days already in the lands of Men than for a child to drink who knows but little else; yet even these did we keep a long while ere we gave them the wine of song, teaching them first much lore and testing their hearts and souls. Therefore I bid you now bide still longer and learn all that you may in this our isle. Lo, what do you know of the world, or of the ancient days of Men, or of the roots which those things that now are have far back in time, or what of the Eldalië and all their wisdom, that you should claim our cup of youth and poesy?'

'The tongue of Tol Eressëa do I know, and of the Valar have I heard, and the great world's beginning, and the building of Valinor; to musics have I hearkened and to poesy and the laughter of the Elves, and all I have found true and good, and my heart knows and it saith to me that these shall I always henceforth love, and love alone' – thus answered Eriol, and his heart was sore for the refusal of the Queen.

'Yet nothing do you know of the coming of the Elves, of the fates wherein they move, nor their nature and the place that Ilúvatar has given to them. Little do you reck of that great splendour of their home in Eldamar upon the hill of Kôr, nor all the sorrow of our parting. What know you of our travail down all the dark ways of the world, and the anguish we have known because of Melko; of the sorrows we have suffered, and do yet, because of Men, of all the fears that darken our hopes because of Men? Know you the wastes of tears that lie between our life in Tol Eressëa and that time of laughter that we knew in Valinor? O child of Men who wouldst be sharer of the fates of the Eldalië, what of our high desires and all those things we look for still to be – for lo! if you drink this drink all these must you know and love, having one heart with us – nay, even at the Faring Forth, should Eldar and Men fall into war at the last, still must you stand by us against the children of your kith and kin, but until then never may you fare away home though longings gnaw you – and the desires that at whiles consume a full-grown man who drinketh *limpë* are a fire of unimagined torture – knew you these things, O Eriol, when you fared hither with your request?'

'Nay, I knew them not,' said Eriol sadly, 'though often have I questioned folk thereof.'

'Then lo!' said Meril, 'I will begin a tale, and tell you some of it ere the long afternoon grows dim – but then must you fare hence again in patience'; and Eriol bowed his head.

'Then,' said Meril, 'now I will tell you of a time of peace the world once knew, and it is known as "Melko's Chains".[3] Of the Earth I will tell you as the Eldar found it and of the manner of their awakening into it.

Behold, Valinor is built, and the Gods dwell in peace, for Melko is far in the world delving deep and fortifying himself in iron and cold, but Makar and Meássë ride upon the gales and rejoice in earthquakes and the overmastering furies of the ancient seas. Light and beautiful is Valinor, but there is a deep twilight upon the world, for the Gods have gathered so much of that light that had before flowed about the airs. Seldom now falls the shimmering rain as it was used, and there reigns a gloom lit with pale streaks or shot with red where Melko spouts to heaven from a fire-torn hill.

Then Palúrien Yavanna fared forth from her fruitful gardens to survey the wide lands of her domain, and wandered the dark continents sowing seed and brooding upon hill and dale. Alone in that agelong gloaming she sang songs of the utmost enchantment, and of such deep magic were they that they floated about the rocky places and their echoes lingered for years of time in hill and empty plain, and all the good magics of all later days are whispers of the memories of her echoing song.

Then things began to grow there, fungus and strange growths heaved in damp places and lichens and mosses crept stealthily across the rocks and ate their faces, and they crumbled and made dust, and the creeping plants died in the dust, and there was mould, and ferns and warted plants grew in it silently, and strange creatures thrust their heads from crannies and crept over the stones. But Yavanna wept, for this was not the fair vigour that she had thought of – and thereupon Oromë came to her leaping in the dusk, but Tuivána would not leave the radiance of Kulullin nor Nessa the green swards of her dancing.

Then Oromë and Palúrien put forth all their might, and Oromë blew great blasts upon his horn as though he would awake the grey rocks to life and lustihead. Behold, at these blasts the great forest reared and moaned about the hills, and all the trees of dark leaf came to being, and the world was shaggy with a growth of pines and odorous with resinous trees, and firs and cedars hung their blue and olive draperies about the slopes, and yews began the centuries of their growth. Now was Oromë less gloomy and Palúrien was comforted, seeing the beauty of the first stars of Varda gleaming in the pale heavens through the shadows of the first trees' boughs, and hearing the murmur of the dusky forests and the creaking of the branches when Manwë stirred the airs.

At that time did many strange spirits fare into the world, for there were pleasant places dark and quiet for them to dwell in. Some came from Mandos, aged spirits that journeyed from Ilúvatar with him who are older than the world and very gloomy and secret, and some from the fortresses of the North where Melko then dwelt in the deep dungeons of Utumna. Full of evil and unwholesome were they; luring and restlessness and horror they brought, turning the dark into an ill and fearful thing, which it was not before. But some few danced thither with gentle feet exuding evening scents, and these came from the gardens of Lórien.

Still is the world full of these in the days of light, lingering alone in shadowy hearts of primeval forests, calling secret things across a starry waste, and haunting caverns in the hills that few have found: – but the pinewoods are yet too full of these old unelfin and inhuman spirits for the quietude of Eldar or of Men.

When this great deed was done then Palúrien would fain rest from her long labours and return to taste the sweet fruits of Valinor, and be refreshed beneath the tree of Laurelin whose dew is light, and Oromë was for beechwoods on the plains of the great Gods; but Melko who long time had delved in fear because of the wrath of the

Valar at his treacherous dealing with their lamps burst forth now into a great violence, for he had thought the world abandoned by the Gods to him and his. Beneath the very floors of Ossë he caused the Earth to quake and split and his lower fires to mingle with the sea. Vaporous storms and a great roaring of uncontrolled sea-motions burst upon the world, and the forests groaned and snapped. The sea leapt upon the land and tore it, and wide regions sank beneath its rage or were hewn into scattered islets, and the coast was dug into caverns. The mountains rocked and their hearts melted, and stone poured like liquid fire down their ashen sides and flowed even to the sea, and the noise of the great battles of the fiery beaches came roaring even through the Mountains of Valinor and drowned the singing of the Gods. Then rose Kémi Palúrien, even Yavanna that giveth fruits, and Aulë who loveth all her works and the substances of the earth, and they climbed to the halls of Manwë and spake to him, saying that all that goodliness was going utterly to wreck for the fiery evil of Melko's untempered heart, and Yavanna pleaded that all her agelong labour in the twilight be not drowned and buried. Thither, as they spake, came Ossë raging like a tide among the cliffs, for he was wroth at the upheaval of his realm and feared the displeasure of Ulmo his overlord. Then arose Manwë Súlimo, Lord of Gods and Elves, and Varda Tinwetári was beside him, and he spake in a voice of thunder from Taniquetil, and the Gods in Valmar heard it, and Vefántur knew the voice in Mandos, and Lórien was aroused in Murmuran.

Then was a great council held between the Two Trees at the mingling of the lights, and Ulmo came thither from the outer deeps; and of the redes there spoken the Gods devised a plan of wisdom, and the thought of Ulmo was therein and much of the craft of Aulë and the wide knowledge of Manwë.

Behold, Aulë now gathered six metals, copper, silver, tin, lead, iron, and gold, and taking a portion of each made with his magic a seventh which he named therefore *tilkal*,* and this had all the properties of the six and many of its own. Its colour was bright green or red in varying lights and it could not be broken, and Aulë alone could forge it. Thereafter he forged a mighty chain, making it of all seven metals welded with spells to a substance of uttermost hardness and brightness and smoothness, but of *tilkal* he had not sufficient to add more than a little to each link. Nonetheless he made two manacles of *tilkal* only and four fetters likewise. Now the chain was

---

* Footnote in the manuscript: '*T*(*ambë*) *I*(*lsa*) *L*(*atúken*) *K*(*anu*) *A*(*nga*) *L*(*aurë*). *ilsa* and *laurë* are the 'magic' names of ordinary *telpë* and *kulu*.'

named *Angaino*, the oppressor, and the manacles *Vorotemnar* that bind for ever, but the fetters *Ilterendi* for they might not be filed or cleft.

But the desire of the Gods was to seek out Melko with great power – and to entreat him, if it might be, to better deeds; yet did they purpose, if naught else availed, to overcome him by force or guile, and set him in a bondage from which there should be no escape.

Now as Aulë smithied the Gods arrayed themselves in armour, which they had of Makar, and he was fain to see them putting on weapons and going as to war, howso their wrath be directed against Melko. But when the great Gods and all their folk were armed, then Manwë climbed into his blue chariot whose three horses were the whitest that roamed in Oromë's domain, and his hand bore a great white bow that would shoot an arrow like a gust of wind across the widest seas. Fionwë his son stood behind him and Nornorë who was his herald ran before; but Oromë rode alone upon a chestnut horse and had a spear, and Tulkas strode mightily beside his stirrup, having a tunic of hide and a brazen belt and no weapon save a gauntlet upon his right hand, iron-bound. Telimektar his son but just war-high was by his shoulder with a long sword girt about his waist by a silver girdle. There rode the Fánturi upon a car of black, and there was a black horse upon the side of Mandos and a dappled grey upon the side of Lórien, and Salmar and Ómar came behind running speedily, but Aulë who was late tarrying overlong at his smithy came last, and he was not armed, but caught up his long-handled hammer as he left his forge and fared hastily to the borders of the Shadowy Sea, and the fathoms of his chain were borne behind by four of his smithy-folk.

Upon those shores Falman-Ossë met them and drew them across on a mighty raft whereon he himself sat in shimmering mail; but Ulmo Vailimo was far ahead roaring in his deep-sea car and trumpeting in wrath upon a horn of conches. Thus was it that the Gods got them over the sea and through the isles, and set foot upon the wide lands, and marched in great power and anger ever more to the North. Thus they passed the Mountains of Iron and Hisilómë that lies dim beyond, and came to the rivers and hills of ice. There Melko shook the earth beneath them, and he made snow-capped heights to belch forth flame, yet for the greatness of their array his vassals who infested all their ways availed nothing to hinder them on their journey. There in the deepest North beyond even the shattered pillar Ringil they came upon the huge gates of deep Utumna, and Melko shut them with great clangour before their faces.

Then Tulkas angered smote them thunderously with his great fist, and they rang and stirred not, but Oromë alighting grasped his horn and blew such a blast thereon that they fled open instantly, and Manwë raised his immeasurable voice and bade Melko come forth.

But though deep down within those halls Melko heard him and was in doubt, he would not come, but sent Langon his servant and said by him that "Behold, he was rejoiced and in wonder to see the Gods before his gates. Now would he gladly welcome them, yet for the poverty of his abode not more than two of them could he fitly entertain; and he begged that neither Manwë nor Tulkas be of the two, for the one merited and the other demanded hospitality of great cost and richness. Should this not be to their mind then would he fain hearken to Manwë's herald and learn what it were the Gods so greatly desired that they must leave their soft couches and indolence of Valinor for the bleak places where Melko laboured humbly and did his toilsome work."

Then Manwë and Ulmo and all the Gods were exceeding wroth at the subtlety and fawning insolence of his words, and Tulkas would have started straightway raging down the narrow stairs that descended out of sight beyond the gates, but the others withheld him, and Aulë gave counsel that it was clear from Melko's words that he was awake and wary in this matter, and it could most plainly be seen which of the Gods he was most in fear of and desired least to see standing in his halls – "therefore," said he, "let us devise how these twain may come upon him unawares and how fear may perchance drive him into betterment of ways." To this Manwë assented, saying that all their force might scarce dig Melko from his stronghold, whereas that deceit must be very cunningly woven that would ensnare the master of guile. "Only by his pride is Melko assailable," quoth Manwë, "or by such a struggle as would rend the earth and bring evil upon us all," and Manwë sought to avoid all strife twixt Ainur and Ainur. When therefore the Gods had concerted a plan to catch Melko in his overweening pride they wove cunning words purporting to come from Manwë himself, and these they put in the mouth of Nornorë, who descended and spoke them before the seat of Melko. "Behold," said he, "the Gods be come to ask the pardon of Melko, for seeing his great anger and the rending of the world beneath his rage they have said one to another: 'Lo! wherefore is Melko displeased?' and one to another have answered beholding the tumults of his power: 'Is he not then the greatest among us – why dwells not the mightiest of the Valar in Valinor? Of a surety he has cause for indignation. Let us get us to Utumna and beseech him to dwell in

Valinor that Valmar be not empty of his presence.' To this,'' said he, ''Tulkas alone would not assent, but Manwë bowed to the common voice (this the Gods said knowing the rancour that Melko had for Poldórëa) and now have they come constraining Tulkas with violence to beg thee to pardon them each one and to fare home with them and complete their glory, dwelling, if it be thy pleasure, in the halls of Makar, until such time as Aulë can build thee a great house; and its towers shall overtop Taniquetil.'' To this did Melko answer eagerly, for already his boundless pride surged up and drowned his cunning.

''At last do the Gods speak fair words and just, but ere I grant their boon my heart must be appeased for old affronts. Therefore must they come putting aside their weapons at the gate, and do homage to me in these my deep halls of Utumna: – but lo! Tulkas I will not see, and if I come to Valinor then will I thrust him out.'' These things did Nornorë report, and Tulkas smote his hands in wrath, but Manwë returned answer that the Gods would do as Melko's heart desired, yet would Tulkas come and that in chains and be given to Melko's power and pleasure; and this was Melko eager to grant for the humiliation of the Valar, and the chaining of Tulkas gave him great mirth.

Then the Valar laid aside their weapons at the gates, setting however folk to guard them, and placed the chain Angaino about the neck and arms of Tulkas, and even he might scarce support its great weight alone; and now they follow Manwë and his herald into the caverns of the North. There sat Melko in his chair, and that chamber was lit with flaming braziers and full of evil magic, and strange shapes moved with feverish movement in and out, but snakes of great size curled and uncurled without rest about the pillars that upheld that lofty roof. Then said Manwë: ''Behold, we have come and salute you here in your own halls; come now and be in Valinor.''

But Melko might not thus easily forgo his sport. ''Nay first,'' said he, ''wilt thou come Manwë and kneel before me, and after you all the Valar; but last shall come Tulkas and kiss my foot, for I have in mind something for which I owe Poldórëa no great love.'' Now he purposed to spurn Tulkas in the mouth in payment of that buffet long ago, but the Valar had foreseen something of this and did but make play of humiliation that Melko might thereby be lured from his stronghold of Utumna. In sooth Manwë hoped even to the end for peace and amity, and the Gods would at his bidding indeed have received Melko into Valinor under truce and pledges of friendship, had not his pride been insatiate and his obstinacy in evil unconquerable. Now however was scant mercy left for him within their hearts, seeing that he abode in his demand that Manwë should do homage and Tulkas bend to those ruthless feet; nonetheless the Lord of Gods and Elves approaches now the chair of Melko and makes to kneel, for such was their plan the more to ensnare that evil one; but lo, so fiercely did wrath blaze up in the hearts of Tulkas and Aulë at that sight that Tulkas leapt across the hall at a bound despite Angaino, and Aulë was behind him and Oromë followed his father and the hall was full of tumult. Then Melko sprang to his feet shouting in a loud voice and his folk came through all those dismal passages to his aid. Then lashed he at Manwë with an iron flail he bore, but Manwë breathed gently upon it and its iron tassels were blown backward, and thereupon Tulkas smote Melko full in his teeth with his fist of iron, and he and Aulë grappled with him, and straight he was wrapped thirty times in the fathoms of Angaino.

Then said Oromë: "Would that he might be slain" – and it would have been well indeed, but the great Gods may not yet be slain.[4] Now is Melko held in dire bondage and beaten to his knees, and he is constrained to command all his vassalage that they molest not the Valar – and indeed the most of these, affrighted at the binding of their lord, fled away to the darkest places.

Tulkas indeed dragged Melko out before the gates, and there Aulë set upon each wrist one of the Vorotemnar and upon each ankle twain of the Ilterendi, and *tilkal* went red at the touch of Melko, and those bands have never since been loosened from his hands and feet. Then the chain is smithied to each of these and Melko borne thus helpless away, while Tulkas and Ulmo break the gates of Utumna and pile hills of stone upon them. And the saps and cavernous places beneath the surface of the earth are full yet of the dark spirits that were prisoned that day when Melko was taken, and yet many are the ways whereby they find the outer world from time to time – from fissures where they shriek with the voices of the tide on rocky coasts, down dark water-ways that wind unseen for many leagues, or out of the blue arches where the glaciers of Melko find their end.

After these things did the Gods return to Valmar by long ways and dark, guarding Melko every moment, and he gnawed his consuming rage. His lip was split and his face has had a strange leer upon it since that buffet dealt him by Tulkas, who even of policy could not endure to see the majesty of Manwë bow before the accursed one.

Now is a court set upon the slopes of Taniquetil and Melko arraigned before all the Vali[5] great and small, lying bound before the silver chair of Manwë. Against him speaketh Ossë, and Oromë, and Ulmo in deep ire, and Vána in abhorrence, proclaiming his deeds of cruelty and violence; yet Makar still spake for him, although not warmly, for said he: "'Twere an ill thing if peace were for always: already no blow echoes ever in the eternal quietude of Valinor, wherefore, if one might neither see deed of battle nor riotous joy even in the world without, then 'twould be irksome indeed, and I for one long not for such times!" Thereat arose Palúrien in sorrow and tears, and told of the plight of Earth and of the great beauty of her designs and of those things she desired dearly to bring forth; of all the wealth of flower and herbage, of tree and fruit and grain that the world might bear if it had but peace. "Take heed, O Valar, that both Elves and Men be not devoid of all solace whenso the times come for them to find the Earth"; but Melko writhed in rage at the name of Eldar and of Men and at his own impotence.

Now Aulë mightily backed her in this and after him many else of the Gods, yet Mandos and Lórien held their peace, nor do they ever speak much at the councils of the Valar or indeed at other times, but Tulkas arose angrily from the midst of the assembly and went from among them, for he could not endure parleying where he thought the guilt to be clear. Liever would he have unchained Melko and fought him then and there alone upon the plain of Valinor, giving him many a sore buffet in meed of his illdoings, rather than making high debate of them. Howbeit Manwë sate and listened and was moved by the speech of Palúrien, yet was it his thought that Melko was an Ainu and powerful beyond measure for the future good or evil of the world; wherefore he put away harshness and his doom was this. For three ages during the displeasure of the Gods should Melko be chained in a vault of Mandos by that chain Angaino, and thereafter should he fare into the light of the Two Trees, but only so that he might for four ages yet dwell as a servant in the house of Tulkas, and obey him in requital of his ancient malice. "Thus," said Manwë, "and yet but hardly, mayst thou win favour again sufficient that the Gods suffer thee to abide thereafter in an house of thine own and to have some slight estate among them as befitteth a Vala and a lord of the Ainur."

Such was the doom of Manwë, and even to Makar and Meássë it seemed good, albeit Tulkas and Palúrien thought it merciful to peril. Now doth Valinor enter upon its greatest time of peace, and all the earth beside, while Melko bideth in the deepest vaults of Mandos and his heart grows black within him.

Behold the tumults of the sea abate slowly, and the fires beneath the mountains die; the earth quakes no more and the fierceness of

the cold and the stubbornness of the hills and rivers of ice is melted
to the uttermost North and to the deepest South, even to the regions
about Ringil and Helkar. Then Palúrien goes once more out over the
Earth, and the forests multiply and spread, and often is Oromë's
horn heard behind her in the dimness: now do nightshade and
bryony begin to creep about the brakes, and holly and ilex are seen
upon the earth. Even the faces of the cliffs are grown with ivies and
trailing plants for the calm of the winds and the quietude of the sea,
and all the caverns and the shores are festooned with weeds, and great
sea-growths come to life swaying gently when Ossë moves the waters.

Now came that Vala and sat upon a headland of the Great Lands,
having leisure in the stillness of his realm, and he saw how Palúrien
was filling the quiet dusk of the Earth with flitting shapes. Bats
and owls whom Vefántur set free from Mandos swooped about the
sky, and nightingales sent by Lórien from Valinor trilled beside still
waters. Far away a nightjar croaked, and in dark places snakes that
slipped from Utumna when Melko was bound moved noiselessly
about; a frog croaked upon a bare pool's border.

Then he sent word to Ulmo of the new things that were done, and
Ulmo desired not that the waters of the inner seas be longer un-
peopled, but came forth seeking Palúrien, and she gave him spells,
and the seas began to gleam with fish or strange creatures crawled at
bottom; yet the shellfish and the oysters no-one of Valar or of Elves
knows whence they are, for already they gaped in the silent waters
or ever Melko plunged therein from on high, and pearls there were
before the Eldar thought or dreamed of any gem.

Three great fish luminous in the dark of the sunless days went
ever with Ulmo, and the roof of Ossë's dwelling beneath the Great
Sea shone with phosphorescent scales. Behold that was a time of
great peace and quiet, and life struck deep roots into the new-made
soils of Earth, and seeds were sown that waited only for the light to
come, and it is known and praised as the age of "Melko's Chains".'

NOTES

1 The following passage was added here, apparently very soon after the
writing of the text, but was later firmly struck through:

The truth is that he is a son of Linwë Tinto King of the Pipers who
was lost of old upon the great march from Palisor, and wandering in
Hisilómë found the lonely twilight spirit (Tindriel) Wendelin
dancing in a glade of beeches. Loving her he was content to leave

his folk and dance for ever in the shadows, but his children Timpinen and Tinúviel long after joined the Eldar again, and tales there are concerning them both, though they are seldom told.

The name *Tindriel* stood alone in the manuscript as written, but it was then bracketed and *Wendelin* added in the margin. These are the first references in the consecutive narrative to Thingol (Linwë Tinto), Hithlum (Hisilómë), Melian (Tindriel, Wendelin), and Lúthien Tinúviel; but I postpone discussion of these allusions.

2 Cf. the explanation of the names *Eriol* and *Angol* as 'ironcliffs' referred to in the Appendix on Names (entry *Eriol*).

3 Associated with the story of the sojourn of Eriol (Ælfwine) in Tol Eressëa, and the 'Lost Tales' that he heard there, are two 'schemes' or synopses setting out the plan of the work. One of these is, for much of its length, a résumé of the *Tales* as they are extant; the other, certainly the later, is divergent. In this second scheme, in which the voyager is called Ælfwine, the tale on the second night by the Tale-fire is given to 'Evromord the Door-ward', though the narrative-content was to be the same (The Coming of the Gods; the World-fashioning and the Building of Valinor; the Planting of the Two Trees). After this is written (a later addition): 'Ælfwine goes to beg *limpë* of Meril; she sends him back.' The third night by the Tale-fire is thus described:

> The Door-ward continues of the Primeval Twilight. The Furies of Melko. Melko's Chains and the awakening of the Elves. (How Fankil and many dark shapes escape into the world.) [Given to Meril but to be placed as here and much abridged.]

It seems certain that this was a revision in intention only, never achieved. It is notable that in the actual text, as also in the first of these two 'schemes', Rúmil's function in the house is that of door-ward – and Rúmil, not Evromord, was the name that was preserved long after as the recounter of The Music of the Ainur.

4 The text as originally written read: 'but the great Gods may not be slain, though their children may and all those lesser people of the Vali, albeit only at the hands of some one of the Valar.'

5 *Vali* is an emendation from *Valar*. Cf. Rúmil's words (p. 58): 'they whom we now call the Valar (or Vali, it matters not).'

Commentary on
The Chaining of Melko

In the interlude between this tale and the last we encounter the figure of Timpinen or Tinfang. This being had existed in my father's mind for some years, and there are two poems about him. The first is entitled *Tinfang Warble*; it is very brief, but exists in three versions. According to a note by my father the original was written at Oxford in 1914, and it was rewritten at Leeds in '1920–23'. It was finally published in 1927 in a further altered form, which I give here.*

Tinfang Warble

O the hoot! O the hoot!
How he trillups on his flute!
O the hoot of Tinfang Warble!

Dancing all alone,
Hopping on a stone,
Flitting like a fawn,
In the twilight on the lawn,
And his name is Tinfang Warble!

The first star has shown
And its lamp is blown
to a flame of flickering blue.
He pipes not to me,
He pipes not to thee,
He whistles for none of you.
His music is his own,
The tunes of Tinfang Warble!

In the earliest version Tinfang is called a 'leprawn', and in the early glossary of the Gnomish speech he is a 'fay'.

The second poem is entitled *Over Old Hills and Far Away*. This exists in five texts, of which the earliest bears an Old English title as well (of the same meaning): *Ʒeond fyrne beorgas ⁊ heonan feor*. Notes by my father state that it was written at Brocton Camp in Staffordshire between December 1915 and February 1916, and rewritten at Oxford in 1927. The final version given here differs in many details of wording and in places whole lines from earlier versions, from which I note at the end a few interesting readings.

Over Old Hills and Far Away

It was early and still in the night of June,
And few were the stars, and far was the moon,
The drowsy trees drooping, and silently creeping
Shadows woke under them while they were sleeping.

I stole to the window with stealthy tread
Leaving my white and unpressed bed;
And something alluring, aloof and queer,
Like perfume of flowers from the shores of the mere

* Publication was in a periodical referred to in the cutting preserved from it as 'I.U.M[agazine]').

That in Elvenhome lies, and in starlit rains
10   Twinkles and flashes, came up to the panes
Of my high lattice-window. Or was it a sound?
I listened and marvelled with eyes on the ground.
For there came from afar a filtered note
Enchanting sweet, now clear, now remote,
15   As clear as a star in a pool by the reeds,
As faint as the glimmer of dew on the weeds.

Then I left the window and followed the call
Down the creaking stairs and across the hall
Out through a door that swung tall and grey,
20   And over the lawn, and away, away!

It was Tinfang Warble that was dancing there,
Fluting and tossing his old white hair,
Till it sparkled like frost in a winter moon;
And the stars were about him, and blinked to his tune
25   Shimmering blue like sparks in a haze,
As always they shimmer and shake when he plays.

My feet only made there the ghost of a sound
On the shining white pebbles that ringed him round,
Where his little feet flashed on a circle of sand,
30   And the fingers were white on his flickering hand.
In the wink of a star he had leapt in the air
With his fluttering cap and his glistening hair;
And had cast his long flute right over his back,
Where it hung by a ribbon of silver and black.

35   His slim little body went fine as a shade,
And he slipped through the reeds like a mist in the glade;
And he laughed like thin silver, and piped a thin note,
As he flapped in the shadows his shadowy coat.
O! the toes of his slippers were twisted and curled,
40   But he danced like a wind out into the world.

He is gone, and the valley is empty and bare
Where lonely I stand and lonely I stare.
Then suddenly out in the meadows beyond,
Then back in the reeds by the shimmering pond,
45   Then afar from a copse where the mosses are thick
A few little notes came trillaping quick.

I leapt o'er the stream and I sped from the glade,
For Tinfang Warble it was that played;
I must follow the hoot of his twilight flute

50   Over reed, over rush, under branch, over root,
        And over dim fields, and through rustling grasses
        That murmur and nod as the old elf passes,
        Over old hills and far away
        Where the harps of the Elvenfolk softly play.

Earlier readings:

1–2   'Twas a very quiet evening once in June –
        And I thought that stars had grown bright too soon –

        Cf. the prose text, p. 94: 'The Noldoli say that [the stars] come
        out too soon if Tinfang Warble plays'.

8   from the shores of the mere] by the fairies' mere

9   Elvenhome] emendation made on the text of the final version,
        replacing 'Fairyland'.

24   Till the stars came out, as it seemed, too soon.

        Cf. the note to line 2.

25–6   They always come out when he warbles and plays,
        And they shine bright blue as long as he stays.

        Cf. the prose text, p. 95: 'or will he play beneath a goodly moon
        and the stars go bright and blue.'

54   Elvenfolk] emendation made on the text of the final version,
        replacing 'fairies'.

★

The first part of this story of *The Chaining of Melko* came to have a very
different form in later versions, where (*The Silmarillion* p. 35) it was
during the sojourn of the Valar on the Isle of Almaren, under the light of
the Two Lamps, that 'the seeds that Yavanna had sown began swiftly to
sprout and to burgeon, and there arose a multitude of growing things
great and small, mosses and grasses and great ferns, and trees whose tops
were crowned with cloud'; and that 'beasts came forth and dwelt in the
grassy plains, or in the rivers and the lakes, or walked in the shadows of
the woods'. This was the Spring of Arda; but after the coming of Melkor
and the delving of Utumno 'green things fell sick and rotted, and rivers
were choked with weeds and slime, and fens were made, rank and poi-
sonous, the breeding place of flies; and forests grew dark and perilous,
the haunts of fear; and beasts became monsters of horn and ivory and
dyed the earth with blood'. Then came the fall of the Lamps, and 'thus
ended the Spring of Arda' (p. 37). After the building of Valinor and the
arising of the Two Trees 'Middle-earth lay in a twilight beneath the
stars' (p. 39), and Yavanna and Oromë alone of the Valar returned there
at times: 'Yavanna would walk there in the shadows, grieving because the
growth and promise of the Spring of Arda was stayed. And she set a sleep
upon many things that had arisen in the Spring, so that they should not

age, but should wait for a time of awakening that yet should be' (p. 47). 'But already the oldest living things had arisen: in the seas the great weeds, and on earth the shadow of great trees; and in the valleys of the night-clad hills there were dark creatures old and strong.'

In this earliest narrative, on the other hand, there is no mention of the beginning of growth during the time when the Lamps shone (see p. 69), and the first trees and low plants appeared under Yavanna's spells in the twilight after their overthrow. Moreover in the last sentence of this tale 'seeds were sown', in that time of 'quiet dusk' while Melko was chained, 'that waited only for the light to come'. Thus in the early story Yavanna sows in the dark with a view (it seems) to growth and flowering in later days of sunlight, whereas in all the subsequent versions the goddess in the time of darkness sows no more, but rather lays a sleep on many things that had arisen beneath the light of the Lamps in the Spring of Arda. But both in the early tale and in *The Silmarillion* there is a suggestion that Yavanna foresees that light will come in the end to the Great Lands, to Middle-earth.

The conception of a flowing, liquid light in the airs of Earth is again very marked, and it seems that in the original idea the twilight ages of the world east of the sea were still illumined by the traces of this light ('Seldom now falls the shimmering rain as it was used, and there reigns a gloom lit with pale streaks', p. 98) as well as by the stars of Varda, even though 'the Gods have gathered so much of that light that had before flowed about the airs' (*ibid.*).

The renewed cosmic violence is conceivably the precursor of the great Battle of the Powers in the later mythology (*The Silmarillion* p. 51); but in this earliest tale Melko's upheavals are the cause of the Valar's visitation, whereas the Battle of the Powers, in which the shape of Middle-earth was changed, resulted from it. In *The Silmarillion* it was the discovery of the newly-awakened Elves by Oromë that led the Valar to the assault on Utumno.

In its rich narrative detail, as in its 'primitive' air, the tale told by Meril-i-Turinqi of the capture of Melko bears little relation to the later narrative; while the tone of the encounter at Utumna, and the treacherous shifts of the Valar to ensnare him, is foreign to it likewise. But some elements survived: the chain Angainor forged by Aulë (if not the marvellous metal *tilkal* with its most uncharacteristically derived name), the wrestling of Tulkas with Melko, his imprisonment in Mandos for 'three ages', and the idea that his fortress was not destroyed to its foundations. It emerges too that the clement and trustful character of Manwë was early defined; while the reference to Mandos' seldom speaking is possibly a foreshadowing of his pronouncing his judgements only at the bidding of Manwë (see p. 90). The origin of nightingales in the domain of Lórien in Valinor is already present.

Lastly, it may seem from the account of the journey of the Valar in this tale that Hisilómë (which survived without any further change as the

Quenya name of Hithlum) was here a quite distinct region from the later Hithlum, since it is placed *beyond* the Mountains of Iron: in *The Silmarillion* the Mountains of Iron are said to have been reared by Melkor 'as a fence to his citadel of Utumno': 'they stood upon the borders of the regions of everlasting cold, in a great curve from east to west' (p. 118). But in fact the 'Mountains of Iron' here correspond to the later 'Mountains of Shadow' (*Ered Wethrin*). In an annotated list of names accompanying the tale of *The Fall of Gondolin* the name *Dor Lómin* is thus defined:

> *Dor Lómin* or the 'Land of Shadow' was that region named of the Eldar *Hisilómë* (and this means 'Shadowy Twilights') . . . and it is so called by reason of the scanty sun which peeps little over the Iron Mountains to the east and south of it.

On the little map given on p. 81 the line of peaks which I have marked *f* almost certainly represents these mountains, and the region to the north of them, marked *g*, is then Hisilómë.

The manuscript continues, from the point where I have ended the text in this chapter, with no break; but this point is the end of a section in the mythological narrative (with a brief interruption by Eriol), and the remainder of Meril-i-Turinqi's tale is reserved to the next chapter. Thus I make two tales of one.

V
THE COMING OF THE ELVES
AND THE MAKING OF KÔR

I take this title from the cover of the book (which adds also 'How the Elves did fashion Gems'), for as I have already remarked the narrative continues without a new heading.

Then said Eriol: 'Sad was the unchaining of Melko, methinks, even did it seem merciful and just – but how came the Gods to do this thing?'

Then Meril[1] continuing said:

'Upon a time thereafter was the third period of Melko's imprisonment beneath the halls of Mandos come nearly to its ending. Manwë sat upon the top of the mountain and gazed with his piercing eyes into the shades beyond Valinor, and hawks flew to him and from him bearing many great tidings, but Varda was singing a song and looking upon the plain of Valinor. Silpion was at that time glimmering and the roofs of Valmar below were black and silver beneath its rays; and Varda was joyous, but on a sudden Manwë spake, saying: "Behold, there is a gleam of gold beneath the pine-trees, and the deepest gloaming of the world is full of a patter of feet. The Eldar have come, O Taniquetil!" Then Varda arose swiftly and stretched her arms out North and South, and unbraided her long hair, and lifted up the Song of the Valar, and Ilwë was filled with the loveliness of her voice.

Then did she descend to Valmar and to the abode of Aulë; and he was making vessels of silver for Lórien. A bason filled with the radiance of Telimpë[2] was by his side, and this he used cunningly in his craft, but now Varda stood before him and said: "The Eldar have come!" and Aulë flung down his hammer saying: "Then Ilúvatar hath sent them at last," and the hammer striking some ingots of silver upon the floor did of its magic smite silver sparks to life, that flashed from his windows out into the heavens. Varda seeing this took of that radiance in the bason and mingled it with molten silver to make it more stable, and fared upon her wings of speed, and set stars about the firmament in very great profusion, so that the skies grew marvellously fair and their glory was doubled; and those stars that she then fashioned have a power of slumbers, for the silver of their bodies came of the treasury of Lórien and their radiance had lain in Telimpë long time in his garden.

Some have said that the Seven Stars were set at that time by Varda to commemorate the coming of the Eldar, and that Morwinyon who blazes above the world's edge in the west was dropped by her as she fared in great haste back to Valinor. Now this is indeed the true beginning of Morwinyon and his beauty, yet the Seven Stars were not set by Varda, being indeed the sparks from Aulë's forge whose brightness in the ancient heavens urged Varda to make their rivals; yet this did she never achieve.

But now even as Varda is engaged in this great work, behold, Oromë pricks over the plain, and drawing rein he shouts aloud so that all the ears in Valmar may hear him: "*Tulielto! Tulielto!* They have come – they have come!" Then he stands midway between the Two Trees and winds his horn, and the gates of Valmar are opened, and the Vali troop into the plain, for they guess that tidings of wonder have come into the world. Then spake Oromë: "Behold the woods of the Great Lands, even in Palisor the midmost region where the pinewoods murmur unceasingly, are full of a strange noise. There did I wander, and lo! 'twas as if folk arose betimes beneath the latest stars. There was a stir among the distant trees and words were spoken suddenly, and feet went to and fro. Then did I say what is this deed that Palúrien my mother has wrought in secret, and I sought her out and questioned her, and she answered: 'This is no work of mine, but the hand of one far greater did this. Ilúvatar hath awakened his children at the last – ride home to Valinor and tell the Gods that the Eldar have come indeed!' "

Then shouted all the people of Valinor: "*I·Eldar tulier* – the Eldar have come" – and it was not until that hour that the Gods knew that their joy had contained a flaw, or that they had waited in hunger for its completion, but now they knew that the world had been an empty place beset with loneliness having no children for her own.

Now once more is council set and Manwë sitteth before the Gods there amid the Two Trees – and those had now borne light for four ages. Every one of the Vali fare thither, even Ulmo Vailimo in great haste from the Outer Seas, and his face is eager and glad.

On that day Manwë released Melko from Angaino before the full time of his doom, but the manacles and the fetters of *tilkal* were not unloosed, and he bore them yet upon wrist and ankle. Great joy blindeth even the forewisdom of the Gods. Last of all came Palúrien Yavanna hasting from Palisor, and the Valar debated concerning the

Eldar; but Melko sat at the feet of Tulkas and feigned a glad and humble cheer. At length it is the word of the Gods that some of the new-come Eldar be bidden to Valinor, there to speak to Manwë and his people, telling of their coming into the world and of the desires that it awakened in them.

Then does Nornorë, whose feet flash invisibly for the greatness of their speed, hurtle from Valinor bearing the embassy of Manwë, and he goes unstaying over both land and sea to Palisor. There he finds a place deep in a vale surrounded by pine-clad slopes; its floor is a pool of wide water and its roof the twilight set with Varda's stars. There had Oromë heard the awaking of the Eldar, and all songs name that place Koivië-néni or the Waters of Awakening.

Now all the slopes of that valley and the bare margin of the lake, even the rugged fringes of the hills beyond, are filled with a concourse of folk who gaze in wonder at the stars, and some sing already with voices that are very beautiful. But Nornorë stood upon a hill and was amazed for the beauty of that folk, and because he was a Vala they seemed to him marvellously small and delicate and their faces wistful and tender. Then did he speak in the great voice of the Valar and all those shining faces turned towards his voice.

"Behold O Eldalië, desired are ye for all the age of twilight, and sought for throughout the ages of peace, and I come even from Manwë Súlimo Lord of the Gods who abides upon Taniquetil in peace and wisdom to you who are the Children of Ilúvatar, and these are the words he put into my mouth to speak: Let now some few of you come back with me – for am I not Nornorë herald of the Valar – and enter Valinor and speak with him, that he may learn of your coming and of all your desires."

Great was the stir and wonder now about the waters of Koivië, and its end was that three of the Eldar came forward daring to go with Nornorë, and these he bore now back to Valinor, and their names as the Elves of Kôr have handed them on were Isil Inwë, and Finwë Nólemë who was Turondo's father, and Tinwë Lintö father of Tinúviel – but the Noldoli call them Inwithiel, Golfinweg, and Tinwelint. Afterward they became very great among the Eldar, and the Teleri were those who followed Isil, but his kindred and descendants are that royal folk the Inwir of whose blood I am. Nolemë was lord of the Noldoli, and of his son Turondo (or Turgon as they called him) are great tales told, but Tinwë[3] abode not long with his people, and yet 'tis said lives still lord of the scattered Elves of Hisilómë, dancing in its twilight places with Wendelin his spouse, a sprite come long long ago from the quiet gardens of Lórien; yet greatest of all the Elves did Isil Inwë become, and folk reverence his mighty name to this day.

Behold now brought by Nornorë the three Elves stood before the Gods, and it was at that time the changing of the lights, and Silpion was waning but Laurelin was awakening to his greatest glory, even as Silmo emptied the urn of silver about the roots of the other Tree. Then those Elves were utterly dazed and astonied by the splendour of the light, whose eyes knew only the dusk and had yet seen no brighter things than Varda's stars, but the beauty and majestic strength of the Gods in conclave filled them with awe, and the roofs of Valmar blazing afar upon the plain made them tremble, and they bowed in reverence – but Manwë said to them: "Rise, O Children of Ilúvatar, for very glad are the Gods of your coming! Tell us how ye came; how found ye the world; what seemeth it to you who are its first offspring, or with what desires doth it fill you."

But Nólemë answering said: "Lo! Most mighty one, whence indeed come we! For meseems I awoke but now from a sleep eternally profound, whose vast dreams already are forgotten." And Tinwë said thereto that his heart told him that he was new-come from illimitable regions, yet he might not recollect by what dark and strange paths he had been brought; and last spake Inwë, who had been gazing upon Laurelin while the others spake, and he said: "Knowing neither whence I come nor by what ways nor yet whither I go, the world that we are in is but one great wonderment to me, and methinks I love it wholly, yet it fills me altogether with a desire for light."

Then Manwë saw that Ilúvatar had wiped from the minds of the Eldar all knowledge of the manner of their coming, and that the Gods might not discover it; and he was filled with deep astonishment; but Yavanna who hearkened also caught her breath for the stab of the words of Inwë, saying that he desired light. Then she looked upon Laurelin and her heart thought of the fruitful orchards in Valmar, and she whispered to Tuivána who sat beside her, gazing upon the tender grace of those Eldar; then those twain said to Manwë: "Lo! the Earth and its shadows are no place for creatures so fair, whom only the heart and mind of Ilúvatar have conceived. Fair are the pine-forests and the thickets, but they are full of unelfin spirits and Mandos' children walk abroad and vassals of Melko lurk in strange places – and we ourselves would not be without the sight of this sweet folk. Their distant laughter has filtered to our ears from Palisor, and we would have it echo always about us in our halls and pleasaunces in Valmar. Let the Eldar dwell among us, and the well of our joy be filled from new springs that may not dry up."

Then arose a clamour among the Gods and the most spake for Palúrien and Vána, whereas Makar said that Valinor was builded for the Valar – "and already is it a rose-garden of fair ladies rather than an abode of men. Wherefore do ye desire to fill it with the children of the world?" In this Meássë backed him, and Mandos and Fui were cold to the Eldar as to all else; yet was Varda vehement in support of Yavanna and Tuivána, and indeed her love for the Eldar has ever been the greatest of all the folk of Valinor; and Aulë and Lórien, Oromë and Nessa and Ulmo most mightily proclaimed their desire for the bidding of the Eldar to dwell among the Gods. Wherefore, albeit Ossë spake cautiously against it – belike out of that ever-smouldering jealousy and rebellion he felt against Ulmo – it was the voice of the council that the Eldar should be bidden, and the Gods awaited but the judgement of Manwë. Behold even Melko seeing where was the majority insinuated his guileful voice into the pleading, and has nonetheless since those days maligned the Valar, saying they did but summon the Eldar as to a prison out of covetice and jealousy of their beauty. Thus often did he lie to the Noldoli afterwards when he would stir their restlessness, adding beside all truth that he alone had withstood the general voice and spoken for the freedom of the Elves.

Maybe indeed had the Gods decided otherwise the world had been a fairer place now and the Eldar a happier folk, but never would they have achieved such glory, knowledge, and beauty as they did of old, and still less would any of Melko's redes have benefited them.

Now having hearkened to all that was said Manwë gave judgement and was glad, for indeed his heart leaned of itself to the leading of the Eldar from the dusky world to the light of Valinor. Turning to the three Eldar he said: "Go ye back now to your kindreds and Nornorë shall bring you swiftly there, even to Koivië-néni in Palisor. Behold, this is the word of Manwë Súlimo, and the voice of the Valar's desire, that the people of the Eldalië, the Children of Ilúvatar, fare to Valinor, and there dwell in the splendour of Laurelin and the radiance of Silpion and know the happiness of the Gods. An abode of surpassing beauty shall they possess, and the Gods will aid them in its building."

Thereto answered Inwë: "Fain are we indeed of thy bidding, and who of the Eldalië that have already longed for the beauty of the stars will stay or rest till his eyes have feasted on the blessed light of Valinor!" Thereafter Nornorë guided those Elves back to the bare margins of Koivië-néni, and standing upon a boulder Inwë spake the embassy to all those hosts of the Eldalië that Ilúvatar waked first upon the Earth, and all such as heard his words were filled with desire to see the faces of the Gods.

When Nornorë returning told the Valar that the Elves were indeed coming and that Ilúvatar had set already a great multitude upon the Earth, the Gods made mighty preparation. Behold Aulë gathers his tools and stuffs and Yavanna and Tuivána wander about the plain even to the foothills of the mountains and the bare coasts of the Shadowy Seas, seeking them a home and an abiding-place; but Oromë goeth straightway out of Valinor into the forests whose every darkling glade he knew and every dim path had traversed, for he purposed to guide the troops of the Eldar from Palisor over all the wide lands west till they came to the confines of the Great Sea.

To those dark shores fared Ulmo, and strange was the roaring of the unlit sea in those most ancient days upon that rocky coast that bore still the scars of the tumultuous wrath of Melko. Falman-Ossë was little pleased to see Ulmo in the Great Seas, for Ulmo had taken that island whereon Ossë himself had drawn the Gods to Arvalin, saving them from the rising waters when Ringil and Helkar thawed beneath their blazing lamps. That was many ages past in the days when the Gods were new-come strangers in the world, and during all that time the island had floated darkly in the Shadowy Seas, desolate save when Ossë climbed its beaches on his journeys in the deeps; but now Ulmo had come upon his secret island and harnessed thereto a host of the greatest fish, and amidmost was Uin the mightiest and most ancient of whales; and he bid these put forth their strength, and they drew the island mightily to the very shores of the Great Lands, even to the coast of Hisilómë northward of the Iron Mountains whither all the deepest shades withdrew when the Sun first arose.

Now Ulmo stands there and there comes a glint in the woods that marched even down to the sea-foam in those quiet days, and behold! he hears the footsteps of the Teleri crackle in the forest, and Inwë is at their head beside the stirrup of Oromë. Grievous had been their march, and dark and difficult the way through Hisilómë the land of shade, despite the skill and power of Oromë. Indeed long after the joy of Valinor had washed its memory faint the Elves sang still sadly of it, and told tales of many of their folk whom they said and say were lost in those old forests and ever wandered there in sorrow. Still were they there long after when Men were shut in Hisilómë by Melko, and still do they dance there when

Men have wandered far over the lighter places of the Earth. Hisilómë did Men name Aryador, and the Lost Elves did they call the Shadow Folk, and feared them.

Nonetheless the most of the great companies of the Teleri came now to the beaches and climbed therefrom upon the island that Ulmo had brought. Ulmo counselled them that they wait not for the other kindreds, and though at first they will not yield, weeping at the thought, at last are they persuaded, and straightway are drawn with utmost speed beyond the Shadowy Seas and the wide bay of Arvalin to the strands of Valinor. There does the distant beauty of the trees shining down the opening in the hills enchant their hearts, and yet do they stand gazing back across the waters they have passed, for they know not where those other kindreds of their folk may be, and not even the loveliness of Valinor do they desire without them.

Then leaving them silent and wondering on the shore Ulmo draws back that great island-car to the rocks of Hisilómë, and behold, warmed by the distant gleam of Laurelin that lit upon its western edge as it lay in the Bay of Faëry, new and more tender trees begin to grow upon it, and the green of herbage is seen upon its slopes.

Now Ossë raises his head above the waves in wrath, deeming himself slighted that his aid was not sought in the ferrying of the Elves, but his own island taken unasked. Fast does he follow in Ulmo's wake and yet is left far behind, for Ulmo set the might of the Valar in Uin and the whales. Upon the cliffs there stand already the Noldoli in anguish, thinking themselves deserted in the gloom, and Nóleme Finwë who had led them thither hard upon the rear of the Teleri went among them enheartening them. Full of travail their journey too had been, for the world is wide and nigh half across it had they come from most distant Palisor, and in those days neither sun shone nor moon gleamed, and pathways were there none be it of Elves or of Men. Oromë too was far ahead riding before the Teleri upon the march and was now gone back into the lands. There the Solosimpi were astray in the forests stretching deep behind, and his horn wound faintly in the ears of those upon the shore, from whence that Vala sought them up and down the dark vales of Hisilómë.

Therefore now coming Ulmo thinks to draw the Noldoli swiftly to the strand of Valinor, returning once again for those others when Oromë shall have led them to the coast. This does he, and Falman beholds that second ferrying from afar and spumes in rage, but great is the joy of the Teleri and Noldoli upon that shore where the lights are those of late summer afternoons for the distant glow of Lindeloksë. There may I leave them for a while and tell of the strange happenings that befell the Solosimpi by reason of Ossë's wrath, and of the first dwelling upon Tol Eressëa.

Fear falls upon them in that old darkness, and beguiled by the fair music of the fay Wendelin, as other tales set forth more fully elsewhere, their leader Tinwë Linto was lost, and long they sought him, but it was in vain, and he came never again among them.[4] When therefore they heard the horn of Oromë ringing in the forest great was their joy, and gathering to its sound soon are they led to the cliffs, and hear the murmur of the sunless sea. Long time they waited there, for Ossë cast storms and shadows about the return of Ulmo, so that he drove by devious ways, and his great fish faltered in their going; yet at the last do they too climb upon that island and are drawn towards Valinor; and one Ellu they chose in place of Tinwë, and he has ever since been named the Lord of the Solosimpi.[5]

Behold now less than half the distance have they traversed, and the Twilit Isles float still far aloof, when Ossë and Ónen waylay them in the western waters of the Great Sea ere yet the mists of the Shadowy Seas are reached. Then Ossë seizes that island in his great hand, and all the great strength of Uin may scarcely drag it onward, for at swimming and in deeds of bodily strength in the water none of the Valar, not even Ulmo's self, is Ossë's match, and indeed Ulmo was not at hand, for he was far ahead piloting the great craft in the glooms that Ossë had gathered, leading it onward with the music of his conches. Now ere he can return Ossë with Ónen's aid had brought the isle to a stand, and was anchoring it even to the sea-bottom with giant ropes of those leather-weeds and polyps that in those dark days had grown already in slow centuries to unimagined girth about the pillars of his deep-sea house. Thereto as Ulmo urges the whales to put forth all their strength and himself aids with all his godlike power, Ossë piles rocks and boulders of huge mass that Melko's ancient wrath had strewn about the seafloor, and builds these as a column beneath the island.

Vainly doth Ulmo trumpet and Uin with the flukes of his un-measured tail lash the seas to wrath, for thither Ossë now brings every kind of deep sea creature that buildeth itself a house and dwelling of stony shell; and these he planted about the base of the island: corals there were of every kind and barnacles and sponges like stone. Nonetheless for a very great while did that struggle endure, until at length Ulmo returned to Valmar in wrath and dismay. There did he warn the other Valar that the Solosimpi may not yet be brought thither, for that the isle has grown fast in the most lonely waters of the world.

There stands that island yet – indeed thou knowest it, for it is called "the Lonely Isle" – and no land may be seen for many leagues' sail from its cliffs, for the Twilit Isles upon the bosom of the Shadowy Seas are deep in the dim West, and the Magic Isles lie backward in the East.

Now therefore do the Gods bid the Elves build a dwelling, and Aulë aided them in that, but Ulmo fares back to the Lonely Island, and lo! it stands now upon a pillar of rock upon the seas' floor, and Ossë fares about it in a foam of business anchoring all the scattered islands of his domain fast to the ocean-bed. Hence came the first dwelling of the Solosimpi on the Lonely Island, and the deeper sundering of that folk from the others both in speech and customs; for know that all these great deeds of the past that make but a small tale now were not lightly achieved and in a moment of time, but rather would very many men have grown and died betwixt the binding of the Islands and the making of the Ships.

Twice now had that isle of their dwelling caught the gleam of the glorious Trees of Valinor, and so was it already fairer and more fertile and more full of sweet plants and grasses than the other places of all the world beside where great light had not been seen; indeed the Solosimpi say that birches grew there already, and many reeds, and turf there was upon the western slopes. There too were many caverns, and there was a stretching shoreland of white sand about the feet of black and purple cliffs, and here was the dwelling even in those deepest days of the Solosimpi.

There Ulmo sate upon a headland and spake to them words of comfort and of the deepest wisdom; and all sea-lore he told them, and they hearkened; and music he taught them, and they made slender pipes of shells. By reason of that labour of Ossë there are no strands so strewn with marvellous shells as were the white beaches and the sheltered coves of Tol Eressëa, and the Solosimpi dwelt much in caves, and adorned them with those sea-treasures, and the sound of their wistful piping might be heard for many a long day come faintly down the winds.

Then Falman-Ossë's heart melted towards them and he would have released them, save for the new joy and pride he had that their beauty dwelt thus amidmost of his realm, so that their pipes gave perpetual pleasure to his ear, and Uinen[6] and the Oarni and all the spirits of the waves were enamoured of them.

So danced the Solosimpi upon the waves' brink, and the love of the sea and rocky coasts entered in their hearts, even though they gazed in longing towards the happy shores whither long ago the Teleri and Noldoli had been borne.

Now these after a season took hope and their sorrow grew less bitter, learning how their kindred dwelt in no unkindly land, and Ulmo had them under his care and guardianship. Wherefore they heeded now the Gods' desire and turned to the building of their home; and Aulë taught them very much lore and skill, and Manwë also. Now Manwë loved more the Teleri, and from him and from Ómar did they learn deeper of the craft of song and poesy than all the Elves beside; but the Noldoli were beloved most by Aulë, and they learned much of his science, till their hearts became unquiet for the lust of more knowing, but they grew to great wisdom and to great subtlety of skill.

Behold there is a low place in that ring of mountains that guards Valinor, and there the shining of the Trees steals through from the plain beyond and gilds the dark waters of the bay of Arvalin,[7] but a great beach of finest sand, golden in the blaze of Laurelin, white in the light of Silpion, runs inland there, where in the trouble of the ancient seas a shadowy arm of water had groped in toward Valinor, but now there is only a slender water fringed with white. At the head of this long creek there stands a lonely hill which gazes at the loftier mountains. Now all the walls of that inlet of the seas are luxuriant with a marvellous vigour of fair trees, but the hill is covered only with a deep turf, and harebells grow atop of it ringing softly in the gentle breath of Súlimo.

Here was the place that those fair Elves bethought them to dwell, and the Gods named that hill Kôr by reason of its roundness and its smoothness. Thither did Aulë bring all the dust of magic metals that his great works had made and gathered, and he piled it about the foot of that hill, and most of this dust was of gold, and a sand of gold stretched away from the feet of Kôr out into the distance where the Two Trees blossomed. Upon the hill-top the Elves built fair abodes of shining white – of marbles and stones quarried from the Mountains of Valinor that glistened wondrously,[8] silver and gold and a substance of great hardness and white lucency that they contrived of shells melted in the dew of Silpion, and white streets there were bordered with dark trees that wound with graceful turns or climbed with flights of delicate stairs up from the plain of Valinor to topmost Kôr; and all those shining houses clomb each shoulder higher than the others till the house of Inwë was reached that was the uppermost, and had a slender silver tower shooting skyward like a needle, and a white lamp of piercing ray was set therein that shone upon the shadows of the bay, but every window of the city on the hill of Kôr looked out toward the sea.

Fountains there were of great beauty and frailty and roofs and pinnacles of bright glass and amber that was made by Palúrien and Ulmo, and trees stood thick on the white walls and terraces, and their golden fruit shone richly.

Now at the building of Kôr the Gods gave to Inwë and to Nólemë a shoot each of either of those glorious trees, and they grew to very small and slender elfin trees, but blossomed both eternally without abating, and those of the courts of Inwë were the fairest, and about them the Teleri sang songs of happiness, but others singing also fared up and down the marble flights and the wistful voices of the Noldoli were heard about the courts and chambers; but yet the Solosimpi dwelt far off amid the sea and made windy music on their pipes of shell.

Now is Ossë very fain of those Solosimpi, the shoreland pipers, and if Ulmo be not nigh he sits upon a reef at sea and many of the Oarni are by him, and hearkens to their voice and watches their flitting dances on this shore, but to Valmar he dare not fare again for the power of Ulmo in the councils of the Valar and . . . . the wrath of that mighty one at the anchoring of the islands.

Indeed war had been but held off by the Gods, who desired peace and would not suffer Ulmo to gather the folk of the Valar and assail Ossë and rend the islands from their new roots. Therefore does Ossë sometimes ride the foams out into the bay of Arvalin[9] and gaze upon the glory on the hills, and he longs for the light and happiness upon the plain, but most for the song of birds and the swift movement of their wings into the clear air, grown weary of his silver and dark fish silent and strange amid the deep waters.

But on a day some birds came flying high from the gardens of Yavanna, and some were white and some black and some both black and white; and being dazed among the shadows they had not where to settle, and Ossë coaxed them, and they settled about his mighty shoulders, and he taught them to swim and gave them great strength of wing, for of such strength of shoulder he had more than any [?other] being and was the greatest of swimmers; and he poured fishy oils upon their feathers that they might bear the waters, and he fed them on small fish.

Then did he turn away to his own seas, and they swam about him or fared above him on low wing crying and piping; and he showed them dwellings on the Twilit Isles and even about the cliffs of Tol Eressëa, and the manner of diving and of spearing fish they learned there, and their voices became harsh for the rugged places of their life far from the soft regions of Valinor or wailing for the music of the Solosimpi and sighing of the sea. And now have all that great folk of gulls and seamews and petrels come into their kingdom; and puffins are there, and eider-duck, and cormorants, and gannets, and rock-doves, and the cliffs are full of a chattering and a smell of fish, and great conclaves are held upon their ledges, or among spits and reefs among the waters. But the proudest of all these birds were the swans, and these Ossë let dwell in Tol Eressëa, [?flying] along its coasts or paddling inland up its streams; and he set them there as a gift and joy to the Solosimpi. But when Ulmo heard of these new deeds he was ill-pleased for the havoc wrought amid the fishes wherewith he had filled the waters with the aid of Palúrien.

Now do the Solosimpi take great joy of [?their] birds, new creatures to them, and of swans, and behold upon the lakes of Tol Eressëa already they fare on rafts of fallen timber, and some harness thereto swans and speed across the waters; but the more hardy dare out upon the sea and the gulls draw them, and when Ulmo saw that he was very glad. For lo! the Teleri and Noldoli complain much to Manwë of the separation of the Solosimpi, and the Gods desire them to be drawn to Valinor; but Ulmo cannot yet think of any device save by help of Ossë and the Oarni, and will not be humbled to this. But now does he fare home in haste to Aulë, and those twain got them speedily to Tol Eressëa, and Oromë was with them, and there is the first hewing of trees that was done in the world outside Valinor. Now does Aulë of the sawn wood of pine and oak make great vessels like to the bodies of swans, and these he covers with the bark of silver birches, or . . . . . with gathered feathers of the oily plumage of Ossë's birds, and they are nailed and [?sturdily] riveted and fastened with silver, and he carves prows for them like the upheld necks of swans, but they are hollow and have no feet; and by cords of great strength and slimness are gulls and petrels harnessed to them, for they were tame to the hands of the Solosimpi, because their hearts were so turned by Ossë.

Now are the beaches upon the western shores of Tol Eressëa, even at Falassë Númëa (Western Surf), thronged with that people of the Elves, and drawn up there is a very great host indeed of those swanships, and the cry of the gulls above them is unceasing. But the Solosimpi arise in great numbers and climb into the hollow bodies of these new things of Aulë's skill, and more of their kin fare ever to the shores, marching to the sound of innumerable pipes and flutes.

Now all are embarked and the gulls fare mightily into the twilit sky, but Aulë and Oromë are in the foremost galley and the mightiest, and seven hundred gulls are harnessed thereto and it gleams with silver and white feathers, and has a beak of gold and eyes of jet and amber. But Ulmo fares at the rear in his fishy car and trumpets loudly for the discomfiture of Ossë and the rescue of the Shoreland Elves.

But Ossë seeing how these birds have been to his undoing is very downcast, yet for the presence of those three Gods and indeed for his love of the Solosimpi that had grown by now very great he molested not their white fleet, and they came thus over the grey leagues of the ocean, through the dim sounds, and the mists of the Shadowy Seas, even to the first dark waters of the bay of Arvalin.

Know then that the Lonely Island is upon the confines of the Great Sea. Now that Great Sea or the Western Water is beyond the westernmost limits of the Great Lands, and in it are many lands and islands ere beyond their anchorage you reach the Magic Isles, and beyond these still lies Tol Eressëa. But beyond Tol Eressëa is the misty wall and those great sea glooms beneath which lie the Shadowy Seas, and thereon float the Twilit Isles whither only pierced at clearest times the faintest twinkle of the far gleam of Silpion. But in the westernmost of these stood the Tower of Pearl built in after days and much sung in song; but the Twilit Isles are held the first of the Outer Lands, which are these and Arvalin and Valinor, and Tol Eressëa is held neither of the Outer Lands or of the Great Lands where Men after roamed. But the farthest shore of those Shadowy Seas is Arvalin or Erumáni to the far south, but more northerly do they lap the very coasts of Eldamar, and here are they broader to one faring west. Beyond Arvalin tower those huge Mountains of Valinor which are in a great ring bending slowly west, but the Shadowy Seas make a vast bay to the north of Arvalin running right up to the black feet of the mountains, so that here they border upon the waters and not upon the lands, and there at the bay's innermost stands Taniquetil, glorious to behold, loftiest of all mountains clad in purest snow, looking across Arvalin half south and half north across that mighty Bay of Faëry, and so beyond the Shadowy Seas themselves, even so that all the sails upon the sunlit waters of the Great Sea in after days (when the Gods had made that lamp) and all the throngs about the western havens of the Lands of Men could be seen from its summit; and yet is that distance counted only in unimagined leagues.

But now comes that strange fleet nigh these regions and eager eyes look out. There stands Taniquetil and he is purple and dark of one side with gloom of Arvalin and of the Shadowy Seas, and lit in glory of the other by reason of the light of the Trees of Valinor. Now where the seas lapped those shores of old their waves long ere their breaking were suddenly lit by Laurelin were it day or by Silpion were it night, and the shadows of the world ceased almost abruptly and the waves laughed. But an opening in the mountains on those shores let through a glimpse of Valinor, and there stood the hill of Kôr, and the white sand runs up the creek to meet it, but its feet are in green water, and behind the sand of gold fares away farther than eye can guess, and indeed beyond Valinor who has heard or seen anything save Ulmo, yet of a certainty here spread the dark waters of the Outer Seas: tideless are they and very cool, and so thin that no boat can float upon their bosom, and few fish swim beneath their depths.

But now upon the hill of Kôr is a running and a joyous concourse, and all the people of the Teleri and Noldoli fare out of the gates and wait to welcome the coming of the fleet upon the shore. And now those ships leave the shadows and now are caught in the bright gleam about the inner bay, and now are they beached high and the Solosimpi dance and pipe, and mingle with the singing of the Teleri and the Noldoli's faint music.

Far behind lay Tol Eressëa in silence and its woods and shores were still, for nearly all that host of sea-birds had flown after the Eldar and wailed now about the shores of Eldamar: but Ossë dwelt in despondency and his silver halls in Valmar abode long empty, for he came no nearer to them for a great while than the shadow's edge, whither came the wailing of his sea-birds far away.

Now the Solosimpi abode not much in Kôr but had strange dwellings among the shoreland rocks, and Ulmo came and sat among them as aforetime in Tol Eressëa, and that was his time of greatest mirth and gentleness, and all his lore and love of music he poured out to them, and they drank it eagerly. Musics did they make and weave catching threads of sound whispered by waters in caverns or by wave-tops brushed by gentle winds; and these they twined with the wail of gulls and the echoes of their own sweet voices in the places of their home. But the Teleri and Inwir gathered [?harvest] of poesy and song, and were oftenest among the Gods, dancing in the skiey halls of Manwë for the joy of Varda of the Stars, or filling the streets and courts of Valmar with the strange loveliness of their pomps and revelry; for Oromë and for Nessa they danced upon green swards, and the glades of Valinor knew them as they flitted among the gold-lit trees, and Palúrien was very merry for the sight of them. Often were the Noldoli with them and made much music for the multitude of their harps and viols was very sweet, and Salmar loved them; but their greatest delight was in the courts of Aulë, or in their own dear homes in Kôr, fashioning many beautiful things and weaving many stories. With paintings and broidered hangings and carvings of great delicacy they filled all their city, and even did Valmar grow more fair beneath their skilful hands.

Now is to tell how the Solosimpi fared often about the near seas in their swanships, or drawn by the birds, or paddling themselves with great oars that they had made to the likeness of the webs of swan or duck; and they dredged the sea-beds and won wealth of the slim shells of those magic waters and uncounted store of pearls of a most pure and starry lustre: and these were both their glory and delight and the envy of the other Eldar who longed for them to shine in the adornment of the city of Kôr.

But those of the Noldoli whom Aulë had most deeply taught laboured in secret unceasingly, and of Aulë they had wealth of metals and of stones and marbles, and of the leave of the Valar much store too was granted to them of the radiance of Kulullin and of Telimpë held in hidden bowls. Starlight they had of Varda and strands of the bluest *ilwë* Manwë gave them; water of the most limpid pools in that creek of Kôr, and crystal drops from all the sparkling founts in the courts of Valmar. Dews did they gather in the woods of Oromë, and flower-petals of all hues and honeys in Yavanna's gardens, and they chased the beams of Laurelin and Silpion amongst the leaves. But when all this wealth of fair and radiant things was gathered, they got of the Solosimpi many shells white and pink, and purest foam, and lastly some few pearls. These pearls were their model, and the lore of Aulë and the magic of the Valar were their tools, and all the most lovely things of the substance of the Earth the matters of their craft – and therefrom did the Noldoli with great labour invent and fashion the first gems. Crystals did they make of the waters of the springs shot with the lights of Silpion; amber and chrysoprase and topaz glowed beneath their hands, and garnets and rubies they wrought, making their glassy substance as Aulë had taught them but dyeing them with the juices of roses and red flowers, and to each they gave a heart of fire. Emeralds some made of the water of the creek of Kôr and glints among the grassy glades of Valinor, and sapphires did they fashion in great profusion, [?tingeing] them with the airs of Manwë; amethysts there were and moonstones, beryls and onyx, agates of blended marbles and many lesser stones, and their hearts were very glad, nor were they content with a few, but made them jewels in immeasurable number till all the fair substances were well nigh exhausted and the great piles of those gems might not be concealed but blazed

in the light like beds of brilliant flowers. Then took they those
pearls that had and some of wellnigh all their jewels and made a
new gem of a milky pallor shot with gleams like echoes of all other
stones, and this they thought very fair, and they were opals; but
still some laboured on, and of starlight and the purest water-drops,
of the dew of Silpion, and the thinnest air, they made diamonds,
and challenged any to make fairer.

Then arose Fëanor of the Noldoli and fared to the Solosimpi and
begged a great pearl, and he got moreover an urn full of the most
luminous phosphor-light gathered of foam in dark places, and with
these he came home, and he took all the other gems and did gather
their glint by the light of white lamps and silver candles, and he took
the sheen of pearls and the faint half-colours of opals, and he
[?bathed] them in phosphorescence and the radiant dew of Silpion,
and but a single tiny drop of the light of Laurelin did he let fall
therein, and giving all those magic lights a body to dwell in of such
perfect glass as he alone could make nor even Aulë compass, so
great was the slender dexterity of the fingers of Fëanor, he made a
jewel – and it shone of its own . . . .[10] radiance in the uttermost dark; and he set it therein and sat a very long while and gazed
at its beauty. Then he made two more, and had no more stuffs:
and he fetched the others to behold his handiwork, and they were
utterly amazed, and those jewels he called Silmarilli, or as we say
the name in the speech of the Noldoli today Silubrilthin.[11] Wherefore
though the Solosimpi held ever that none of the gems of the Noldoli,
not even that majestic shimmer of diamonds, overpassed their tender
pearls, yet have all held who ever saw them that the Silmarils of
Fëanor were the most beautiful jewels that ever shone or [?glowed].

Now Kôr is lit with this wealth of gems and sparkles most marvellously, and all the kindred of the Eldalië are made rich in their
loveliness by the generosity of the Noldoli, and the Gods' desire of
their beauty is sated to the full. Sapphires in great [?wonder] were
given to Manwë and his raiment was crusted with them, and Oromë
had a belt of emeralds, but Yavanna loved all the gems, and Aulë's
delight was in diamonds and amethysts. Melko alone was given none
of them, for that he had not expiated his many crimes, and he lusted
after them exceedingly, yet said nought, feigning to hold them of
lesser worth than metals.

But now all the kindred of the Eldalië has found its greatest bliss,
and the majesty and glory of the Gods and their home is augmented
to the greatest splendour that the world has seen, and the Trees shone
on Valinor, and Valinor gave back their light in a thousand scintilla-

tions of splintered colours; but the Great Lands were still and dark and very lonesome, and Ossë sat without the precincts and saw the moongleam of Silpion twinkle on the pebbles of diamonds and of crystals which the Gnomes cast in prodigality about the margin of the seas, and the glassy fragments splintered in their labouring glittered about the seaward face of Kôr; but the pools amid the dark rocks were filled with jewels, and the Solosimpi whose robes were sewn with pearls danced about them, and that was the fairest of all shores, and the music of the waters about those silver strands was beyond all sounds enchanting.

These were the rocks of Eldamar, and I saw them long ago, for Inwë was my grandsire's sire[12]; and [?even] he was the eldest of the Elves and had lived yet in majesty had he not perished in that march into the world, but Ingil his son went long ago back to Valinor and is with Manwë. And I am also akin to the shoreland dancers, and these things that I tell you I know they are true; and the magic and the wonder of the Bay of Faëry is such that none who have seen it as it was then can speak without a catch of the breath and a sinking of the voice.'

Then Meril the Queen ceased her long tale, but Eriol said nought, gazing at the long radiance of the westering sun gleaming through the apple boles, and dreaming of Faëry. At length said Meril: 'Fare now home, for the afternoon has waned, and the telling of the tale has set a weight of desire in my heart and in thine. But be in patience and bide yet ere ye seek fellowship with that sad kindred of the Island Elves.'

But Eriol said: 'Even now I know not and it passes my heart to guess how all that loveliness came to fading, or the Elves might be prevailed to depart from Eldamar.'

But Meril said: 'Nay, I have lengthened the tale too much for love of those days, and many great things lie between the making of the gems and the coming back to Tol Eressëa: but these things many know as well as I, and Lindo or Rúmil of Mar Vanwa Tyaliéva would tell them more skilfully than I.' Then did she and Eriol fare back to the house of flowers, and Eriol took his leave ere the western face of Ingil's tower was yet grown grey with dusk.

NOTES

1 The manuscript has *Vairë*, but this can only be a slip.
2 The occurrence of the name *Telimpë* here, and again later in the tale, as also in that of *The Sun and Moon*, is curious; in the tale of *The

Coming of the Valar and the Building of Valinor the name was changed at its first appearance from *Telimpë* (*Silindrin*) to *Silindrin*, and at subsequent occurrences *Silindrin* was written from the first (p. 79).

3   The manuscript has *Linwë* here, and again below; see under *Tinwë Linto* in 'Changes made to names' at the end of these notes.

4   This sentence, from 'and beguiled . . .', was added after, though not to all appearance much after, the writing of the text.

5   This sentence, from 'and one Ellu . . .', was added at the same time as that referred to in note 4.

6   The first occurrence of the form *Uinen*, and so written at the time of composition (i.e. not corrected from *Ónen*).

7   *Arvalin*: thus written at the time of composition, not emended from *Habbanan* or *Harmalin* as previously.

8   When my father wrote these texts, he wrote first in pencil, and then subsequently wrote over the top of it in ink, erasing the pencilled text – of which bits can be read here and there, and from which one can see that he altered the pencilled original somewhat as he went along. At the words 'glistened wondrously', however, he abandoned the writing of the new text in ink, and from this point we have only the original pencilled manuscript, which is in places exceedingly difficult to read, being more hasty, and also soft and smudged in the course of time. In deciphering this text I have been in places defeated, and I use brackets and question-marks to indicate uncertain readings, and rows of dots to show roughly the length of illegible words.

It is to be emphasized therefore that from here on there is only a *first draft*, and one written very rapidly, dashed onto the page.

9   *Arvalin*: here and subsequently emended from *Habbanan*; see note 7. The explanation is clearly that the name *Arvalin* came in at or before the time of the rewriting in ink over the pencilled text; though further on in the narrative we are here at an earlier stage of composition.

10   The word might be read as 'wizardous'.

11   Other forms (beginning *Sigm-*) preceded *Silubrilthin* which cannot be read with certainty. Meril speaks as if the Gnomish name was the form used in Tol Eressëa, but it is not clear why.

12   'my grandsire's sire': the original reading was 'my grandsire'.

Changes made to names in
The Coming of the Elves and the Making of Kôr

Tinwë Linto ⟨ *Linwë Tinto* (this latter is the form of the name in an interpolated passage in the preceding tale, see p. 106 note 1). At two subsequent occurrences of *Linwë* (see note 3 above) the name was not changed, clearly through oversight; in the two added passages where the name occurs (see notes 4 and 5 above) the form is *Tinwë* (*Linto*).

Inwithiel ⟨ *Gim-githil* (the same change in *The Cottage of Lost Play*, see p. 22).

Tinwelint ⟨ *Tintoglin*.

Wendelin ⟨ *Tindriel* (cf. the interpolated passage in the previous tale, p. 106 note 1).

Arvalin ⟨ *Habbanan* throughout the tale except once, where the name was written *Arvalin* from the first; see notes 7 and 9 above.

Lindeloksë ⟨ *Lindelótë* (the same change in *The Coming of the Valar and the Building of Valinor*, see p. 79).

Erumáni ⟨ *Harwalin*.

Commentary on
The Coming of the Elves and the Making of Kôr

I have already (p. 111) touched on the great difference in the structure of the narrative at the beginning of this tale, namely that here the Elves awoke *during* Melko's captivity in Valinor, whereas in the later story it was the very fact of the Awakening that brought the Valar to make war on Melkor, which led to his imprisonment in Mandos. Thus the ultimately very important matter of the capture of the Elves about Cuiviénen by Melkor (*The Silmarillion* pp. 49–50) is necessarily entirely absent. The release of Melko from Mandos here takes place far earlier, before the coming of the Elvish 'ambassadors' to Valinor, and Melko plays a part in the debate concerning the summons.

The story of Oromë's coming upon the newly-awakened Elves is seen to go back to the beginnings (though here Yavanna Palúrien was also present, as it appears), but its singular beauty and force is the less for the fact of their coming being known independently to Manwë, so that the great Valar did not need to be told of it by Oromë. The name *Eldar* was already in existence in Valinor before the Awakening, and the story of its being given by Oromë ('the People of the Stars') had not arisen – as will be seen from the Appendix on Names, *Eldar* had a quite different etymology at this time. The later distinction between the *Eldar* who followed Oromë on the westward journey to the ocean and the *Avari*, the Unwilling, who would not heed the summons of the Valar, is not present, and indeed in this tale there is no suggestion that any Elves who heard the summons refused it; there were however, according to another (later) tale, Elves who never left Palisor (pp. 231, 234).

Here it is Nornorë, Herald of the Gods, not Oromë, who brought the three Elves to Valinor and afterwards returned them to the Waters of Awakening (and it is notable that even in this earliest version, given more than the later to 'explanations', there is no hint of how they passed from the distant parts of the Earth to Valinor, when afterwards the Great March was only achieved with such difficulty). The story of the questioning of the three Elves by Manwë concerning the nature of their coming into the world, and their loss of all memory of what preceded their awakening, did not survive the *Lost Tales*. A further important shift in the structure is seen in Ulmo's eager support of the party favouring the summoning of the Elves to Valinor; in *The Silmarillion* (p. 52) Ulmo was the chief of those who 'held that the Quendi should be left free to walk as they would in Middle-earth'.

I set out here the early history of the names of the chief Eldar.

Elu Thingol (Quenya *Elwë Singollo*) began as *Linwë Tinto* (also simply *Linwë*); this was changed to *Tinwë Linto* (*Tinwë*). His Gnomish name was at first *Tintoglin*, then *Tinwelint*. He was the leader of the Solosimpi (the later Teleri) on the Great Journey, but he was beguiled in Hisilómë by the 'fay' (*Tindriel* >) *Wendelin* (later *Melian*), who came from the gardens of Lórien in Valinor; he became lord of the Elves of Hisilómë, and their daughter was *Tinúviel*. The leader of the Solosimpi in his place was, confusingly, *Ellu* (afterwards *Olwë*, brother of Elwë).

The lord of the Noldoli was *Finwë Nólemë* (also *Nólemë Finwë*, and most commonly simply *Nólemë*); the name *Finwë* remained throughout the history. In the Gnomish speech he was *Golfinweg*. His son was *Turondo*, in Gnomish *Turgon* (later Turgon became Finwë's grandson, being the son of Finwë's son Fingolfin).

The lord of the Teleri (afterwards the Vanyar) was (*Ing* >) *Inwë*, here called *Isil Inwë*, named in Gnomish (*Gim-githil* >) *Inwithiel*. His son, who built the great tower of Kortirion, was (*Ingilmo* >) *Ingil*. The 'royal clan' of the Teleri were the Inwir. Thus:

Lost Tales (later forms of names)	*The Silmarillion*
Isil Inwë (Gnomish Inwithiel) lord of the Teleri	Ingwë lord of the Vanyar
(his son Ingil)	
Finwë Nólemë (Gnomish Golfinweg) lord of the Noldoli	Finwë lord of the Noldor
(his son Turondo, Gnomish Turgon)	(his grandson Turgon)
Tinwë Linto (Gnomish Tinwelint) lord of the Solosimpi, later lord of the Elves of Hisilómë	Elwë Singollo (Sindarin Elu Thingol) lord of the Teleri, later lord of the Grey-elves of Beleriand
Wendelin	Melian
(their daughter Tinúviel)	(their daughter Lúthien Tinúviel)

| Ellu, lord of the Solosimpi after the loss of Tinwë Linto | Olwë, lord of the Teleri after the loss of his brother Elwë Singollo |

★

In *The Silmarillion* (p. 48) is described the second star-making of Varda before and in preparation for the coming of the Elves:

> Then Varda went forth from the council, and she looked out from the height of Taniquetil, and beheld the darkness of Middle-earth beneath the innumerable stars, faint and far. Then she began a great labour, greatest of all the works of the Valar since their coming into Arda. She took the silver dews from the vats of Telperion, and therewith she made new stars and brighter against the coming of the First-born . . .

In the earliest version we see the conception already present that the stars were created in two separate acts – that a new star-making by Varda celebrated the coming of the Elves, even though here the Elves were already awakened; and that the new stars were derived from the liquid light fallen from the Moon-tree, Silpion. The passage just cited from *The Silmarillion* goes on to tell that it was at the time of the second star-making that Varda 'high in the north as a challenge to Melkor set the crown of seven mighty stars to swing, Valacirca, the Sickle of the Valar and sign of doom'; but here this is denied, and a special origin is claimed for the Great Bear, whose stars were not of Varda's contriving but were sparks that escaped from Aulë's forge. In the little notebook mentioned on p. 23, which is full of disjointed jottings and hastily noted projects, a different form of this myth appears:

> The Silver Sickle
> The seven butterflies
> Aulë was making a silver sickle. Melko interrupted his work telling him a lie concerning the lady Palúrien. Aulë so wroth that he broke the sickle with a blow. Seven sparks leapt up and winged into the heavens. Varda caught them and gave them a place in the heavens as a sign of Palúrien's honour. They fly now ever in the shape of a sickle round and round the pole.

There can be no doubt, I think, that this note is earlier than the present text.

The star Morwinyon, 'who blazes above the world's edge in the west', is Arcturus; see the Appendix on Names. It is nowhere explained why Morwinyon-Arcturus is mythically conceived to be always in the west.

Turning now to the Great March and the crossing of the ocean, the origin of Tol Eressëa in the island on which Ossë drew the Gods to the western lands at the time of the fall of the Lamps (see p. 70) was necessarily lost afterwards with the loss of that story, and Ossë ceased to have any proprietary right upon it. The idea that the Eldar came to the shores of the Great Lands in three large and separated companies (in the order Teleri – Noldori – Solosimpi, as later Vanyar – Noldor – Teleri) goes back to the beginning; but here the first people and the second people each crossed the ocean alone, whereas afterwards they crossed together.

In *The Silmarillion* (p. 58) 'many years' elapsed before Ulmo returned for the last of the three kindreds, the Teleri, so long a time that they came to love the coasts of Middle-earth, and Ossë was able to persuade some of them to remain (Círdan the Shipwright and the Elves of the Falas, with their havens at Brithombar and Eglarest). Of this there is no trace in the earliest account, though the germ of the idea of the long wait of the lastcomers for Ulmo's return is present. In the published version the cause of Ossë's rage against the transportation of the Eldar on the floating island has disappeared, and his motive for anchoring the island in the ocean is wholly different: indeed he did this at the bidding of Ulmo (*ibid.* p. 59), who was opposed to the summoning of the Eldar to Valinor in any case. But the anchoring of Tol Eressëa as a rebellious act of Ossë's long remained an element in the story. It is not made clear what other 'scattered islands of his domain' (p. 121) Ossë anchored to the sea-bottom; but since on the drawing of the World-Ship the Lonely Isle, the Magic Isles, and the Twilit Isles are all shown in the same way as 'standing like pinnacles from the weedy depths' (see pp. 84–6) it was probably these that Ossë now established (though Rúmil and Meril still speak of the Twilit Isles as 'floating' on the Shadowy Seas, pp. 68, 125).

In the old story it is made very clear that Tol Eressëa was made fast far out in the mid-ocean, and 'no land may be seen for many leagues' sail from its cliffs'. That was indeed the reason for its name, which was diminished when the Lonely Isle came to be set in the Bay of Eldamar. But the words used of Tol Eressëa, 'the Lonely Isle, that looks both west and east', in the last chapter of *The Silmarillion* (relatively very little worked on and revised), undoubtedly derive from the old story; in the tale of *Ælfwine of England* is seen the origin of this phrase: 'the Lonely Island looking East to the Magic Archipelago and to the lands of Men beyond it, and West into the Shadows beyond which afar off is glimpsed the Outer Land, the kingdom of the Gods'. The deep sundering of the speech of the Solosimpi from that of the other kindreds, referred to in this tale (p. 121), is preserved in *The Silmarillion*, but the idea arose in the days when Tol Eressëa was far further removed from Valinor.

As is very often to be observed in the evolution of these myths, an early idea survived in a wholly altered context: here, the growth of trees and plants on the westward slopes of the floating island began with its twice lying in the Bay of Faëry and catching the light of the Trees when the Teleri and Noldoli disembarked, and its greater beauty and fertility remained from those times after it was anchored far away from Valinor in the midst of the ocean; afterwards, this idea survived in the context of the light of the Trees passing through the Calacirya and falling on Tol Eressëa near at hand in the Bay of Eldamar. Similarly, it seems that Ulmo's instruction of the Solosimpi in music and sea-lore while sitting 'upon a headland' of Tol Eressëa after its binding to the sea-bottom was shifted to Ossë's instruction of the Teleri 'in all manner of sea-lore and sea-music' sitting on a rock off the coast of Middle-earth (*The Silmarillion* p. 58).

Very noteworthy is the account given here of the gap in the Mountains of Valinor. In *The Silmarillion* the Valar made this gap, the Calacirya or Pass of Light, only after the coming of the Eldar to Aman, for 'even among the radiant flowers of the Tree-lit gardens of Valinor they [the Vanyar and Noldor] longed still at times to see the stars' (p. 59); whereas in this tale it was a 'natural' feature, associated with a long creek thrust in from the sea.

From the account of the coming of the Elves to the shores of the Great Lands it is seen (p. 118) that Hisilómë was a region bordering the Great Sea, agreeing with its identification as the region marked *g* on the earliest map, see pp. 81, 112; and most remarkably we meet here the idea that Men were shut in Hisilómë by Melko, an idea that survived right through to the final form in which the Easterling Men were rewarded after the Nirnaeth Arnoediad for their treacherous service to Morgoth by being confined in Hithlum (*The Silmarillion* p. 195).

In the description of the hill and city of Kôr appear several features that were never lost in the later accounts of Tirion upon Túna. Cf. *The Silmarillion* p. 59:

> Upon the crown of Túna the city of the Elves was built, the white walls and terraces of Tirion; and the highest of the towers of that city was the Tower of Ingwë, Mindon Eldaliéva, whose silver lamp shone far out into the mists of the sea.

The dust of gold and 'magic metals' that Aulë piled about the feet of Kôr powdered the shoes and clothing of Eärendil when he climbed the 'long white stairs' of Tirion (*ibid.* p. 248).

It is not said here whether the shoots of Laurelin and Silpion that the Gods gave to Inwë and Nólemë, which 'blossomed both eternally without abating', were also givers of light, but later in the *Lost Tales* (p. 213), after the Flight of the Noldoli, the Trees of Kôr are again referred to, and there the trees given to Inwë 'shone still', while the trees given to Nólemë had been uprooted and 'were gone no one knew whither.' In *The Silmarillion* it is said that Yavanna made for the Vanyar and the Noldor 'a tree like to a lesser image of Telperion, save that it did not give light of its own being'; it was 'planted in the courts beneath the Mindon and there flourished, and its seedlings were many in Eldamar'. Thence came the Tree of Tol Eressëa.

In connection with this description of the city of the Elves in Valinor I give here a poem entitled *Kôr*. It was written on April 30th, 1915 (two days after *Goblin Feet* and *You and Me*, see pp. 27, 32), and two texts of it are extant: the first, in manuscript, has a subtitle 'In a City Lost and Dead'. The second, a typescript, was apparently first entitled *Kôr*, but this was changed to *The City of the Gods*, and the subtitle erased; and with this title the poem was published at Leeds in 1923.* No changes were made to the text except that in the penultimate line 'no bird sings' was altered already in the manuscript to 'no voice stirs'. It seems possible, especially in view of the original subtitle, that the poem described Kôr after the Elves had left it.

Kôr

In a City Lost and Dead

A sable hill, gigantic, rampart-crowned
Stands gazing out across an azure sea
Under an azure sky, on whose dark ground
Impearled as 'gainst a floor of porphyry
Gleam marble temples white, and dazzling halls;
And tawny shadows fingered long are made
In fretted bars upon their ivory walls
By massy trees rock-rooted in the shade
Like stony chiselled pillars of the vault
With shaft and capital of black basalt.
There slow forgotten days for ever reap
The silent shadows counting out rich hours;
And no voice stirs; and all the marble towers
White, hot and soundless, ever burn and sleep.

★

The story of the evolution of sea-birds by Ossë, and of how the Solosimpi went at last to Valinor in ships of swan-shape drawn by gulls, to the chagrin of Ossë, is greatly at variance with the account in *The Silmarillion* (p. 61):

Through a long age they [the Teleri] dwelt in Tol Eressëa; but slowly their hearts were changed, and were drawn towards the light that flowed out over the sea to the Lonely Isle. They were torn between the love of the music of the waves upon their shores, and the desire to see

* Publication was in a magazine called *The Microcosm*, edited by Dorothy Ratcliffe, Volume VIII no. 1, Spring 1923.

again their kindred and to look upon the splendour of Valinor; but in the end desire of the light was the stronger. Therefore Ulmo, submitting to the will of the Valar, sent to them Ossë, their friend, and he though grieving taught them the craft of ship-building; and when their ships were built he brought them as his parting gift many strong-winged swans. Then the swans drew the white ships of the Teleri over the windless sea; and thus at last and latest they came to Aman and the shores of Eldamar.

But the swans remained as a gift of Ossë to the Elves of Tol Eressëa, and the ships of the Teleri retained the form of the ships built by Aulë for the Solosimpi: they 'were made in the likeness of swans, with beaks of gold and eyes of gold and jet' (ibid.).

The passage of geographical description that follows (p. 125) is curious; for it is extremely similar to (and even in some phrases identical with) that in the tale of The Coming of the Valar and the Building of Valinor, p. 68. An explanation of this repetition is suggested below. This second version gives in fact little new information, its chief difference of substance being the mention of Tol Eressëa. It is now made clear that the Shadowy Seas were a region of the Great Sea west of Tol Eressëa. In The Silmarillion (p. 102) the conception had changed, with the change in the anchorage of Tol Eressëa: at the time of the Hiding of Valinor

the Enchanted Isles were set, and all the seas about them were filled with shadows and bewilderment. And these isles were strung as a net in the Shadowy Seas from the north to the south, before Tol Eressëa, the Lonely Isle, is reached by one sailing west.

There is a further element of repetition in the account of the gap in the Mountains of Valinor and the hill of Kôr at the head of the creek (p. 126), which have already been described earlier in this same tale (p. 122). The explanation of this repetition is almost certainly to be found in the two layers of composition in this tale (see note 8 above); for the first of these passages is in the revised portion and the second in the original, pencilled text. My father in his revision had, I think, simply taken in earlier the passage concerning the gap in the Mountains, the hill and the creek, and if he had continued the revision of the tale to its end the second passage would have been excised. This explanation may be suggested also for the repetition of the passage concerning the islands in the Great Sea and the coast of Valinor from the tale of The Coming of the Valar and the Building of Valinor; but in that case the implication must be that the revision in ink over the original pencilled manuscript was carried out when the latter was already far ahead in the narrative.

In *The Silmarillion* the entire account of the making of gem-stones by the Noldoli has become compressed into these words (p. 60):

> And it came to pass that the masons of the house of Finwë, quarrying in the hills after stone (for they delighted in the building of high towers), first discovered the earth-gems, and brought them forth in countless myriads; and they devised tools for the cutting and shaping of gems, and carved them in many forms. They hoarded them not, but gave them freely, and by their labour enriched all Valinor.

Thus the rhapsodic account at the end of this tale of the making of gems out of 'magic' materials – starlight, and *ilwë*, dews and petals, glassy substances dyed with the juice of flowers – was abandoned, and the Noldor became miners, skilful indeed, but mining only what was there to be found in the rocks of Valinor. On the other hand, in an earlier passage in *The Silmarillion* (p. 39), the old idea is retained: 'The Noldor also it was who first achieved the making of gems.' It need not be said that everything was to be gained by the discretion of the later writing; in this early narrative the Silmarils are not strongly marked out from the accumulated wonder of all the rest of the gems of the Noldoli's making.

Features that remained are the generosity of the Noldor in the giving of their gems and the scattering of them on the shores (cf. *The Silmarillion* p. 61: 'Many jewels the Noldor gave them [the Teleri], opals and diamonds and pale crystals, which they strewed upon the shores and scattered in the pools'); the pearls that the Teleri got from the sea (*ibid.*); the sapphires that the Noldor gave to Manwë ('His sceptre was of sapphire, which the Noldor wrought for him', *ibid.* p. 40); and, of course, Fëanor as the maker of the Silmarils – although, as will be seen in the next tale, Fëanor was not yet the son of Finwë (Nólemë).

★

I conclude this commentary with another early poem that bears upon the matter of this tale. It is said in the tale (p. 119) that Men in Hisilómë feared the Lost Elves, calling them the Shadow Folk, and that their name for the land was *Aryador*. The meaning of this is given in the early Gnomish word-list as 'land or place of shadow' (cf. the meanings of *Hisilómë* and *Dor Lómin*, p. 112).

The poem is called *A Song of Aryador*, and is extant in two copies; according to notes on these it was written in an army camp near Lichfield on September 12th, 1915. It was never, to my knowledge, printed. The first copy, in manuscript, has the title also in Old English: *Án léoþ Éargedores*; the second, in typescript, has virtually no differences in the text, but it may be noted that the first word of the third verse, 'She', is an emendation from 'He' in both copies.

A Song of Aryador

In the vales of Aryador
By the wooded inland shore
Green the lakeward bents and meads
Sloping down to murmurous reeds
That whisper in the dusk o'er Aryador:

'Do you hear the many bells
Of the goats upon the fells
Where the valley tumbles downward from the pines?
Do you hear the blue woods moan
When the Sun has gone alone
To hunt the mountain-shadows in the pines?

She is lost among the hills
And the upland slowly fills
With the shadow-folk that murmur in the fern;
And still there are the bells
And the voices on the fells
While Eastward a few stars begin to burn.

Men are kindling tiny gleams
Far below by mountain-streams
Where they dwell among the beechwoods near the shore,
But the great woods on the height
Watch the waning western light
And whisper to the wind of things of yore,

When the valley was unknown,
And the waters roared alone,
And the shadow-folk danced downward all the night,
When the Sun had fared abroad
Through great forests unexplored
And the woods were full of wandering beams of light.

Then were voices on the fells
And a sound of ghostly bells
And a march of shadow-people o'er the height.
In the mountains by the shore
In forgotten Aryador
There was dancing and was ringing;
There were shadow-people singing
Ancient songs of olden gods in Aryador.'

VI

THE THEFT OF MELKO
AND THE DARKENING OF VALINOR

This title is again taken from the cover of the book containing the text; the narrative, still written rapidly in pencil (see note 8 to the last chapter), with some emendations from the same time or later, continues without a break.

Now came Eriol home to the Cottage of Lost Play, and his love for all the things that he saw about him and his desire to understand them all became more deep. Continually did he thirst to know yet more of the history of the Eldar; nor did he ever fail to be among those who fared each evening to the Room of the Tale-fire; and so on a time when he had already sojourned some while as a guest of Vairë and Lindo it so passed that Lindo at his entreaty spake thus from his deep chair:

'Listen then, O Eriol, if thou wouldst [know] how it so came that the loveliness of Valinor was abated, or the Elves might ever be constrained to leave the shores of Eldamar. It may well be that you know already that Melko dwelt in Valmar as a servant in the house of Tulkas in those days of the joy of the Eldalië; there did he nurse his hatred of the Gods, and his consuming jealousy of the Eldar, but it was his lust for the beauty of the gems for all his feigned indifference that in the end overbore his patience and caused him to design deep and evilly.

Now the Noldoli alone at those times had the art of fashioning these beautiful things, and despite their rich gifts to all whom they loved the treasure they possessed of them was beyond count the greatest, wherefore Melko whenever he may consorteth with them, speaking cunning words. In this way for long he sought to beg gifts of jewels for himself, and maybe also catching the unwary to learn something of their hidden art, but when none of these devices succeeded he sought to sow evil desires and discords among the Gnomes, telling them that lie concerning the Council when the Eldar were first bidden to Valinor.[1] "Slaves are ye," he would say, "or children, an you will, bidden play with toys and seek not to stray or know too much. Good days mayhap the Valar give you, as ye say; seek but to cross their walls and ye shall know the hardness of their hearts. Lo, they use your skill, and to your beauty they hold fast as an adornment of their realms. This is not love, but selfish desire – make test of it. Ask for your inheritance that Ilúvatar designed for you – the whole wide world to roam, with all its mysteries to explore, and all its substances to be material of such mighty crafts as never can be realised in these narrow gardens penned by the mountains, hemmed in by the impassable sea."

Hearing these things, despite the true knowledge which Nólemë had and spread abroad, there were many who hearkened with half their hearts to Melko, and restlessness grew amongst them, and Melko poured oil on their smouldering desires. From him they learnt many things it were not good for any but the great Valar to know, for being half-comprehended such deep and hidden things slay happiness; and besides many of the sayings of Melko were cunning lies or were but partly true, and the Noldoli ceased to sing, and their viols fell silent upon the hill of Kôr, for their hearts grew somewhat older as their lore grew deeper and their desires more swollen, and the books of their wisdom were multiplied as the leaves of the forest. For know that in those days Aulë aided by the Gnomes contrived alphabets and scripts, and on the walls of Kôr were many dark tales written in pictured symbols, and runes of great beauty were drawn there too or carved upon stones, and Eärendel read many a wondrous tale there long ago, and mayhap still is many a one still there to read, if it be not corrupted into dust. The other Elves heeded these things not over much, and were at times sad and fearful at the lessened gladness of their kinsmen. Great mirth had Melko at this and wrought in patience biding his time, yet no nearer did he get to his end, for despite all his labours the glory of the Trees and the beauty of the gems and the memory of the dark ways from Palisor held back the Noldoli – and ever Nólemë spake against Melko, calming their restlessness and discontents.

At length so great became his care that he took counsel with Fëanor, and even with Inwë and Ellu Melemno (who then led the Solosimpi), and took their rede that Manwë himself be told of the dark ways of Melko.

And Melko knowing this was in great anger against the Gnomes, and going first before Manwë bowed very low, and said how the Noldoli dared murmur to his ears against Manwë's lordship, claiming that in skill and beauty they (whom Ilúvatar had destined to possess all the earth) far surpassed the Valar, for whom they must labour unrecompensed. Heavy was Manwë's heart at these words, for he had feared long that that great amity of the Valar and Eldar be ever perchance broken, knowing that the Elves were children of the world and must one day return to her bosom. Nay, who shall say but that all these deeds, even the seeming needless evil of Melko, were but a portion of the destiny of old? Yet cold was the Lord of the Gods to the informer, and lo! even as he questioned him further the embassy of Nólemë came thither, and being granted leave spake the truth before him. By reason of the presence of Melko perchance they spoke somewhat less skilfully in their own cause than they might, and perchance even the heart of Manwë Súlimo was tainted with the poison of Melko's words, for that venom of Melko's malice is very strong and subtle indeed.

Howbeit, both Melko and the Noldoli were chidden and dismissed. Melko indeed was bidden get him back to Mandos and there dwell awhile in penitence, nor dare to walk in Valmar for many moons, not until the great festival that now approached had come and gone; but Manwë fearing lest the pollution of their discontent spread among the other kindreds commanded Aulë to find other places and thither lead the Noldoli, and build them a new town where they might dwell.

Great was the sorrow upon the hill of Kôr when those tidings were brought thither, and though all were wroth with the treachery of Melko, yet was there now a new bitterness against the Gods, and the murmuring louder than before.

A little stream, and its name was *Híri*, ran down from the hills, northward of the opening to the coast where Kôr was built, and it wandered thence across the plain no one knew whither. Maybe it found the Outer Seas, for north of the roots of Silpion it dived into the earth and there was a rugged place and a rock-ringed dale; and here the Noldoli purposed to abide, or rather to await the passing of wrath from Manwë's heart, for in no way as yet would they accept the thought of leaving Kôr for ever.

Caves they made in the walls of that dale, and thither they bore their wealth of gems, of gold and silver and fair things; but their ancient homes in Kôr were empty of their voices, filled only with their paintings and their books of lore, and the streets of Kôr and all the ways of Valmar shone still with [?gems] and carven marbles telling of the days of the happiness of the Gnomes that cometh now upon its waning.

Now Melko gets him gone to Mandos, and far from Valinor he plans rebellion and vengeance upon both Gnomes and Gods. Indeed, dwelling for nigh three ages in the vaults of Mandos Melko had made friends to himself of certain gloomy spirits there and perverted them to ill, promising them great lands and regions on the Earth for their [?having] if they aided him when he called on them in need; and now he gathers them to him in the dark ravines of the mountains about Mandos. Thence sends he spies, invisible as fleeting shades when Silpion is in bloom, and learns of those doings of the Noldoli and of all that passes in the plain. Now soon after it chanced indeed that the Valar and Eldar held a great feast, even that one that Manwë had spoken of, bidding Melko rid Valmar of his presence at that time; for know that they made merry on one day every seventh year to celebrate the coming of the Eldar into Valinor, and every third year a lesser feast to commemorate the coming of the white fleet of the Solosimpi to the shores of Eldamar; but at every twenty-first year when both these feasts fell together they held one of the greatest magnificence, and it endured for seven days, and for this cause such years were called "Years of Double Mirth";* and these feasts all the Koreldar wherever they now may be in the wide world still do celebrate. Now that feast that approacheth is one of Double Mirth, and all the hosts of the Gods and Elves made ready to celebrate it most gloriously. Pomps there were and long processions of the Elves, dancing and singing, that wound from Kôr to Valmar's gates. A road had been laid against this festival from the westward gate of Kôr even to the turrets of the mighty arch which opened in the walls of Valmar northward towards the Trees. Of white marble it was and many a gentle stream flowing from the far mountains crossed its path. Here it would leap into slender bridges marvellously fenced with delicate balustrades that shone like pearls; scarcely did these clear the water, so that lilies of great beauty growing upon the bosom of the streams that fared but gently in the plain thrust their wide blossoms about its borders and iris marched along its flanks; for by cunning delving runnels of clearest water were made to flow from stream to stream bordering that whole long way with the cool noise of rippling water. At places mighty trees grew on either side, or at places the road would open to a glade and fountains spring by magic high into the air for the refreshment of all who sped that way.

Now came the Teleri led by the white-robed people of the Inwir, and the throbbing of their congregated harps beat the air most sweetly; and after them went the Noldoli mingling once more with their own dear folk by Manwë's clemency, that his festival might be duly kept, but the music that their viols and instruments awoke was now more sweetly sad than ever before. And last came the people

* Added in the margin here: *Samírien*.

of the shores, and their piping blent with voices brought the sense of tides and murmurous waves and the wailing cry of the coast-loving birds thus inland deep upon the plain.

Then was all that host marshalled before the gate of Valmar, and at the word and sign from Inwë as one voice they burst in unison into the Song of Light. This had Lirillo[2] written and taught them, and it told of the longing of the Elves for light, of their dread journey through the dark world led by the desire of the Two Trees, and sang of their utmost joy beholding the faces of the Gods and their renewed desire once more to enter Valmar and tread the Valar's blessed courts. Then did the gates of Valmar open and Nornorë bid them enter, and all that bright company passed through. There Varda met them, standing amid the companies of the Mánir and the Súruli, and all the Gods made them welcome, and feasts there were in all the great halls thereafter.

Now their custom was on the third day to robe themselves all in white and blue and ascend to the heights of Taniquetil, and there would Manwë speak to them as he thought fit of the Music of the Ainur and the glory of Ilúvatar, and of things to be and that had been. And on that day would Kôr and Valmar be silent and still, but the roof of the world and the slope of Taniquetil shine with the gleaming raiment of the Gods and Elves, and all the mountains echo with their speech — but afterward on the last day of merriment the Gods would come to Kôr and sit upon the slopes of its bright hill, gazing in love upon that slender town, and thereafter blessing it in the name of Ilúvatar would depart ere Silpion came to bloom; and so would end the days of Double Mirth.

But in this fateful year Melko dared of his blasphemous heart to choose that very day of Manwë's speech upon Taniquetil for the carrying out of his designs; for then would Kôr and Valmar and the rock-ringed dale of Sirnúmen be unguarded: for against whom indeed had Elf or Vala need to guard in those old days?

Creeping then down with his dark people on the third day of Samírien, as that feast was named, he passed the dark halls of Makar's abode (for even that wild Vala had gone to Valmar to honour the time, and indeed all of the Gods went there saving Fui and Vefántur only, and Ossë even was there, dissembling for those seven days his feud and jealousy with Ulmo). Here does a thought come to Melko's heart, and he arms himself and his band stealthily with swords very sharp and cruel, and this was well for them: for now do they all steal into the vale of Sirnúmen where the Noldoli had their present dwelling, and behold the Gnomes by reason of the workings in their hearts of Melko's own teaching had become wary and suspicious beyond the wont of the Eldar of those days. Guards of some strength were set over the treasures there that went not to the feast, albeit this was contrary to the customs and ordinances of the Gods. Now is there suddenly bitter war awake in the heart of Valinor and those guards are slain, even while the peace and gladness upon Taniquetil afar is very great – indeed for that reason none heard their cries. Now Melko knew that it was indeed war for ever between himself and all those other folk of Valinor, for he had slain the Noldoli – guests of the Valar – before the doors of their own homes. With his own hand indeed he slew Bruithwir father of Fëanor,[3] and bursting into that rocky house that he defended laid hands upon those most glorious gems, even the Silmarils, shut in a casket of ivory. Now all that great treasury of gems he despoiled, and lading himself and all his companions to the utmost he seeks how he may escape.

Know then that Oromë had great stables and a breeding ground of good horses not so far from this spot, where a wild forest land had grown up. Thither Melko steals, and a herd of black horses he captures, cowing them with the terror that he could wield. Astride those his whole company of thieves rides far away, after destroying what things of lesser value they deemed it impossible to carry thence. Making a wide circuit and faring with the speed of hurricanes such as only the divine horses of Oromë ridden by the children of the Gods could compass they pass far to the west of Valmar in the untracked regions where the light of the Trees was thin. Long ere the folk had come down from Taniquetil and long ere the end of the feast or ever the Noldoli fared back to find their homes despoiled, Melko and his [?thieves] were ridden to the deep south, and finding there a low place in the hills they passed into the plains of Eruman. Well might Aulë and Tulkas bemoan their carelessness in leaving that low place long ago when they reared those hills to fend all evil from the plain – for that was the place where they were accustomed to enter Valinor after their quarryings in the fields of Arvalin.[4] It is said indeed that this riding in a half-circle, laborious and perilous as it was, was at first no part of Melko's design, for rather had he purposed to get to northward over the passes nigh to Mandos; but this he was warned might not be done, for Mandos and Fui never left those realms, and all the ravines and chasms of the northward mountains were infested with their folk, nor for all his gloom was Mandos any rebel against Manwë or an abetter of evil deeds.

Far to the north if one may endure the colds as Melko could it is said in ancient lore that the Great Seas narrow to a little thing, and without aid of ships Melko and his company might thus have got into the world safely; but this was not done, and the sad tale took its appointed course, or the Two Trees might yet have shone and the Elves sung still in Valinor.

At length that daytide of festival is over and the Gods are turned back towards Valmar, treading the white road from Kôr. The lights twinkle in the city of the Elves and peace dwells there, but the Noldoli fare over the plain to Sirnúmen sadly. Silpion is gleaming in that hour, and ere it wanes the first lament for the dead that was heard in Valinor rises from that rocky vale, for Fëanor laments the death of Bruithwir; and many of the Gnomes beside find that the spirits of their dead have winged their way to Vê. Then messengers ride hastily to Valmar bearing tidings of the deeds, and there they find Manwë, for he has not yet left that town for his abode upon Taniquetil.

"Alas, O Manwë Súlimo," they cry, "evil has pierced the Mountains of Valinor and fallen upon Sirnúmen of the Plain. There lies Bruithwir sire of Fëanor[5] dead and many of the Noldoli beside, and all our treasury of gems and fair things and the loving travail of our hands and hearts through many years is stolen away. Whither O Manwë whose eyes see all things? Who has done this evil, for the Noldoli cry for vengeance, O most [?just] one!"

Then said Manwë to them: "Behold O Children of the Noldoli, my heart is sad towards you, for the poison of Melko has already changed you, and covetice has entered your hearts. Lo! had ye not thought your gems and fabrics[6] of better worth than the festival of the folk or the ordinances of Manwë your lord, this had not been, and Bruithwir go-Maidros and those other hapless ones still had lived, and your jewels been in no greater peril. Nay, my wisdom teaches me that because of the death of Bruithwir and his comrades shall the greatest evils fall on Gods and Elves, and Men to be. Without the Gods who brought you to the light and gave you all the materials of your craft, teaching your first ignorance, none of these fair things you love now so well ever would have been; what has been done may again be done, for the power of the Valar does not change; but of more worth than all the glory of Valinor and all the grace and beauty of Kôr is peace and happiness and wisdom, and these once lost are harder to recapture. Cease then to murmur and to speak against the Valar, or to set yourselves in your hearts as equals to their majesty; rather depart now in penitence knowing full well that Melko has wrought this evil against you, and that your secret trafficking with him has brought you all this loss and sorrow. Trust him not again therefore, nor any others that whisper secret words of discontent among you, for its fruit is humiliation and dismay."

And the embassy was abashed and afraid and went back unto Sirnúmen utterly cast down; yet was Manwë's heart heavier than theirs, for things had gone ill indeed, and yet he foresaw that worse would be; and so did the destinies of the Gods work out, for lo! to the Noldoli Manwë's words seemed cold and heartless, and they knew not his sorrow and his tenderness; and Manwë thought them strangely changed and turned to covetice, who longed but for comfort, being like children very full of the loss of their fair things.

Now Melko findeth himself in the wastes of Arvalin and knoweth not how he may escape, for the gloom there is very great, and he knoweth not those regions that stretch there unto the utmost south. Therefore he sent a messenger claiming the inviolable right of a herald (albeit this was a renegade servant of Mandos whom Melko had perverted) over the pass to Valinor, and there standing before the gates of Valmar[7] he demanded audience of the Gods; and it was asked of him whence he came, and he said from Ainu Melko, and Tulkas would have hurled stones at him from the walls and slain him, but the others as yet suffered him not to be mishandled, but despite their anger and loathing they admitted him to the great square of gold that was before Aulë's courts. And at the same hour riders were sent to Kôr and to Sirnúmen summoning the Elves, for it was guessed that this matter touched them near. When all was made ready the messenger took stand beside the needle of pure gold whereon Aulë had written the story of the kindling of the Tree of gold (in Lórien's courts stood one of silver with another tale), and on a sudden Manwë said: "Speak!" and his voice was as a clap of wrathful thunder, and the courts rang, but the envoy unabashed uttered his message, saying:

"The Lord Melko, ruler of the world from the darkest east to the outer slopes of the Mountains of Valinor unto his kinsmen the Ainur. Behold, in compensation for divers grievous affronts and for long times of unjust imprisonment despite his noble estate and blood that he has at your hands suffered, now has he taken, as is due to him, certain small treasures held by the Noldoli, your slaves. Great grief is it to him that of these he has slain some, in that they would do him hurt in the evil of their hearts; yet their blasphemous intent will he now put from memory, and all the past injuries that ye the

Gods have wrought him will he so far forget as once again to show his presence in that place that is called Valmar, if ye will hearken to his conditions and fulfil them. For know that the Noldoli shall be his servants and shall adorn him a house; moreover of right he does demand —" but hereon even as the herald lifted up his voice yet louder swelling with his words of insolence, so great became the wrath of the Valar that Tulkas and several of his house leapt down and seizing him stopped his mouth, and the place of council was in uproar. Indeed Melko had not thought to gain aught but time and the confusion of the Valar by this embassage of insolence.

Then Manwë bid him unhand the herald, but the Gods arose crying with one voice: "This is no herald, but a rebel, a thief, and a murderer." "He hath defiled the sanctity of Valinor," shouted Tulkas, "and cast his insolence in our teeth." Now the mind of all the Elves was as one in this matter. Hope they had none of the recovery of the jewels save by the capture of Melko, which was now a matter beyond hope, but they would have no parley with Melko whatsoever and would treat him as an outlaw and all his folk. (And this was the meaning of Manwë, saying that the death of Bruithwir would be the root of the greatest evil, for it was that slaying that most inflamed both Gods and Elves.)[8]

To this end they spoke in the ears of Varda and Aulë, and Varda befriended their cause before Manwë, and Aulë yet more stoutly, for his heart was sore too for the theft of so many things of exquisite craft and workmanship; but Tulkas Poldórëa needed no pleading, being hot with ire. Now these great advocates moved the council with their words, so that in the end it is Manwë's doom that word he sent back to Melko rejecting him and his words and outlawing him and all his followers from Valinor for ever. These words would he now speak to the envoy, bidding him begone to his master with them, but the folk of the Vali and the Elves would have none of it, and led by Tulkas they took that renegade to the topmost peak of Taniquetil, and there declaring him no herald and taking the mountain and the stars to witness of the same they cast him to the boulders of Arvalien so that he was slain, and Mandos received him into his deepest caves.

Then Manwë seeing in this rebellion and their violent deed the seed of bitterness cast down his sceptre and wept; but the others spake unto Sorontur King of Eagles upon Taniquetil and by him were the words of Manwë sent to Melko: "Begone for ever, O accursed, nor dare to parley more with Gods or Elves. Neither shall thy foot nor that of any who serve thee tread the soil of Valinor again while the world endures." And Sorontur sought out Melko and said as he was bidden, and of the death of his envoy he told [?too]. Then Melko would have slain Sorontur, being mad with anger at the death of his messenger; and verily this deed was not in accord with the strict justice of the Gods, yet was the anger of those at Valmar sorely tempted; but Melko has ever cast it against the Gods most bitterly, twisting it into a black tale of wrong; and between that evil one and Sorontur has there ever since been hate and war, and that was most bitter when Sorontur and his folk fared to the Iron Mountains and there abode, watching all that Melko did.

Now Aulë goeth to Manwë and speaketh enheartening words, saying how Valmar still stands and the Mountains are high and a sure bulwark against evil. "Lo! if Melko sets once more turmoils in the world, was he not bound in chains aforetime, and so may be again: – but behold, soon will I and Tulkas fill that pass that leads to Erumáni and the seas, that Melko come not ever that way hither again."

But Manwë and Aulë plan to set guards about all those mountains until such time as Melko's deeds and places of abode without become known.

Then does Aulë fall to speech with Manwë concerning the Noldoli, and he pleads much for them, saying that Manwë wrought with anxiety has done hardly by them, for that of Melko in sooth alone is the evil come, whereas the Eldar are not slaves nor servants but beings of a wondrous sweetness and beauty – that they were guests for ever of the Gods. Therefore does Manwë bid them now, an they will, go back to Kôr, and, if they so desire, busy themselves in fashioning gems and fabrics anew, and all things of beauty and cost that they may need in their labour shall be given to them even more lavishly than before.

But when Fëanor heard this saying, he said: "Yea, but who shall give us back the joyous heart without which works of loveliness and magic cannot be? – and Bruithwir is dead, and my heart also." Many nonetheless went then back to Kôr, and some semblance of old joy is then restored, though for the lessened happiness of their hearts their labours do not bring forth gems of the old lustre and glory. But Fëanor dwelt in sorrow with a few folk in Sirnúmen, and though he sought day and night to do so he could in no wise make other jewels like to the Silmarils of old, that Melko snatched away; nor indeed has any craftsman ever done so since. At length does he abandon the attempt, sitting rather beside the tomb of Bruithwir, that is called the Mound of the First Sorrow,* and is well named for

* In the margin are written Gnomish names: '*Cûm a Gumlaith* or *Cûm a Thegranaithos*'.

all the woe that came from the death of him who was laid there. There brooded Fëanor bitter thoughts, till his brain grew dazed by the black vapours of his heart, and he arose and went to Kôr. There did he speak to the Gnomes, dwelling on their wrongs and sorrows and their minished wealth and glory – bidding them leave this prison-house and get them into the world. "As cowards have the Valar become; but the hearts of the Eldar are not weak, and we will see what is our own, and if we may not get it by stealth we will do so by violence. There shall be war between the Children of Ilúvatar and Ainu Melko. What if we perish in our quest? The dark halls of Vê be little worse than this bright prison . . . ."[9] And he prevailed thus upon some to go before Manwë with himself and demand that the Noldoli be suffered to leave Valinor in peace and set safely by the Gods upon the shores of the world whence they had of old been ferried.

Then Manwë was grieved by their request and forbade the Gnomes to utter such words in Kôr if they desired still to dwell there among the other Elves; but then changing from harshness he told them many things concerning the world and its fashion and the dangers that were already there, and the worse that might soon come to be by reason of Melko's return. "My heart feels, and my wisdom tells me," said he, "that no great age of time will now elapse ere those other Children of Ilúvatar, the fathers of the fathers of Men, do come into the world – and behold it is of the unalterable Music of the Ainur that the world come in the end for a great while under the sway of Men; yet whether it shall be for happiness or sorrow Ilúvatar has not revealed, and I would not have strife or fear or anger come ever between the different Children of Ilúvatar, and fain would I for many an age yet leave the world empty of beings who might strive against the new-come Men and do hurt to them ere their clans be grown to strength, while the nations and peoples of the Earth are yet infants." To this he added many words concerning Men and their nature and the things that would befall them, and the Noldoli were amazed, for they had not heard the Valar speak of Men, save very seldom; and had not then heeded overmuch, deeming these creatures weak and blind and clumsy and beset with death, nor in any ways likely to match the glory of the Eldalië. Now therefore, although Manwë had unburdened his heart in this way hoping that the Noldoli, seeing that he did not labour without a purpose or a reason, would grow calmer and more trustful of his love, rather were they astonished to discover that the Ainur made the thought of Men so great a matter, and Manwë's words achieved the opposite of his wish; for Fëanor in his misery twisted them into an evil

semblance, when standing again before the throng of Kôr he spake
these words:

"Lo, now do we know the reason of our transportation hither as
it were cargoes of fair slaves! Now at length are we told to what end
we are guarded here, robbed of our heritage in the world, ruling not
the wide lands, lest perchance we yield them not to a race unborn.
To these foresooth – a sad folk, beset with swift mortality, a race of
burrowers in the dark, clumsy of hand, untuned to songs or musics,
who shall dully labour at the soil with their rude tools, to these
whom still he says are of Ilúvatar would Manwë Súlimo lordling of
the Ainur give the world and all the wonders of its land, all its
hidden substances – give it to these, that is our inheritance. Or
what is this talk of the dangers of the world? A trick to deceive us;
a mask of words! O all ye children of the Noldoli, whomso will no
longer be house-thralls of the Gods however softly held, arise I bid
ye and get you from Valinor, for now is the hour come and the world
awaits."

In sooth it is a matter for great wonder, the subtle cunning of
Melko – for in those wild words who shall say that there lurked not
a sting of the minutest truth, nor fail to marvel seeing the very words
of Melko pouring from Fëanor his foe, who knew not nor remembered
whence was the fountain of these thoughts; yet perchance the
[?outmost] origin of these sad things was before Melko himself, and
such things must be – and the mystery of the jealousy of Elves and
Men is an unsolved riddle, one of the sorrows at the world's dim
roots.

Howso these deep things be, the fierce words of Fëanor got him
instantly a mighty following, for a veil there seemed before the hearts
of the Gnomes – and mayhap even this was not without the knowledge of Ilúvatar. Yet would Melko have been rejoiced to hear it,
seeing his evil giving fruit beyond his hopes. Now however that evil
one wanders the dark plains of Eruman, and farther south than anyone had yet penetrated he found a region of the deepest gloom, and
it seemed to him a good place wherein for the time to hide his stolen
treasure.

Therefore he seeks until he finds a dark cavern in the hills, and
webs of darkness lie about so that the black air might be felt heavy
and choking about one's face and hands. Very deep and winding
were those ways having a subterranean outlet on the sea as the
ancient books say, and here on a time were the Moon and Sun
imprisoned afterward;[10] for here dwelt the primeval spirit Móru
whom even the Valar know not whence or when she came, and the

folk of Earth have given her many names. Mayhap she was bred of mists and darkness on the confines of the Shadowy Seas, in that utter dark that came between the overthrow of the Lamps and the kindling of the Trees, but more like she has always been; and she it is who loveth still to dwell in that black place taking the guise of an unlovely spider, spinning a clinging gossamer of gloom that catches in its mesh stars and moons and all bright things that sail the airs. Indeed it was because of her labours that so little of that overflowing light of the Two Trees flowed ever into the world, for she sucked light greedily, and it fed her, but she brought forth only that darkness that is a denial of all light. Ungwë Lianti the great spider who enmeshes did the Eldar call her, naming her also Wirilómë or Gloom-weaver, whence still do the Noldoli speak of her as Ungoliont the spider or as Gwerlum the Black.

Now between Melko and Ungwë Lianti was there friendship from the first, when she found him and his comrades straying in her caves, but Gloomweaver was ahungered of the brightness of that hoard of jewels so soon as she saw them.

Now Melko having despoiled the Noldoli and brought sorrow and confusion into the realm of Valinor through less of that hoard than aforetime, having now conceived a darker and deeper plan of aggrandisement; therefore seeing the lust of Ungwë's eyes he offers her all that hoard, saving only the three Silmarils, if she will abet him in his new design. This she granteth readily, and so came all that treasury of most lovely gems fairer than any others that the world has seen into the foul keeping of Wirilómë, and was wound in webs of darkness and hidden deep in the caverns of the eastern slopes of the great hills that are the southern boundary of Eruman.

Deeming that now is the time to strike while Valinor is yet in uproar nor waiting for Aulë and Tulkas to block the passage in the hills, Melko and Wirilómë crept into Valinor and lay hidden in a valley of the foothills until Silpion was in bloom; but all the while was Gloomweaver spinning her most lightless webs and ill-enchanted shades. These she lets float down so that in place of the fair silver light of Silpion all about the western plain of Valinor there creeps now a dim uncertain darkness and faint lights waver in it. Then does she throw a black cloak of invisibility about Melko and herself and they steal across the plain, and the Gods are in wonder and the Elves in Kôr are afraid; nonetheless they do not as yet suspect the hand of Melko in this, thinking rather it is some work of Ossë's, who at times with his storms caused great mists and darkness to be wafted off the Shadowy Seas, encroaching even the bright airs of Valinor;

though in this he met the anger both of Ulmo and of Manwë. Then Manwë sent forth a sweet westerly breath wherewith he was accustomed at such times to blow all sea-humours back eastward over the waters, but such gentle breathing availed nothing against the woven night heavy and clinging that Wirilómë had spread far abroad. Thus was it that unmarked Melko and the Spider of Night reached the roots of Laurelin, and Melko summoning all his godlike might thrust a sword into its beauteous stock, and the fiery radiance that spouted forth assuredly had consumed him even as it did his sword, had not Gloomweaver cast herself down and lapped it thirstily, plying even her lips to the wound in the tree's bark and sucking away its life and strength.

By accursed fortune this deed was not straightway marked, for it was the time of Laurelin's accustomed deepest repose; and now behold, never more would it wake to glory, scattering beauty and joy upon the faces of the Gods. Because of that great draught of light suddenly pride surged in Gwerlum's heart, and she heeded not Melko's warnings, but sate herself now nigh to the roots of Silpion and spouted forth evil fumes of night that flowed like rivers of blackness even to the gates of Valmar. Now Melko takes the weapon that remains to him, a knife, and will injure the bole of Silpion as much as time will allow; but a Gnome called Daurin (Tórin) wandering from Sirnúmen in great boding of ill sees him and makes for him, crying aloud. So great was the onrush of that impetuous Gnome that ere Melko is aware he has hewn at Wirilómë where in the likeness of a spider she sprawls upon the ground. Now the slender blade that Daurin wielded came from the forge of Aulë and was steeped in *miruvor*, or never had he done harm to that secret [?being], but now he cleaves one of her great legs, and his blade is stained with her black gore, a poison to all [?things] whose life is light. Then Wirilómë writhing throws a thread about him and he may not get free, and Melko ruthless stabs him. Then wresting that bright slender blade from his dying grasp he thrusts it deep into Silpion's trunk, and the poison of Gwerlum black upon it dried the very sap and essence of the tree, and its light died suddenly to a dismal glow lost in impenetrable dusk.

Then did Melko and Wirilómë turn in flight, nor is it too soon, for some that were behind Daurin seeing his fate fled in terror both to Kôr and Valmar, stumbling madly in the darkness, but indeed already the Valar are riding forth upon the plain speeding as fast as may be yet too late to defend the Trees which they now know to be in danger.

Now do those Noldoli confirm their fears, saying how Melko is indeed the author of the mischief, and they have but one desire and that is to lay hands upon him and his accomplices ere they can escape beyond the mountains.

Tulkas is in the van of that great hunt leaping surefooted in the dimness, and Oromë may not keep up with him, for even his divine steed cannot rush as headlong in the gathering night as does Poldórëa in the fire of his wrath. Ulmo hears the shouting in his house in Vai, and Ossë [?thrusteth] his head above the Shadowy Seas and seeing no longer any light come down the valley of Kôr he leaps upon the beach of Eldamar and runs in haste to join the Ainur in their hunt. Now is the only light place left in Valinor that garden where the golden fountain sprang from Kulullin, and then were Vána and Nessa and Urwen and many maids and ladies of the Valar in tears, but Palúrien girds her lord as he stands impatiently, and Varda has ridden forth from Taniquetil by her lord's side bearing a blazing star before him as a torch.

Telimektar son of Tulkas is with those noble ones, and his face and weapons gleam as silver in the dark, but now all the Gods and all their folk ride this way and that, and some have [?hasty] torches in their hands, so that the plain is full of pale wandering lights and the sound of voices hallooing in the dusk.

Even as Melko speeds away a vanguard of the chase sweeps by the Trees, and well nigh the Vali faint for anguish at the ruin they see there; but now Melko and certain of his comrades, aforetime children of Mandos, are separated from Ungwë, who wrapped in night gets her gone southward and over the mountains to her home, nor does that chase ever draw nigh to her; but the others flee northward with great speed, for Melko's comrades have knowledge of the mountains there, and hope to get [?him] through. There came a place at length where the shadow-veils were thin and they were viewed by a scattered band of the Vali, and Tulkas was amongst them; who now with a great roar leaps at them. Indeed it might have come to battle upon the plain betwixt Tulkas and Melko had not the distance been overgreat, so that even as Tulkas gained to within spearcast of Melko a belt of mist took the fugitives again and the mocking laugh of Melko seems to come first from one side and then from the other, now from his elbow almost, now from far ahead, and Tulkas turns wildly about and Melko slips away.

Then Makar and Meássë rode in all haste north with their folk, arousing Mandos and ordering the guarding of the mountain paths, but either Makar was too late or Melko's cunning defeated him —

and the mind of Makar was not oversubtle, for no glimpse of that Ainu did they see, though assuredly he did escape that way, and worked much evil after in the world, yet none are there whom I have heard tell ever of the manner of his perilous flight back to the ice-kingdoms of the North.'

NOTES

1 See p. 117.
2 *Lirillo* appears in the list of secondary names of the Valar referred to on p. 93 as a name of Salmar-Noldorin.
3 'father of Fëanor' is the final reading after a prolonged hesitation between 'son of Fëanor' and 'brother of Fëanor'.
4 For the story of the taking of rock and stone from Arvalin (Eruman) for the raising of the Mountains of Valinor see p. 70.
5 'sire of Fëanor' is an emendation from 'son of Fëanor'; see note 3.
6 After the word 'fabrics' there stood the following sentence, which was struck through: 'which the Gods could an they listed have created in an hour' – a sentence notable in itself and also for its excision.
7 The MS page beginning with the words 'before the gates of Valmar' and ending with 'unabashed uttered his message, saying' is written round the little world-map reproduced and described on pp. 81 ff.
8 In this part of the tale the manuscript consists of detached passages, with directions from one to another; the place of this sentence is not perfectly clear, but seems most probably to belong here.
9 The dots are in the original.
10 'afterward' is an emendation from 'of old'. A question mark is written in the margin against this sentence.

Changes made to names in
The Theft of Melko and the Darkening of Valinor

Ellu Melemno ⟨ *Melemno* (in Chapter V, p. 120, in an added sentence, the leader of the Solosimpi is *Ellu*).
Sirnúmen ⟨ *Numessir* (at the first two occurrences; subsequently *Sirnú-men* was the form first written).
Eruman ⟨ *Harmalin* (pp. 145, 152), ⟨ *Habbanan* (p. 151).
Arvalin ⟨ *Harvalien* ⟨ *Habbanan* (p. 145), ⟨ *Harvalien* ⟨ *Harmalin* (p. 147); *Arvalien* thus first written p. 148.
Bruithwir replaces an earlier name, probably *Maron*.
Bruithwir go-Maidros ⟨ *Bruithwir go-Fëanor*. go- is a patronymic, 'son of'. See notes 3 and 5 above.

Móru   This name could equally well be read, as also at its occasional
    occurrences elsewhere, as *Morn* (see the Appendix on Names). It
    replaces here another name, probably *Mordi*.

Ungoliont ⟨ *Gungliont*.

Daurin (*Tórin*)   The original reading at the first occurence was *Fëanor*,
    changed to (?)*Daurlas* . . . . *akin to Fëanor*, and then to *a Gnome
    called Daurin* (*Tórin*). The subsequent occurrences of *Daurin* are
    emendations of *Fëanor*.

Commentary on
The Theft of Melko and the Darkening of Valinor

The story of the corruption of the Noldoli by Melko was ultimately told
quite differently; for there entered the matter of the strife between Finwë's
sons Fëanor and Fingolfin (*The Silmarillion* p. 69), of which in the tale
there is no trace, and where in any case Fëanor is not the son of Finwë
Nólemë but of one Bruithwir. The primary motive in the later story of
Melkor's desire for the Silmarils (*ibid.* p. 67) is here represented only by
a lust for the gems of the Noldoli in general: it is indeed a remarkable
feature of the original mythology that though the Silmarils were present
they were of such relatively small importance. There is essential agreement with the later story in its being the Noldoli at whom Melko aimed his
attack, and there is a quite close, if limited, similarity in the arguments he
used: the confinement of the Elves in Valinor by the Valar, and the broad
realms in the East that were rightly theirs – but notably absent from Melko's
words is any reference to the coming of Men: this element is in the tale
introduced later and quite differently, by Manwë himself (p. 150). Moreover the particular association of the Noldoli with the evil Vala arises
from his desire for their gems: in *The Silmarillion* (p. 66) the Noldor
turned to him for the instruction he could give, while the other kindreds
held aloof.

From this point the narratives diverge altogether; for the secret evil
of Melkor was in *The Silmarillion* laid bare as a result of the enquiry
held into the quarrel of the Noldorin princes, whereas here its revelation
came about more simply from the anxiety of Finwë Nólemë about the
unrest of his people. The later story is of course far superior, in that
Melkor was sought by the Valar as a known enemy as soon as his machina-
tions were uncovered (though he escaped), whereas in the tale, despite
there being now every evidence that he was by no means reformed, he
was merely told to go and think things over in Mandos. The germ of the
story in *The Silmarillion* of Fëanor's banishment to Formenos, where he
was accompanied by Finwë, is present, though here the entire people of
the Noldoli are ordered to leave Kôr for the rugged dale northwards
where the stream Híri plunged underground, and the command to do so

seems to have been less a punishment meted out to them by Manwë than a precaution and a safeguard.

In connection with the place of the banishment of the Noldoli, here called *Sirnúmen* ('Western Stream'), it may be mentioned that in an isolated note found in the little book referred to on p. 23 it is stated: 'The river of the second rocky dwelling of the Gnomes in Valinor was *kelusindi* and the spring at its source *kapalinda*.'

Very remarkable is the passage (p. 142) where Manwë is said to know that 'the Elves were children of the world and must one day return to her bosom'. As I have noticed earlier (p. 82) 'the world' is often equated with the Great Lands, and this usage occurs repeatedly in the present tale, but it is not clear to me whether this sense is intended here. I incline to think that the meaning of the phrase is that at 'the Great End' the Eldar, being bound to the Earth, cannot return with the Valar and spirits that were 'before the world' (p. 66) to the regions whence they came (cf. the conclusion of the original *Music of the Ainur*, p. 60).

Coming to the account of the theft of the jewels, the structure of the narrative is again radically different from the later story, in that there Melkor's attack on the Noldor of Formenos, the theft of the Silmarils and the slaying of Finwë, was accomplished *after* his meeting with Ungoliant in the South and the destruction of the Two Trees; Ungoliant was with him at Formenos. Nor in the earliest version is there any mention of Melko's previous visit to Formenos (*The Silmarillion* pp. 71–2), after which he passed through the Calacirya and went northwards up the coast, returning later in secret to Avathar (Arvalin, Eruman) to seek out Ungoliant.

On the other hand the great festival was already the occasion for Melko's theft of the Silmarils from the dwelling of the Noldoli, though the festival was wholly different in having a purely commemorative purpose (see *The Silmarillion* pp. 74–5), and it was a necessary part of that purpose that the Solosimpi should be present (in *The Silmarillion* 'Only the Teleri beyond the mountains still sang upon the shores of the sea; for they recked little of seasons or times . . .').

Of Melko's dark accomplices out of Mandos (some of them said to be 'aforetime children of Mandos', p. 154) there is no trace later, nor of his theft of Oromë's horses; and while Melko is here said to have wished to leave Valinor by passes over the northern mountains, but to have thought better of it (leading to a reflection on what might have been the fate of Valinor had he not), in the later story his movement northwards was a feint. But it is interesting to observe the germ of the one in the other, the underlying idea never lost of a northward and then a southward movement, even though it takes place at a different point in the narrative and has a different motivation.

Interesting also is the emergence of the idea that a close kinsman of Fëanor's – only after much hesitation between brother and son becoming fixed on the father – was slain by Melkor in the dwelling of the Noldoli, Sirnúmen, precursor of Formenos; but the father had yet to be identified with the lord of the Noldoli.

In this passage there are some slight further geographical indications. The Two Trees stood to the north of the city of Valmar (p. 143), as they are shown on the map (see pp. 81–2); and, again in agreement with the map, the Great Lands and the Outer Lands came very close together in the far North (p. 146). Most notably, the gap in the Mountains of Valinor shown on the map and which I marked with the letter *e* is now explained: 'the low place in the hills' by which Melko and his following passed out of Valinor into Arvalin-Eruman, a gap left by Tulkas and Aulë for their own entry into Valinor at the time of the raising of the mountains (p. 145).

Of the next part of this tale (pp. 146–9) almost nothing survived. Manwë's lecture to the Noldoli disappeared (but some of its content is briefly expressed at another place in the narrative of *The Silmarillion*, p. 68: 'The Noldor began to murmur against [the Valar], and many became filled with pride, forgetting how much of what they had and knew came to them in gift from the Valar'). Manwë's naming of Fëanor's father Bruithwir by the patronymic *go-Maidros* is notable: though the name *Maidros* was subsequently to be that of Fëanor's eldest son, not of his grandfather, it was from the outset associated with the 'Fëanorians'. There is no trace later of the strange story of the renegade servant of Mandos, who brought Melko's outrageous message to the Valar, and who was hurled to his death from Taniquetil by the irrepressible Tulkas in direct disobedience to Manwë; nor of the sending of Sorontur to Melko as the messenger of the Gods (it is not explained how Sorontur knew where to find him). It is said here that afterwards 'Sorontur and his folk fared to the Iron Mountains and there abode, watching all that Melko did'. I have noticed in commenting (pp. 111–12) on *The Chaining of Melko* that the Iron Mountains, said to be south of Hisilómë (pp. 101, 118), there correspond to the later Mountains of Shadow (*Ered Wethrin*). On the other hand, in the *Tale of the Sun and Moon* (p. 176) Melko after his escape from Valinor makes himself 'new dwellings in that region of the North where stand the Iron Mountains very high and terrible to see'; and in the original *Tale of Turambar** it is said that Angband lay beneath the roots of the northernmost fastnesses of the Iron Mountains, and that these mountains were so named from 'the Hells of Iron' beneath them. The statement in the present tale that Sorontur 'watched all that Melko did' from his abode in the Iron Mountains obviously implies likewise that Angband was beneath them; and the story that Sorontur (Thorondor) had his eyries on Thangorodrim before he removed them to Gondolin survived long in the 'Silmarillion' tradition (see *Unfinished Tales* p. 43 and note 25). There is thus, apparently, a contradictory usage of the term

* The actual title of this tale is *The Tale of Turambar and the Foalókë*, the *Foalókë* being the Dragon.

'Iron Mountains' within the *Lost Tales*; unless it can be supposed that these mountains were conceived as a continuous range, the southerly extension (the later Mountains of Shadow) forming the southern fence of Hisilómë, while the northern peaks, being above Angband, gave the range its name. Evidence that this is so will appear later.

In the original story the Noldoli of Sirnúmen were given permission (through the intercession of Aulë) to return to Kôr, but Fëanor remained there in bitterness with a few others; and thus the situation of the later narrative – the Noldor in Tirion, but Fëanor at Formenos – is achieved, with the element absent of Fëanor's banishment and unlawful return to the city of the Elves. An underlying difference to be noted is that in *The Silmarillion* (pp. 61–2) the Vanyar had long since departed from Tirion and gone to dwell on Taniquetil or in Valinor: of this there is no suggestion in the old tale; and of course there is the central structural difference between the early and late narratives – when Fëanor raises his standard of rebellion the Trees are still shining in Valinor.

In the tale, a good while seems to elapse after the loss of the treasures of the Noldoli, during which they set to work again with lessened joy and Fëanor sought in vain to remake the Silmarils: this element must of course disappear in the later, much tauter structure, where Fëanor (refusing to hand over the Silmarils to the Valar for the healing of the Trees and not yet knowing that Melko has taken them) knows without attempting it that he cannot remake them any more than Yavanna can remake the Trees.

The embassage of Fëanor and other Noldoli to Manwë, demanding that the Gods ferry them back to the Great Lands, was excised, and with it Manwë's remarkable instruction to them concerning the coming of Men – and his expressed reluctance to have the Eldar return to 'the world' while Men were still in their infancy. No such idea is represented in *The Silmarillion* as being in Manwë's mind (nor is there any suggestion that Manwë's knowledge was so great); and indeed, where in the old story it was Manwë's very description of Men and account of his policy with regard to them that gave rise to Fëanor's rhetoric against them, and which gave strong colour to his assertion of the Valar's true motive for bringing the Eldar to Valinor, in *The Silmarillion* (p. 68) these ideas are a part of the lies of Melkor (I have noticed above that in Melko's persuasions of the Noldoli in the tale there is no reference to the coming of Men).

An otherwise unknown element in the Music of the Ainur is revealed in Manwë's words: that the world shall come in the end for a great while under the sway of Men. In the original version there are several suggestions in reflective asides that all was fated: so here 'the jealousy of Elves and Men' is seen as perhaps a necessary part of the unfolding of the history of the world, and earlier in the tale (p. 142) it is asked: 'Who shall say but that all these deeds, even the seeming needless evil of Melko, were but a portion of the destiny of old?'

But for all the radical changes in the narrative the characteristic note of Fëanor's rhetoric remained; his speech to the Noldoli of Kôr rises in the same rhythms as his speech by torchlight to the Noldor of Tirion (*The Silmarillion* pp. 82–3).

In the story of Melko and Ungoliont it is seen that essential elements were present *ab initio*: the doubt as to her origin, her dwelling in the desolate regions in the south of the Outer Lands, her sucking in of light to bring forth webs of darkness; her alliance with Melko, his rewarding her with the gems stolen from the Noldoli (though this was differently treated later), the piercing of the Trees by Melko and Ungoliont's sucking up the light; and the great hunt mounted by the Valar, which failed of its object through darkness and mist, allowing Melko to escape out of Valinor by the northward ways.

Within this structure there are as almost always a great many points of difference between the first story and the later versions. In *The Silmarillion* (p. 73) Melkor went to Avathar because he knew of Ungoliant's dwelling there, whereas in the tale she found him wandering there seeking a way of escape. In the tale her origin is unknown, and though this element may be said to have remained in *The Silmarillion* ('The Eldar know not whence she came', *ibid.*), by the device of 'Some have said . . .' a clear explanation is in fact given: she was a being from 'before the world', perverted by Melkor, who had been her lord, though she denied him. The original idea of 'the primeval spirit Móru' (p. 151) is made explicit in an entry in the early word-list of the Gnomish language, where the name *Muru* is defined as 'a name of the Primeval Night personified as Gwerlum or Gungliont'.*

The old story markedly lacks the quality of the description in *The Silmarillion* of the descent of Melkor and Ungoliant from Mount Hyarmentir into the plain of Valinor; and there too the great festival of the Valar and Eldar was in progress at the time: here it is long since over. In *The Silmarillion* the assault on the Trees came at the time of the mingling of the lights (p. 75), while here Silpion was in full bloom; and the detail of the account of the destruction of the Trees is rendered quite different through the presence of the Gnome Daurin, afterwards abandoned without trace. Thus in the old story it is not actually said that Ungoliont drank the light of Silpion, but only that the tree died from her poison on Daurin's blade, with which Melko stabbed its trunk; and in *The Silmarillion* Ungoliant went to 'the Wells of Varda' and drank them dry also. It is puzzling that the Gnome was first named Fëanor, since he was slain by Melko. It would seem that my father was at least momentarily entertaining the idea that Fëanor would play no part in the story of the Noldoli in the Great Lands; but in outlines for a later tale (pp. 238-9) he died in Mithrim. In this passage is the first appearance of *miruvor*, defined in the early Qenya word-list as 'nectar, drink of the Valar'; with this cf. *The Road Goes Ever On*, p. 61, where my father stated that it was the name given by the Valar to the drink poured at their festivals,

---

* In the tale (see p. 156) the name *Gungliont* was originally written, but was emended to *Ungoliont*.

and compared it to the nectar of the Olympian Gods (in the translation of *Namárië* he rendered *miruvórë* 'nectar', *ibid.* p. 58).

Most important of the differences in the tale is the immediate return of Ungoliont to her lair in the south, so that all the story in *The Silmarillion* (pp. 80–1) of 'the Thieves' Quarrel', the rescue of Melkor by the Balrogs, and Ungoliant's coming into Nan Dungortheb, is absent from the narrative in the *Lost Tales*; the surrender of the gems of the Noldoli to Ungoliont takes place in the early version at the time of her first meeting with Melko – in *The Silmarillion* he did not then possess them, for the attack on Formenos had not yet taken place.

VII

THE FLIGHT OF THE NOLDOLI

There is no break in Lindo's narrative, which continues on in the same hastily-pencilled form (and near this point passes to another similar note-book, clearly with no break in composition), but I have thought it convenient to introduce a new chapter, or a new 'Tale', here, again taking the title from the cover of the book.

'Nonetheless the Gods did not give up hope, but many a time would meet beneath the ruined tree of Laurelin and thence break and scour the land of Valinor once more unwearingly, desiring fiercely to avenge the hurts done to their fair realm; and now the Eldar at their summons aided in the chase that labours not only in the plain but toils both up and down the slopes of the mountains, for there is no escape from Valinor to west, where lie the cold waters of the Outer Seas.

But Fëanor standing in the square about Inwë's house in topmost Kôr will not be silenced, and cries out that all the Noldoli shall gather about him and hearken, and many thousands of them come to hear his words bearing slender torches, so that that place is filled with a lurid light such as has never before shone on those white walls. Now when they are gathered there and Fëanor sees that far the most of the company is of the kin of the Noldor[1] he exhorts them to seize now this darkness and confusion and the weariness of the Gods to cast off the yoke – for thus demented he called the days of bliss in Valinor – and get them hence carrying with them what they might or listed. "If all your hearts be too faint to follow, behold I Fëanor go now alone into the wide and magic world to seek the gems that are my own, and perchance many great and strange adventures will there befall me more worthy of a child of Ilúvatar than a servant of the Gods."[2]

Then is there a great rush of those who will follow him at once, and though wise Nólemë speaks against this rashness they will not hear him, and ever the tumult groweth wilder. Again Nólemë pleads that at least they send an embassy to Manwë to take due farewell and maybe get his goodwill and counsel for their journeying, but Fëanor persuades them to cast away even such moderate wisdom, saying that to do so were but to court refusal, and that Manwë would forbid them and prevent them: "What is Valinor to us," say they, "now that its light is come to little – as lief and liever would we have the untrammeled world." Now then they arm themselves as best they may – for nor Elves nor Gods in those days bethought themselves overmuch of weapons – and store of jewels they took and stuffs of raiment; but all their books of their lore they left behind, and indeed there was not much therein that the wise men among them could not match from memory. But Nólemë seeing that his counsel prevailed not would not be separated from his folk, and went with them and aided them in all their preparations. Then did they get them down the hill of Kôr lit by the flame of torches, and so faring in haste along the creek and the shores of that arm of the Shadowy Sea that encroached here upon the hills they found the seaward dwellings of the Solosimpi.

The next short section of the text was struck through afterwards, the words 'Insert the Battle of Kópas Alqalunten' written across it, and replaced by a rider. The rejected section reads:

The most of that folk were gone a-hunting with the Gods, but some of those that remained they suaded to cast in their lot with them, as already had some of the Teleri, but of the Inwir none would hearken to their words. Now having nigh as many maids and women as of men and boys (albeit many especially of the youngest children were left in Kôr and Sirnúmen) they were at a loss, and in this extremity, being distraught with sorrows and wildered in mind, the Noldoli did those deeds which afterwards they most bitterly rued – for by them was the displeasure laid heavily on all their folk and the hearts even of their kindred were turned against them for a while.

Coming upon Cópas where was a haven of great quiet beloved of the Solosimpi they seized all the ships of that people and embarked thereon their womenfolk and children and some few [?others] wherewith were those of the Solosimpi who had joined them, for these had a skill in navigation. In this way marching endlessly along the beach that grew wilder and more evil going as it trended to the North, while the fleet coasted beside them not far out to sea, it has been said to me that the Noldoli got them from Valinor; however I know not the matter deeply, and maybe there are tales known to none of the Gnome-kin that relate more clearly the sad happenings of that time. Moreover have I heard say

The rider that replaces this passage was written carefully and very legibly in ink on separate sheets, at how great an interval of time I cannot say.

The Kinslaughter
(Battle of Kópas Alqalunten)

The most of that folk were gone a-hunting with the Gods, but many there were gathered about the beaches before their dwellings and dismay was abroad among them, yet still were no few busy about the places of their ships, and the chief of these was that one they named Kópas, or more fully Kópas Alqaluntë, the Haven of the Swanships.* Now Swanhaven was like a bason of quiet waters, save that towards the eastward and the seas the ring of rocks that enclosed it sank somewhat, and there did the sea pierce through, so that there was a mighty arch of living stone. So great was this that save of the mightiest ships two might pass therethrough, one going out maybe and another seeking inward to the quiet blue waters of the haven, nor would the mast-tops come nigh to grazing on the rock. Not much of the light of the Trees came thither aforetime by reason of the wall, wherefore was it lit ever with a ring of lamps of gold, and lanterns there were too of many colours tokening the wharves and landings of the different houses; but through the arch the pale waters of the Shadowy Seas might distantly be glimpsed, lit faintly with the shining of the Trees. Very beautiful was that harbour to gaze upon, what time the white fleets came shimmering home and the troubled waters broke the mirrored radiance of the lamps into rippling lights, weaving strange patterns of many twinkling lines. But now were all those vessels lying still, and a deep gloom was settled on the place at the fading of the Trees.

Of the Solosimpi none would hearken to the wild words of the Noldoli, save a few that might be counted on two hands; and so did that folk wander unhappily northward along the shores of Eldamar, even till they came to the cliff-tops that gazed down upon Swanhaven, and therefrom had the Solosimpi of old cut winding stairs in the rock leading down to the harbour's edge. Now northward thence the way was very rugged and evil, and the Noldoli had with them nigh as many maids and women as of men and boys (albeit many especially of the youngest children were left in Kôr and in Sirnúmen and many tears were shed thereat); wherefore were they now at a loss, and in this extremity, distraught with sorrows and wildered in mind, they here wrought those deeds which afterwards they have most bitterly

---

* In the margin is written *Ielfethýp*. This is Old English, representing the interpretation of the Elvish name made by Eriol in his own language: the first element meaning 'swan' (*ielfetu*), and the second (later 'hithe') meaning 'haven, landing-place'.

repented – for by them was for a while the displeasure of the Gods laid heavily upon all their folk and the hearts even of the Eldalië were turned against them.

Behold, the counsel of Fëanor is that by no means can that host hope to win swiftly along the coast save by the aid of ships; "and these," said he, "an the shore-elves will not give them, we must take". Wherefore going down to the harbour they essayed to go upon those ships that there lay, but the Solosimpi said them nay, yet for the great host of the Gnome-folk they did not as yet resist; but a new wrath awoke there between Eldar and Eldar. So did the Noldoli embark all their womenfolk and children and a great host beside upon those ships, and casting them loose they oared them with a great multitude of oars towards the seas. Then did a great anger blaze in the hearts of the Shoreland Pipers, seeing the theft of those vessels that their cunning and long labours had fashioned, and some there were that the Gods had made of old on Tol Eressëa as has been recounted, wondrous and magic boats, the first that ever were. So sprang up suddenly a voice among them: "Never shall these thieves leave the Haven in our ships", and all those of the Solosimpi that were there ran swiftly atop of the cliff-wall to where the archway was wherethrough that fleet must pass, and standing there they shouted to the Gnomes to return; but these heeded them not and held ever on their course, and the Solosimpi threatened them with rocks and strung their elfin bows.

Seeing this and believing war already to be kindled came now those of the Gnomes who might not fare aboard the ships but whose part it was to march along the shores, and they sped behind the Solosimpi, until coming suddenly upon them nigh the Haven's gate they slew them bitterly or cast them in the sea; and so first perished the Eldar neath the weapons of their kin, and that was a deed of horror. Now the number of the Solosimpi that fell was very many, and of the Gnomes not a few, for they had to fight hard to win their way back from those narrow cliff-top paths, and many of the shoreland folk hearing the affray were gathered in their rear.

At length however it is done, and all those ships have passed out to the wide seas, and the Noldoli fared far away, but the little lamps are broken and the Haven is dark and very still, save for the faint sound of tears. Of like kind were all the works of Melko in this world.

Now tells the tale that as the Solosimpi wept and the Gods scoured all the plain of Valinor or sat despondent neath the ruined Trees a great age passed and it was one of gloom, and during that time the Gnome-folk suffered the very greatest evils and all the unkindliness of the world beset them. For some marched endlessly along that shore until Eldamar was dim and forgotten far behind, and wilder grew the ways and more impassable as it trended to the North, but the fleet coasted beside them not far out to sea and the shore-farers might often see them dimly in the gloom, for they fared but slowly in those sluggish waves.

Yet of all the sorrows that walked those ways I know not the full tale, nor have any told it, for it would be an ill tale, and though the Gnomes relate many things concerning those days more clearly than I can, yet do they in no wise love to dwell upon the sad happenings of that time and will not often awake its memory. Nonetheless have I heard it said

The inserted rider ends here and we return to the original roughly-pencilled text:

that never would they have made the dreadful passage of the Qerka-ringa³ had they or yet been subject to weariness, sickness, and the many weaknesses that after became their lot dwelling far from Valinor. Still was the blessed food of the Gods and their drink rich in their veins and they were half-divine – but no *limpë* had they as yet to bring away, for that was not given to the fairies until long after, when the March of Liberation was undertaken, and the evils of the world which Melko poisoned with his presence soon fell upon them.'

'Nay, if thou wilt forgive me bursting in upon thy tale,' quoth Eriol, 'what meaneth thy saying "the dread passage of the Qerka-ringa"?'

'Know then,' said Lindo, 'that the trend of the coasts of Eldamar and those coasts that continue that strand northward beyond the wide haven of Kópas is ever to the East, so that after uncounted miles, more northward even than the Mountains of Iron and upon the confines of the Icy Realms, the Great Seas aided by a westerly bend of the shores of the Great Lands dwindle to a narrow sound. Now the passage of that water is of impassable peril, for it is full of evil currents and eddies of desperate strength, and islands of floating ice swim therein, grinding and crashing together with a dread noise and destroying both great fish and vessels, do any ever dare to venture there. In those days however a narrow neck, which the Gods after destroyed, ran out from the western land almost to the eastern shores, yet it was of ice and snow [?pillared] and torn into gaps and cliffs and was all but untraversable, and that was the

Helkaraksë or Icefang,[4] and it was a remnant of the old and terrible ices that crept throughout those regions ere Melko was chained and the North became clement for a while, and it maintained itself there by reason of the narrowness of the seas and the [?jamming] of the ice-isles floating down from the deepest North whither winter had withdrawn. Now that strip of water that flowed still between Icefang's tip and the Great Lands was called Qerkaringa or Chill Gulf.[5]

Had Melko indeed known of the Gnomes' wild attempt to cross it he might have overwhelmed them all in that ill place or done whatso he willed, but many months had gone since he himself had fled perchance by that very way, and he was now far afield. Say I not well, Rúmil, with regard to these things?'

'Thou hast told the true tale,' said Rúmil, 'yet hast thou not said how ere they came to Helkaraksë the host passed by that place where Mornië is wont to be beached, for there a steep and rugged path winds down from Mandos deep in the mountains that the souls whom Fui sends to Arvalin must tread.[6] There did a servant of Vefántur spy them and asking what might that wayfaring mean pled with them to return, but they answered him scornfully, so that standing upon a high rock he spoke to them aloud and his voice came even to the fleet upon the waves; and he foretold to them many of the evil adventures that after came to them, warning them against Melko, and at last he said: "Great is the fall of Gondolin", and none there understood, for Turondo son of Nólemë[7] was not yet upon the Earth. But the wise men stored his sayings, for Mandos and all his people have a power of prophecy, and these words were treasured long among them as the Prophecies of Amnos, for thus was the place where they were spoken called at that time, which now is Hanstová-nen[8] or the beaching place of Mornië.

After that the Noldoli journeyed slowly, and when the awful isthmus of Helkaraksë was before them some were for ferrying all the host, part at a time, across the sea, venturing rather over the perilous waters than seeking to find passage over the gulfs and treacherous crevasses of the isthmus of ice. This they tried, and a great ship was lost with all aboard by reason of a certain fearsome eddy that was in the bay nigh where Helkaraksë jutted from the western mainland; and that eddy at times spins around like a vast top and shrieks with a loud wailing noise most terrible to hear, and such things as approach are sucked down to its monstrous deep and crushed there upon jags of ice and rock; and the name of the eddy is Wiruin. Wherefore are the Noldoli in great anguish and perplexity, for even could they find a way through the terrors of the Helkaraksë, behold they cannot even so reach the inner world, for still there lies that gap at the far end, and though but narrow the screech of water rushing therethrough can be heard thus far away, and the boom of ice splitting from the cape came to them, and the crash and buffet of the ice-isles that thrust down from the North through that dreadful strait.

Now the presence of those floating isles of ice no doubt was due to the presence of Melko once more in the far North, for winter had retreated to the uttermost North and South, so that almost it had no foothold in the world remaining in those days of peace that are called Melko's Chains; but nonetheless it was this very activity of Melko that in the end proved the salvation of the Noldoli, for behold they now are constrained to lead all their womenfolk and the mariners of their host out of the ships, and there on those bleak shores they beach them and set now a miserable encampment.

Songs name that dwelling[9] the Tents of Murmuring, for there arose much lamentation and regret, and many blamed Fëanor bitterly, as indeed was just, yet few deserted the host for they suspected that there was no welcome ever again for them back to Valinor – and this some few who sought to return indeed found, though this entereth not into this tale.

When their woes are now at the blackest and scarce any look for return of any joy again, behold winter unfurls her banners again and marches slowly south clad in ice with spears of frost and lashes of hail. Yet so great is the cold that the floating ice packs and jams and piles like hills between the end of Helkaraksë[10] and the Eastern land, and in the end does it become so strong that the current moves it not. Then abandoning their stolen ships they leave their sorrowful encampment and strive to cross the terrors of the Qerkaringa. Who shall tell of their misery in that march or of those numbers who were lost, falling into great pits of ice where far below hidden water boiled, or losing their way until cold overcame them – for evil as it was so many and desperate things befell them after in the Great Lands that it was lessened in their minds to a thing of less worth, and in sooth tales that told of the leaving of Valinor were never sweet in the ears of the Noldoli after, were they thralls or citizens of Gondolin. Yet even so such things may not slay the Gnome-kin, and of those there lost still 'tis said some wander sadly there among the icehills, unknowing of all things that have befallen their folk, and some essayed to get them back to Valinor, and Mandos has them, and some following after found in long days their unhappy kin again. Howso it be, a gaunt and lessened band indeed did in the end reach the rocky soil of the Eastern lands, and there stood looking backward over the ice of Helkaraksë and of Qerkaringa at the spurs of hills beyond the sea, for far away in the gathering southward mists rose those most glorious heights of Valinor, fencing them for ever from their kindred and their homes.

Thus came the Noldoli into the world.'

And with those words of Rúmil's the story of the darkening of Valinor was at an end.

'Great was the power of Melko for ill,' saith Eriol, 'if he could indeed destroy with his cunning the happiness and glory of the Gods and of the Elves, darkening the light of their hearts no less than of their dwelling, and bringing all their love to naught! This must surely be the worst deed that ever he has done.'

'Of a truth never has such evil again been done in Valinor,' said Lindo, 'but Melko's hand has laboured at worse things in the world, and the seeds of his evil have waxen since those days to a great and terrible growth.'

'Nay,' said Eriol, 'yet can my heart not think of other griefs, for sorrow at the destruction of those most fair Trees and the darkness of the world.'

NOTES

1   The manuscript seems certainly to have the form *Noldor* here. – It is to be remembered that in the old story the Teleri (i.e. the later Vanyar) had not departed from Kôr; see p. 159.

2   At the top of the manuscript page and fairly clearly referring to Fëanor's words my father wrote: 'Increase the element of the desire for Silmarils'. Another note refers to the section of the narrative that begins here and says that it 'wants a lot of revision: the [?thirst ?lust] for jewels – especially for the sacred Silmarils – wants emphasizing. And the all-important battle of Cópas Alqaluntë where the Gnomes slew the Solosimpi must be inserted.' This note was then struck through and marked 'done', but only the latter direction was in fact followed: this is the rider on the Kinslaughter given on pp. 164–6.

3   Against this my father wrote in the margin: '*Helkaraksë* Icefang *Qerkaringa* the water'; see note 5.

4   *Helkaraksë or Icefang*: earlier reading *Qerkaringa*; see note 5.

5   This passage, from ' "Know then," said Lindo . . .', replaces an earlier version which I do not give, for it contains almost nothing that is not in the replacement; and the last sentence of the replacement is a later addition still. It is to be noted however that in the first version the neck of land is called *Qerkaringa* (as also in the replacement passage at first, see note 4), with the remark that 'the name has also

been given to the sound beyond'. This then was the earlier idea: *Qerkaringa* the name primarily of the neck of land, but extended also to the sound (presumably at that stage *querka* did not mean 'gulf'). My father than decided that *Qerkaringa* was the name of the sound and introduced the name *Helkaraksë* for the neck of land; hence the marginal annotation given in note 3 above. At this point he added the last sentence of the replacement passage, 'Now that strip of water that flowed still between Icefang's tip and the Great Lands was called Qerkaringa or Chill Gulf', and emended *Qerkaringa* in the body of the passage (note 4) to *Helkaraksë or Icefang*, carrying this change through the rest of the tale (on p. 169 *of Qerkaringa* > *of Helkaraksë and of Qerkaringa*).

6 For the path down from Mandos, the black ship Mornië, and its journey down the coast to Arvalin, see pp. 77, 90 ff.

7 Turondo or Turgon, son of Nólemë, has been named previously, p. 115.

8 The reading *Hanstovánen* is slightly uncertain, and another name 'or . . . . . . *Mornien*' follows it. See under 'Changes made to names' below.

9 After the word 'dwelling' there is a space left for the insertion of an Elvish name.

10 MS *Qerkaringa* unemended, but clearly the western promontory (the Icefang) is referred to, and I therefore read *Helkaraksë* in the text (see note 5).

Changes made to names in
The Flight of the Noldoli

Helkaraksë < *Qerkaringa* (for the details of, and the explanation of this change see note 5 above).
Arvalin < *Habbanan*.
Amnos < *Emnon* < *Morniento*.
Hanstovánen The name of 'the beaching place of Mornië' was first written *Mornielta* (last letters uncertain), then *Vane* (or *Vone*) *Hansto*; this latter was not struck out, but the form in the text (which may also be read as *Hanstavánen*) seems to be the final one. After *Hanstovánen* follows 'or . . . . . . *Mornien*'.

Commentary on
The Flight of the Noldoli

In this 'tale' (in reality the conclusion of the long tale of 'The Theft of Melko and the Darkening of Valinor' told by Lindo and finished by

Rúmil) is found the oldest account of the departure of the Gnomes out of Valinor. Here the Gods continue the vain pursuit and search long after Melko has escaped, and moreover are aided in it by the Eldar (including the Solosimpi, who as the later Teleri portrayed in *The Silmarillion* would hardly have left their shores and their ships). Fëanor's return to Kôr and his haranguing of the Noldoli (and, in this account, others) by the light of their torches is seen to be an original feature; but his sons have not yet appeared, nor indeed any of the Noldorin princes descended from Finwë save Turondo (Turgon), of whom it is specifically stated (p. 167) that he was 'not yet upon the Earth'. There is no Oath of Fëanor, and the later story of the divided counsels of the Noldor appears only in the attempt of Nólemë (Finwë) to calm the people – Nólemë thus playing the later part of Finarfin (*The Silmarillion* p. 83). In *The Silmarillion*, after the Kinslaying at Alqualondë and the Prophecy of the North, Finarfin and many of his people returned to Valinor and were pardoned by the Valar (p. 88); but here those few who went back found there was no welcome for them, or else 'Mandos has them' (p. 168).

In the rejected section given on p. 163, which was replaced by the account of the battle of Kópas Alqualunten, the reference to 'those deeds which afterwards the Noldoli most bitterly rued' must be simply to the theft of the ships of the Solosimpi, since there is no suggestion of any worse actions (in the replacement passage almost the same words are used of the Kinslaying). The actual emergence of the idea that the Noldoli were guilty of worse than theft at Kópas is seen in a note in the little book (see p. 23) that my father used to jot down thoughts and suggestions – many of these being no more than single sentences, or mere isolated names, serving as reminders of work to be done, stories to be told, or changes to be made. This note reads:

> The wrath of the Gods and Elves very great – even let some Noldoli slay some Solosimpi at Kópas – and let Ulmo plead for them (? if Ulmo so fond of the Solosimpi).

This was struck through and marked 'done', and the recommendation here that Ulmo should plead for the Noldoli is found in the tale of *The Hiding of Valinor* (p. 209).

In the description of Kópas the 'mighty arch of living stone' survived into the 'arch of living rock sea-carved' in the much briefer description of Alqualondë in *The Silmarillion* (p. 61); and we see here the reason for the Haven's being 'lit with many lamps' (*ibid.*) – because little light came there from the Two Trees on account of the rock-wall around it (though the darkness of Alqualondë is implied by the statement in *The Silmarillion* that it 'lay upon the confines of Eldamar, north of the Calacirya, where the light of the stars was bright and clear').

The events at the Haven were differently conceived in detail from the later story, but still with much general agreement; and though the storm raised by Uinen (*ibid.* p. 87) does not appear in the original version, the picture of the Noldoli journeying northward some along the shore and some in the vessels remained.

There are interesting indications of the geography of the northern regions. There is no suggestion of a great wasteland (later Araman) between the northern Mountains of Valinor and the sea, a conclusion reached earlier (p. 83), and supported incidentally by the accounts of the steep path from Mandos in the mountains down to the beaching place of the black ship Mornië (pp. 77, 167). The name *Helkaraksë*, 'Icefang', first appearing in emendations to the text and given to the neck or promontory running out from the western land, was afterwards re-applied to what is here called *Qerkaringa*, the strait filled with ice-floes that 'grind and crash together'; but this was when the *Helcaraxë*, 'the Grinding Ice', had come to have a quite different geographical significance in the much more sophisticated world-picture that my father evolved during the next 'phase' of the mythology.

In *The Silmarillion* (p. 87) there is a suggestion that the speaker of the Prophecy of the North was Mandos himself 'and no lesser herald of Manwë', and its gravity, indeed its centrality in the mythology, is far greater; here there is no suggestion of a 'doom' or 'curse', but only a foretelling. This foretelling included the dark words 'Great is the fall of Gondolin'. In the tale of *The Fall of Gondolin* (but in an interpolated sentence very possibly later than the present tale) Turgon, standing upon the stairs of his palace amid the destruction of the city, uttered these same words, 'and men shuddered, for such were the words of Amnon the prophet of old'. Here *Amnon* (rather than *Amnos* as in the present text, itself an emendation from *Emnon*) is not a place but a person (the servant of Vefántur who uttered the prophecy?). In the little notebook referred to above occurs the following jotting:

> Prophecy of Amnon. Great is the fall of Gondolin. Lo Turgon shall not fade till the lily of the valley fadeth.

In some other notes for the *Lost Tales* this takes the form:

> Prophecy of Amnon. 'Great is the fall of Gondolin' and 'When the lily of the valley withers then shall Turgon fade'.

In these notes *Amnon* might be either place or person. The 'lily of the valley' is Gondolin itself, one of whose Seven Names was *Losengriol*, later *Lothengriol*, which is translated 'flower of the vale or lily of the valley'.

There is an interesting statement in the old story (p. 166) that the Noldoli would never have passed the ice if they had yet been subject to the 'weariness, sickness, and the many weaknesses that after became their lot dwelling far from Valinor', but 'still was the blessed food of the Gods and their drink rich in their veins and they were half-divine'. This is echoed in the words of *The Silmarillion* (p. 90) that the Noldor were 'but new-come from the Blessed Realm, and not yet weary with the weariness of Earth'. On the other hand it was specifically said in the Prophecy of the North (*ibid.* p. 88) that 'though Eru appointed you to die not in Eä, *and no sickness may assail you*, yet slain ye may be, and slain ye shall be,' &c.

Of the treachery of the Fëanorians, sailing away in the ships and leaving the host of Fingolfin on the shores of Araman, there is of course in the old story no trace; but the blaming of Fëanor was already present ('the Tents of Murmuring', p. 168). It is a remarkable aspect of the earliest version of the mythology that while so much of the narrative structure was firm and was to endure, the later 'genealogical' structure had scarcely emerged. Turgon existed as the son of (Finwë) Nólemë, but there is no suggestion that Fëanor was close akin to the lord of the Noldoli, and the other princes, Fingolfin, Finarfin, Fingon, Felagund, do not appear at all, in any form, or by any name.

VIII

THE TALE OF THE SUN AND MOON

The *Tale of the Sun and Moon* is introduced by an 'Interlude' (as it is called in the manuscript) in which there appears, as a guest at Mar Vanwa Tyaliéva, one Gilfanon of Tavrobel. This interlude exists also in a rejected earlier version.

The tale itself is for most of its length a manuscript in ink over an erased pencilled original, but towards its end (see note 19) it becomes a primary manuscript in ink with the pencilled draft extant in another book.

The *Tale of the Sun and Moon* is very long, and I have shortened it in places in brief paraphrase, without omitting any detail of interest. (A note of my father's refers to this tale as 'in need of great revision, cutting-down, and [?reshaping]'.)

Gilfanon a·Davrobel

Now it is not to be thought that as Eriol hearkened to many tales which spake of divers sorrows of the Elves that the thirst for *limpë* grew less within him, for it was not so, and ever as the throng sat about the Tale-fire he was an eager questioner, seeking to learn all the history of the folk even down to those days that then were, when the elfin people dwelt again together in the isle.

Knowing now therefore something of the glorious fashion of their ancient home and of the splendour of the Gods, he pondered often on the coming of the days of Sunlight and of Moonsheen, and of the doings of the Elves in the world without, and of their adventures there with Men ere Melko compassed their estrangement; wherefore one night he said, sitting before the Tale-fire: 'Whence be the Sun and Moon, O Lindo? For as yet have I heard only of the Two Trees and their sad fading, but of the coming of Men, or of the deeds of the Elves beyond Valinor has no one told me.'

Now there happened that night to be present a guest both at their board and at their tale-telling, and his name was Gilfanon, and all named him beside Gilfanon a·Davrobel,[1] for he came from that region of the isle where stands the Tower of Tavrobel beside the rivers,[2] and about it dwelt the Gnome-folk still as one people, naming the places in their own tongue. That region was Gilfanon wont to name the fairest of all the isle, and the Gnome-kin its best folk, albeit ere the coming of the folk thither long had he dwelt away from the Noldoli, faring with Ilkorins in Hisilómë and Artanor,[3] and thereto had he become as few Elves did a great friend and companion of the Children of Men of those days. To their legends and their memories he added his own knowledge, for he had been deep-versed in many lores and tongues once in the far days of Kôr, and experience had he beside of many very ancient deeds, being indeed one of the oldest of the fairies[4] and the most aged that now dwelt in the isle, albeit Meril held the title of Lady of the Isle by reason of her blood.

Therefore said Lindo now, answering Eriol: 'Behold, Gilfanon here can tell thee much of such matters, and it were well if you fared hence away with him to sojourn awhile in Tavrobel. – Nay, look not thus,' he laughed, seeing Eriol's face, 'for we do not banish thee yet – but of a sooth he who would drink of *limpë* were wise first to seek the guestkindliness of Gilfanon, in whose ancient house – the House of the Hundred Chimneys, that stands nigh the bridge of Tavrobel[5] – may many things be heard of both past and that are to come.'

'Methinks,' said Gilfanon to Eriol, 'that Lindo seeks to rid himself of two guests at once; howso he may not do so yet, for I purpose to stay in Kortirion a sennight yet, and moreover to feast at his good board meanwhile, and stretch me by the Tale-fire too – thereafter maybe thou and I will fare away and thou shalt see the full loveliness of the fairies' isle – but now let Lindo raise up his voice and tell us yet more of the splendour of the Gods and their works, a theme that never wearies him!'

At that was Lindo well-pleased, for of a truth he loved to tell such tales and sought often an occasion for recalling them, and said he: 'Then will I tell the story of the Sun and Moon and of the Stars, that Eriol may hearken to his desire,' and Eriol was well pleased, but Gilfanon said: 'Speak on, my Lindo – yet lengthen not the tale for ever.'

Then did Lindo lift up his voice,[6] and it was the most pleasant to hearken to of all tale-tellers, and he said:*

'A tale I tell of that time of the first flight of the Gnomes, and behold they are but newly fled. Now came that grievous news to the Gods and the other Elves, and at first none believed. Nonetheless the tidings came still unto them, and by many different messengers. Some were of the Teleri, who had heard the speech of Fëanor in the square of Kôr and had seen the Noldoli depart thence with all

* Written in the margin: 'Beginning of The Sun and Moon'.

the goods they might convey; others were of the Solosimpi, and these brought the dire tidings of the swanships' rape and the dread kinslaughter of the Haven, and the blood that lay on the white shores of Alqaluntë.

Lastly came some hotfoot from Mandos who had gazed upon that sad throng nigh the strands of Amnor, and the Gods knew that the Gnomes were far abroad, and Varda and all the Elves wept, for now seemed the darkness black indeed and that more than the outward light of the fair Trees was slain.

Strange is to tell that albeit Aulë had loved the Noldoli above all the Elves and had taught them all they knew and given them great stores of wealth, now was his heart most turned against them, for he deemed them ingrate in that they had bidden him no farewell, and for their ill deeds among the Solosimpi he was grieved to the heart. "Speak not," said he, "the name of the Noldoli ever again unto me," and albeit he gave still his love to those few faithful Gnomes who remained still about his halls, yet did he name them thereafter "Eldar".

But the Teleri and the Solosimpi having wept at first, when the onslaught of the Haven became known to all dried their tears and horror and anguish held their hearts, and they too spake seldom of the Noldoli, save sadly or in whispers behind closed doors; and those few of the Noldoli that remained behind were named the Aulenossë or kindred of Aulë, or were taken into the other kindreds, and the Gnome-folk has no place or name remaining now in all Valinor.

Now is it to tell that after a great while it seemed to Manwë that the hunt of the Gods availed nothing, and that surely Melko is now escaped out of Valinor; wherefore he sent Sorontur into the world, and Sorontur came not back for long, and still Tulkas and many others ranged the land, but Manwë stood beside the darkened Trees and his heart was very heavy as he pondered deep and gloomily, but at that time could he see little light of hope. Suddenly there is a sound of wings in that place, for Sorontur King of Eagles is come again on strong wings through the dusk, and behold alighting on the boughs of darkened Silpion he tells how Melko is now broken into the world and many evil spirits are gathered to him: "but," quoth he, "methinks never more will Utumna open unto him, and already is he busy making himself new dwellings in that region of the North where stand the Iron Mountains very high and terrible to see. Yet O Manwë Lord of the Air, other tidings have I also for thy ear, for lo! as I winged my way homeward hither over the black seas and over the unkindly lands a sight I saw of greatest wonder and amaze:

a fleet of white ships that drifted empty in the gales, and some were burning with bright fires, and as I marvelled behold I saw a great concourse of folk upon the shores of the Great Lands, and they gazed all westward, but some were still wandering in the ice – for know, this was at that place where are the crags of Helkaraksë and the murderous waters of Qerkaringa flowed of old, which now are stopped with ice. Swooping methought I heard the sound of wailing and of sad words spoken in the Eldar tongue; and this tale do I bring to thee for thy unravelling."

But Manwë knew thereby that the Noldoli were gone for ever and their ships burned or abandoned, and Melko too was in the world, and the hunt of no avail; and belike it is in memory of those deeds that it has ever been a saying in the mouths of Elves and Men that those burn their boats who put all hope from them of change of mind or counsel. Therefore now Manwë lifted up his unmeasurable voice calling to the Gods, and all those about the wide lands of Valinor hearkened and returned.

There first came Tulkas weary and dust-covered, for none had leapt about that plain as he. Seven times had he encompassed all its width and thrice had he scaled the mountain-wall, and all those measureless slopes and pastures, meads and forests, he had traversed, burnt by his desire to punish the spoiler of Valinor. There came Lórien and leaned against the withered bole of Silpion, and wept the wrack of his quiet gardens by the trampling hunt; there too was Meássë and with her Makar, and his hand was red for he had come upon twain of Melko's comrades as they fled, and he slew them as they ran, and he alone had aught of joy in those ill times. Ossë was there and his beard of green was torn and his eyes were dim, and he gasped leaning on a staff and was very much athirst, for mighty as he was about the seas and tireless, such desperate travail on the bosom of Earth spent his vigour utterly.

Salmar and Ómar stood by and their instruments of music made no sound and they were heavy of heart, yet not so bitterly as was Aulë, lover of the earth and of all things made or gained by good labour therefrom, for of all the Gods he had loved Valmar most wholly and Kôr and all their treasures, and the smile of the fair plains without, and its ruin cut his heart. With him was Yavanna, Earth-queen, and she had hunted with the Gods and was spent; but Vána and Nessa wept as maidens still beside the founts of gold Kulullin.

Ulmo alone came not to the Trees, but went down to the beach of Eldamar, and there he stood gazing into the gloom far out to sea, and he called often with his most mighty voice as though he would draw back those truants to the bosom of the Gods, and whiles he played deep longing music on his magic conches, and to him alone, lest it be[7] Varda lady of the stars, was the going of the Gnomes a greater grief than even the ruin of the Trees. Aforetime had Ulmo loved the Solosimpi very dearly, yet when he heard of their slaughter by the Gnomes he grieved indeed but anger hardened not his heart, for Ulmo was foreknowing more than all the Gods, even than great Manwë, and perchance he saw many of the things that should spring from that flight and the dread pains of the unhappy Noldoli in the world, and the anguish wherewith they would expiate the blood of Kópas, and he would that it need not be.

Now when all were thus come together, then spake Manwë to them and told the tidings of Sorontur and how the chase had failed, but at that time the Gods were wildered in the gloom and had little counsel, and sought each one his home and places of old delight now dead, and there sat in silence and dark pondering. Yet some fared ever and anon out upon the plain and gazed wistfully at the faded Trees as though those withered boughs would one day burgeon with new light: but this came not to pass, and Valinor was full of shadows and of gloom, and the Elves wept and could not be comforted, and the Noldoli had bitter sorrow in the northern lands.

Thereafter in a great time it pierced the grief and the weariness of the Gods that light is gone from Valinor for ever, and that never again will those Trees bloom again at their appointed times. Only the light of the stars remained, save where a glow lay about the fountain of Kulullin playing still or a pale gleam lingered nigh deep Telimpë,[8] vat of dreams. Yet even these were dimmed and tarnished, for the Trees bore dew no more for their replenishment.

Wherefore does Vána arise and seek Lórien, and with them go Urwendi and Silmo[9] and many of both Vali and the Elves; and they gather much light of gold and silver in great vessels and fare sadly to the ruined Trees. There singeth Lórien most wistful songs of magic and enchantment about the stock of Silpion, and he bid water his roots with the radiance of Telimpë; and this was lavishly done, albeit small store thereof remained now in the dwellings of the Gods. In like manner doth Vána, and she sings old golden songs of the happier days, and bids her maidens dance their bright dances even such as they were used to dance upon the sward of the rose-gardens nigh Kulullin, and as they danced she flooded the roots of Laurelin with streams from out her golden jars.

Yet all their singing and enchantment is of little worth, and

though the roots of the Trees seem to drink all that they may pour
yet can they see no stir of life renewed nor faintest gleam of light;
nor withered leaf glows with sap nor blossom lifts its drooping stem.
Indeed in the frenzy of their grief they had poured out all the last
remaining stores of brightness that the Gods retained, had not of a
fortune Manwë and Aulë come upon them in that hour, being drawn
thither by their singing in the gloom, and stayed them, saying: "Lo,
O Vána, and thou O Lórien, what is this rashness? And wherefore
did ye not first take counsel of your brethren? For know ye not that
that which ye spill unthinking upon the earth is become more
precious than all the things the world contains; and when it is gone
perchance not all the wisdom of the Gods may get us more."

Then Vána said: "Pardon, O Manwë Súlimo, and let my sorrow
and my tears be my excuse; yet aforetime did this draught fail never
to refresh the heart of Laurelin, and she bare ever in return a fruit
of light more plentiful than we gave; and methought the Gods sat
darkly in their halls and for the weight of their grief essayed no
remedy of their ills. But behold now have Lórien and I put forth
our spells and nought may they avail," and Vána wept.

Now was it the thought of many that those twain Lórien and
Vána might not avail to heal the wounds of Laurelin and Silpion,
in that no word of the Earth-lady, mother of magics, was mingled
in their spells. Therefore many said: "Let us seek Palúrien, for of
her magic maybe these Trees shall again know some portion of
their ancient glory – and then if light be renewed Aulë and his
craftsmen may repair the hurts of our fair realm, and happiness will
be once more twixt Erumáni and the Sea"[10] – but of the darkness
and ill days that had long been without the hills few recked or
thought.

Now therefore they called for Yavanna, and she came and asked
them what they would, and hearing she wept and spake before them,
saying: "Know ye, O Valar, and ye sons and daughters of the Eldar,
Children of Ilúvatar, first offspring of the forests of the Earth, that
never may these Two Trees bloom again, and others like them may
not be brought to life for many many ages of the world. Many things
shall be done and come to pass, and the Gods grow old, and the
Elves come nigh to fading, ere ye shall see the rekindling of these
Trees or the Magic Sun relit," and the Gods knew not what she
meant, speaking of the Magic Sun, nor did for a long while after. But
Tulkas hearing said: "Why speakest thou these words, O Kémi
Palúrien, for foretelling is not thy wont, and that of evil least of all?"
And others there were who said: "Ay, and never before has Kémi

the Earth-lady been hard of counsel or lacked a spell of deepest virtue," and they besought her to put forth her power. But Yavanna said: " 'Tis of fate and the Music of the Ainur. Such marvels as those Trees of gold and silver may even the Gods make but once, and that in the youth of the world; nor may all my spells avail to do what ye now ask."

Then said Vána: "How then sayest thou, Aulë, mighty contriver, who art called *i·Talka Marda* – Smith of the World – for the might of thy works, how are we to obtain light that is needful to our joy? For what is Valinor without light, or what art thou an thou losest thy skill, as, meseems, in this hour thy spouse has done?"

"Nay," said Aulë, "light may not be fashioned by smithcraft, O Vána-Laisi, nor can any even of the Gods devise it, if the sap of the Trees of wonder be dried for ever." But Palúrien answering also said: "Lo, O Tuivána, and ye beside of the Vali and of the Elves, think ye only and always of Valinor, forgetting the world without? – for my heart saith to me that already were it time for the Gods to take up once more the battle for the world and expel therefrom the powers of Melko ere they be waxen to o'erwhelming strength." But Vána comprehended not Palúrien's mind, thinking only of her Tree of gold, and she abode ill-content; but Manwë and Varda, and with them Aulë and Yavanna, fared thence, and in secret conclave they took deep and searching counsel one of another, and at the last they bethought them of a rede of hope. Then did Manwë call together all the folk of Valinor once more; and that great throng was gathered even in Vána's bower amidst her roses, where Kulullin's fountains were, for the plain without lay now all cold and dark. There came even the leaders of the Elves and sat at the feet of the Gods, nor had that before been done; but when all were come together Aulë arose and said: "Hearken ye all. A rede has Manwë Súlimo Valatúru* to declare, and the mind of the Earth-lady and of the Queen of the Stars is therein, nor yet is my counsel absent."

Then was there a great silence that Manwë might speak, and he said: "Behold O my people, a time of darkness has come upon us, and yet I have it in mind that this is not without the desire of Ilúvatar. For the Gods had well-nigh forgot the world that lies without expectant of better days, and of Men, Ilúvatar's younger sons that soon must come. Now therefore are the Trees withered that so filled our land with loveliness and our hearts with mirth that wider desires came not into them, and so behold, we must turn now

---

* In margin: 'also *Valahíru*'.

our thoughts to new devices whereby light may be shed upon both the world without and Valinor within.''

Then told he them concerning those stores of radiance they still possessed; for of silver light they had no great store save only that that yet lay in Telimpë, and a lesser measure that Aulë had in basons in his smithy. Some indeed had the Eldar lovingly saved in tiny vessels as it flowed and wasted in the soils about the stricken bole, but it was little enough.

Now the smallness of their store of white light was due to many causes, in that Varda had used greatly of it when she kindled mighty stars about the heavens, both at the coming of the Eldar and at other times. Moreover that Tree Silpion bore dew of light less richly far than Laurelin had been wont to do, and nonetheless, for it was less hot and fiery-subtle, did the Gods and Elves have need of it always in their magic crafts, and had mingled it with all manner of things that they devised, and in this were the Noldoli the chief.

Now golden light not even the Gods could tame much to their uses, and had suffered it to gather in the great vat Kulullin to the great increase of its fountains, or in other bright basons and wide pools about their courts, for the health and glory of its radiance was very great. 'Tis said indeed that those first makers of jewels, of whom Fëanor has the greatest fame, alone of the Eldar knew the secret of subtly taming golden light to their uses, and they dared use their knowledge but very sparingly, and now is that perished with them out of the Earth. Yet even of this golden radiance was there no unfailing source, now that Laurelin dripped her sweet dew no more. Of this necessity did Manwë shape his plan, and it was caught from that very sowing of the stars that Varda did of yore; for to each of the stars had she given a heart of silver flame set in vessels of crystals and pale glass and unimagined substances of faintest colours: and these vessels were some made like to boats, and buoyed by their hearts of light they fared ever about Ilwë, yet could they not soar into the dark and tenuous realm of Vaitya that is outside all. Now winged spirits of the utmost purity and beauty – even the most ethereal of those bright choirs of the Mánir and the Súruli who fare about the halls of Manwë on Taniquetil or traverse all the airs that move upon the world – sate in those starry boats and guided them on mazy courses high above the Earth, and Varda gave them names, but few of these are known.

Others there were whose vessels were like translucent lamps set quivering above the world, in Ilwë or on the very confines of Vilna and the airs we breathe, and they flickered and waned for the stirring of the upper winds, yet abode where they hung and moved not; and of these some were very great and beautiful and the Gods and Elves among all their riches loved them; and thence indeed the jewel-makers catch their inspiration. Not least did they love Morwinyon of the west, whose name meaneth the glint at dusk, and of his setting in the heavens much has been told; and of Nielluin too, who is the Bee of Azure, Nielluin whom still may all men see in autumn or in winter burning nigh the foot of Telimektar son of Tulkas whose tale is yet to tell.

But lo! (said Lindo) the beauty of the stars hath drawn me far afield, and yet I doubt not in that great speech, the mightiest Manwë ever spake before the Gods, mention he made of them yet more loving than was mine. For behold, he desired in this manner to bring the hearts of the Gods to consider his design, and having spoken of the stars he shaped thus his final words: "Behold," said Manwë, "this is now the third essay of the Gods to bring light into dark places, and both the Lamps of the North and South, and the Trees of the plain, Melko hath brought to ruin. Now in the air only hath Melko no power for ill, wherefore it is my rede that we build a great vessel brimming with golden light and the hoarded dews of Laurelin, and this do set afloat like a mighty ship high above the dark realms of the Earth. There shall it thread far courses through the airs and pour its light on all the world twixt Valinórë and the Eastern shores."

Now Manwë designed the course of the ship of light to be between the East and West, for Melko held the North and Ungweliant the South, whereas in the West was Valinor and the blessed realms, and in the East great regions of dark lands that craved for light.

Now it is said (quoth Lindo) that, whereas certain of the Gods of their divine being might, an they wished, fare with a great sudden-ness of speed through Vilna and the low airs, yet might none even of the Valar, not Melko himself, nor any other save Manwë and Varda and their folk alone avail to pass beyond: for this was the word of Ilúvatar when he sped them to the world at their desire, that they should dwell for ever within the world if once they entered it, nor should leave it, until its Great End came, being woven about it in the threads of its fate and becoming part thereof. Yet more, to Manwë alone, knowing the purity and glory of his heart, did Ilúvatar grant the power of visiting the uttermost heights; and breathing the great clear Serene which lies so far above the world that no finest dust of it, nor thinnest odour of its lives, nor faintest echo of its song or sorrow comes there; but far below it gleams palely beneath the stars and the shadows of the Sun and Moon faring back and forth from Valinor flutter upon its face. There walks Manwë Súlimo often far out beyond the stars and watches it with love, and he is very near the heart of Ilúvatar.

But this has ever been and is yet the greatest bitterness to Melko, for in no wise of himself could he now forsake the bosom of the Earth, and belike ye shall yet hear how mightily his envy was increased when the great vessels of radiance set sail; but now is it to tell that so moving were the words and so great their wisdom that[11] the most part of the Gods thought his purpose good, and they said: "Let Aulë busy himself then with all his folk in the fashioning of this ship of light", and few said otherwise, though 'tis told that Lórien was little pleased, fearing lest shadow and quiet and secret places ceased to be, and of a surety Vána might think of little else for the greatness of her vain desire to see the rekindling of the Trees.

Then said Aulë: "The task ye set me is of the utmost difficulty, yet will I do all that I may therein," and he begged the aid of Varda the starfashioner, and those twain departed and were lost in the gloom a great while.

The narrative continues with an account of the failure of Aulë and Varda to devise any substance that was not 'too gross to swim the airs or too frail to bear the radiance of Kulullin'; and when this was made known Vána and Lórien asked that, since Manwë's design had failed, he should command Yavanna to attempt the healing of the Trees.

At length therefore did Manwë bid Yavanna to put forth her power, and she was loath, but the clamour of the folk constrained her, and she begged for some of the radiance of white and gold; but of this would Manwë and Aulë spare only two small phials, saying that if the draught of old had power to heal the Trees already had they been blooming, for Vána and Lórien had poured it unstintingly upon their roots. Then sorrowfully Yavanna stood upon the plain and her form trembled and her face was very pale for the greatness of the effort that her being put forth, striving against fate. The phial of gold she held in her right hand and the silver in her left, and standing between the Trees she lifted them on high, and flames of red and of white arose from each like flowers, and the ground shook, and the earth opened, and a growth of flowers and plants leapt up therefrom about her feet, white and blue about her left side and red and gold about her right, and the Gods sat still and in amaze. Then going she cast each phial upon its proper Tree and sang the songs of unfading growth and a song of resurrection after death and withering; and suddenly she sang no more. Midway she stood between the

Trees and utter silence fell, then there was a great noise heard and none knew what passed, but Palúrien lay swooning on the Earth; but many leapt beside her and raised her from the ground, and she trembled and was afraid.

"Vain, O children of the Gods," she cried, "is all my strength. Lo, at your desire I have poured my power upon the Earth like water, and like water the Earth has sucked it from me — it is gone and I can do no more." And the Trees stood still gaunt and stark, and all the companies wept beholding her, but Manwë said: "Weep not, O children of the Gods, the irreparable harm, for many fair deeds may be yet to do, and beauty hath not perished on the earth nor all the counsels of the Gods been turned to nought"; but nonetheless folk left that place in sorrow, save Vána only, and she clung to the bole of Laurelin and wept.

Now was the time of faintest hope and darkness most profound fallen on Valinor that was ever yet; and still did Vána weep, and she twined her golden hair about the bole of Laurelin and her tears dropped softly at its roots; and even as the dew of her gentle love touched that tree, behold, a sudden pale gleam was born in those dark places. Then gazed Vána in wonder, and even where her first tears fell a shoot sprang from Laurelin, and it budded, and the buds were all of gold, and there came light therefrom like a ray of sunlight beneath a cloud.

Then sped Vána a little way out upon the plain, and she lifted up her sweet voice with all her power and it came trembling faintly to the gates of Valmar, and all the Valar heard. Then said Ómar: "'Tis the voice of Vána's lamentation," but Salmar said: "Nay, listen more, for rather is there joy in that sound," and all that stood by hearkened, and the words they heard were *I·kal'antúlien*, Light hath returned.

Loud then was the murmur about the streets of Valmar, and folk sped thronging over the plain, and when they beheld Vána beneath the Tree and the new shoot of gold then suddenly did a song of very mighty praise and joy burst forth on every tongue; and Tulkas said: "Lo, mightier have the spells of Yavanna proved than her foretelling!" But Yavanna gazing upon Vána's face said: "Alas, 'tis not so, for in this have my spells played but a lesser part, and more potent has the gentle love of Vána been and her falling tears a dew more healing and more tender than all the radiance of old: yet as for my foretelling, soon wilt thou see, O Tulkas, if thou dost but watch."

Then did all the folk gaze on Laurelin, and behold, those buds opened and put forth leaves, and these were of finest gold and of other kind to those of old, and even as they watched the branch bore golden blossom, and it was thronged with flowers. Now as swiftly as its blossoms opened full it seemed a gust of wind came suddenly and shook them from their slender stems, blowing them about the heads of those that watched like jets of fire, and folk thought there was evil in that; but many of the Eldar chased those shining petals far and wide and gathered them in baskets, yet save such as were of golden threads or of other metals these might not contain those ardent blooms and were all consumed and burnt, that the petals were lost again.

One flower there was however greater than the others, more shining, and more richly golden, and it swayed to the winds but fell not; and it grew, and as it grew of its own radiant warmth it fructified. Then as its petals fell and were treasured a fruit there was of great beauty hanging from that bough of Laurelin, but the leaves of the bough grew sere and they shrivelled and shone no more. Even as they dropped to earth the fruit waxed wonderfully, for all the sap and radiance of the dying Tree were in it, and the juices of that fruit were like quivering flames of amber and of red and its pips like shining gold, but its rind was of a perfect lucency smooth as a glass whose nature is transfused with gold and therethrough the moving of its juices could be seen within like throbbing furnace-fires. So great became the light and richness of that growth and the weight of its fruitfulness that the bough bent thereunder, and it hung as a globe of fires before their eyes.

Then said Yavanna to Aulë: "Bear thou up the branch, my lord, lest it snap and the fruit of wonder be dashed rudely to the ground; and the greatest ruth would that be, for know ye all that this is the last flame of life that Laurelin shall show." But Aulë had stood by as one lost in sudden thought since first that fruit came to ripening, and he answered now saying: "Very long indeed did Varda and I seek through the desolate homes and gardens for materials of our craft. Now do I know that Ilúvatar has brought my desire into my hand." Then calling to Tulkas to aid him he severed the stem of that fruit, and they that behold gasped and were astonied at his ruthlessness.

Loudly they murmured, and some cried: "Woe to him that ravishes anew our Tree," and Vána was in great ire. Yet did none dare to draw nigh, for those twain Aulë and Tulkas might scarcely bear up even upon their godlike shoulders that great globe of flame and were tottering beneath it. Hearing their anger indeed Aulë stayed, saying: "Cease ye of little wisdom and have a patience," but even with those words his foot went astray and he stumbled, and even Tulkas might not bear that fruit alone, so that it fell, and striking stony ground burst asunder. Straightway such a blinding radiance leapt forth as even the full bloom of Laurelin had not yielded of old, and the darkened eyes of the Vali were dazzled so that they fell back stunned; but a pillar of light rose from that place smiting the heavens that the stars paled above it and the face of Taniquetil went red afar off, and Aulë alone of all those there was unmoved by sorrow. Then said Aulë: "Of this can I make a ship of light – surpassing even the desire of Manwë," and now Varda and many others, even Vána, understood his purpose and were glad. But they made a mighty corbel of twisted gold, and strewing it with ardent petals of its own bloom they laid therein the halves of the fruit of noon and uplifting it with many hands bore it away with much singing and great hope. Then coming to the courts of Aulë they set it down, and thereupon began the great smithying of the Sun; and this was the most cunning-marvellous of all the works of Aulë Talkamarda, whose works are legion. Of that perfect rind a vessel did he make, diaphanous and shining, yet of a tempered strength, for with spells of his own he overcame its brittleness, nor in any way was its subtle delicacy thereby diminished.

Now the most ardent radiance poured therein neither spilled nor dimmed, nor did that vessel receive any injury therefrom, yet would it swim the airs more lightly than a bird; and Aulë was overjoyed, and he fashioned that vessel like a great ship broad of beam, laying one half of the rind within the other so that its strength might not be broken.

There follows an account of how Vána, repenting of her past murmurings, cut short her golden hair and gave it to the Gods, and from her hair they wove sails and ropes 'more strong than any mariner hath seen, yet of the slenderness of gossamer'. The masts and spars of the ship were all of gold.

Then that the Ship of the Heavens might be made ready unto the last, the unfading petals of the latest flower of Laurelin were gathered like a star at her prow, and tassels and streamers of glancing light were hung about her bulwarks, and a flash of lightning was caught in her mast to be a pennant; but all that vessel was filled to the brim with the blazing radiance of gold Kulullin and mingled therein drops of the juices of the fruit of noon, and these were very hot, and thereafter scarcely might the bosom of the Earth withhold her, and she leapt at her cords like a captive bird that listeth for the airs. Then did the Gods name that ship, and they called her Sári which

is the Sun, but the Elves Úr which is fire;[12] but many other names
does she bear in legend and in poesy. The Lamp of Vána is she
named among the Gods in memory of Vána's tears and her sweet
tresses that she gave; and the Gnomes call her Galmir the goldgleamer[13] and Glorvent the ship of gold, and Bráglorin the blazing
vessel, and many a name beside; and her names among Men no man
has counted them.

Behold now it is to be told how while that galleon was a-building
others nigh to where the Two Trees once grew fashioned a great
bason and folk laboured mightily at it. Its floor they made of gold
and its walls of polished bronze, and an arcade of golden pillars
topped with fires engirdled it, save only on the East; but Yavanna
set a great and nameless spell around it, so that therein was poured
the most of the waters of the fruit of noon and it became a bath
of fire. Indeed is it not called Tanyasalpë, the bowl of fire, even
Faskalanúmen, the Bath of the Setting Sun, for here when Urwendi
after returned from the East and the first sunset came on Valinor the
ship was drawn down and its radiance refreshed against new voyagings
on the morrow while the Moon held High Heaven.

Now the making of this place of fire is more wondrous than seems,
for so subtle were those radiances that set in the air they spilled not
nor sank, nay rather they rose and floated away far above Vilna,
being of the utmost buoyancy and lightness; yet now did nought
escape from Faskalan which burnt amid the plain, and light came to
Valinor therefrom, yet by reason of the deepness of the bason it
fared not far abroad and the ring of shadows stood close in.

Then said Manwë, looking upon the glory of that ship as it strained
to be away: "Who shall steer us this boat and guide its course above
the realms of Earth, for even the holy bodies of the Valar, meseems,
may not for long endure to bathe in this great light."

But a great thought came into the heart of Urwendi, and she said
that she was not adread, and begged leave to become the mistress
of the Sun and to make herself ready for that office as Ilúvatar set it
in her heart to do. Then did she bid a many of her maidens follow
her, even of those who had aforetime watered the roots of Laurelin
with light, and casting aside their raiment they went down into that
pool Faskalan as bathers into the sea, and its golden foams went over
their bodies, and the Gods saw them not and were afraid. But after
a while they came again to the brazen shores and were not as before,
for their bodies were grown lucent and shone as with an ardour
within, and light flashed from their limbs as they moved, nor might
any raiment endure to cover their glorious bodies any more. Like

air were they, and they trod as lightly as does sunlight on the earth, and saying no word they climbed upon the ship, and that vessel heaved against its great cords and all the folk of Valinor might scarce restrain it.

Now at last by Manwë's command do they climb the long slopes of Taniquetil and draw i·Kalaventë the Ship of Light along with them, nor is that any great task; and now do they stand on the wide space before great Manwë's doors, and the ship is on the western slope of the mountain trembling and tugging at its bonds, and already so great is its glory become that sunbeams pour out over the shoulders of Taniquetil and a new light is in the sky, and the waters of the Shadowy Seas beyond are touched with such fire as they never yet had seen. In that hour 'tis said that all creatures that wandered in the world stood still and wondered, even as Manwë going spake to Urwendi and said: "Go now, most wondrous maiden washed in fire, and steer the ship of divine light above the world, that joy may search out its narrowest crannies and all the things that sleep within its bosom may awake";[14] but Urwendi answered not, looking only eagerly to the East, and Manwë bade cast the ropes that held her, and straightway the Ship of the Morning arose above Taniquetil and the bosom of the air received it.

Ever as it rose it burned the brighter and the purer till all Valinor was filled with radiance, and the vales of Erúmáni and the Shadowy Seas were bathed in light, and sunshine was spilled on the dark plain of Arvalin, save only where Ungweliantë's clinging webs and darkest fumes still lay too thick for any radiance to filter through.

Then all looking up saw that heaven was blue, and very bright and beautiful, but the stars fled as that great dawn came upon the world; and a gentle wind blew from the cold lands to meet the vessel and filled its gleaming sails, and white vapours mounted from off the misty seas below toward her, that her prow seemed to cleave a white and airy foam. Yet did she waver not, for the Mánir that fared about her drew her by golden cords, and higher and higher the Sun's great galleon arose, until even to the sight of Manwë it was but a disc of fire wreathed in veils of splendour that slowly and majestically wandered from the West.

Now ever as it drew further on its way so grew the light in Valinor more mellow, and the shadows of the houses of the Gods grew long, slanting away towards the waters of the Outer Seas, but Taniquetil threw a great westering shadow that waxed ever longer and deeper, and it was afternoon in Valinor.'

Then said Gilfanon laughing: 'Nay, but, good sir, you lengthen the tale mightily, for methinks you love to dwell upon the works and deeds of the great Gods, but an you set not a measure to your words our stranger here will live not to hear of those things that happened in the world when at length the Gods gave to it the light they so long had withholden – and such tales, methinks, were a variety pleasing to hear.'

But Eriol had of a sooth been listening very eagerly to the sweet voice of Lindo, and he said: 'But a little while agone, a day perchance the Eldar would esteem it, did I come hither, yet no longer do I love the name of stranger, neither will Lindo ever lengthen the tale beyond my liking, whatsoever he tells, but behold this history is all to my heart.'

But Lindo said: 'Nay, nay, I have indeed more to tell; yet, O Eriol, the things that Gilfanon hath upon his lips are well worth the hearing – indeed never have I nor any here heard a full count of these matters. As soon therefore as may be will I wind up my tale and make an end, but three nights hence let us have another tale-telling, and it shall be one of greater ceremony, and musics there shall be, and all the children of the House of Lost Play shall here be gathered together at his feet to hear Gilfanon relate the travail of the Noldoli and the coming of Mankind.'

Now these words mightily pleased Gilfanon and Eriol, and many beside were glad, but now doth Lindo proceed:

'Know then that to such vast heights did the Sunship climb, and climbing blazed ever hotter and brighter, that ere long its glory was wider than ever the Gods conceived of when that vessel was still harboured in their midst. Everywhere did its great light pierce and all the vales and darkling woods, the bleak slopes and rocky streams, lay dazzled by it, and the Gods were amazed. Great was the magic and wonder of the Sun in those days of bright Urwendi, yet not so tender and so delicately fair as had the sweet Tree Laurelin once been; and thus whisper of new discontent awoke in Valinor, and words ran among the children of the Gods, for Mandos and Fui were wroth, saying that Aulë and Varda would for ever be meddling with the due order of the world, making it a place where no quiet or peaceful shadow could remain; but Lórien sat and wept in a grove of trees beneath the shade of Taniquetil and looked upon his gardens stretching beneath, still disordered by the great hunt of the Gods, for he had not had the heart for their mending. There the nightingales were silent for the heat danced above the trees, and his poppies were withered, and his evening flowers drooped and gave no scent; and Silmo stood sadly by Telimpë that gleamed wanly as still waters rather than the shining dew of Silpion, so overmastering was the great light of day. Then Lórien arose and said to Manwë: "Call back your glittering ship, O Lord of the Heavens, for the eyes of us ache by reason of its flaming, and beauty and soft sleep is driven far away. Rather the darkness and our memories than this, for this is not the old loveliness of Laurelin, and Silpion is no more." Nor were any of the Gods utterly content, knowing in their hearts that they had done a greater thing than they at first knew, and never again would Valinor see such ages as had passed; and Vána said that Kulullin's fount was dulled and her garden wilted in the heat, and her roses lost their hues and fragrance, for the Sun then sailed nearer to the Earth than it now does.

Then Manwë chid them for their flickleness and discontent, but they were not appeased; and suddenly spake Ulmo, coming from outer Vai: "Lord Manwë, neither are their counsels nor thine to be despised. Have ye then not yet understood, O Valar, wherein lay much of the great beauty of the Trees of old? – In change, and in slow alternation of fair things, the passing blending sweetly with that which was to come."

But Lórien said suddenly: "O Valatúru, the Lord of Vai speaketh words wiser than ever before, and they fill me with a great longing," and he left them thereupon and went out upon the plain, and it was then three daytimes, which is the length of three blossomings of Laurelin of old, since the Ship of Morning was unmoored. Then for four daytimes more sate Lórien beside the stock of Silpion and the shadows gathered shyly round him, for the Sun was far to the East, beating about the heavens where it listed, since Manwë had not as yet ruled its course and Urwendi was bidden fare as seemed good to her. Yet even so Lórien is not appeased, not though the darkness of the mountains creep across the plain, and a mist bloweth in from off the sea and a vague and flitting twilight gathers once more in Valinor, but long he sits pondering why the spells of Yavanna wrought only upon Laurelin.

Then Lórien sang to Silpion, saying that the Valar were lost 'in a wilderness of gold and heat, or else in shadows full of death and unkindly glooms,' and he touched the wound in the bole of the Tree.

Lo, even as he touched that cruel hurt, a light glowed faintly there as if radiant sap still stirred within, but a low branch above Lórien's bowed head burgeoned suddenly, and leaves of a very dark green, long and oval, budded and unfolded upon it, yet was all the Tree beside bare and dead and has ever been so since. Now it was at that time seven times seven days since the fruit of noon was born upon Laurelin, and many of the Eldar and of the sprites and of the Gods were drawn nigh, listening to Lórien's song; but he heeded them not, gazing upon the Tree.

Lo, its new leaves were crusted with a silver moisture, and their undersides were white and set with pale gleaming filaments. Buds there were of flowers also upon the bough, and they opened, but a dark mist of the sea gathered about the tree, and the air grew bitterly cold as it never before had been in Valinor, and those blossoms faded and fell and none heeded them. One only was there at the branch's end that opening shone of its own light and no mist or cold harmed it, but indeed waxing it seemed to suck the very vapours and transform them subtly to the silver substance of its body; and it grew to be a very pale and wondrous glistering flower, nor did even the purest snow upon Taniquetil gleaming in the light of Silpion outrival it, and its heart was of white flame and it throbbed, waxing and waning marvellously. Then said Lórien for the joy of his heart: "Behold the Rose of Silpion", and that rose grew till the fruit of Laurelin had been but little greater, and ten thousand crystal petals were in that flower, and it was drenched in a fragrant dew like honey and this dew was light. Now Lórien would suffer none to draw near, and this will he rue for ever: for the branch upon which the Rose hung yielded all its sap and withered, nor even yet would he suffer that blossom to be plucked gently down, being enamoured of its loveliness and lusting to see it grow mightier than the fruit of noon, more glorious than the Sun.

Then snapped the withered bough and the Rose of Silpion fell, and some of its dewy light was roughly shaken from it, and here and there a petal was crushed and tarnished, and Lórien cried aloud and sought to lift it gently up, but it was too great. Therefore did the Gods let send to Aulë's halls, for there was a great silver charger, like to a table of the giants, and they set the latest bloom of Silpion upon it, and despite its hurts its glory and fragrance and pale magic were very great indeed.

Now when Lórien had mastered his grief and ruth he spake the counsel that Ulmo's words had called to his heart: that the Gods build another vessel to match the galleon of the Sun, "and it shall be made from the Rose of Silpion," said he, "and in memory of the waxing and waning of these Trees for twelve hours shall the Sunship sail the heavens and leave Valinor, and for twelve shall Silpion's pale bark mount the skies, and there shall be rest for tired eyes and weary hearts."

This then was the manner of the shaping of the Moon, for Aulë would not dismember the loveliness of the Rose of Silver, and he called rather to him certain of those Eldar of his household who were of the Noldoli of old[15] and had consorted with the jewel-makers. Now these revealed to him much store of crystals and delicate glasses that Fëanor and his sons[16] had laid up in secret places in Sirnúmen, and with the aid of those Elves and of Varda of the stars, who gave even of the light of those frail boats of hers to give limpid clearness to their fashioning, he brought to being a substance thin as a petal of a rose, clear as the most transparent elfin glass, and very smooth, yet might Aulë of his skill bend it and fashion it, and naming it he called it *virin*. Of *virin* now he built a marvellous vessel, and often have men spoken of the Ship of the Moon, yet is it scarce like to any bark that sailed or sea or air. Rather was it like an island of pure glass, albeit not very great, and tiny lakes there were bordered with snowy flowers that shone, for the water of those pools that gave them sap was the radiance of Telimpë. Midmost of that shimmering isle was wrought a cup of that crystalline stuff that Aulë made and therein the magic Rose was set, and the glassy body of the vessel sparkled wonderfully as it gleamed therein. Rods there were and perchance they were of ice, and they rose upon it like aëry masts, and sails were caught to them by slender threads, and Uinen wove them of white mists and foam, and some were sprent with glinting scales of silver fish, some threaded with tiniest stars like points of light – sparks caught in snow when Nielluin was shining.

Thus was the Ship of the Moon, the crystal island of the Rose, and the Gods named it Rána, the Moon, but the fairies Sil, the Rose,[17] and many a sweet name beside. Ilsaluntë or the silver shallop has it been called, and thereto the Gnomes have called it Minethlos or the argent isle and Crithosceleg the disc of glass.

Now Silmo begged to sail upon the oceans of the firmament therein, but he might not, for neither was he of the children of the air nor might he find a way to cleanse his being of its earthwardness as had Urwendi[18] done, and little would it have availed to enter Faskalan had he dared essay it, for then would Rána have shrivelled before him. Manwë bade therefore Ilinsor, a spirit of the Súruli who loved the snows and the starlight and aided Varda in many of her works, to pilot this strange-gleaming boat, and with him went many another spirit of the air arrayed in robes of silver and white, or else of palest gold; but an aged Elf with hoary locks stepped upon the Moon unseen and hid him in the Rose, and there dwells he ever since and tends that flower, and a little white turret has he builded on the Moon where often he climbs and watches the heavens, or the world beneath, and that is Uolë Kúvion who sleepeth never. Some indeed have named him the Man in the Moon, but Ilinsor is it rather who hunts the stars.

Now is to tell how the plan that Lórien devised was changed, for the white radiance of Silpion is by no means so buoyant and ethereal as is the flame of Laurelin, nor *vírin* so little weighty as the rind of the bright fruit of noon; and when the Gods laded the white ship with light and would launch it upon the heavens, behold, it would not rise above their heads. Moreover, behold, that living Rose continued to give forth a honey as of light that distills upon the isle of glass, and a dew of moonbeams glistens there, yet rather does this weigh the vessel than buoy it as did the increase of the Sunship's flames. So is it that Ilinsor must return at times, and that overflowing radiance of the Rose is stored in Valinor against dark days – and it is to tell that such days come ever and anon, for then the white flower of the isle wanes and scarcely shines, and then must it be refreshed and watered with its silver dew, much as Silpion was wont of old to be.

Hence was it that a pool was builded hard by the dark southern wall of Valmar, and of silver and white marbles were its walls, but dark yews shut it in, being planted in a maze most intricate about it. There Lórien hoarded the pale dewy light of that fair Rose, and he named it the Lake Irtinsa.

So comes it that for fourteen nights men may see Rána's bark float upon the airs, and for other fourteen the heavens know it not; while even on those fair nights when Rána fares abroad it showeth not ever the same aspect as doth Sári the glorious, for whereas that bright galleon voyageth even above Ilwë and beyond the stars and cleaveth a dazzling way blinding the heavens, highest of all things recking little of winds or motions of the airs, yet Ilinsor's bark is heavier and less filled with magic and with power, and fareth never above the skies but saileth in the lower folds of Ilwë threading a white swathe among the stars. For this reason the high winds trouble it at times, tugging at its misty shrouds; and often are these torn and scattered, and the Gods renew them. At times too are the petals of the Rose ruffled, and its white flames blown hither and thither like a silver candle guttering in the wind. Then doth Rána heave and toss about the air, as often you may see him, and mark the slender curve of his bright keel, his prow now dipping, now his stern; and whiles again he sails serenely to the West, and up through the pure lucency of his frame the wide Rose of Silpion is seen, and some say the aged form of Uolë Kúvion beside.

Then indeed is the Ship of the Moon very fair to look upon, and the Earth is filled with slender lights and deep quick-moving shadows, and radiant dreams go with cool wings about the world, but Lórien has ruth amid his gladness, because his flower bears yet, and will for ever, the faint marks of its bruising and its fall; and all men can see them clearly.

But[19] lo,' saith Lindo, 'I run on ahead, for yet have I only told that the silver ship is newly built, and Ilinsor yet but first stepped aboard – and now do the Gods draw that vessel once again up the steep sides of old Taniquetil singing as they go songs of Lórien's folk that long have been dumb in Valinor. Slower was that wayfaring than the lifting of the Ship of Morn, and all the folk strain lustily at the ropes, until Oromë coming harnesses thereto a herd of wild white horses, and thus comes the vessel to the topmost place.

Then behold, the galleon of the Sun is seen afar beating golden from the East, and the Valar marvel to descry the glowing peaks of many a mountain far away, and isles glimmering green in seas once dark. Then cried Ossë: "Look, O Manwë, but the sea is blue, as blue wellnigh as Ilwë that thou lovest!" and "Nay," said Manwë, "envy we not Ilwë, for the sea is not blue alone, but grey and green and purple, and most beauteous-flowered with foaming white. Nor jade nor amethyst nor porphyry set with diamonds and with pearls outrival the waters of the Great and little seas when the sunlight drenches them."

So saying Manwë sent Fionwë his son, swiftest of all to move about the airs, and bade him say to Urwendi that the bark of the Sun come back awhile to Valinor, for the Gods have counsels for her ear; and Fionwë fled most readily, for he had conceived a great love for that bright maiden long ago, and her loveliness now, when bathed in fire she sate as the radiant mistress of the Sun, set him aflame with the eagerness of the Gods. So was it that Urwendi brought her ship unwilling above Valinor, and Oromë cast a noose of gold about it, and it was drawn slowly down upon the Earth, and behold, the woods upon Taniquetil glowed once more in the mingled light of silver and of gold, and all were minded of the ancient blending of the Trees; but Ilsaluntë paled before the galleon of the Sun till almost it seemed to burn no more. So ended the first day upon the world, and it was very long and full of many marvellous deeds that Gilfanon may tell; but now the Gods beheld the evening deepen over the world as the Sunship was drawn down and the glow upon the mountains faded, and the sparkle of the seas went out. Then the primeval darkness crept out again once more from many stealthy lairs, but Varda was

glad to see the steady shining of the stars. Far upon the plain was
Sári drawn, and when she was gone Ilsaluntë was haled upon the
topmost peak so that his white lucency fell out thence over the wide
world and the first night was come. Indeed in these days darkness
is no more within the borders of the world, but only night, and night
is another and a different thing, by reason of the Rose of Silpion.

Now however does Aulë fill the brimming vessel of that flower
with white radiance, and many of the Súruli white-winged glide
beneath and bear it slowly up and set it among the company of the
stars. There does it swim slowly, a pale and glorious thing, and
Ilinsor and his comrades sit them upon its rim and with shimmering
oars urge it bravely through the sky; and Manwë breathed upon its
bellying sails till it was wafted far away, and the beat of the unseen
oars against the winds of night faded and grew faint.

Of this manner was the first rising of the Moon above Taniquetil,
and Lórien rejoiced, but Ilinsor was jealous of the supremacy of the
Sun, and he bade the starry mariners flee before him and the constellate lamps go out, but many would not, and often he set sail in
chase of them, and the little ships of Varda fled before the huntsman
of the firmament, and were not caught: – and that, said Lindo, 'is
all, methinks, I know to tell of the building of those marvellous
ships and their launching on the air.'[20]

'But,' said Eriol, 'nay, surely that is not so, for at the tale's beginning methought you promised us words concerning the present
courses of the Sun and Moon and their rising in the East, and I for
one, by the leave of the others here present am not minded to release
you of your word.'

Then quoth Lindo laughing, 'Nay, I remember not the promise,
and did I make it then it was rash indeed, for the things you ask are
nowise easy to relate, and many matters concerning the deeds in
those days in Valinor are hidden from all save only the Valar. Now
however am I fain rather to listen, and thou Vairë perchance will
take up the burden of the tale.'

Thereat did all rejoice, and the children clapped their hands, for
dearly did they love those times when Vairë was the teller of the
tale; but Vairë said:

'Lo, tales I tell of the deep days, and the first is called *The Hiding
of Valinor*.'

NOTES

1 The manuscript has here *Gilfan a·Davrobel*, but in the rejected

earlier version of this passage the reading is *Gilfanon a·Davrobel*,
suggesting that *Gilfan* was not intentional.

2 See pp. 24–5 on the relation of Tavrobel to the Staffordshire village
   of Great Haywood. At Great Haywood the river Sow joins the Trent.

3 In the rejected version of this 'interlude' Gilfanon's history is
   differently recounted: 'he was long before an Ilkorin and had dwelt
   ages back in Hisilómë'; 'he came to Tol Eressëa after the great
   march [i.e. Inwë's 'march into the world', the great expedition from
   Kôr, see p. 26], for he had adopted blood-kinship with the Noldoli.' –
   This is the first occurrence of the term *Ilkorin*, which refers to Elves
   who were 'not of Kôr' (cf. the later term *Úmanyar*, Elves 'not of
   Aman'). *Artanor* is the precursor of Doriath.

4 Gilfanon, a Gnome, is here called the oldest of the *fairies*; see p. 51.

5 No explanation of 'the House of the Hundred Chimneys', near the bridge
   of Tavrobel, is known to me, but I have never visited Great Haywood,
   and it may be that there was (or is) a house there that gave rise to it.

6 The rejected form of the 'interlude' is quite different in its latter part:

> Therefore said Lindo in answer to Eriol: 'Behold, Gilfanon here
> can tell you much of such matters, but first of all must you be
> told of the deeds that were done in Valinor when Melko slew the
> Trees and the Gnomes marched away into the darkness. 'Tis a long
> tale but well worth the hearkening.' For Lindo loved to tell such
> tales and sought often an occasion for recalling them; but Gilfanon
> said: 'Speak on, my Lindo, but methinks the tale will not be told
> tonight or for many a night after, and I shall have fared long back
> to Tavrobel.' 'Nay,' said Lindo, 'I will not make the tale overlong,
> and tomorrow shall be all your own.' And so saying Gilfanon sighed,
> but Lindo lifted up his voice . . .

7 'lest it be': this curious expression is clear in the manuscript; the
   usage seems wholly unrecorded, but the meaning intended must be
   'unless it be', i.e. 'to him alone, unless also to Varda . . .'

8 On *Telimpë* as the name of the 'Moon-cauldron', rather than *Silindrin*,
   see pp. 79 and 129 note 2.

9 See pp. 73, 88. At previous occurrences the name is *Urwen*, not *Urwendi*.

10 'twixt Erumáni and the Sea': i.e., the Outer Sea, Vai, the western
   bound of Valinor.

11 The passage beginning 'For behold, he desired in this manner . . .'
   on p. 182 and continuing to this point was added on a detached sheet
   and replaced a very much shorter passage in which Manwë briefly
   declared his plan, and nothing was said about the powers of the
   Valar. But I do not think that the replacement was composed signi-
   ficantly later than the body of the text.

12 The earlier reading here was: 'Then did the Gods name that ship,
   and they called her Ûr which is the Sun', etc.

13 The earlier reading here was: 'and the Gnomes call her Aur the Sun,
   and Galmir the goldgleamer', etc.

14 An isolated note refers to the coming forth of more wholesome creatures when the Sun arose (i.e. over the Great Lands), and says that 'all the birds sang in the first dawn'.

15 The Aulenossë: see p. 176.

16 This is the first appearance of the Sons of Fëanor.

17 Earlier reading: 'the silver rose'.

18 *Urwendi*: manuscript *Urwandi*, but I think that this was probably unintended.

19 From this point the text of the *Tale of the Sun and Moon* ceases to be written over an erased pencilled original, and from the same point the original text is extant in another book. In fact, to the end of the *Tale of the Sun and Moon* the differences are slight, no more than alterations of wording; but the original text does explain the fact that at the first occurrence of the name *Gilfanon* on p. 189 the original reading was *Ailios*. One would guess in any case that this was a slip, a reversion to an earlier name, and that this is so is shown by the first version, which has, for 'many marvellous deeds that Gilfanon may tell' (p. 194), 'many marvellous deeds as Ailios shall tell'.

20 From this point the second version diverges sharply from the first. The first reads as follows:

> And that is all, methinks,' said Lindo, 'that I know to tell of those fairest works of the Gods'; but Ailios said: 'Little doth it cost thee to spin the tale, an it be of Valinor; it is a while since ye offered us a . . . . . tale concerning the rising of the Sun and Moon in the East, and a flow of speech has poured from thee since then, but now art thou minded to [?tease], and no word of that promise.' Of a truth Ailios beneath his roughness liked the words of Lindo as well as any, and he was eager to learn of the matter.
>
> 'That is easy told,' said Lindo . . .

> What follows in the original version relates to the matter of the next chapter (see p. 220 note 2).

> Ailios here claims that a promise made by Lindo has not been fulfilled, just as does Eriol, more politely, in the second version. The beginning of the tale in the first version is not extant, and perhaps as it was originally written Lindo did make this promise; but in the second he says no such thing (indeed Eriol's question was 'Whence be the Sun and Moon?'), and at the end of his tale denies that he had done so, when Eriol asserts it.

Changes made to names in
The Tale of the Sun and Moon

Amnor < *Amnos* (*Amnos* is the form in *The Flight of the Noldoli*, < *Emnon*; the form *Amnon* also occurs, see p. 172).

For changes in the passage on the names of the Sun see notes 12 and 13.

Gilfanon 〈 *Ailios* (p. 189, at the first occurrence only, see note 19).

Minethlos 〈 *Mainlos*.

Uolë Kúvion 〈 *Uolë Mikúmi*, only at the second occurrence on p. 193; at the first occurrence, *Uolë Mikúmi* was left unchanged, though I have given *Uolë Kúvion* in the text.

Ship of Morning 〈 *Kalaventë* (p. 190; *i·Kalaventë* 'the Ship of Light' occurs unemended in the text on p. 188).

the Sunship's flames 〈 *the flames of Kalaventë* (p. 193).

Sári 〈 *Kalavénë* (pp. 193, 195. *Kalavénë* is the form in the original version, see note 19).

Commentary on
The Tale of the Sun and Moon

The effect of the opening of this tale is undoubtedly to emphasize more strongly than in the later accounts the horror aroused by the deeds of the Noldoli (notable is Aulë's bitterness against them, of which nothing is said afterwards), and also the finality and absoluteness of their exclusion from Valinor. But the idea that some Gnomes remained in Valinor (the Aulenossë, p. 176) survived; cf. *The Silmarillion* p. 84:

> And of all the Noldor in Valinor, who were grown now to a great people, but one tithe refused to take the road: some for the love that they bore to the Valar (and to Aulë not least), some for the love of Tirion and the many things that they had made; none for fear of peril by the way.

Sorontur's mission and the tidings that he brought back were to be abandoned. Very striking is his account of the empty ships drifting, of which 'some were burning with bright fires': the origin of Fëanor's burning of the ships of the Teleri at Losgar in *The Silmarillion* (p. 90), where however there is a more evident reason for doing so. That Melko's second dwelling-place in the Great Lands was distinct from Utumna is here expressly stated, as also that it was in the Iron Mountains (cf. pp. 149, 158); the name *Angamandi* 'Hells of Iron' has occurred once in the *Lost Tales*, in the very strange account of the fate of Men after death (p. 77). In later accounts Angband was built on the site of Utumno, but finally they were separated again, and in *The Silmarillion* Angband had existed from ancient days before the captivity of Melkor (p. 47). It is not explained in the present tale why 'never more will Utumna open to him' (p. 176), but doubtless it was because Tulkas and Ulmo broke its gates and piled hills of stone upon them (p. 104).

In the next part of the tale (pp. 177 ff.) much light is cast on my father's early conception of the powers and limitations of the great Valar. Thus

Yavanna and Manwë (brought to this realization by Yavanna?) are shown
to believe that the Valar have done ill, or at least failed to achieve the
wider designs of Ilúvatar ('I have it in mind that this [time of darkness]
is not without the desire of Ilúvatar'): the idea of 'selfish', inward-looking
Gods is plainly expressed, Gods content to tend their gardens and devise
their devisings behind their mountains, leaving 'the world' to shape itself
as it may. And this realization is an essential element in their conceiving
the making of the Sun and Moon, which are to be such bodies as may light
not only 'the blessed realms' (an expression which occurs here for the
first time, p. 182) but all the rest of the dark Earth. Of all this there is
only a trace in *The Silmarillion* (p. 99):

> These things the Valar did, recalling in their twilight the darkness of
> the lands of Arda; and they resolved now to illumine Middle-earth and
> with light to hinder the deeds of Melkor.

Of much interest also is the 'theological' statement in the early narrative
concerning the binding of the Valar to the World as the condition of their
entering it (p. 182); cf. *The Silmarillion* p. 20:

> But this condition Ilúvatar made, or it is the necessity of their love,
> that their power should thenceforward be contained and bounded in
> the World, to be within it for ever, until it is complete, so that they are
> its life and it is theirs.

In the tale this condition is an express physical limitation: none of the
Valar, save Manwë and Varda and their attendant spirits, could pass into
the higher airs above Vilna, though they could move at great speed within
the lowest air.

From the passage on p. 178, where it is said that Ulmo, despite his love
for the Solosimpi and grief at the Kinslaying, was yet not filled with anger
against the Noldoli, for he 'was foreknowing more than all the Gods,
even than great Manwë', it is seen that Ulmo's peculiar concern for the
exiled Eldar – which plays such an important if mysterious part in the
development of the story – was there from the beginning; as also was
Yavanna's thought, expressed in *The Silmarillion* p. 78:

> Even for those who are mightiest under Ilúvatar there is some work
> that they may accomplish once, and once only. The Light of the Trees
> I brought into being, and within Eä I can do so never again.

Yavanna's reference to the Magic Sun and its relighting (which has appeared
in the toast drunk in the evening in the Cottage of Lost Play, pp. 17, 65)
is obviously intended to be obscure at this stage.

There is no later reference to the story of the wastage of light by Lórien
and Vána, pouring it over the roots of the Trees unavailingly.

Turning to Lindo's account of the stars (pp. 181–2), *Morwinyon* has appeared in an earlier tale (p. 114), with the story that Varda dropped it 'as she fared in great haste back to Valinor', and that it 'blazes above the world's edge in the west'; in the present tale Morwinyon (which according to both the Qenya and Gnomish word-lists is Arcturus) is again strangely represented as being a luminary always of the western sky. It is said here that while some of the stars were guided by the Mánir and the Súruli 'on mazy courses', others, including Morwinyon and Nielluin, 'abode where they hung and moved not'. Is the explanation of this that in the ancient myths of the Elves there was a time when the regular apparent movement of all the heavenly bodies from East to West had not yet begun? This movement is nowhere explained mythically in my father's cosmology.

Nielluin ('Blue Bee') is Sirius (in *The Silmarillion* called *Helluin*), and this star had a place in the legend of Telimektar son of Tulkas, though the story of his conversion into the constellation of Orion was never clearly told (cf. *Telumehtar* 'Orion' in *The Lord of the Rings* Appendix E, I). Nielluin was Inwë's son Ingil, who followed Telimektar 'in the likeness of a great bee bearing honey of flame' (see the Appendix on Names under *Ingil* and *Telimektar*).

The course of the Sun and Moon between East and West (rather than in some other direction) is here given a rationale, and the reason for avoiding the South is Ungweliant's presence there. This seems to give Ungweliant a great importance and also a vast area subject to her power of absorbing light. It is not made clear in the tale of *The Darkening of Valinor* where her dwelling was. It is said (p. 151) that Melko wandered 'the dark plains of Eruman, and farther south than anyone yet had penetrated he found a region of the deepest gloom' – the region where he found the cavern of Ungweliant, which had 'a subterranean outlet on the sea'; and after the destruction of the Trees Ungweliant 'gets her gone southward and over the mountains to her home' (p. 154). It is impossible to tell from the vague lines on the little map (p. 81) what was at this time the configuration of the southern lands and seas.

In comparison with the last part of the tale, concerning the last fruit of Laurelin and the last flower of Silpion, the making from them of the Sun and Moon, and the launching of their vessels (pp. 183–95), Chapter XI of *The Silmarillion* (constituted from two later versions not greatly dissimilar the one from the other) is extremely brief. Despite many differences the later versions read in places almost as summaries of the early story, but it is often hard to say whether the shortening depends rather on my father's feeling (certainly present, see p. 174) that the description was too long, was taking too large a place in the total structure, or an actual rejection of some of the ideas it contains, and a desire to diminish the extreme 'concreteness' of its images. Certainly there is here a revelling in materials of 'magic' property, gold, silver, crystal, glass, and above all light conceived as a liquid element, or as dew, as honey, an element that can be bathed in and gathered into vessels, that has quite largely disappeared from *The Silmarillion* (although, of course, the idea of light as liquid, dripping down, poured and hoarded, sucked up by Ungoliant, remained essential to the conception of the Trees, this idea becomes in the later writing less palpable and the divine operations are given less 'physical' explanation and justification).

As a result of this fullness and intensity of description, the origin of the Sun and Moon in the last fruit and last flower of the Trees has less of mystery than in the succinct and beautiful language of *The Silmarillion*; but also much is said here to emphasize the great size of the 'Fruit of Noon', and the increase in the heat and brilliance of the Sunship after its launching, so that the reflection rises less readily that if the Sun that brilliantly illumines the whole Earth was but one fruit of Laurelin then Valinor must have been painfully bright and hot in the days of the Trees. In the early story the last outpourings of life from the dying Trees are utterly strange and 'enormous', those of Laurelin portentous, even ominous; the Sun is astoundingly bright and hot even to the Valar, who are awestruck and disquieted by what has been done (the Gods knew 'that they had done a greater thing than they at first knew', p. 190); and the anger and distress of certain of the Valar at the burning light of the Sun enforces the feeling that in the last fruit of Laurelin a terrible and unforeseen power has been released. This distress does indeed survive in *The Silmarillion* (p. 100), in the reference to 'the prayers of Lórien and Estë, who said that sleep and rest had been banished from the Earth, and the stars were hidden'; but in the tale the blasting power of the new Sun is intensely conveyed in the images of 'the heat dancing above the trees' in the gardens of Lórien, the silent nightingales, the withered poppies and the drooping evening flowers.

In the old story there is a mythical explanation of the Moon's phases (though not of eclipses), and of the markings on its face through the story of the breaking of the withered bough of Silpion and the fall of the Moonflower – a story altogether at variance with the explanation given in *The Silmarillion* (*ibid.*). In the tale the fruit of Laurelin also fell to the ground, when Aulë stumbled and its weight was too great for Tulkas to bear alone: the significance of this event is not made perfectly clear, but it seems that, had the Fruit of Noon not burst asunder, Aulë would not have understood its structure and conceived that of the Sunship.

To whatever extent the great differences between the versions in this part of the Mythology may be due to later compression, there remain a good many actual contradictions, of which I note here only some of the more important, in addition to that concerning the markings on the Moon already mentioned. Thus in *The Silmarillion* the Moon rose first, 'and was the elder of the new lights as was Telperion of the Trees' (*ibid.*); in the old story the reverse is true both of the Trees and of the new lights. Again, in *The Silmarillion* it is Varda who decides their motions, and she changes these from her first plan at the plea of Lórien and Estë, whereas here it is Lórien's very distress at the coming of Sunlight that leads to the last blossoming of Silpion and the making of the Moon. The Valar indeed play different roles throughout; and here far greater importance attaches to the acts of Vána and Lórien, whose relations with the Sun and Moon are at once deeper and more explicit than they afterwards became, as they had been with the Trees (see p. 71); in *The Silmarillion* it was Nienna who watered the Trees with her tears (p. 98). In *The Silmarillion* the Sun and Moon move nearer to Arda than 'the ancient stars' (p. 99), but here they move at quite different levels in the firmament.

But a feature in which later compression can be certainly discerned is the elaborate description in the tale of the Moon as 'an island of pure glass', 'a shimmering isle', with little lakes of the light from Telimpë bordered with shining flowers and a crystalline cup amidmost in which was set the Moonflower; only from this is explicable the reference in *The Silmarillion* to Tilion's steering 'the island of the Moon'. The aged Elf Uolë Kúvion (whom 'some indeed have named the Man in the Moon') seems almost to have strayed in from another conception; his presence gives difficulty in any case, since we have just been told (p. 192) that Silmo could not sail in the Moonship because he was not of the children of the air and could not 'cleanse his being of its earthwardness'. – An isolated heading 'Uolë and Erinti' in the little pocket-book used among things for suggestions of stories to be told (see p. 171) no doubt implies that a tale was preparing on the subject of Uolë; cf. the Tale of Qorinómi concerning Urwendi and Erinti's brother Fionwë (p. 215). No traces of these tales are to be found and they were presumably never written. Another note in the pocket-book calls Uolë Mikúmi (the earlier name of Uolë Kúvion, see p. 198) 'King of the Moon'; and a third refers to a poem 'The Man in the Moon' which is to be sung by Eriol, 'who says he will sing them a song of a legend touching Uolë Mikúmi as Men have it'. My father wrote a poem about the Man in the Moon in March 1915, but if it was this that he was thinking of including it would have startled the company of Mar Vanwa Tyaliéva – and he would have had to change its references to places in England which were not yet in existence. Although it is very probable that he had something quite different in mind, I think it may be of interest to give this poem in an early form (see p. 204).

As the mythology evolved and changed, the Making of the Sun and Moon became the element of greatest difficulty; and in the published *Silmarillion* this chapter does not seem of a piece with much of the rest of the work, and could not be made to be so. Towards the end of his life my father was indeed prepared to dismantle much of what he had built, in the attempt to solve what he undoubtedly felt to be a fundamental problem.

Note on the order of the Tales

The development of the *Lost Tales* is here in fact extremely complex. After the concluding words of *The Flight of the Noldoli*, 'the story of the darkening of Valinor was at an end' (p. 169), my father wrote: 'See on beyond in other books', but in fact he added subsequently the short dialogue between Lindo and Eriol ('Great was the power of Melko for ill . . .') which is given at the end of *The Flight of the Noldoli*.

The page-numbering of the notebooks shows that the next tale was to be the *Tale of Tinúviel*, which is written in another book. This long story (to be given in Part II), the oldest extant version of 'Beren and Lúthien', begins with a long *Link* passage; and the curious thing is that this *Link* begins with the very dialogue between Lindo and Eriol just referred to, in almost identical wording, and this can be seen to be its original place; but here it was struck through.

I have mentioned earlier (p. 45) that in a letter written by my father in 1964 he said that he wrote *The Music of the Ainur* while working in Oxford on the staff of the Dictionary, a post that he took up in November 1918 and relinquished in the spring of 1920. In the same letter he said that he wrote ' "The Fall of Gondolin" during sick-leave from the army in 1917', and 'the original version of the "Tale of Lúthien Tinúviel and Beren" later in the same year'. There is nothing in the manuscripts to suggest that the tales that follow *The Music of the Ainur* to the point we have now reached were not written consecutively and continuously from *The Music*, while my father was still in Oxford.

At first sight, then, there is a hopeless contradiction in the evidence: for the *Link* in question refers explicitly to the Darkening of Valinor, a tale written *after* his appointment in Oxford at the end of 1918, but is a link to the *Tale of Tinúviel*, which he said that he wrote in 1917. But the *Tale of Tinúviel* (and the *Link* that precedes it) is in fact a text in ink written over an erased pencilled original. It is, I think, certain that this *rewriting* of Tinúviel was considerably later. It was linked to *The Flight of the Noldoli* by the speeches of Lindo and Eriol (the link-passage is integral and continuous with the *Tale of Tinúviel* that follows it, and was not added afterwards). At this stage my father must have felt that the *Tales* need not necessarily be told in the actual sequence of the narrative (for *Tinúviel* belongs of course to the time after the making of the Sun and Moon).

The rewritten *Tinúviel* was followed with no break by a first form of the 'interlude' introducing Gilfanon of Tavrobel as a guest in the house, and this led into the *Tale of the Sun and Moon*. But subsequently my father changed his mind, and so struck out the dialogue of Lindo and Eriol from the beginning of the *Link* to *Tinúviel*, which was not now to follow *The Flight of the Noldoli*, and wrote it out again in the other book at the end of that tale. At the same time he rewrote the Gilfanon 'interlude' in an extended form, and placed it at the end of *The Flight of the Noldoli*. Thus:

Flight of the Noldoli	Flight of the Noldoli
Words of Lindo and Eriol	Words of Lindo and Eriol

Tale of Tinúviel	Gilfanon 'interlude' (rewritten)
Gilfanon 'interlude'	Tale of the Sun and Moon and
Tale of the Sun and Moon and	the Hiding of Valinor
the Hiding of Valinor	

That the rewriting of *Tinúviel* was one of the latest elements in the composition of the *Lost Tales* seems clear from the fact that it is followed by the first form of the Gilfanon 'interlude', written at the same time: for Gilfanon replaced Ailios, and Ailios, not Gilfanon, is the guest in the house in the earlier versions of the *Tale of the Sun and Moon* and *The Hiding of Valinor*, and is the teller of the *Tale of the Nauglafring*.

The poem about the Man in the Moon exists in many texts, and was published at Leeds in 1923;* long after and much changed it was included in *The Adventures of Tom Bombadil* (1962). I give it here in the earlier published form, which was only a little retouched from the earliest workings – where it has the title 'Why the Man in the Moon came down too soon: an East Anglian phantasy'; in the first finished text the title is 'A Faërie: Why the Man in the Moon came down too soon', together with one in Old English: *Se Móncyning*.

Why the Man in the Moon
came down too soon

The Man in the Moon had silver shoon
    And his beard was of silver thread;
He was girt with pale gold and inaureoled
    With gold about his head.   4
Clad in silken robe in his great white globe
    He opened an ivory door
With a crystal key, and in secrecy
    He stole o'er a shadowy floor;   8

Down a filigree stair of spidery hair
    He slipped in gleaming haste,
And laughing with glee to be merry and free
    He swiftly earthward raced.   12
He was tired of his pearls and diamond twirls;
    Of his pallid minaret
Dizzy and white at its lunar height
    In a world of silver set;   16

* *'A Northern Venture:* verses by members of the Leeds University English School Association' (Leeds, at the Swan Press, 1923). I have not seen this publication and take these details from Humphrey Carpenter, *Biography*, p. 269.

And adventured this peril for ruby and beryl
   And emerald and sapphire,
And all lustrous gems for new diadems,
   Or to blazon his pale attire.   20
He was lonely too with nothing to do
   But to stare at the golden world,
Or strain for the hum that would distantly come
   As it gaily past him whirled;   24

And at plenilune in his argent moon
   He had wearily longed for Fire –
Not the limpid lights of wan selenites,
   But a red terrestrial pyre   28
With impurpurate glows of crimson and rose
   And leaping orange tongue;
For great seas of blues and the passionate hues
   When a dancing dawn is young;   32

For the meadowy ways like chrysoprase
   By winding Yare and Nen.
How he longed for the mirth of the populous Earth
   And the sanguine blood of men;   36
And coveted song and laughter long
   And viands hot and wine,
Eating pearly cakes of light snowflakes
   And drinking thin moonshine.   40

He twinkled his feet as he thought of the meat,
   Of the punch and the peppery brew,
Till he tripped unaware on his slanting stair,
   And fell like meteors do;   44
As the whickering sparks in splashing arcs
   Of stars blown down like rain
From his laddery path took a foaming bath
   In the Ocean of Almain;   48

And began to think, lest he melt and stink,
   What in the moon to do,
When a Yarmouth boat found him far afloat,
   To the mazement of the crew   52
Caught in their net all shimmering wet
   In a phosphorescent sheen
Of bluey whites and opal lights
   And delicate liquid green.   56

With the morning fish — 'twas his regal wish —
   They packed him to Norwich town,
To get warm on gin in a Norfolk inn,
   And dry his watery gown.   60
Though Saint Peter's knell waked many a bell
   In the city's ringing towers
To shout the news of his lunatic cruise
   In the early morning hours,   64

No hearths were laid, not a breakfast made,
   And no one would sell him gems;
He found ashes for fire, and his gay desire
   For chorus and brave anthems   68
Met snores instead with all Norfolk abed,
   And his round heart nearly broke,
More empty and cold than above of old,
   Till he bartered his fairy cloak   72

With a half-waked cook for a kitchen nook,
   And his belt of gold for a smile,
And a priceless jewel for a bowl of gruel,
   A sample cold and vile   76
Of the proud plum-porridge of Anglian Norwich —
   He arrived so much too soon
For unusual guests on adventurous quests
   From the Mountains of the Moon.   80

It seems very possible that the 'pallid minaret' reappears in the 'little white turret' which Uolë Kúvion built on the Moon, 'where often he climbs and watches the heavens, or the world beneath'. The minaret of the Man in the Moon survives in the final version.

The Ocean of Almain is the North Sea (*Almain* or *Almany* was a name of Germany in earlier English); the Yare is a Norfolk river which falls into the sea at Yarmouth, and the Nene (pronounced also with a short vowel) flows into the Wash.

IX
THE HIDING OF VALINOR

The link to this tale, which is told by Vairë, has been given at the end of the last (p. 195). The manuscript continues as in the latter part of *The Tale of the Sun and Moon* (see p. 197 note 19), with an earlier draft also extant, to which reference is made in the notes.

'Lo, tales I tell of the deep days, and the first is called *The Hiding of Valinor*.

Already have ye heard,' said she, 'of the setting forth of the Sun and Moon upon their wayward journeyings, and many things are there to tell concerning the awakening of the Earth beneath their light; but hear now of the thoughts and deeds of the dwellers in Valinor in those mighty days.

Now is it to tell that so wide were the wanderings of those boats of light that the Gods found it no easy thing to govern all their comings and their goings as they had purposed at the first, and Ilinsor was loath to yield the heaven to Urwendi, and Urwendi set sail often before Ilinsor's due return, being eager and hot of mood. Wherefore were both vessels often far afloat at one and the same time, and the glory of them sailing most nigh to the very bosom of the Earth, as often they did at that time, was very great and very terrible to see.

Then did a vague uneasiness begin to stir anew in Valinor, and the hearts of the Gods were troubled, and the Eldar spake one to another, and this was their thought.

"Lo, all the world is grown clear as the courtyards of the Gods, straight to walk upon as are the avenues of Vansamírin or the terraces of Kôr; and Valinor no longer is safe, for Melko hates us without ceasing, and he holds the world without and many and wild are his allies there" – and herein in their hearts they[1] numbered even the Noldoli, and wronged them in their thought unwittingly, nor did they forget Men, against whom Melko had lied of old. Indeed in the joy of the last burgeoning of the Trees and the great and glad labour of that fashioning of ships the fear of Melko had been laid aside, and the bitterness of those last evil days and of the Gnome-folk's flight was fallen into slumber – but now when Valinor had peace once more and its lands and gardens were mended of their hurts memory awoke their anger and their grief again.

Indeed if the Gods forgot not the folly of the Noldoli and hardened their hearts, yet more wroth were the Elves, and the Solosimpi were full of bitterness against their kin, desiring never more to see their faces in the pathways of their home. Of these the chief were those whose kin had perished at the Haven of the Swans, and their leader was one Ainairos who had escaped from that fray leaving his brother dead; and he sought unceasingly with his words to persuade the Elves to greater bitterness of heart.

Now this was a grief to Manwë, yet did he see that as yet his design was not complete, and that the wisdom of the Valar must needs be bent once more to the more perfect government of the Sun and Moon. Wherefore he summoned the Gods and Elves in conclave, that their counsel might better his design, and moreover he hoped with soft words of wisdom to calm their anger and uneasiness ere evil came of it. For clearly he saw herein the poison of Melko's lies that live and multiply wherever he may cast them more fruitfully than any seed that is sown upon the Earth; and already it was reported to him that the ancient murmuring of the Elves was begun anew concerning their freedom, and that pride made some full of folly, so that they might not endure the thought of the coming of Mankind.

Now then sat Manwë in heavy mood before Kulullin and looked searchingly upon the Valar gathered nigh and upon the Eldar about his knees, but he opened not his full mind, saying to them only that he had called them in council once more to determine the courses of the Sun and Moon and devise an order and wisdom in their paths. Then straightway spake Ainairos before him saying that other matters were deeper in their hearts than this, and he laid before the Gods the mind of the Elves concerning the Noldoli and of the nakedness of the land of Valinor toward the world beyond. Thereat arose much tumult and many of the Valar and their folk supported him loudly, and some others of the Eldar cried out that Manwë and Varda had caused their kindred to dwell in Valinor promising them unfailing joy therein — now let the Gods see to it that their gladness was not minished to a little thing, seeing that Melko held the world and they dared not fare forth to the places of their awakening even an they would. The most of the Valar moreover were fain of their ancient ease and desired only peace, wishing neither rumour of Melko and his violence nor murmur of the restless Gnomes to come ever again among them to disturb their happiness; and for such reasons they also clamoured for the concealment of the land. Not the least among these were Vána and Nessa, albeit most even of the great Gods were of one mind. In vain did Ulmo of his foreknowing plead before them for pity and pardon on the Noldoli, or Manwë unfold the secrets of the Music of the Ainur and the purpose of the world; and long and very full of that noise was that council, and more filled with bitterness and burning words than any that had been; wherefore did Manwë Súlimo depart at length from among them, saying that no walls or bulwarks might now fend Melko's evil from them which lived already among them and clouded all their minds.

So came it that the enemies of the Gnomes carried the council of the Gods and the blood of Kópas began already its fell work; for now began that which is named the Hiding of Valinor, and Manwë and Varda and Ulmo of the Seas had no part therein, but none others of the Valar or the Elves held aloof therefrom, albeit Yavanna and Oromë her son were uneasy in their hearts.

Now Lórien and Vána led the Gods and Aulë lent his skill and Tulkas his strength, and the Valar went not at that time forth to conquer Melko, and the greatest ruth was that to them thereafter, and yet is; for the great glory of the Valar by reason of that error came not to its fullness in many ages of the Earth, and still doth the world await it.[2]

In those days however they were unwitting of these things, and they set them to new and mighty labours such as had not been seen among them since the days of the first building of Valinor. The encircling mountains did they make more utterly impassable of their eastern side than ever were they before, and such earth-magics did Kémi weave about their precipices and inaccessible peaks that of all the dread and terrible places in the mighty Earth was that rampart of the Gods that looked upon Eruman the most dire and perilous, and not Utumna nor the places of Melko in the Hills of Iron were so filled with insuperable fear. Moreover even upon the plains about their eastward . . .[3] were heaped those impenetrable webs of clinging dark that Ungweliantë sloughed in Valinor at the Trees' destroying. Now did the Gods cast them forth from their bright land, that they might entangle utterly the steps of all who fared that way, and they flowed and spread both far and wide, lying even upon the bosom of the Shadowy Seas until the Bay of Faëry grew dim and no radiance of Valinor filtered there, and the twinkling of the lamps of Kôr died or ever it passed the jewelled shores. From North to South marched the enchantments and inaccessible magic of the Gods, yet were they not content; and they said: Behold, we will cause all the paths that fare to Valinor both known and secret to fade utterly from the world, or wander treacherously into blind confusion.

This then they did, and no channel in the seas was left that was not beset with perilous eddies or with streams of overmastering strength for the confusion of all ships. And spirits of sudden storms and winds unlooked-for brooded there by Ossë's will, and others of inextricable mist. Neither did they forget even the long circuitous ways that messengers of the Gods had known and followed through the dark wildernesses of the North and the deepest South; and when all was done to their mind Lórien said: "Now doth Valinor stand alone, and we have peace," and Vána sang once more about her garden in the lightness of her heart.

Alone among all did the hearts of the Solosimpi misgive them, and they stood upon the coasts nigh to their ancient homes and laughter came not easily again amongst them, and they looked upon the Sea and despite its peril and its gloom they feared it lest it still might bring evil into the land. Then did some of them going speak to Aulë and to Tulkas who stood nigh, saying: "O great ones of the Valar, full well and wondrously have the Gods laboured, yet do we think in our hearts that something is yet lacking; for we have not heard that the way of the escape of the Noldoli, even the dread passage of Helkaraksë's cliffs, is destroyed. Yet where the children of the Eldar have trodden so may the sons of Melko return, despite all your enchantments and deceits; neither are we in peace at heart by reason of the undefended sea."

Thereat did Tulkas laugh, saying that naught might come now to Valinor save only by the topmost airs, "and Melko hath no power there; neither have ye, O little ones of the Earth". Nonetheless at Aulë's bidding he fared with that Vala to the bitter places of the sorrow of the Gnomes, and Aulë with the mighty hammer of his forge smote that wall of jagged ice, and when it was cloven even to the chill waters Tulkas rent it asunder with his great hands and the seas roared in between, and the land of the Gods was sundered utterly from the realms of Earth.[4]

This did they at the Shoreland Elves' behest, yet by no means would the Gods suffer that low place in the hills beneath Taniquetil that lets upon the Bay of Faëry to be piled with rocks as the Solosimpi desired, for there had Oromë many pleasant woods and places of delight, and the Teleri[5] would not endure that Kôr should be destroyed or pressed too nearly by the gloomy mountain walls.

Then spake the Solosimpi to Ulmo, and he would not listen to them, saying that never had they learnt such bitterness of heart of his music, and that rather had they been listening to whispers of Melko the accursed. And going from Ulmo some were abashed, but others went and sought out Ossë, and he aided them in Ulmo's despite; and of Ossë's labour in those days are come the Magic Isles; for Ossë set them in a great ring about the western limits of the mighty sea, so that they guarded the Bay of Faëry, and albeit in those days the huge glooms of that far water overreached all the Shadowy Seas and stretched forth tongues of darkness towards them, still were they themselves surpassing fair to look upon. And such ships as fare that way must needs espy them or ever they reach the last waters that wash the elfin shores, and so alluring were they that few had power to pass them by, and did any essay to then sudden storms drove them perforce against those beaches whose pebbles shone like silver and like gold. Yet all such as stepped thereon came never thence again, but being woven in the nets of Oinen's[6] hair the Lady of the Sea, and whelmed in agelong slumber that Lórien set there, lay upon the margin of the waves, as those do who being drowned are cast up once more by the movements of the sea; yet rather did these hapless ones sleep unfathomably and the dark waters laved their limbs, but their ships rotted, swathed in weeds, on those enchanted sands, and sailed never more before the winds of the dim West.[7]

Now when Manwë gazing in sorrow from high Taniquetil saw all these things done he sent for Lórien and for Oromë, thinking them less stubborn of heart than the others, and when they were come he spoke earnestly with them; yet he would not that the labour of the Gods be undone, for he thought it not altogether ill, but he prevailed on those twain to do his bidding in certain matters. And in this manner did they so; for Lórien wove a way of delicate magic, and it fared by winding roads most secret from the Eastern lands and all the great wildernesses of the world even to the walls of Kôr, and it ran past the Cottage of the Children of the Earth[8] and thence down the "lane of whispering elms" until it reached the sea.

But the gloomy seas and all the straits it bridged with slender bridges resting on the air and greyly gleaming as it were of silken mists lit by a thin moon, or of pearly vapours; yet beside the Valar and the Elves have no Man's eyes beheld it save in sweet slumbers in their heart's youth. Longest of all ways is it and few are there ever reach its end, so many lands and marvellous places of allurement and of loveliness doth it pass ere it comes to Elfinesse, yet smooth is it to the feet and none tire ever who fare that way.

Such,' then said Vairë, 'was and still is the manner of Olórë Mallë, the Path of Dreams; but of far other sort was the work of Oromë, who hearing the words of Manwë went speedily to Vána his wife, and begged of her a tress of her long golden hair. Now the hair of Vána the fair had become more long and radiant still since the days of her offering to Aulë, and she gave to Oromë of its golden threads. Then did he dip these in the radiance of Kulullín, but Vána wove them cunningly to a leash immeasurable, and therewith Oromë strode swiftly to the gatherings of Manwë on the mountain.

Then calling loudly that Manwë and Varda and all their folk come forth he held before their eyes his thong of gold, and they knew not his purpose; but Oromë bid them cast their eyes on that Hill that is called Kalormë standing hugely in the lands most distant from Valinor, and is held most lofty save Taniquetil, yet seemeth therefrom a dim thing fading afar off. Even as they watched Oromë stepped back, and putting all his cunning and his strength thereto he made a mighty cast, and that golden cord sped in a curve through the sky until its noose caught Kalormë's topmost pinnacle. Then by the magic of its making and the cunning of Oromë's hand it stayed a bright golden curve and neither drooped nor sagged; but Oromë fastened its hither end to a pillar in Manwë's courts, and turning to those who gazed upon him said: "Who then listeth to wander in the Great Lands, let him follow me," and thereat he set foot upon the thong and sped like the wind out over the gulf even to Kalormë, while all upon Taniquetil were silent in amaze. Now did Oromë loosen the thong from Kalormë's peak and run as swiftly back, ravelling it as he came, until once more he stood before Manwë. Then said he: "Lo, O Súlimo Lord of the Airs, a way I have devised whereby any of the Valar of good heart may fare whithersoever they list in the Great Lands; for whither they wish I will cast my slender bridge, and its hither end wilt thou securely guard."

And of this work of Oromë's came that mighty wonder of the heavens that all men look upon and marvel at, and some fear much, pondering what it may portend. Yet doth that bridge wear a different aspect at different times and in various regions of the Earth, and seldom is it visible to Men and Elves. Now because it glistens most marvellously in the slanting rays of the Sun, and when the rains of heaven moisten it it shines most magically therein and the gold light breaks upon its dripping cords to many hues of purple, green, and red, so do men most often name it the Rainbow, but many other names have they fashioned also, and the fairies call it Ilweran the Bridge of Heaven.

Now living Men may not tread the swaying threads of Ilweran and few of the Eldar have the heart, yet other paths for Elves and Men to fare to Valinor are there none since those days save one alone, and it is very dark; yet is it very short, the shortest and swiftest of all roads, and very rough, for Mandos made it and Fui set it in its place. Qalvanda is it called, the Road of Death, and it leads only to the halls of Mandos and Fui. Twofold is it, and one way tread the Elves and the other the souls of Men, and never do they mingle.[9]

'Thus,' said Vairë, 'was the Hiding of Valinor achieved, and the Valar let slip the chance of a glory more splendid and enduring even than that great glory which was theirs and still is. Nonetheless are there still very mighty tidings of those days to tell, of which perchance I may now recount to you a few; and one I will name *The Haven of the Sun*.

Behold, now are the hearts of all set at rest by the truce[10] of Manwë and the Valar, and while the Gods feast in Valmar and the heaven is full of the ungoverned glory of the Ships of Light the Elves go back at last to rebuild the happiness of Kôr; and there they seek to forget all the sorrows and all the labours that had come among them since the Release of Melko. Now does Kôr become the fairest and most delicate-lovely of all the realms of Valinor, for in the courtyard of Inwë those two elfin trees shone still tenderly; and they were shoots of the glorious Trees now dead given by the Gods to Inwë in the first days of that town's building. Others too had been given to Nólemë, but these were uprooted and were gone no one knew whither, and more had there never been.[11]

Yet even though the Elves trusted the Valar to shield the land and weave protection about them, and though the days of sorrow faring into the past grew dim, still could they not yet utterly shake away the memory of their unhappiness; nor did they ever so, until after the magic way of Lórien was complete and the children of the fathers of the fathers of Men first were suffered to come there in sweet sleep; then did a new joy burn very brightly in their hearts, but these things were not yet come to pass and Men were yet but new-wakened on the Earth.

But Manwë and Ulmo knowing their hour was come held high councils for their protection. Many designs they made therein, and they were weighed down by the thought of Melko and the wandering of the Gnomes; yet did the other folk of Valinor trouble themselves little with such matters yet. Nonetheless Manwë ventured to speak once more to the Valar, albeit he uttered no word of Men, and he

reminded them that in their labours for the concealment of their
land they had let slip from thought the waywardness of the Sun
and Moon. Now it was the fear of Manwë lest the Earth become
unbearable by reason of the great light and heat of those bright
things, and Yavanna's heart was in accord with him in that, but the
most of the Valar and the Elves saw good in his design because in
the lifting of the Sun and Moon to higher paths they thought to set
a final end to all their labours, removing those piercing beams more
far, that all those hills and regions of their abode be not too bright
illumined, and that none might ever again espy them afar off.

Wherefore said some: "Let us send now messengers to discover
the fashion of the world in the uttermost East beyond even the
sight of Manwë from the Mountain of the World." Then arose
Oromë: "That I can tell you, for I have seen. In the East beyond the
tumbled lands there is a silent beach and a dark and empty sea."
And the Gods marvelled at these tidings, yet never before had any
save Oromë listed to see or hear such things, not even Yavanna the
Earth-lady. Nought do I say of Ulmo Vailimo, Lord of Vai, for of
a truth all such matters he knew from the beginning of the Earth.
Now therefore did that ancient one follow Oromë, expounding to the
Valar what was the secret nature of the Earth, and he said:

"Lo, there is but one Ocean, and that is Vai, for those that Ossë
esteemeth as oceans are but seas, waters that lie in the hollows of
the rock; but Vai runneth from the Wall of Things unto the Wall
of Things whithersoever you may fare. Now to the North is it so
cold that even its pale waters are frozen to a depth beyond thought
or sounding, and to the South is such utter darkness and deceit by
reason of Ungoliont[12] that none save I alone may find a way. In
this vast water floateth the wide Earth upheld by the word of Ilúvatar,
for nought else or fish or bark will swim therein to whom I have not
spoken the great word that Ilúvatar said to me and bound them
with the spell; but of the wide Earth is even Valinor a part, and the
substance of the Earth is stone and metal, and the seas are pools in
its hollows, and the islands save some few that swim still unfettered
stand now like pinnacles from their weedy depths. Know then that
somewhat nearer stands Valinor to the great Wall of Things wherein
Ilúvatar hath enclosed us than doth that furthest Eastern shore:
and this do I know, for diving beneath the world often have I
visited those unharboured beaches; for lo, O Valar, ye know not all
wonders, and many secret things are there beneath the Earth's dark
keel, even where I have my mighty halls of Ulmonan, that ye have
never dreamed on."

But said Manwë: "True is that, O Ulmo Vailimo; but what is it to our present purpose?" And Ulmo answered: "Lo, I will take Aulë the Smith with me and convey him safe and swift beneath the waters of Vai in my deep-sea car, even to the Eastern shores, and there will he and I build havens for the Ships, and from the East hereafter shall they arise and give their fullest light and glory to Men who need them, and to the unhappy Noldoli, following one the other over the sky, and coming home to Valinor. Here, when their hearts wax faint by reason of their journeyings, shall they rest awhile upon the Outer Seas and Urwendi bathe in Faskalan and Ilinsor drink of the quiet waters of the Lake Irtinsa, ere ever they return again."

Now this speech had Manwë and Ulmo designed in collusion, and the Valar and Eldar hearkened for divers reasons as before; wherefore was Aulë sped now with Ulmo, and they builded great havens in the East beside the soundless sea; and the haven of the Sun was wide and golden, but the haven of the Moon was set within the same harbourage, and it was white, having gates of silver and of pearl that shone faintly so soon as the Sun sank from the heavens into Valinor; at that hour do those gates open of themselves before the issuing Moon, but none of the Eldar have seen these things save Uolë Kúvion, and he has told no tale.

Now at first the Valar purposed to draw the Sun and Moon beneath the Earth, hallowing them with Ulmo's spell that Vai harm them not, each at its appointed time; yet in the end they found that Sári[13] might not, even so, safely come beneath the world, for it was too frail and lissom; and much precious radiance was spilled in their attempts about the deepest waters, and escaped to linger as secret sparks in many an unknown ocean cavern. These have many elfin divers, and divers of the fays, long time sought beyond the outmost East, even as is sung in the song of the Sleeper in the Tower of Pearl.[14]

Indeed for a while mishap fell even upon bright Urwendi, that she wandered the dark grots and endless passages of Ulmo's realm until Fionwë found her and brought her back to Valinor – but the full tale is called the Tale of Qorinómi and may not here be told.[15]

Thus came it that the Gods dared a very great deed, the most mighty of all their works; for making a fleet of magic rafts and boats with Ulmo's aid – and otherwise had none of these endured to sail upon the waters of Vai – they drew to the Wall of Things, and there they made the Door of Night (Moritarnon or Tarn Fui as the Eldar name it in their tongues). There it still stands, utterly black and huge against the deep-blue walls. Its pillars are of the mightiest basalt and its lintel likewise, but great dragons of black stone are carved thereon, and shadowy smoke pours slowly from their jaws. Gates it has unbreakable, and none know how they were made or set, for the Eldar were not suffered to be in that dread building, and it is the last secret of the Gods; and not the onset of the world will force that door, which opens to a mystic word alone. That word Urwendi only knows and Manwë who spake it to her; for beyond the Door of Night is the outer dark, and he who passes therethrough may escape the world and death and hear things not yet for the ears of Earth-dwellers, and this may not be.

In the East however was the work of the Gods of other sort, for there was a great arch made, and, 'tis said, 'tis all of shining gold and barred with silver gates, yet few have beheld it even of the Gods for the wealth of glowing vapours that are often swathed about it. Now the Gates of Morn open also before Urwendi only, and the word she speaks is the same that she utters at the Door of Night, but it is reversed.

So comes it that ever now, as the Ship of the Moon leaves his haven in the East and his gates of pearl, Ulmo draws the galleon of the Sun before the Door of Night. Then speaks Urwendi the mystic word, and they open outward before her, and a gust of darkness sweeps in but perishes before her blazing light; and the galleon of the Sun goes out into the limitless dark, and coming behind the world finds the East again. There doth Sári filled with the lightness of the morning ride through the gates and Urwendi and her maidens make a sound of golden horns, and dawn is spilt upon the eyes of Men.[16]

Yet many a time and oft a tiny star-ship of Varda that has dipped into the Outer Seas, as often they will, is sucked through that Door of Night behind the Sun; and some track her galleon through the starless vast back unto the Eastern Wall, and some are lost for ever, and some glimmer beyond the Door until the Sunship issues forth again.[17] Then do these leap back and rush up into the sky again, or flee across its spaces; and this is a very beautiful thing to see – the Fountains of the Stars.

Behold, the Moon dares not the utter loneliness of the outer dark by reason of his lesser light and majesty, and he journeys still beneath the world and many are the chances of that way; wherefore is it that he is often less timely than the Sun and is more fickle. Sometimes he comes not after Sári at all, and other times is late and maketh but a little voyage or even dares the heavens while Urwendi still is there. Then smile the Gods wistfully and say: "It is the mingling of the lights once more."[18]

Long was this indeed the manner of the ships' guidance, and long was it after those days that the Gods grew afraid once more for the Sun and Moon because of certain tidings of those days, which perchance may after be told; and because of their fear a new and strange thing befell. Now the manner of this mayhap I may tell before I make an end; and it is called *The Weaving of the Days and Months and of the Years*.

For know that even as the great Gods sat in conclave pondering how they might fetter the lamps of heaven ever to their hand and guide their goings even as a charioteer doth guide his galloping horses, behold three aged men stood before them and saluted Manwë.

But Manwë asked them who they were, "for well I know," quoth he, "that ye are not of the glad folk that dwell in Valmar or the gardens of the Gods," and the Valar marvelled how they came unaided to their land. Now those men were of strange aspect, seeming aged beyond count albeit of strength untamed. And one that stood at the left was exceeding small and short, and another amidmost of middle stature, and the third was long and tall; and the first had short hair and a small beard, and the other's was neither long nor short, but the beard of the third swept the earth before his feet as he walked. Now after a while he that was short and small spake in answer to Manwë, and he said: "Brothers are we; and men of exceeding subtle craft"; and the other answered: "Lo, Danuin, Ranuin, and Fanuin are we called,* and I am Ranuin, and Danuin has spoken." Then said Fanuin: "And we will offer thee our skill in your perplexity – yet who we are and whence we come or whither we go that we will tell to you only if ye accept our rede and after we have wrought as we desire."

Then some of the Gods said them nay, fearing a trick (even perhaps of Melko), and others would grant their request, and such was the counsel that in the end prevailed because of the great perplexity of the time. Then did those three Danuin and Ranuin and Fanuin beg that a room might be set apart for them; and this was done in Aulë's house. There did they spin and weave in secret, and after a space of twice twelve hours Danuin came forth and spake to Manwë, saying: "Behold my handicraft!"; and none knew his intent, for his hands were empty. But when the Ship of the Sun returned then went Danuin to her stern, and laying his hand thereon he bid Ulmo draw her, as was his wont, over the waters to the Door of Night; and when Ulmo was gone a little way from the further

* In the margin is written *Dōgor Mōnaþ 7 Missére*, Old English words meaning 'Day, Month, and Year'.

shore of Valinor Danuin stepped back, and behold Ulmo might not draw the Sunship further, not though he put forth all his strength. Then were Manwë and Ulmo and all that beheld afraid, but Danuin after released the Sun and went from among them, and they might not find him; but after twenty nights and eight came forth Ranuin and he said also: "Behold my handicraft!" and yet no more could be seen in his outstretched hands than before in those of Danuin. Now Ranuin waited until Ilinsor brought the Rose of Silpion unto Valinor, and then going he set his hands against a jag of glass upon that isle, and thereafter might no man stir Ilinsor's bark far from Ranuin against his will; but again Ranuin spake no word and went from among them; then Rána was released, but Ranuin no man could find.

Now the Gods pondered long what this might portend, but nought more betid until thirteen times had Rána waxed and waned. Then came forth Fanuin, and he bid the Gods detain Ilinsor that at Sári's coming both ships might stand in Valinor at once. But when this was done he begged aid of the Gods, "for," said he, "I have fashioned somewhat of great weight that I would fain show to you, yet cannot of my own strength hale it forth." And seven of the stoutest from the halls of Tulkas went to the place of Fanuin's labouring and could not see aught therein; but he bid them stoop, and them seemed they laid hands upon a mighty cable and staggered beneath it as they laid it upon their shoulders, yet could they not see it.

Then going unto Sári and to Rána in turn Fanuin moved his hands as though he were making fast a great rope to each of those vessels; but when all was done he said to Manwë: "Lo, O Súlimo Lord of the Gods, the work is wrought and the ships of light are set in the unbreakable fetters of time, which neither ye, nor they, may ever break, nor may they escape therefrom, albeit these fetters are invisible to all beings that Ilúvatar has made; for nonetheless are they the strongest of things."

Then suddenly behold Danuin and Ranuin stood beside him, and Danuin going to Manwë placed in his hand a slender cord, but Manwë saw it not. "Herewith," said Danuin, "O Manwë Súlimo, canst thou govern the goings and comings of the Sun, and never may she be brought beyond the guidance of your hand, and such is the virtue of this cord that the goings and returnings of the Sun shall be accounted the most timely and inevitable of all things on Earth." Thereafter did Ranuin in like manner, and behold Manwë felt a stout rope within his palm invisible. "Herewith," said Ranuin, "shalt thou hold and steer the wayward Moon, as well as may be, and so great is the virtue of the 'thong of Ranuin' that even the fickle and untimely Moon shall be a measure of time to Elves and Men." Lastly did Fanuin bid bear his mighty cable's end to Manwë, and Manwë touched it, and it was made fast to a great rock upon Taniquetil (that is called therefore Gonlath), and Fanuin said: "Now doth this mightiest cable hold both the Moon and Sun in tow; and herewith mayest thou coordinate their motions and interweave their fates; for the rope of Fanuin is the Rope of Years, and Urwendi issuing through the Door of Night shall wind it all tangled with the daycord's slender meshes, round and about the Earth until the Great End come – and so shall all the world and the dwellers within it, both Gods and Elves and Men, and all the creatures that go and the things that have roots thereon, be bound about in the bonds of Time."

Then were all the Gods afraid, seeing what was come, and knowing that hereafter even they should in counted time be subject to slow eld and their bright days to waning, until Ilúvatar at the Great End calls them back. But Fanuin said: "Nay, it is but the Music of the Ainur: for behold, who are we, Danuin, Ranuin, and Fanuin, Day and Month and Year, but the children of Aluin, of Time, who is the oldest of the Ainur, and is beyond, and subject to Ilúvatar; and thence came we, and thither go we now." Then did those three vanish from Valinor; but of such is the framing of the moveless courses of the Sun and Moon, and the subjection of all things within the world to time and change.

But as for the Ships of Light themselves, behold! O Gilfanon and all that hearken, I will end the tale of Lindo and Vairë concerning the building of the Sun and Moon with that great foreboding that was spoken among the Gods when first the Door of Night was opened. For 'tis said that ere the Great End come Melko shall in some wise contrive a quarrel between Moon and Sun, and Ilinsor shall seek to follow Urwendi through the Gates, and when they are gone the Gates of both East and West will be destroyed, and Urwendi and Ilinsor shall be lost. So shall it be that Fionwë Úrion, son of Manwë, of love for Urwendi shall in the end be Melko's bane, and shall destroy the world to destroy his foe, and so shall all things then be rolled away.'[19]

And thus ended Vairë, and the great tale fell silent in the room.

NOTES

1 'they': original reading 'the Solosimpi'.

2   The rejected draft text of the tale to this point is remarkably brief, and reads as follows (following on from Ailios' remarks given on p. 197, note 20):

> 'That is easy told,' said Lindo; 'for the murmurings that I have spoken of grew ever louder, and came to speech at that council which was now summoned to fix the courses of the Sun and Moon; and all the ancient grievance that had flamed before at Melko's instigation concerning the freedom of the Elves − even that strife that ended in the Exile of the Noldoli − grew sore again. Yet were few now in pity of the Gnomes, and such of the Eldar whom the newlit world allured dared not for the power of Melko break from Valinor; wherefore in the end the enemies of the Gnomes, despite all that Ulmo might say or plead, and despite the clemency of Manwë, carried the counsels of the Gods − and so came that which stories name the [Closing >] Hiding of Valinor. And the Gods went not at that time forth to fight Melko, and their greatest opportunity for glory and eternal honour was let slip, [even as the Music of Ilúvatar had foreboded − and they little understood it − and who knows if the salvation of the world and the freeing of Men and Elves shall ever come from them again? Some there are who whisper that it is not so, and hope dwelleth only in a far land of Men, but how so that may be I do not know.]

The concluding passage is thus bracketed in the manuscript, with a question-mark against it.

3   The word looks like 'east'. The word 'eastward' was added to the text, and it may be that my father intended to change 'east' to 'eastward edge' or something similar.

4   Here 'Earth' is clearly used, if strangely so, in the same way as is 'the world', to mean the Great Lands as distinguished from the Outer Lands of the West.

5   The Teleri (i.e. the later Vanyar) had not in the old story departed from Kôr (see p. 159).

6   Originally *Ówen* and then *Ónen*, the name of Ossë's wife has already appeared in the final form *Uinen* (pp. 121, 192); but *Oinen* here is clear, and clearly intended.

7   In the draft text the account of the Hiding of Valinor is very brief, and moves on quickly to the Path of Dreams. The webs of darkness laid on the eastward slopes of the mountains were not those 'sloughed in Valinor' by Ungweliantë, but are merely compared to 'the most clinging that ever Ungweliantë wove'. Helkaraksë and the Magic Isles are only mentioned in a marginal direction that they are to be included.

8   'Earth' is again used in the sense of the Great Lands (see note 4). The draft has here 'Children of the World'.

9   While there are no differences of any substance in the account of the Olórë Mallë in the two texts, in the first there is no mention of Oromë's

Path of the Rainbow. – An isolated note, obviously written before the present Tale, says: 'When the Gods close Valinor . . . Lórien leaves a path across the mountains called Olórë Mallë, and Manwë the Rainbow where he walks to survey the world. It is only visible after rain, for then it is wet.'

10 'truce': earlier reading 'compromise'. It is notable how Manwë is portrayed as *primus inter pares* rather than as ruler over the other Valar.

11 On the Trees of Kôr see pp. 123, 135.

12 See p. 200.

13 *Sári* is here (and subsequently) the name as written, not an emendation from *Kalavénë*, the name in the draft texts of *The Sun and Moon* and *The Hiding of Valinor* (see p. 198). The reading of the draft in this place is 'the Sunship', itself an alteration from 'the ships', for my father first wrote that neither ship could safely be drawn beneath the Earth.

14 The Sleeper in the Tower of Pearl is named in *The Cottage of Lost Play*, p. 15. The song of the sleeper is virtually certainly the poem *The Happy Mariners*, originally written in 1915 and published in 1923 (see Humphrey Carpenter, *Biography*, Appendix C, p. 269); this will be given in two versions in connection with the materials for the *Tale of Eärendel* in the second part of the *Lost Tales*. The poem contains a reference to the boats that pass the Tower of Pearl, piled 'with hoarded sparks of orient fire / that divers won in waters of the unknown Sun'.

15 The original draft has here: 'but that is the tale of Qorinómi and I dare not tell it here, for friend Ailios is watching me' (see p. 197, notes 19 and 20).

16 The draft text had here at first: 'and the galleon of the Sun goes out into the dark, and coming behind the world finds the East again, but there there is no door and the Wall of Things is lower; and filled with the lightness of the morning Kalavénë rides above it and dawn is split upon the Eastern hills and falls upon the eyes of Men.' Part of this, from 'but there there is no door', was bracketed, and the passage about the great arch in the East and the Gates of Morn introduced. In the following sentence, the draft had 'back over the Eastern Wall', changed to the reading of the second text, 'back unto the Eastern Wall'. For the name *Kalavénë* see p. 198.

17 I.e., until the Sunship issues forth, through the Door of Night, into the outer dark; as the Sunship leaves, the shooting stars pass back into the sky.

18 The second version of this part of Vairë's tale, 'The Haven of the Sun', follows the original draft (as emended) fairly closely, with no differences of any substance; but the part of her tale that now follows, 'The Weaving of the Days and Months and Years', is wholly absent from the draft text.

19   This concluding passage differs in several points from the original
version. In that, Ailios appears again, for Gilfanon; the 'great foreboding' was spoken among the Gods 'when they designed first to
build the Door of Night'; and when Ilinsor has followed Urwendi
through the Gates 'Melko will destroy the Gates and raise the Eastern
Wall beyond the [?skies] and Urwendi and Ilinsor shall be lost'.

Changes made to names in
The Hiding of Valinor

Vansamirin ⟨ *Samirien's road* (*Samirien* occurs as the name of the Feast
of Double Mirth, pp. 143-4).
Kôr ⟨ *Kortirion* (p. 207). Afterwards, though *Kôr* was not struck out,
my father wrote above it *Tûn*, with a query, and the same at the
occurrence of *Kôr* on p. 210. This is the first appearance in the
text of the *Lost Tales* of this name, which ultimately gave rise to
Túna (the hill on which Tirion was built).
Ainairos ⟨ *Oivárin*.
Moritarnon, Tarn Fui The original draft of the tale has '*Móritar* or
Tarna Fui'.
Sári The original draft has *Kalavéné* (see p. 198 and note 13 above).
At the first occurrence of the names of the three Sons of Time the sequence
of forms was:
Danuin ⟨ *Danos* ⟨ an illegible form *Dan..*
Ranuin ⟨ *Ranos* ⟨ *Ranoth* ⟨ *Rôn*
Fanuin ⟨ *Lathos* ⟨ *Lathweg*
Throughout the remainder of the passage: *Danuin* ⟨ *Dana; Ranuin* ⟨
Ranoth; Fanuin ⟨ *Lathweg*.
Aluin ⟨ *Lúmin*.

Commentary on
The Hiding of Valinor

The account of the Council of the Valar and Eldar in the opening of this
tale (greatly developed from the preliminary draft given in note 2) is
remarkable and important in the history of my father's ideas concerning
the Valar and their motives. In *The Silmarillion* (p. 102) the Hiding of
Valinor sprang from the assault of Melkor on the steersman of the Moon:

> But seeing the assault upon Tilion the Valar were in doubt, fearing
> what the malice and cunning of Morgoth might yet contrive against
> them. Being unwilling to make war upon him in Middle-earth, they
> remembered nonetheless the ruin of Almaren; and they resolved that
> the like should not befall Valinor.

A little earlier in *The Silmarillion* (p. 99) reasons are given for the unwillingness of the Valar to make war:

> It is said indeed that, even as the Valar made war upon Melkor for the sake of the Quendi, so now for that time they forbore for the sake of the Hildor, the Aftercomers, the younger Children of Ilúvatar. For so grievous had been the hurts of Middle-earth in the war upon Utumno that the Valar feared lest even worse should now befall; whereas the Hildor should be mortal, and weaker than the Quendi to withstand fear and tumult. Moreover it was not revealed to Manwë where the beginning of Men should be, north, south, or east. Therefore the Valar sent forth light, but made strong the land of their dwelling.

In *The Silmarillion* there is no vestige of the tumultuous council, no suggestion of a disagreement among the Valar, with Manwë, Varda and Ulmo actively disapproving the work and holding aloof from it; no mention, equally, of any pleading for pity on the Noldor by Ulmo, nor of Manwë's disgust. In the old story it was the hostility of some of the Eldar towards the Noldoli, led by an Elf of Kópas (Alqualondë) – who likewise disappeared utterly: in the later account there is never a word about the feelings of the Elves of Valinor for the exiled Noldor – that was the starting-point of the Hiding of Valinor; and it is most curious to observe that the action of the Valar here sprang essentially from indolence mixed with fear. Nowhere does my father's early conception of the *fainéant* Gods appear more clearly. He held moreover quite explicitly that their failure to make war upon Melko then and there was a deep error, diminishing themselves, and (as it appears) irreparable. In his later writing the Hiding of Valinor remained indeed, but only as a great fact of mythological antiquity; there is no whisper of its condemnation.

The blocking-up and utter isolation of Valinor from the world without is perhaps even more strongly emphasized in the early narrative. The cast-off webs of Ungweliant and the use to which the Valar put them disappeared in the later story. Most notable is the different explanation of the fact that the gap in the encircling heights (later named the Calacirya) was not blocked up. In *The Silmarillion* (p. 102) it is said that the pass was not closed

> because of the Eldar that were faithful, and in the city of Tirion upon the green hill Finarfin yet ruled the remnant of the Noldor in the deep cleft of the mountains. For all those of elven-race, even the Vanyar and Ingwë their lord, must breathe at times the outer air and the wind that comes over the sea from the lands of their birth; and the Valar would not sunder the Teleri wholly from their kin.

The old motive of the Solosimpi (> Teleri) wishing this to be done (sufficiently strange, for did the Shoreland Pipers wish to abandon the shores?) disappeared in the general excision of their bitter resentment against the Noldoli, as did Ulmo's refusal to aid them, and Ossë's willing-ness to do so in Ulmo's despite. The passage concerning the Magic Isles, made by Ossë, is the origin of the conclusion of Chapter XI of *The Silmarillion*:

> And in that time, which songs call *Nurtalë Valinoréva*, the Hiding of Valinor, the Enchanted Isles were set, and all the seas about them were filled with shadows and bewilderment. And these isles were strung as a net in the Shadowy Seas from the north to the south, before Tol Eressëa, the Lonely Isle, is reached by one sailing west. Hardly might any vessel pass between them, for in the dangerous sounds the waves sighed for ever upon dark rocks shrouded in mist. And in the twilight a great weariness came upon mariners and a loathing of the sea; but all that ever set foot upon the islands were there entrapped, and slept until the Change of the World.

It is clear from this passage in the tale that the Magic Isles were set to the east of the Shadowy Seas, though 'the huge glooms . . . . stretched forth tongues of darkness towards them'; while in an earlier passage (p. 125) it is said that beyond Tol Eressëa (which was itself beyond the Magic Isles) 'is the misty wall and those great sea-glooms beneath which lie the Shadowy Seas'. The later 'Enchanted Isles' certainly owe much as a conception to the Magic Isles, but in the passage just cited from *The Silmarillion* they were set in the Shadowy Seas and were in twilight. It is possible therefore that the Enchanted Isles derive also from the Twilit Isles (pp. 68, 125).

The account of the works of Tulkas and Aulë in the northern regions (p. 210) does not read as perfectly in accord with what has been said previously, though a real contradiction is unlikely. On pp. 166-7 it is plainly stated that there was a strip of water (Qerkaringa, the Chill Gulf) between the tip of the 'Icefang' (Helkaraksë) and the Great Lands at the time of the crossing of the Noldoli. In this same passage the Icefang is referred to as 'a narrow neck, which the Gods after destroyed'. The Noldoli were able to cross over to the Great Lands despite 'that gap at the far end' (p. 168) because in the great cold the sound had become filled with un-moving ice. The meaning of the present passage may be, however, that by the destruction of the Icefang a much wider gap was made, so that there was now no possibility of any crossing by that route.

Of the three 'roads' made by Lórien, Oromë, and Mandos there is no vestige in my father's later writing. The Rainbow is never mentioned, nor is there ever any hint of an explanation of how Men and Elves pass to the halls of Mandos. But it is difficult to interpret this conception of the 'roads' – to know to what extent there was a purely figurative content in the idea.

For the road of Lórien, Olóre Mallë the Path of Dreams, which is described by Vairë in *The Cottage of Lost Play*, see pp. 18, 27 ff. There Vairë told that Olóre Mallë came from the lands of Men, that it was 'a lane of deep banks and great overhanging hedges, beyond which stood many tall trees wherein a perpetual whisper seemed to live', and that from this lane a high gate led to the Cottage of the Children or of the Play of Sleep. This was not far from Kôr, and to it came 'the children of the fathers of the fathers of Men'; the Eldar guided them into the Cottage and its garden if they could, 'lest they strayed into Kôr and became enamoured of the glory of Valinor'. The accounts in the two tales seem to be in general agreement, though it is difficult to understand the words in the present passage 'it ran past the Cottage of the Children of the Earth and *thence* down the "lane of whispering elms" *until it reached* the sea'. It is very notable that still at this stage in the development of the mythology, when so much more had been written since the coming of Eriol to Tol Eressëa, the conception of the children of Men coming in sleep by a mysterious 'road' to a cottage in Valinor had by no means fallen away.

In the account of Oromë's making of the Rainbow-bridge, the noose that he cast caught on the summit of the great mountain Kalormë ('Sun-rising-hill') in the remotest East. This mountain is seen on the 'World-Ship' drawing, p. 84.

The story that Vairë named 'The Haven of the Sun' (pp. 213 ff.) provides the fullest picture of the structure of the world that is to be found in the earliest phase of the mythology. The Valar, to be sure, seem strangely ignorant on this subject – the nature of the world that came into being so largely from their own devising, if they needed Ulmo to acquaint them with such fundamental truths. A possible explanation of this ignorance may be found in the radical difference in the treatment of the Creation of the World between the early and later forms of *The Music of the Ainur*. I have remarked earlier (p. 62) that originally the Ainur's first sight of the world was already in its actuality, and Ilúvatar said to them: 'even now the world unfolds and its history begins'; whereas in the developed form it was a vision that was taken away from them, and only given existence in the word of Ilúvatar: *Eä! Let these things Be!* It is said in *The Silmarillion* (p. 20) that

> when the Valar entered into Eä they were at first astounded and at a loss, for it was as if naught was yet made which they had seen in vision, and all was but on point to begin and yet unshaped . . .

and there follows (pp. 21–2) an account of the vast labours of the Valar in the actual 'construction' of the world:

> They built lands and Melkor destroyed them; valleys they delved and Melkor raised them up; mountains they carved and Melkor threw them down; seas they hollowed and Melkor spilled them . . .

In the old version there is none of this, and one gains the impression (though nothing is explicit) that the Valar came into a world that was already 'made', and unknown to them ('the Gods stalked north and south and could see little; indeed in the deepest of these regions they found great cold and solitude . . .', p. 69). Although the conception of the world was indeed derived in large measure from their own playing in the Music, its reality came from the creative act of Ilúvatar ('We would have the guarding of those fair things of our dreams, which of thy might have now attained to reality', p. 57); and the knowledge possessed by the Valar of the actual properties and dimensions of their habitation was correspondingly smaller (so we may perhaps assume) than it was afterwards conceived to be.

But this is to lean rather heavily on the matter. More probably, the ignorance of the Valar is to be attributed to their curious collective isolation and indifference to the world beyond their mountains that is so much emphasized in this tale.

However this may be, Ulmo at this time informed the Valar that the whole world is an Ocean, Vai, on which the Earth floats, 'upheld by the word of Ilúvatar'; and all the seas of the Earth, even that which divides Valinor from the Great Lands, are hollows in the Earth's surface, and are thus distinct from Vai, which is of another nature. All this we have already seen (pp. 84 ff.); and in an earlier tale something has been said (p. 68) of the nature of the upholding waters:

Beyond Valinor I have never seen or heard, save that of a surety there are the dark waters of the Outer Seas, that have no tides, and they are very cool and thin, that no boat can sail upon their bosom or fish swim within their depths, save the enchanted fish of Ulmo and his magic car.

So here Ulmo says that neither fish nor boat will swim in its waters 'to whom I have not spoken the great word that Ilúvatar said to me and bound them with the spell'.

At the outer edge of Vai stands the Wall of Things, which is described as 'deep-blue' (p. 215). Valinor is nearer to the Wall of Things than is the eastern shore of the Great Lands, which must mean that Vai is narrower in the West than in the East. In the Wall of Things the Gods at this time made two entrances, in the West the Door of Night and in the East the Gates of Morn; and what lies beyond these entrances in the Wall is called 'the starless vast' and 'the outer dark'. It is not made clear how the outer air ('the dark and tenuous realm of Vaitya that is outside all', p. 181) is to be related to the conception of the Wall of Things or the Outer Dark. In the rejected preliminary text of this tale my father wrote at first (see note 16 above) that in the East 'the Wall of Things is lower', so that when the Sun returns from the Outer Dark it does not enter the eastern sky by a door but 'rides above' the Wall. This was then changed, and the idea of the Door in the Eastern Wall, the Gates of Morn, introduced; but the implication seems clear that the Walls were originally conceived like the walls of terrestrial cities, or gardens – walls with a top: a 'ring-fence'. In the cosmological essay of the 1930s, the *Ambarkanta*, the Walls are quite other:

> About the World are the *Ilurambar*, or Walls of the World. They are as ice and glass and steel, being above all imagination of the Children of Earth cold, transparent, and hard. They cannot be seen, nor can they be passed, save by the Door of Night.
>
> Within these walls the Earth is globed: above, below, and upon all sides is *Vaiya*, the Enfolding Ocean. But this is more like to sea below the Earth and more like to air above the Earth.

See further p. 86.

The Tale of Qorinómi (p. 215) was never in fact told – in the first version of the present tale (see note 15 above) it seems that Vairë would have liked to tell it, but felt the beady eye of the captious Ailios upon her. In the early Qenya word-list *Qorinómi* is defined as 'the name of the Sun', literally 'Drowned in the Sea', the name being a derivative from a root meaning 'choke, suffocate, drown', with this explanation: 'The Sun, after fleeing from the Moon, dived into the sea and wandered in the caverns of the Oaritsi.' *Oaritsi* is not given in the word-list, but *oaris* = 'mermaid'. Nothing is said in the *Lost Tales* of the Moon giving chase to the Sun; it was the stars of Varda that Ilinsor, 'huntsman of the firmament', pursued, and he was 'jealous of the supremacy of the Sun' (p. 195).

The conclusion of Vairë's tale, 'The Weaving of Days, Months, and Years', shows (as it seems to me) my father exploring a mode of mythical imagining that was for him a dead end. In its formal and explicit symbolism it stands quite apart from the general direction of his thought, and he excised it without trace. It raises, also, a strange question. In what possible sense were the Valar 'outside Time' before the weavings of Danuin, Ranuin, and Fanuin? In *The Music of the Ainur* (p. 55) Ilúvatar said: 'even now the world unfolds *and its history begins*'; in the final version (*The Silmarillion* p. 20) it is said that

> The Great Music had been but the growth and flowering of thought in the Timeless Halls, and the Vision only a foreshowing; but now they had entered in at the beginning of Time . . .

(It is also said in *The Silmarillion* (p. 39) that when the Two Trees of Valinor began to shine there began the Count of Time; this refers to the beginning of the measurement of Time from the waxing and the waning of the Trees.)

In the present tale the works of Danuin, Ranuin, and Fanuin are said to be the cause of 'the subjection of all things within the world to time and change'. But the very notion of a history, a consecutive story, self-

evidently implies time and change; how then can Valinor be said only
now to come under the necessity of change, with the ordering of the motions
of the Sun and Moon, when it has undergone vast changes in the course
of the story of the *Lost Tales*? Moreover the Gods now know 'that *hereafter*
even they should in counted time be subject to slow eld and their bright
days to waning'. But the very statement (for instance) that Ómar-Amillo
was 'the youngest of the great Valar' who entered the world (p. 67) is an
assertion that the other Valar, older than he, were 'subject to eld'. 'Age'
has of course for mortal beings two aspects, which draw always closer:
time passes, and the body decays. But of the 'natural' immortality of the
Eldar it is said (p. 59): 'nor doth eld subdue their strength, unless it may
be in ten thousand centuries'. Thus they 'age' (so Gilfanon is 'the most
aged that now dwelt in the isle' and is 'one of the oldest of the fairies', p.
175), but they do not 'age' (do not become enfeebled). Why then do the
Gods know that 'hereafter' they will be 'subject to slow eld' – which can
only mean ageing in the latter sense? It may well be that there is a deeper
thought here than I can fathom; but certainly I cannot explain it.

Finally, at the end of all the early writing concerning it, it may be
remarked how major a place was taken in my father's original conception
by the creation of the Sun and the Moon and the government of their
motions: the astronomical myth is central to the whole. Afterwards it was
steadily diminished, until in the end, perhaps, it would have disappeared
altogether.

X

GILFANON'S TALE: THE TRAVAIL
OF THE NOLDOLI AND THE
COMING OF MANKIND

The rejected draft text of *The Hiding of Valinor* continues a little way beyond the end of Vairë's tale, thus:

> Now after the telling of this tale no more was there of speaking for that night, but Lindo begged Ailios to consent to a tale-telling of ceremony to be held the next night or as soon as might be; but Ailios would not agree, pleading matters that he must needs journey to a distant village to settle. So was it that the tale-telling was fixed ere the candles of sleep were lit for a sevennight from that time – and that was the day of Turuhalmë[1] or the Logdrawing. ''Twill be a fitting day,' saith Lindo, 'for the sports of the morning in the snow and the gathering of the logs from the woods and the songs and drinking of Turuhalmë will leave us of right mood to listen to old tales beside this fire.'

As I have noticed earlier (p. 204), the original form of the *Tale of the Sun and Moon* and *The Hiding of Valinor* belonged to the phase before the entry of Gilfanon of Tavrobel, replacing Ailios.

Immediately following this rejected draft text, on the same manuscript page, the text in ink of the *Tale of Turambar* (Túrin) begins, with these words:

> When then Ailios had spoken his fill the time for the lighting of candles was at hand, and so came the first day of Turuhalmë to an end; but on the second night Ailios was not there, and being asked by Lindo one Eltas began a tale . . .

What was Ailios' tale to have been? (for I think it certain that it was never written). The answer becomes clear from a separate short text, very rough, which continues on from the discussion at the end of *The Hiding of Valinor*, given above. This tells that at length the day of Turuhalmë was come, and the company from Mar Vanwa Tyaliéva went into the snowy woods to bring back firewood on sleighs. Never was the Tale-fire allowed to go out or to die into grey ash, but on the eve of Turuhalmë it sank always to a smaller blaze until Turuhalmë itself, when great logs were brought into the Room of the Tale-fire and being blessed by Lindo with ancient magic roared and flared anew upon the hearth. Vairë blessed the door and lintel of the hall and gave the key to Rúmil, making him once again the Door-ward, and to Littleheart was given the hammer of his gong. Then Lindo said, as he said each year:

> 'Lift up your voices, O Pipers of the Shore, and ye Elves of Kôr sing aloud; and all ye Noldoli and hidden fairies of the world dance ye and sing, sing and dance O little children of Men that the House of Memory resound with your voices . . .'

Then was sung a song of ancient days that the Eldar made when they dwelt beneath the wing of Manwë and sang on the great road from Kôr to the city of the Gods (see pp. 143-4).

It was now six months since Eriol went to visit Meril-i-Turinqi beseech-ing a draught of *limpë* (see pp. 96-8), and that desire had for a time fallen from him; but on this night he said to Lindo: 'Would I might drink with thee!' To this Lindo replied that Eriol should not 'think to overpass the bounds that Ilúvatar hath set', but also that he should consider that 'not yet hath Meril denied thee thy desire for ever'. Then Eriol was sad, for he guessed in his deepest heart that 'the savour of *limpë* and the blessed-ness of the Elves might not be his for ever'.

The text ends with Ailios preparing to tell a tale:

'I tell but as I may those things I have seen and known of very ancient days within the world when the Sun rose first, and there was travail and much sorrow, for Melko reigned unhampered and the power and strength that went forth from Angamandi reached almost to the ends of the great Earth.'

It is clear that no more was written. If it had been completed it would have led into the opening of *Turambar* cited above ('When then Ailios had spoken his fill . . .'); and it would have been central to the history of the Great Lands, telling of the coming of the Noldoli from Valinor, the Awakening of Men, and the Battle of Unnumbered Tears.

The text just described, linking *The Hiding of Valinor* to Ailios' un-written tale, was not struck out, and my father later wrote on it: 'To come after the Tale of Eärendel and before Eriol fares to Tavrobel – after Tavrobel he drinks of *limpë*.' This is puzzling, since he cannot have intended the story of the Coming of Men to follow that of Eärendel; but it may be that he intended only to use the substance of this short text, describing the Turuhalmë ceremonies, without its ending.

However this may be, he devised a new framework for the telling of these tales, though he did not carry it through, and the revised account of the arranging of the next tale-telling has appeared in the *Tale of the Sun and Moon*, where after Gilfanon's interruption (p. 189) it was agreed that three nights after that on which *The Sun and Moon* and *The Hiding of Valinor* were told by Lindo and Vairë there should be a more ceremonial occasion, on which Gilfanon should relate 'the travail of the Noldoli and the coming of Mankind'.

Gilfanon's tale follows on, with consecutive page-numbers, from the second version of Vairë's tale of *The Hiding of Valinor*; but Gilfanon here tells it on the night following, not three days later. Unhappily Gilfanon was scarcely better served than Ailios had been, for if Ailios scarcely got started Gilfanon stops abruptly after a very few pages. What there is of his tale is very hastily written in pencil, and it is quite clear that it ends where it does because my father wrote no more of it. It was here that my father abandoned the *Lost Tales* – or, more accurately, abandoned those that still waited to be written; and the effects of this withdrawal never ceased to be felt throughout the history of 'The Silmarillion'. The major stories to follow Gilfanon's, those of Beren and Tinúviel, Túrin Turambar, the Fall of Gondolin, and the Necklace of the Dwarves, had been written and (in the first three cases) rewritten; and the last of these was to lead on to 'the great tale of Eärendel'. But that was not even begun. Thus the *Lost Tales* lack their middle, and their end.

I give here the text of Gilfanon's Tale so far as it goes.

Now when Vairë made an end, said Gilfanon: 'Complain not if on the morrow I weave a long tale, for the things I tell of cover many years of time, and I have waited long to tell them,' and Lindo laughed, saying he might tell to his heart's desire all that he knew.

But on the morrow Gilfanon sat in the chair and in this wise he began:

'Now many of the most ancient things of the Earth are forgotten, for they were lost in the darkness that was before the Sun, and no lore may recover them; yet mayhap this is new to the ears of many here that when the Teleri, the Noldoli, and the Solosimpi fared after Oromë and afterward found Valinor, yet was that not all of the race of the Eldalië that marched from Palisor, and those who remained behind are they whom many call the Qendi, the lost fairies of the world, but ye Elves of Kôr name Ilkorins, the Elves that never saw the light of Kôr. Of these some fell out upon the way, or were lost in the trackless glooms of those days, being wildered and but newly awakened on the Earth, but the most were those who left not Palisor at all, and a long time they dwelt in the pine-woods of Palisor, or sat in silence gazing at the mirrored stars in the pale still Waters of Awakening. Such great ages fared over them that the coming of Nornorë among them faded to a distant legend, and they said one to another that their brethren had gone westward to the Shining Isles. There, said they, do the Gods dwell, and they called them the Great Folk of the West, and thought they dwelt on firelit islands in the sea; but many had not even seen the great waves of that mighty water.

Now the Eldar or Qendi had the gift of speech direct from Ilúvatar, and it is but the sunderance of their fates that has altered them and made them unlike; yet is none so little changed as the tongue of the Dark Elves of Palisor.[2]

Now the tale tells of a certain fay, and names him Tû the wizard, for he was more skilled in magics than any that have dwelt ever yet beyond the land of Valinor; and wandering about the world he found the . . .[3] Elves and he drew them to him and taught them many deep things, and he became as a mighty king among them, and their tales name him the Lord of Gloaming and all the fairies of his realm Hisildi or the twilight people. Now the places about Koivië-néni the Waters of Awakening are rugged and full of mighty rocks, and the stream that feeds that water falls therein down a deep cleft . . . . a pale and slender thread, but the issue of the dark lake was beneath the earth into many endless caverns falling ever more deeply into the bosom of the world. There was the dwelling of Tû the wizard, and fathomless hollow are those places, but their doors have long been sealed and none know now the entry.

There was . . . . a pallid light of blue and silver flickering ever, and many strange spirits fared in and out beside the [?numbers] of the Elves. Now of those Elves there was one Nuin, and he was very wise, and he loved much to wander far abroad, for the eyes of the Hisildi were become exceeding keen, and they might follow very faint paths in those dim days. On a time did Nuin wander far to the east of Palisor, and few of his folk went with him, nor did Tû send them ever to those regions on his business, and strange tales were told concerning them; but now[4] curiosity overcame Nuin, and journeying far he came to a strange and wonderful place the like of which he had not seen before. A mountainous wall rose up before him, and long time he sought a way thereover, till he came upon a passage, and it was very dark and narrow, piercing the great cliff and winding ever down. Now daring greatly he followed this slender way, until suddenly the walls dropped upon either hand and he saw that he had found entrance to a great bowl set in a ring of unbroken hills whose compass he could not determine in the gloom.

Suddenly about him there gushed the sweetest odours of the Earth – nor were more lovely fragrances ever upon the airs of Valinor, and he stood drinking in the scents with deep delight, and amid the fragrance of [?evening] flowers came the deep odours that many pines loosen upon the midnight airs.

Suddenly afar off down in the dark woods that lay above the valley's bottom a nightingale sang, and others answered palely afar off, and Nuin well-nigh swooned at the loveliness of that dreaming place, and he knew that he had trespassed upon Murmenalda or the "Vale of Sleep", where it is ever the time of first quiet dark beneath young stars, and no wind blows.

Now did Nuin descend deeper into the vale, treading softly by reason of some unknown wonder that possessed him, and lo, beneath the trees he saw the warm dusk full of sleeping forms, and some were twined each in the other's arms, and some lay sleeping gently all alone, and Nuin stood and marvelled, scarce breathing.

Then seized with a sudden fear he turned and stole from that hallowed place, and coming again by the passage through the mountain he sped back to the abode of Tû; and coming before that oldest of wizards he said unto him that he was new come from the Eastward Lands, and Tû was little pleased thereat; nor any the more when Nuin made an end of his tale, telling of all he there saw – "and methought," said he, "that all who slumbered there were children, yet was their stature that of the greatest of the Elves."

Then did Tû fall into fear of Manwë, nay even of Ilúvatar the Lord of All, and he said to Nuin:

Here *Gilfanon's Tale* breaks off. The wizard Tû and the Dark Elf Nuin disappeared from the mythology and never appear again, together with the marvellous story of Nuin's coming upon the forms of the Fathers of Mankind still asleep in the Vale of Murmenalda – though from the nature of the work and the different degrees of attention that my father later gave to its different parts one cannot always distinguish between elements definitively abandoned and elements held in 'indefinite abeyance'. And unhappy though it is that this tale should have been abandoned, we are nonetheless by no means entirely in the dark as to how the narrative would have proceeded.

I have referred earlier (p. 107, note 3) to the existence of two 'schemes' or outlines setting out the plan of the *Lost Tales*; and I have said that one of these is a résumé of the *Tales* as they are extant, while the other is divergent, a project for a revision that was never undertaken. There is no doubt that the former of these, which for the purposes of this chapter I will call 'B', was composed when the *Lost Tales* had reached their furthest point of development, as represented by the latest texts and arrangements given in this book. Now when this outline comes to the matter of *Gilfanon's Tale* it becomes at once very much fuller, but then contracts again to cursory references for the tales of Tinúviel, Túrin, Tuor, and the Necklace of the Dwarves, and once more becomes fuller for the tale of Eärendel. It is clear, therefore, that B is the preliminary form, according to the method that my father regularly used in those days, of *Gilfanon's Tale*, and indeed the part of the tale that was written as a proper narrative is obviously following the outline quite closely, while substantially expanding it.

There is also an extremely rough, though full, outline of the matter of *Gilfanon's Tale* which though close to B has things that B does not, and vice versa; this is virtually certainly the predecessor of B, and in this chapter will be called 'A'.

The second outline referred to above, an unrealized project for the revision of the whole work, introduces features that need not be discussed here; it is sufficient to say that the mariner was now Ælfwine, not Eriol, and that his previous history was changed, but that the general plan of the *Tales* themselves was largely intact (with several notes to the effect that they needed abridging or recasting). This outline I shall call 'D'. How much time elapsed between B and D cannot be said, but I think probably not much. It seems possible that this new scheme was associated with the sudden breaking-off of *Gilfanon's Tale*. As with B, D suddenly expands to a much fuller account when this point is reached.

Lastly, a much briefer and more cursory outline, which however adds one or two interesting points, also has Ælfwine instead of Eriol; this followed B and preceded D, and is here called 'C'.

I shall not give all these outlines *in extenso*, which is unnecessary in view of the amount of overlap between them; on the other hand to combine them all into one would be both inaccurate and confusing. But since A and B are very close they can be readily combined into one; and I follow this account by that of D, with C in so far as it adds anything of note. And since in the matter of *Gilfanon's Tale* the outlines are clearly divided into two parts, the Awakening of Men and the history of the Gnomes in the Great Lands, I treat the narrative in each case in these two parts, separately.

There is no need to give the material of the outlines in the opening passage of *Gilfanon's Tale* that was actually written, but there are some points of difference between the outlines and the tale to be noted.

A and B call the wizard-king Túvo, not Tû; in C he is not named, and in D he is Tû 'the fay', as in the tale. Evil associations of this being appear in A: 'Melko meets with Túvo in the halls of Mandos during his enchainment. He teaches Túvo much black magic.' This was struck out, and nothing else is said of the matter; but both A and B say that it was after the escape of Melko and the ruin of the Trees that Túvo entered the world and 'set up a wizard kingship in the middle lands'.

In A, only, the Elves who remained behind in Palisor are said to have been of the people of the Teleri (the later Vanyar). This passage of *Gilfanon's Tale* is the first indication we have had that there were any such Elves (see p. 131); and I incline to think that the conception of the Dark Elves (the later Avari) who never undertook the journey from the Waters of Awakening only emerged in the course of the composition of the *Lost Tales*. But the name *Qendi*, which here first appears in the early narratives, is used somewhat ambiguously. In the fragment of the written tale, the words 'those who remained behind are they whom many call the Qendi, the lost fairies of the world,[5] but ye Elves of Kôr name Ilkorins' seem an altogether explicit statement that Qendi=Dark Elves; but a little later Gilfanon speaks of 'the Eldar or Qendi', and in the outline B it is said that 'a number of the original folk called Qendi (the name Eldar being given by the Gods) remained in Palisor'. These latter statements seem to show equally clearly that *Qendi* was intended as a term for all Elves.

The contradiction is however only apparent. *Qendi* was indeed the original name of all the Elves, and *Eldar* the name given by the Gods and adopted by the Elves of Valinor; those who remained behind preserved the old name *Qendi*. The early word-list of the Gnomish tongue states explicitly that the name *Elda* was given to the 'fairies' by the Valar and was 'adopted largely by them; the Ilkorins still preserved the old name *Qendi*, and this was adopted as the name of the reunited clans in Tol Eressëa'.[6]

In both A and B it is added that 'the Gods spoke not among themselves the tongues of the Eldalië, but could do so, and they comprehended all tongues. The wiser of the Elves learned the secret speech of the Gods and long treasured it, but after the coming to Tol Eressëa none remembered it save the Inwir, and now that knowledge has died save in the house of Meril.' With this compare Rúmil's remarks to Eriol, p. 48: 'There is beside the secret tongue in which the Eldar wrote many poesies and books of wisdom and histories of old and earliest things, and yet speak not. This tongue do only the Valar use in their high counsels, and not many of the Eldar of these days may read it or solve its characters.'

Nuin's words to Tû on the stature of the sleepers in the Vale of Murmenalda are curious. In A is added: 'Men were almost of a stature at first with Elves, the fairies being far greater and Men smaller than now. As the power of Men has grown the fairies have dwindled and Men waxed somewhat.' Other early statements indicate that Men and Elves were originally of very similar stature, and that the diminishing in that of the Elves was closely related to the coming of, and the dominance of, Men. Nuin's words are therefore puzzling, especially since in A they immediately precede the comment on the original similarity of size; for he can surely only mean that the sleepers in Murmenalda were very large by comparison with the Elves. That the sleepers were in fact children, not merely likened in some way to children, is made clear in D: 'Nuin finds the Slumbrous Dale (Murmenalda) where countless sleeping children lie.'

We come now to the point where the narrative is carried forward only in the outlines.

The Awakening of Men
according to the earlier outlines

The wizard Túvo told Nuin that the sleepers he had found were the new Children of Ilúvatar, and that they were waiting for light. He forbade any of the Elves to wake them or to visit those places, being frightened of the wrath of Ilúvatar; but despite this Nuin went there often and watched, sitting on a rock. Once he stumbled against a sleeper, who stirred but did not wake. At last, overcome by curiosity, he awakened two, named Ermon and Elmir; they were dumb and very much afraid, but he taught them much of the Ilkorin tongue, for which reason he is called Nuin Father of Speech. Then came the First Dawn; and Ermon and Elmir alone of Men saw the first Sun rise in the West and come over to the Eastward Haven. Now Men came forth from Murmenalda as 'a host of sleepy children'.

(In the tale of *The Hiding of Valinor* it was long after the first rising of the Sunship from Valinor that its Haven in the East was built; see pp. 214-15. It is interesting that the first Men, Ermon and Elmir, were woken by Nuin before the first rising of the Sun, and although it was known to Túvo that Men were 'waiting for light' no connection is made between Nuin's act and the Sunrise. But of course one cannot judge the inner tenor of the narrative from such summaries. It is notable also that whereas the tongue of the Elves, in origin one and the same, was a direct gift of Ilúvatar (p. 232), Men were born into the world without language and received it from the instruction of an Ilkorin. Cf. *The Silmarillion*, p. 141: 'It is said also that these Men [the people of Bëor] had long had dealings with the Dark Elves east of the mountains, and from them had learned much of their speech; and since all the languages of the Quendi were of one origin, the language of Bëor and his folk resembled the Elven-tongue in many words and devices.')

At this point in the story the agents of Melko appear, the Úvanimor, 'bred in the earth' by him (Úvanimor, 'who are monsters, giants, and ogres', have been mentioned in an earlier tale, p. 75); and Túvo protected Men and Elves from them and from 'evil fays'. A makes mention of Orcs besides.

A servant of Melko named 'Fúkil or Fangli' entered the world, and coming among Men perverted them, so that they fell treacherously upon the Ilkorins; there followed the Battle of Palisor, in which the people of Ermon fought beside Nuin. According to A 'the fays and those Men that aided them were defeated', but B calls it an 'undecided battle'; and the Men corrupted by Fangli fled away and became 'wild and savage tribes', worshipping Fangli and Melko. Thereafter (in A only) Palisor was possessed by 'Fangli and his hosts of Nauglath (or Dwarves)'. (In the early writings the Dwarves are always portrayed as an evil people.)

From this outline it is seen that the corruption of certain Men in the beginning of their days by the agency of Melko was a feature of the earliest phase of the mythology; but of all the story here sketched there is no more than a hint or suggestion, at most, in *The Silmarillion* (p. 141): ' "A darkness lies behind us," Bëor said; "and we have turned our backs upon it, and we do not desire to return thither even in thought." '[7]

The Awakening of Men
according to the later outline

Here it is told at the beginning of the narrative that Melko's Úvanimor had escaped when the Gods broke the Fortress of the North, and were wandering in the forests; Fankil servant of Melko dwelt uncaptured in the world. (Fankil=Fangli / Fúkil of A and B. In C he is called 'child of Melko'. Fankil has been mentioned at an earlier point in D, when at the time of the Awakening of the Elves 'Fankil and many dark shapes escaped into the world'; see p. 107, note 3.)

Nuin 'Father of Speech', who went again and again to Murmenalda despite the warnings of Tû (which are not here specified), woke Ermon and Elmir, and taught them speech and many things else. Ermon and Elmir alone of Mankind saw the Sun arising in the West, and the seeds of Palúrien bursting forth into leaf and bud. The hosts of Men came forth as sleepy children, raising a dumb clamour at the Sun; they followed it westward when it returned, and were grievously afraid of the first Night. Nuin and Ermon and Elmir taught them speech.

Men grew in stature, and gathered knowledge of the Dark Elves,[8] but Tû faded before the Sun and hid in the bottomless caverns. Men dwelt in the centre of the world and spread thence in all directions; and a very great age passed.

Fankil with the Dwarves and Goblins went among Men, and bred estrangement between them and the Elves; and many Men aided the Dwarves. The folk of Ermon alone stood by the fairies in the first war of Goblins and Elves (Goblins is here an emendation from Dwarves, and that from Men), which is called the War of Palisor. Nuin died at the hands of the Goblins through the treachery of Men. Many kindreds of Men were driven to the eastern deserts and the southern forests, whence came dark and savage peoples.

The hosts of Tareg the Ikorin marched North-west hearing a rumour of the Gnomes; and many of the lost kindreds joined him.

The History of the Exiled Gnomes
according to the earlier outlines

The Gnomes, after the passage of Helkaraksë, spread into Hisilómë, where they had 'trouble' with the ancient Shadow Folk in that land – in A called 'fay-people', in B '*Úvalear* fays'. (We have met the Shadow Folk of Hisilómë before, in the tale of *The Coming of the Elves*, p. 119, but there this is a name given by Men, after they were shut in Hisilómë by Melko, to the Lost Elves who remained there after straying on the march from Palisor. It will be seen in the later outlines that these Shadow Folk were an unknown people wholly distinct from Elves; and it seems therefore that the name was preserved while given a new interpretation.)

The Gnomes found the Waters of Asgon* and encamped there; then took place the Counting of the Folk, the birth of Turgon with 'prophecies', and the death of Fëanor. On this last matter the outlines are divergent. In A it was Nólemë, called also Fingolma, who died: 'his bark vanishes down a hidden way – said to be the way that Tuor after escaped by. He sailed to offer sacrifice in the islanded rock in Asgon.' (To whom was he sacrificing?) In B, as first written, it was likewise 'Fingolma (Nólemë)' who died, but this was emended to Fëanor; 'his bark vanished down a hidden [way] – said to be that opening that the Noldoli after enlarged and fashioned to a path, so that Tuor escaped that way. He sailed to the Islanded Rock in Asgon because he saw something brightly glitter there and sought his jewels.'

Leaving Asgon the Gnomes passed the Bitter Hills and fought their first battle with Orcs in the foothills of the Iron Mountains. (For the Iron Mountains as the southern border of Hisilómë see pp. 111–12, 158–9.) In the *Tale of Tinúviel* Beren came from Hisilómë, from 'beyond the Bitter Hills', and 'through the terrors of the Iron Mountains', and it thus seems clear that the Bitter Hills and the Iron Mountains may be equated.)

The next camp of the Gnomes was 'by Sirion' (which here first appears); and here the Gnomes first met the Ilkorins – A adding that these Ilkorins were originally of the Noldoli, and had been lost on the march from Palisor. The Gnomes learned from them of the coming of Men and of the Battle of Palisor; and they told the Ilkorins of the tidings in Valinor, and of their search for the jewels.

Now appears for the first time Maidros son of Fëanor (previously, in the tale of *The Theft of Melko*, the name was given to Fëanor's grandfather, pp. 146, 158). Maidros, guided by Ilkorins, led a host into the hills, either 'to seek for the jewels' (A), or 'to search the dwellings of Melko' (B – this should perhaps read 'search for the dwellings of Melko', the reading of C), but they were driven back with slaughter from the doors of Angamandi; and Maidros himself was taken alive, tortured – because he would not reveal the secret arts of the Noldoli in the making of jewels – and sent back to the Gnomes maimed. (In A, which still had Nólemë rather than Fëanor die in the Waters of Asgon, it was Fëanor himself who led the host against Melko, and it was Fëanor who was captured, tortured, and maimed.)

Then the Seven Sons of Fëanor swore an oath of enmity for ever against any that should hold the Silmarils. (This is the first appearance of the Seven Sons, and of the Oath, though that Fëanor had sons is mentioned in the *Tale of the Sun and Moon*, p. 192.)

The hosts of Melko now approached the camp of the Gnomes by Sirion, and they fled south, and dwelt then at Gorfalon, where they made the acquaintance of Men, both good and bad, but especially those of Ermon's folk; and an embassy was sent to Túvo, to Tinwelint (i.e. Thingol,

* later Lake Mithrim.

see p. 132), and to Ermon.[9] A great host was arrayed of Gnomes, Ilkorins, and Men, and Fingolma (Nólemë) marshalled it in the Valley of the Fountains, afterwards called the Vale of Weeping Waters. But Melko himself went into the tents of Men and beguiled them, and some of them fell treacherously on the rear of the Gnomes even as Melko's host attacked them; others Melko persuaded to abandon their friends, and these, together with others that he led astray with mists and wizardries, he beguiled into the Land of Shadows. (With this cf. the reference in the tale of *The Coming of the Elves* to the shutting of Men in Hisilómë by Melko, p. 118.)

Then took place 'the terrible Battle of Unnumbered Tears'. The Children of Úrin* (Sons of Úrin, A) alone of Men fought to the last, and none (save two messengers) came out of the fray; Turgon and a great regiment, seeing the day lost, turned and cut their way out, and rescued a part of the women and children. Turgon was pursued, and there is a reference to 'Mablon the Ilkorin's sacrifice to save the host'; Maidros and the other sons of Fëanor quarrelled with Turgon – because they wanted the leadership, A – and departed into the south. The remainder of the survivors and fugitives were surrounded, and swore allegiance to Melko; and he was wrathful, because he could not discover whither Turgon had fled.

After a reference to 'the Mines of Melko' and 'the Spell of Bottomless Dread' (the spell that Melko cast upon his slaves), the story concludes with 'the Building of Gondolin' and 'the estrangement of Men and Elves in Hisilómë, owing to the Battle of Unnumbered Tears': Melko fostered distrust and kept them spying on each other, so that they should not combine against him; and he fashioned the false-fairies or Kaukareldar in their likeness, and these deceived and betrayed Men.[10]

Since the outlines at this point return to mere headings for the tales of Tinúviel, Túrin, etc., it is clear that *Gilfanon's Tale* would have ended here.

The History of the Exiled Gnomes
according to the later outline

The Gnomes sojourned in the Land of Shadows (i.e. Hisilómë), and had dealings with the Shadow Folk. These were fays (C); no one knows whence they came: they are not of the Valar nor of Melko, but it is thought that they came from the outer void and primeval dark when the world was first fashioned. The Gnomes found 'the Waters of Mithrim (Asgon)', and here Fëanor died, drowned in the Waters of Mithrim. The Gnomes devised weapons for the first time, and quarried the dark hills. (This is curious, for it has been said in the account of the Kinslaughter at Alqaluntë that 'so first perished the Eldar neath the weapons of their kin', p. 165.

* later Húrin.

The first acquisition of weapons by the Eldar remained a point of uncertainty for a long time.)

The Gnomes now fought for the first time with the Orcs and captured
the pass of the Bitter Hills; thus they escaped out of the Land of Shadows,
to Melko's fear and amazement. They entered the Forest of Artanor (later
Doriath) and the Region of the Great Plains (perhaps the forerunner of
the later Talath Dirnen, the Guarded Plain of Nargothrond); and the
host of Nólemë grew to a vast size. They practised many arts, but would
dwell no longer in settled abodes. The chief camp of Nólemë was about
the waters of Sirion; and the Gnomes drove the Orcs to the foothills of
the Iron Mountains. Melko gathered his power in secret wrath.

Turgon was born to Nólemë.

Maidros, 'chief son of Fëanor', led a host against Angband, but was
driven back with fire from its gates, and he was taken alive and tortured —
according to C, repeating the story of the earlier outline, because he would
not reveal the secret arts of jewel-making. (It is not said here that Maidros
was freed and returned, but it is implied in the Oath of the Seven Sons
that follows.)

The Seven Sons of Fëanor swore their terrible oath of hatred for ever
against all, Gods or Elves or Men, who should hold the Silmarils; and
the Children of Fëanor left the host of Nólemë and went back into Dor
Lómin, where they became a mighty and a fierce race.

The hosts of Tareg the Ilkorin (see p. 237) found the Gnomes at the
Feast of Reunion; and the Men of Ermon first saw the Gnomes. Then
Nólemë's host, swollen by that of Tareg and by the sons of Ermon, pre-
pared for battle; and messengers were sent out North, South, East, and
West. Tinwelint alone refused the summons, and he said: 'Go not into
the hills.' Úrin and Egnor* marched with countless battalions.

Melko withdrew all his forces and Nólemë believed that he was afraid.
The hosts of Elfinesse drew into the Tumbled Lands and encamped in
the Vale of Fountains (Gorfalong), or as it was afterwards called the
Valley of Weeping Waters.

(The outline D differs in its account of the events before the Battle of
Unnumbered Tears from that in the earlier ones, here including C. In
the earlier, the Gnomes fled from the camp by Sirion when Melko's hosts
approached, and retreated to Gorfalon, where the great host of Gnomes,
Ilkorins, and Men was gathered, and arrayed in the Valley of the Fountains.
In D, there is no mention of any retreat by Nólemë's hosts: rather, it
seems, they advanced from the camp by Sirion into the Vale of Fountains
(Gorfalong). But from the nature of these outlines they cannot be too
closely pressed. The outline C, which ends here, says that when the
Gnomes first encountered Men at Gorfalon the Gnomes taught them
crafts — and this was one of the starting-points, no doubt, of the later
Elf-friends of Beleriand.)

* The father of Beren.

Certain Men suborned by Melko went among the camp as minstrels and betrayed it. Melko fell upon them at early dawn in a grey rain, and the terrible Battle of Unnumbered Tears followed, of which no full tale is told, for no Gnome will ever speak of it. (In the margin here my father wrote: 'Melko himself was there?' In the earlier outline Melko himself entered the camp of his enemies.)

In the battle Nólemë was isolated and slain, and the Orcs cut out his heart; but Turgon rescued his body and his heart, and it became his emblem.[11] Nearly half of all the Gnomes and Men who fought there were slain.

Men fled, and the sons of Úrin alone stood fast until they were slain; but Úrin was taken. Turgon was terrible in his wrath, and his great battalion hewed its way out of the fight by sheer prowess.

Melko sent his host of Balrogs after them, and Mablon the Ilkorin died to save them when pursued. Turgon fled south along Sirion, gathering women and children from the camps, and aided by the magic of the stream escaped into a secret place and was lost to Melko.

The Sons of Fëanor came up too late and found a stricken field: they slew the spoilers who were left, and burying Nólemë they built the greatest cairn in the world over him and the [?Gnomes]. It was called the Hill of Death.

There followed the Thraldom of the Noldoli. The Gnomes were filled with bitterness at the treachery of Men, and the ease with which Melko beguiled them. The outline concludes with references to 'the Mines of Melko' and 'the Spell of Bottomless Dread', and the statement that all the Men of the North were shut in Hisilómë.

The outline D then turns to the story of Beren and Tinúviel, with a natural connection from the tale just sketched: 'Beren son of Egnor wandered out of Dor Lómin* into Artanor . . .' This is to be the next story told by the Tale-fire (as also in outline B); in D the matter of *Gilfanon's Tale* is to take four nights.

★

If certain features are selected from these outlines, and expressed in such a way as to emphasize agreement rather than disagreement, the likeness to the narrative structure of *The Silmarillion* is readily apparent. Thus:

- The Noldoli cross the Helkaraksë and spread into Hisilómë, making their encampment by Asgon (Mithrim);
- They meet Ilkorin Elves (=Úmanyar);
- Fëanor dies;
- First battle with Orcs;
- A Gnomish army goes to Angband;

* i.e. Hisilómë; see p. 112.

- Maidros captured, tortured, and maimed;
- The Sons of Fëanor depart from the host of the Elves (in D only);
- A mighty battle called the Battle of Unnumbered Tears is fought between Elves and Men and the hosts of Melko;
- Treachery of Men, corrupted by Melko, at that battle;
- But the people of Úrin (Húrin) are faithful, and do not survive it;
- The leader of the Gnomes is isolated and slain (in D only);
- Turgon and his host cut their way out, and go to Gondolin;
- Melko is wrathful because he cannot discover where Turgon has gone;
- The Fëanorians come late to the battle (in D only);
- A great cairn is piled (in D only).

These are essential features of the story that were to survive. But the unlikenesses are many and great. Most striking of all is that the entire later history of the long years of the Siege of Angband, ending with the Battle of Sudden Flame (Dagor Bragollach), of the passage of Men over the Mountains into Beleriand and their taking service with the Noldorin Kings, had yet to emerge; indeed these outlines give the effect of only a brief time elapsing between the coming of the Noldoli from Kôr and their great defeat. This effect may be to some extent the result of the compressed nature of these outlines, and indeed the reference in the last of them, D, to the practice of many arts by the Noldoli (p. 240) somewhat counteracts the impression — in any case, Turgon, born when the Gnomes were in Hisilómë or (according to D) when they were encamped by Sirion, is full grown at the Battle of Unnumbered Tears.[12] Even so, the picture in *The Silmarillion* of a period of centuries elapsing while Morgoth was straitly confined in Angband and 'behind the guard of their armies in the north the Noldor built their dwellings and their towers' is emphatically not present. In later 'phases' of the history my father steadily expanded the period between the rising of the Sun and Moon and the Battle of Unnumbered Tears. It is essential, also, to the old conception that Melko's victory was so complete and overwhelming: vast numbers of the Noldoli became his thralls, and wherever they went lived in the slavery of his spell; in Gondolin alone were they free — so in the old tale of *The Fall of Gondolin* it is said that the people of Gondolin 'were that kin of the Noldoli who alone escaped Melko's power, when at the Battle of Unnumbered Tears he slew and enslaved their folk and wove spells about them and caused them to dwell in the Hells of Iron, faring thence at his will and bidding only'. Moreover Gondolin was not founded until *after* the Battle of Unnumbered Tears.[13]

Of Fëanor's death in the early conception we can discern little; but at least it is clear that it bore no relation to the story of his death in *The Silmarillion* (p. 107). In these early outlines the Noldoli, leaving Hisilómë, had their first affray with the Orcs in the foothills of the Iron Mountains or in the pass of the Bitter Hills, and these heights pretty clearly correspond to the later Mountains of Shadow, Ered Wethrin (see pp. 158, 238);

but in *The Silmarillion* (p. 106) the first encounter of the Noldor with the Orcs was in Mithrim.

The meeting of Gnomes and Ilkorins survived in the meeting of the new-come Noldor with the Grey-elves of Mithrim (*ibid.* p. 108); but the Noldor heard rather of the power of King Thingol of Doriath than of the Battle of Palisor.

Whereas in these outlines Maidros son of Fëanor led an attack on Angband which was repulsed with slaughter and his own capture, in *The Silmarillion* it was Fingolfin who appeared before Angband, and being met with silence prudently withdrew to Mithrim (p. 109). Maidros (Maedhros) had been already taken at a meeting with an embassage of Morgoth's that was supposed to be a parley, and he heard the sound of Fingolfin's trumpets from his place of torment on Thangorodrim – where Morgoth set him until, as he said, the Noldor forsook their war and departed. Of the divided hosts of the Noldor there is of course no trace in the old story; and the rescue of Maedhros by Fingon, who cut off his hand in order to save him, does not appear in any form: rather is he set free by Melko, though maimed, and without explanation given. But it is very characteristic that the maiming of Maidros – an important 'moment' in the legends – should never itself be lost, though it came to be given a wholly different setting and agency.

The Oath of the Sons of Fëanor was here sworn after the coming of the Gnomes from Valinor, and after the death of their father; and in the later outline D they then left the host of (Finwë) Nólemë, Lord of the Noldoli, and returned to Dor Lómin (Hisilómë). In this and in other features that appear only in D the story is moved nearer to its later form. In the return to Dor Lómin is the germ of the departure of the Fëanorians from Mithrim to the eastern parts of Beleriand (*The Silmarillion* p. 112); in the Feast of Reunion that of Mereth Aderthad, the Feast of Reuniting, held by Fingolfin for the Elves of Beleriand (*ibid.* p. 113), though the participants are necessarily greatly different; in the latecoming of the Fëanorians to the stricken field of Unnumbered Tears that of the delayed arrival of the host of Maedhros (*ibid.* pp. 190–2); in the cutting-off and death of (Finwë) Nólemë in the battle that of the slaying of Fingon (*ibid.* p. 193 – when Finwë came to be Fëanor's father, and thus stepped into the place of Bruithwir, killed by Melko in Valinor, his position as leader of the hosts in the Battle of Unnumbered Tears was taken by Fingon); and in the great cairn called the Hill of Death, raised by the Sons of Fëanor, that of the Haudh-en-Ndengin or Hill of Slain, piled by Orcs in Anfauglith (*ibid.* p. 197). Whether the embassy to Túvo, Tinwelint, and Ermon (which in D becomes the sending of messengers) remotely anticipates the Union of Maedhros (*ibid.* pp. 188–9) is not clear, though Tinwelint's refusal to join forces with Nólemë survived in Thingol's rejection of Maedhros' approaches (p. 189). I cannot certainly explain Tinwelint's words 'Go not into the hills', but I suspect that 'the hills' are the Mountains of Iron (in *The Hiding of Valinor*, p. 209, called 'the Hills of Iron') above

Angband, and that he warned against an attack on Melko; in the old *Tale of Turambar* Tinwelint said: 'Of the wisdom of my heart and the fate of the Valar did I not go with my folk to the Battle of Unnumbered Tears.'

Other elements in the story of the battle that survived – the steadfastness of the folk of Úrin (Húrin), the escape of Turgon – already existed at this time in a tale that had been written (that of Túrin).

The geographical indications are slight, and there is no map of the Great Lands for the earliest period of the legends; in any case these questions are best left until the tales that take place in those lands. The Vale (or Valley) of the Fountains, afterwards the Valley (or Vale) of Weeping Waters, is in D explicitly equated with Gorfalong, which in the earlier outlines is given as Gorfalon, and seems to be distinct; but in any case neither these, nor 'the Tumbled Lands', can be brought into relation with any places or names in the later geography – unless (especially since in D Turgon is said to have fled 'south down Sirion') it may be supposed that something like the later picture of the Pass of Sirion was already in being, and that the Vale of the Fountains, or of Weeping Waters, was a name for it.

NOTES

1   Above *Turuhalmë* are written *Duruchalm* (struck out) and *Halmadhurwion*.

2   This paragraph is marked with queries.

3   The word may be read equally well as 'dim' or 'dun'.

4   The original reading here was: 'and few of his folk went with him, and this Tû forbade to his folk, fearing the wrath of Ilúvatar and Manwë; yet did' (sc. curiosity overcome Nuin, etc.).

5   Earlier in the *Tales*, 'the Lost Elves' are those who were lost from the great journey and wandered in Hisilómë (see p. 118).

6   In the tale the 'fairies' of Tû's dominion (i.e. the Dark Elves) are given the name *Hisildi*, the twilight people; in outlines A and B, in addition to *Hisildi*, other names are given: *Humarni*, *Kaliondi*, *Lómëarni*.

7   Cf. also Sador's words to Túrin in his boyhood (*Unfinished Tales* p. 61): 'A darkness lies behind us, and out of it few tales have come. The fathers of our fathers may have had things to tell, but they did not tell them. Even their names are forgotten. The Mountains stand between us and the life that they came from, flying from no man now knows what.'

8   Cf. *The Silmarillion* p. 104: 'It is told that ere long they met Dark Elves in many places, and were befriended by them; and Men became the companions and disciples in their childhood of these ancient folk, wanderers of the Elven-race who never set out upon the paths to Valinor, and knew of the Valar only as a rumour and a distant name.'

9   Above *Ermon* is written, to all appearance, the Old English word *Æsc*
    ('ash'). It seems conceivable that this is an anglicizing of Old Norse
    Askr ('ash'), in the northern mythology the name of the first man,
    who with the first woman (*Embla*) were made by the Gods out of
    two trees that they found on the seashore (Völuspá strophe 17;
    Snorra Edda, Gylfaginning §8).

10 The text has here the bracketed word '(Gongs)'. This might be
    thought to be a name for the *Kaukareldar* or 'false-fairies', but in
    the Gnomish word-list *Gong* is defined as 'one of a tribe of the Orcs,
    a goblin'.

11 The cutting out of Nólemë's heart by the Orcs, and its recapture by
    Turgon his son, is referred to in an isolated early note, which says
    also that Turgon encased it in gold; and the emblem of the King's
    Folk in Gondolin, the Scarlet Heart, is mentioned in the tale of
    The Fall of Gondolin.

12 Cf. p. 167: 'Turondo son of Nólemë was not yet upon the Earth.'
    Turgon was the Gnomish name of *Turondo* (p. 115). In the later story
    Turgon was a leader of the Noldor from Valinor.

13 After the story was changed, and the founding of Gondolin was
    placed far earlier, the concluding part of *The Silmarillion* was never
    brought into harmony; and this was a main source of difficulty in
    the preparation of the published work.

APPENDIX
NAMES IN THE *LOST TALES* – PART I

There exist two small books, contemporary with the *Lost Tales*, which contain the first 'lexicons' of the Elvish languages; and both of them are very difficult documents.

One is concerned with the language called, in the book, *Qenya*, and I shall refer to this book as 'QL' (Qenya Lexicon). A good proportion of the entries in the first half of the alphabet were made at one time, when the work was first begun; these were very carefully written, though the pencil is now faint. Among these original entries is this group:

> *Lemin* 'five'
> *Lempe* 'ten'
> *Leminkainen* '23'

The choice of '23' suggests that this was my father's age at the time, and that the book was begun therefore in 1915. This is supported by some of the statements made in the first layer of entries about certain figures of the mythology, statements that are at odds with everything that is said elsewhere, and which give glimpses of a stage even earlier than the *Lost Tales*.

The book naturally continued in use, and many entries (virtually all of those in the second part of the alphabet) are later than this first layer, though nothing more definite can be said than that all entries belong to the period of (or not long preceding) the *Lost Tales*.

The words in QL are arranged according to 'roots', and a note at the beginning states:

> Roots are in capitals, and are not words in use at all, but serve as an elucidation of the words grouped together and a connection between them.

There is a good deal of uncertainty, expressed by queries, in the formulation of the roots, and in the ascription of words to one root or another, as my father moved among different etymological ideas; and in some cases it seems clear that the word was 'there', so to speak, but its etymology remained to be certainly defined, and not vice versa. The roots themselves are often difficult to represent, since certain consonants carry diacritic marks that are not defined. The notes on names that follow inevitably give a slightly more positive impression than does the book itself.

The other book is a dictionary of the Gnomish language, *Goldogrin*, and I shall refer to this as 'GL' (Goldogrin, or Gnomish, Lexicon). This is not arranged historically, by roots (though occasionally roots are given), but rather, in plan at least, as a conventional dictionary; and it contains a remarkable number of words. The book is entitled *i·Lam na·Ngoldathon* (i.e. 'the tongue of the Gnomes'): *Goldogrin*, with a date: 1917. Written beneath the title is *Eriol Sarothron* (i.e. 'Eriol the Voyager'), *who else is called Angol but in his own folk Ottor Wǽfre* (see p. 23).*

The great difficulty in this case is the intensity with which my father used this diminutive book, emending, rejecting, adding, in layer upon layer, so that in places it has become very hard to interpret. Moreover later changes to the forms in one entry were not necessarily made in related entries; thus the stages of a rapidly expanding linguistic conception are very confused in their representation. These little books were working materials, by no means the setting-out of finished ideas (it is indeed quite clear that GL in particular closely accompanied the actual composition of the *Tales*). Further, the languages changed even while the first 'layer' was being entered in GL; for example, the word *mô* 'sheep' was changed later to *moth*, but later in the dictionary *uimoth* 'sheep of the waves' was the form first written.

It is immediately obvious that an already extremely sophisticated and phonetically intricate historical structure lies behind the languages at this stage; but it seems that (unhappily and frustratingly) very little indeed in the way of phonological or grammatical description now survives from those days. I have found nothing, for instance, that sets out even in the sketchiest way the phonological relations between the two languages. Some early phonological description does exist for Qenya, but this became through later alterations and substitutions such a baffling muddle (while the material is in any case intrinsically extremely complex) that I have been unable to make use of it.

To attempt to use later materials for the elucidation of the linguistic ideas of the earliest period would in this book be quite impractical. But the perusal of these two vocabularies shows in the clearest possible way how deeply involved were the developments in the mythology and in the languages, and it would be seriously misleading to publish the *Lost Tales* without some attempt to show the etymological connections of the names that appear in them. I give therefore as much information, derived from these books, as is possible, but without any speculation beyond them. It is evident, for instance, that a prime element in the etymological constructions was slight variation in ancient 'roots' (caused especially by differences in the formation of consonants) that in the course of ages yielded very complex semantic situations; or again, that an old vocalic 'ablaut' (variation, in length or quality, of vowels in series) was present;

---

* The note concerning *Angol* and *Eriollo* referred to on p. 24 is written inside the cover of GL.

but I have thought it best merely to try to present the content of the dictionaries as clearly as I can.

It is noteworthy that my father introduced a kind of 'historical punning' here and there: so for instance the root SAHA 'be hot' yields (beside *saiwa* 'hot' or *sára* 'fiery') *Sahóra* 'the South', and from NENE 'flow' come *nen* 'river', *nénu* 'yellow water-lily', and *nénuvar* 'pool of lilies' – cf. *nenuphar* 'water-lily', modern French *nénufar*. There are also several resemblances to early English that are obviously not fortuitous, as *hôr* 'old', HERE 'rule', *rûm* 'secret (whisper)'.

It will be seen that a great many elements in the later languages, Quenya and Sindarin, as they are known from the published works, go back to the beginning; the languages, like the legends, were a continuous evolution, expansion, and refinement. But the historical status and relationship of the two languages as they were conceived at this time was radically changed later on: see p. 51.

The arrangement of the material has proved difficult, and indeed without a better understanding of relationships and their shifting formulations could scarcely be made satisfactory. The system I have adopted is to give etymologically-connected groups of words, in both Qenya and Gnomish, under an important name that contains one of them; to this entry other occurrences of a word in the group are referred (e.g. *glor-* in *Glorvent*, *Bráglorin* is referred to the entry *Laurelin*, where the etymological associations of Qenya *laurë* 'gold' are given).* Every name in the *Lost Tales* of this volume is given – that is, if any contemporary etymological information is to be found concerning it: any name not found in the following list is either quite opaque to me, or at least cannot be identified with any certainty. Rejected names are also included, on the same basis, but are given under the names that replaced them (e.g. *Dor Uswen* under *Dor Faidwen*).

The list of secondary names of the Valar which is written out on blank facing pages in the tale of *The Coming of the Valar* (see p. 93) is referred to as 'the Valar name-list'. The sign ⟨ is used only where it is used in the Gnomish dictionary, as *alfa* ⟨ *alchwa*, meaning that the one was historically derived from the other: it is not used in this Appendix to refer to alterations made by my father in the dictionaries themselves.

★

Ainur   Among the original entries in QL are *ainu* 'a pagan god' and *aini* 'a pagan goddess', together with *áye* 'hail!' and *Ainatar* 'Ilúvatar, God'. (Of course no one *within* the context of the mythology can call

---

* Later Quenya and Sindarin forms are only exceptionally mentioned. For such words see the vocabularies given in *An Introduction to Elvish*, ed. J. Allan, Bran's Head Books, 1978; also the Appendix to *The Silmarillion*.

the Ainur 'pagan'.) GL has *Ain*: 'also with distinctive masc. and fem. forms *Ainos* and *Ainil*, a God, i.e. one of the Great Valar'.

Alalminórë See *Aldaron, Valinor*. In QL *Alalminórë* is glossed 'Land of Elms, one of the provinces of Inwinórë in which is situated Kortirion (Warwickshire)'; i.e. *Alalminórë*=Warwickshire (see p. 25). Gnomish words are *lalm* or *larm*, also *lalmir*, 'elm'.

Aldaron In QL is a root ALA 'spread', with derivatives *alda* 'tree', *aldëa* 'tree-shadowed', *aldëon* 'avenue of trees', and *alalmë* 'elm' (see *Alalminórë*). In GL this name of Oromë appears as *Aldor* and *Ormaldor* (*Oromë* is *Orma* in Gnomish); *ald* 'wood (material)', later altered to *âl*.

Alqaluntë QL *alqa* 'swan'; GL *alcwi*, with the corresponding word in Qenya here given as *alqë, alcwi* changed later to *alfa* ⟨ *alchwa*.

QL *luntë* 'ship' from root LUTU, with other derivatives *lúto* 'flood' and verb *lutta-, lutu-* 'flow, float' (cf. *Ilsaluntë*). GL has correspondingly *lunta* 'ship', *lud-* 'flow, stream, float'.

Aluin See *Lúmin*.

Amillo This appears in QL but with no indication of meaning; *Amillion* is Amillo's month, February (one of the most 'primitive' entries).

Angaino Together with *angayassë* 'misery', *angaitya* 'torment', *Angaino* is given in QL separately from the 'iron' words (see *Angamandi*) and was first defined as 'a giant', emended to 'the great chain'. In GL Melko has a name *Angainos*, with a note: 'Do not confuse Gnomish *Angainos* with Qenya *Angaino* (Gnomish *Gainu*), the great chain of *tilkal*.' Under *Gainu* there is a later note: 'popularly connected with *ang* "iron" but really = "tormentor".'

Angamandi QL has *anga* 'iron' (which is the *a* of *tilkal*, p. 100), *angaina* 'of iron', *Angaron(ti)* 'Mountains of Iron', and *Angamandu* or *Eremandu* 'Hells of Iron' (added later: 'or *Angamandi*, plural'). The Gnomish forms are *ang* 'iron' (as in *Angol*, see under *Eriol*), *angrin* 'of iron', *Angband* – which, strangely, is said in GL to be 'Melko's great fortress after the battle of Countless Lamentation down to the battle of the Twilit Pool' (when Tulkas finally overthrew Melko). See *Mandos*.

Angol See *Eriol*.

Arvalin See *Eruman*.

Aryador This is said (p. 119) to be the name among Men of Hisilómë; but according to GL it was a word of Ilkorin origin, meaning 'land or place of shadow'; QL *Arëandor, Arëanor* 'name of a mountainous district, the abode of the Shadow Folk' (see p. 237). See *Eruman*.

Asgon GL has *Asgon* 'name of a lake in Dor Lómin (Hisilómë), Q. *Aksanda*'; QL has *aksa* 'waterfall', of which the Gnomish equivalent is given as *acha* of the same meaning. (No light is cast on the later name *Mithrim* in the dictionaries.)

Aulë A word *aulë* 'shaggy' is given in QL as a derivative from a root OWO (whence also *oa* 'wool', *uë* 'fleece'), but without any indication that this is to be connected with the name of the Vala. The Gnomish form of his name is *Óla*, changed to *Óli*, without further information. In the Valar name-list Aulë is called also *Tamar* or *Tamildo*. These are given in QL without translation under root TAMA 'smelt, forge', with *tambë* 'copper' (the *t* of *tilkal*, p. 100), *tambina* 'of copper', *tamin* 'forge'; Gnomish words are *tam* 'copper', *tambin* 'of copper', *tambos* 'cauldron'. For other names of Aulë see *Talka Marda*.

Aulenossë   For *nossë* 'kin, people' see *Valinor*.

Aur   Gnomish name of the Sun; see *Ûr*.

Balrog   GL defines *Balrog* as 'a kind of fire-demon; creatures and servants of Melko'. With the article the form is *i'Malrog*, plural *i'Malraugin*. Separate entries give *bal* 'anguish' (original initial consonant *mb*-), *balc* 'cruel'; and *graug* 'demon'. Qenya forms are mentioned: *araukë* and *Malkaraukë*. In QL *Malkaraukë* with other words such as *malkanë* 'torture' are given under a root MALA (MBALA) '(crush), hurt, damage', but the relation of this to MALA 'crush, squeeze' (see *Olórë Mallë*) was apparently not decided. There are also *Valkaraukë* and *valkanë* 'torture', but again the relationship is left obscure.

Bráglorin   Defined in the text (p. 187) as 'the blazing vessel', but translated in GL as 'Golden Wain, a name of the Sun', with a note: 'also in analytical form *i·Vreda 'Loriol*'; *brada* 'waggon, wain'. For *-glorin* see *Laurelin*.

Bronweg   GL has *Bronweg* '(the constant one), name of a famous Gnome', with related words as *brod*, *bronn* 'steadfast', *bronweth* 'constancy'. In QL *Voronwë* (see p. 48) 'the faithful' is derived from the root VORO, with *vor*, *voro* 'ever', *voronda* 'faithful', *vorima* 'everlasting', etc. Cf. *Vorotemnar*.

The common ending *-weg* is not given in GL, but cf. *gweg* 'man', plural *gwaith*.

Cûm a Gumlaith   'The Mound of the First Sorrow', tomb of Bruithwir, p. 149. GL *cûm* 'mound, especially burial-mound' (also *cum-* 'lie', *cumli* 'couch'); *gumlaith* 'weariness of spirit, grief' (*blaith* 'spirit').

Cûm a Thegranaithos   See preceding entry. GL *thegra* 'first, foremost', *thegor* 'chief'; *naitha-* 'lament, weep, wail for', *naithol* 'miserable'.

Danuin   GL has *dana* 'day (24 hours)', with reference to Qenya *sana* (not in QL); *Dana* was an earlier reading for *Danuin* (p. 222). The same element appears in *Lomendánar* 'Days of Gloaming'.

Dor Faidwen   Gnomish *dôr* (< *ndor-*) '(inhabited) land, country, people of the land'; see *Valinor*.

Dor Faidwen is translated in the text 'Land of Release' (p. 13); GL has *faidwen* 'freedom' and many related words, as *fair* 'free', *faith* 'liberty', etc. In QL under root FAYA appear *fairë* 'free', *fairië* 'freedom', *fainu-* 'release'.

Dor Faidwen was the final Gnomish name of Tol Eressëa after many changes (p. 21), but little light can be cast on the earlier forms. *Gar* in *Gar Eglos* is a Gnomish word meaning 'place, district'. *Dor Us(g)wen*: GL gives the stem *us-* 'leave, depart' (also *uthwen* 'way out, exit'), and QL under root USU 'escape' has *uswë* 'issue, escape' and *usin* 'he escapes'.

Dor Lómin   See *Valinor, Hisilómë*.

Eärendel   In an annotated list of names accompanying *The Fall of Gondolin* there is a suggestion, attributed to Littleheart son of Voronwë, that *Eärendel* had 'some kinship to the Elfin *ea* and *earen* "eagle" and "eyrie" ', and in QL these words (both given the meaning 'eagle') are placed with *Eärendel*, though not explicitly connected. In the tale itself it is said that 'there are many interpretations both among Elves and Men' of the name *Eärendel*, with a suggestion that it was a word of 'some secret tongue' spoken by the people of Gondolin.

GL has an entry: *Ioringli* 'true Gnomish form of Eärendel's name, though the Eldar-form has been also adopted and often is met in transition state as *Iarendel, Iorendel*' (on the distinction between 'Gnomish' and 'Eldar' see p. 50). Gnomish words for 'eagle' are *ior, ioroth*.

In QL is an entry *Eärendilyon* 'son of Eärendel (used of any mariner)'; cf. p. 13.

Eldamar   For the first element see *Eldar*. – In QL the following words are given in a group: *mar* (*mas-*) 'dwelling of men, the Earth, -land', *mardo* 'dweller', *masto* 'village', and *-mas* equivalent to English *-ton, -by* in place-names (cf. *Mar Vanwa Tyaliéva*; *Koromas*; *i·Talka Marda* 'Smith of the World', Aulë). In GL are *bar* 'home' (< *mbar-*), and derivatives, as *baros* 'hamlet', also *-bar* as suffix 'dweller', or 'home, -ham'.

The Gnomish equivalent of *Eldamar* was *Eglobar* (Gnomish *Egla* = Qenya *Elda*): '*Eglobar* "Elfinesse" = Q. *Eldamar*, i.e. Elfhome; the land on the edge of Valinor where the fairies dwelt and built Côr. Also in forms *Eglabar, Eglamar, Eglomar*.' In QL *Eldamar* is said, in a very early entry, to be 'the rocky beach in western Inwinórë (Faëry)'; 'upon this rock was the white town built called Kôr'.

Eldar   In QL *Elda* is given separately, without etymological connections, and defined as 'a beach-fay or *Solosimpë* (shore-piper)'. This is a glimpse of an earlier conception than that found in the *Lost Tales*: the *Eldar* were originally the Sea-elves. GL has the entry *Egla* ' "a being from outside", name of the fairies given by the Valar and largely adopted by them, =Q. *Elda*' (see p. 235); also *eg, êg* 'far away, distant'. The association of *Eldar* with the stars does not go back to the beginning.

Erinti   She appears in QL in an isolated, early entry (afterwards struck through). Nothing is ever told of Erinti in the *Lost Tales*, but in this note she is called the Vala of love, music, and beauty, also named *Lotessë* and *Akairis* ('bride'), sister of Noldorin and Amillo. These three alone (i.e. of the Valar) have left Valinor, and dwell in Inwenórë (Tol Eressëa); she herself dwells in Alalminórë in a *korin* of elms guarded by the fairies. The second half of the month of *avestalis* (January) is called *Erintion*.

There is no trace of this elsewhere; but clearly, when Erinti became the daughter of Manwë and Varda her dwelling in Alalminórë was taken over by Meril-i-Turinqi, the Lady of Tol Eressëa.

In the Valar name-list Erinti is called also *Kalainis*; this word appears in QL with the meaning 'May', one of many derivatives from the root KALA (see *Galmir*).

Eriol In *The Cottage of Lost Play* (p. 14) *Eriol* is translated 'One who dreams alone'. In QL the elements of this interpretation are given under the roots ERE 'remain alone' (see *Tol Eressëa*) and LORO 'slumber' (see *Lórien*). In GL appears the note cited on p. 24 that Gnomish *Angol* and Qenya *Eriollo* were the names of the region 'between the seas' whence Eriol came (=Angeln in the Danish peninsula); and in an isolated note elsewhere *Angol* is derived from *ang* 'iron' and *ôl* 'cliff', while Eriol is said to mean the same – 'this being the name of the fairies for the parts [*sic*] of his home (ironcliffs)'. Meril refers to 'the black coasts of your home' (p. 96). In this note the interpretation 'One who dreams alone' is said to be a pun on Lindo's part.

For *ang* 'iron' see *Angamandi*. GL has *ol, óla* 'cliff, seaward precipice', with Qenya forms *ollo, oldō. ere(n)* 'iron or steel' is given in QL, and this element appears also in the alternative name *Eremandu* for *Angamandu*, 'Hells of Iron'.

Eruman The names of this region are as difficult as the original conception of the region itself (see pp. 91 ff.). The form *Erumáni* (which occurs in the *Tales* as well as *Eruman*) appears in QL under ERE 'out' (cf. *Neni Erúmëar*) without further information. GL has a long entry under *Edhofon*, which=Q. *Erumáni*: it is a 'dark land outside Valinor and to the south of the Bay of Faëry, that ran right up to the bases of the western side of the Mountains of Valinor; its farthest northern point touched upon the roots of Taniquetil, hence *Edhofon* ⟨ *Eöusmānī-*, i.e. beyond the abode of the Mánir. Hence also the Q. title *Afalinan* or *Arvalion*, i.e. nigh Valinor.' The implication of this seems to be that Taniquetil was 'the abode of the Mánir', as is comprehensible, since the Mánir were particularly associated with Manwë (the Gnomish words *móna, móni* are defined as 'spirits of the air, children of Manwë'), and therefore Eruman was beyond (south of) their abode. See *Mánir*.

GL also states that Edhofon was called *Garioth*; and *Garioth* is 'the true Gnome form' of the name *Aryador* (a word of Ilkorin origin) 'land of shadow', though applied not to Hisilómë but to Edhofon / Eruman.

According to QL *Harwalin* 'near the Valar' contains *har(e)* 'near'; the entries in GL are too confusing to cite, for the forms of *Harwalin* / *Arvalin* were changed over and over again. A late entry in GL gives a prefix *ar-* 'beside, along with'. For *Habbanan* see *Valar*.

Falassë Númëa Translated in the text (p. 124) as 'Western Surf'; see *Falman*, *Númë*.

Falman In QL the root FALA has derivatives *falma* 'foam', *falmar* 'wave as it breaks', *falas(s)* 'shore, beach', *Falman*=Ossë; cf. *Falassë Númea, Falmarini*. GL has *falm* 'breaker, wave', *falos* 'sea-marge, surf', *Falmon* or *Falathron* 'names of Otha [Ossë], =Q. *Falman* and *Falassar*'.

Falmaríni See *Falman*.

Fanturi In QL *fantur*, without translation but with reference to Lórien and Mandos, is given under root FANA, with several derivatives all referring to visions, dreams, falling asleep. In GL (a late entry) the form is *Fanthor*, plural *i·Fanthaurin* 'the name of each of the two brothers, of sleep, of death'.

Fanuin GL has *fann* 'a year'. For the rejected names *Lathos, Lathweg* (p. 222) see *Gonlath*.

Faskala-númen, Faskalan Translated in the text (p. 187) as 'Bath of the Setting Sun'. GL has *fas-* 'wash', *fasc* 'clean', *fasca-* 'splash, sprinkle', *fôs* 'bath'. For *-númen* see *Númë*.

Fëanor The only evidence for the meaning of this name is given under *Fionwë-Úrion*.

Fingolma See *Nólemë*.

Finwë As a proper name this is not in the dictionaries, but GL gives a common noun *finweg* 'craftsman, man of skill' (with *fim* 'clever; right hand' and other related words); for *-weg* see *Bronweg*. In QL derivatives of root FINI are *finwa* 'sagacious', *finië, findë* 'cunning'. See *Nólemë*.

Fionwë-Úrion *Fion* 'son' is given separately in QL (a hurried later addition), with the note 'especially Fion(wë) the Vala'. In Gnomish he is '*Auros Fionweg*, or *Fionaur Fionor*'. In a later entry in GL '*Fionaur (Fionor)*=Q. *Fëanor* (goblet-smith)', and among the original entries is *fion* 'bowl, goblet'. There is no indication that this refers to Fëanor the Gnome.

For the second element (*Úrion, Auros*) see *Úr*. In the Valar name-list Fionwë is called *Kalmo*; see *Galmir*.

Fui In QL are *hui* 'fog, dark, murk, night' and *huiva* 'murky', and also '*Fui* (=*hui*) wife of Vê'. In Gnomish she is *Fuil* 'Queen of the Dark', and related words are *fui* 'night', *fuin* 'secret, dark'.

fumellar The 'flowers of sleep' (poppies) in Lórien's gardens (p. 74). QL under root FUMU 'sleep' has *fúmë* 'sleep' (noun), *fúmella, fúmellot* 'poppy'.

Galmir   Translated in the text (p. 187) as 'the goldgleamer' (a name of the Sun). This is a derivative of Gnomish *gal-* 'shine', which in Qenya is KALA 'shine golden', and of which a great many derivatives are given in QL, as *kala-* 'shine', *kálë* 'morning', *kalma* 'daylight', *Kalainis* 'May' (see *Erinti*), *kalwa* 'beautiful', etc. Cf. *Kalormë*, *Kalaventë*, and *i·kal'antúlien* 'Light hath returned' (p. 184).

Gar Lossion   Translated in the text (p. 16) as 'Place of Flowers' (Gnomish name of Alalminórë). For *Gar* see *Dor Faidwen*. GL gives *lost* 'blossom' and *lôs* 'flower', but it is noted that they are probably unconnected and that *lôs* is more likely to be related to *lass* 'leaf', also used to mean 'petal'. (QL has *lassë* 'leaf', *lasselanta* 'the Fall, Autumn'.) See *Lindelos*.

Glorvent   For the element *Glor-* see *Laurelin*. – GL had *Glorben(d)* 'ship of gold', changed later to *Glorvent* 'boat of gold'; *benn* 'shape, cut, fashion', *benc*, *bent* 'small boat'. QL has the root VENE 'shape, cut out, scoop', with derivatives *venië*, *venwë* 'shape, cut' and *venë* 'small boat, vessel, dish'. Cf. the title of the 'World-Ship' drawing, *I Vene Kemen* (see p. 85), and the Sun's name *i·Kalaventë* (*Kalavénë*).

Golfinweg   See *Nólemë*, *Finwë*.

Gondolin   QL does not give this name, but *ondo* 'stone' appears under root ONO 'hard'. In GL *Gondolin* is said to=Qenya *Ondolin* (changed to *Ondolinda*) 'singing stone'. There is also an entry *gond* 'great stone, rock'; later this was changed to *gonn*, and a note added that *Gondolin*= *Gonn Dolin*, together with an entry *dólin* 'song'. See *Lindelos*.

Gong   GL gives no other information beyond that cited on p. 245, note 10, but compares *sithagong* 'dragonfly' (*sitha* 'fly', *Sithaloth* or *Sithaloctha* ('fly-cluster'), the Pleiades).

Gonlath   This is the name of the great rock on Taniquetil to which Fanuin's cable was tied (p. 219); the second element must therefore be Gnomish *lath* 'a year', which appears also in the rejected names for Fanuin, *Lathos* and *Lathweg* (p. 222). For *Gon-* see *Gondolin*.

Gwerlum   This is given in GL with the translation 'Gloomweaver'; *gwer-* 'wind, turn, bend', but also used in the sense of the root *gwidh-* 'plait, weave'. QL has a root GWERE 'whirl, twirl, twist', but the name *Wirilómë* of the great Spider is placed under the root GWIÐI, whence also *windelë* 'loom', *winda* 'woof', *wistë* 'weft'. The name of the great eddy *Wiruin* (p. 167), not in the dictionaries. must belong here. For the element *-lómë*, *-lum* see *Hisilómë*.

Haloisi Velikë   (On the 'World-Ship' drawing, p. 84.) In QL *haloisi* 'the sea (in storm)' is given under a root HALA, with other derivatives *haloitë* 'leaping', *halta-* 'to leap'.

To Qenya *velikë* 'great' corresponds Gnomish *beleg* 'mighty, great' (as in Beleg the Bowman in the tale of Túrin).

Helkar   QL under root HELE has *helkë* 'ice', *helka* 'ice-cold', *hilkin* 'it freezes', *halkin* 'frozen'. GL has *helc*, *heleg* 'ice', *hel-* 'freeze', *heloth* 'frost', etc., and *helcor* 'arctic cold, utter frost'; this last was changed to read *helchor* 'antarctic cold, utter frost of the South (the pillar of the Southern Lamp). Q. *Helkar*.'

Helkaraksë   See *Helkar*; *Helkaraksë* is not in either dictionary and the second element is obscure, unless it is to be connected with Q. *aksa* 'waterfall' (see *Asgon*).

Heskil   The root HESE 'winter' in QL has derivatives *Heskil* 'winter one', *Hesin* 'winter', *hessa* 'dead, withered', *hesta-* 'wither'. In GL are *Hess* 'winter, especially as name of Fuil', and *hesc* 'withered, dead; chill'. For another name of Fui Nienna see *Vailimo*.

Hisildi   See *Hisilómë*.

Hisilómë   Under the root HISI QL gives *hísë*, *histë* 'dusk', *Hisinan* 'Land of Twilight'. For the translation of *Hisilómë* as 'Shadowy Twilights' see p. 112.

The root LOMO has many derivatives, as *lómë* 'dusk, gloom, darkness', *lómëar* 'child of gloom' (cf. *Lómëarni*), *lómin* 'shade, shadow', *lomir* 'I hide', *lomba* 'secret'. Cf. *Wirilómë*. Gnomish words are *lôm* 'gloom, shade', *lómin* 'shadowy, gloomy' and noun 'gloom': so *Dor Lómin*. The same element occurs in *Lomendánar* 'Days of Gloaming'.

Ilinsor   A late entry in GL gives *Glinthos*=Qenya *Ilinsor*, Helmsman of the Moon. The first element is probably *glint* 'crystal'. *Ilinsor* does not appear in QL.

Ilkorin   A negative prefix *il-* is given in both dictionaries; in GL it is said that *il-* 'denotes the opposite, the reversal, i.e. more than the mere negation'. See *Kôr*.

Ilsaluntë   (Name of the Moon.) *Ilsa* is given in QL as 'the mystic name of silver, as *laurë* of gold'; it is the *i* of *tilkal*, p. 100. For *luntë* 'ship' see *Alqaluntë*. The Gnomish name is *Gilthalont*; *giltha* 'white metal' is said to be properly the same as *celeb* 'silver' (Q. *telpë*), but now including *gais* 'steel', *ladog* 'tin', etc., as opposed to *culu* 'gold'; and *culu* is said to be a poetic word for 'gold' but 'also used mythically as a class name of all red and yellow metals, as *giltha* of white and grey'. See *Telimpë*.

Ilterendi   In the text the fetters are called *Ilterendi* 'for they might not be filed or cleft' (p. 101); but root TERE in QL has derivatives with a sense of 'boring' (*tereva* 'piercing', *teret* 'auger, gimlet').

Ilúvatar   There can be no doubt that the original meaning of *Ilúvatar* was 'Sky-father' (in QL is found *atar* 'father'); see *Ilwë*.

Ilverin   Elvish name of Littleheart son of Bronweg. The rejected name *Elwenildo* (p. 52) contains the word *elwen* 'heart' given in QL; GL gives the word *ilf* 'heart (especially used of feelings)', and several names (*Ilfin(g)*, *Ilfiniol*, *Ilfrith*) corresponding to Qenya *Ilwerin*.

Ilwë   In QL the word *ilu* is glossed 'ether, the slender airs among the stars', while in GL the Gnomish name *Ilon* of Illúvatar is said to= Qenya *Ilu*. In QL *ilwë* was first glossed 'sky, heavens', with a later

addition 'the blue air that is about the stars, the middle layers';
to this in Gnomish corresponds *ilwint* – concerning which it is
explained in GL that the true form *ilwi* or *ilwin* was perverted to
ilwint through association with *gwint* 'face', as if it meant 'face of
God'. Other words found in Gnomish are *Ilbar*, *Ilbaroth* 'heaven,
the uttermost region beyond the world'; *Ilador*, *Ilathon*=*Ilúvatar*;
ilbrant 'rainbow' (see *Ilweran*).

Ilweran   QL gives *Ilweran*, *Ilweranta* 'rainbow' (another word for the
rainbow in Qenya is *Iluqinga*, in which *qinga* means 'bow'; *qingi*-
'twang, of strings, harp'). In Gnomish the corresponding forms are
Ilbrant or *Ilvrant*, which are said in GL to be falsely associated with
brant 'bow (for shooting)'; the second element is related rather to
rantha 'arch, bridge', as Q. *Ilweran(ta)* shows.

Ingil   In GL the Gnomish names of Inwë's son are *Gilweth* and *Githilma*;
Gil is the star Sirius, and is said to be the name of Gilweth after he
rose into the heavens and 'in the likeness of a great bee bearing honey
of flame followed Daimord [Telimektar, Orion]'; see entries *Nielluin*,
Telimektar. No explanation of these names is given, but *Gil(weth)*
is clearly connected with *gil-* 'gleam', *gilm* 'moonlight', *giltha* 'white
metal' (see *Ilsaluntë*). For *Githilma* see *Isil*.

Inwë   In QL this, the name of 'the ancient king of the fairies who led
them to the world', is a derivative of a root INI 'small', whence also
the adjective *inya* and the names *Inwilis*, *Inwinórë* 'Faëry' and
'England' (the latter struck out). Tol Eressëa was here said to have
been named *Inwinórë* after Inwë, but this was changed to say that
it was named *Ingilnórë* after his son Ingil. These entries relate to a
very early conception (see *Alalminórë*, *Eldamar*). For other names
of Inwë see *Inwithiel*, *Isil*.

Inwir   See *Inwë*. In GL the 'noble clan of the Tilthin' (Teleri) are called
Imrim, singular *Im* (see *Inwithiel*).

Inwithiel   In the texts *Inwithiel*, Gnomish name of King Inwë, is an
emendation from *(Gim)Githil* (pp. 22, 131). In GL these names
Inwithiel, *Githil* are given as additional to his proper names *Inweg*
or *Im*. See *Isil*.

Isil   In the tale of *The Coming of the Elves* (p. 115) Inwë is called
Isil Inwë, and in GL the Gnomish form corresponding to *Isil* is
Githil (to the name of his son *Githilma* corresponds Qenya *Isilmo*).
In QL is a root ISI (*iska* 'pale', *is* 'light snow'), of which the Gnomish
equivalent is given as *ith-* or *gith-*; GL has a word *ith* 'fine snow'.

Kalaventë   See *Galmir*, *Glorvent*.

Kalormë   This appears in QL among the derivatives of root KALA (see
Galmir), with the meaning 'hill-crest over which the Sun rises'.
ormë='summit, crest', from a root ORO with apparently a base
sense of 'rise': *or* 'on', *oro* 'hill', *oro-* 'rise', *orto-* 'raise', *oronta* 'steep',
orosta 'ascension', etc.; Gnomish *or* 'on, onto, on top', *orod*, *ort*

'mountain', *orm* 'hill-top', *oros*, *orost-* 'rising'. Cf. *Oromë*, *Orossi*, *Tavrobel*.

Kapalinda (The source of the river in the place of the banishment of the Noldoli in Valinor, p. 157.) QL has *kapalinda* 'spring of water' among derivatives of root KAPA 'leap, spring'; *linda* is obscure.

Kaukareldar Under the root KAWA 'stoop' in QL are derivations *kauka* 'crooked, bent, humped', *kauko* 'humpback', *kawin* 'I bow', *kaurë* 'fear', *kaurëa* 'timid'.

Kelusindi (The river in the place of the banishment of the Noldoli in Valinor, p. 157; in the text called *Sirnúmen*.) In QL under root KELE, KELU 'flow, trickle, ooze' are given many derivatives including *kelusindi* 'a river', also *kelu*, *kelumë* 'stream', *kektelë* 'fountain' (also in the form *ektelë*), etc. For *-sindi* see *Sirion*.

Kémi QL gives *kemi* 'earth, soil, land' and *kemen* 'soil', from root KEME. The Gnomish name is *Címir*, which=Q. *Kémi* 'Mother Earth'. There is also a Gnomish word *grosgen* 'soil' in which *-gen* is said to= Q. *kémi*.

Koivië-néni 'Waters of Awakening.' In QL under root KOYO 'have life' are derivatives *koi*, *koirë* 'life', *koitë* 'living being', *koina*, *koirëa* 'alive', *koiva* 'awake', *koivië* 'awakening'. In GL are *cuil* 'life', *cuith* 'life, living body', etc.; *cwiv-* 'be awake', *cwivra-* 'awaken', *cuivros* 'awakening': *Nenin a Gwivros* 'Waters of Awakening'. For *-néni*, *Nenin* see *Neni Erúmëar*.

Kópas QL has *kópa* 'harbour', the only word given under root KOPO 'keep, guard'. GL has *gobos* 'haven', with a reference to Q. *kópa*, *kópas*; also *gob* 'hollow of hand', *gobli* 'dell'.

Kôr In QL this name is given under the root KORO 'revere?', with the note 'the ancient town built above the rocks of Eldamar, whence the fairies marched into the world'; also placed here are *korda* 'temple', *kordon* 'idol'. The Gnomish form is here given as *Côr*, but in GL *Côr* ('the hill of the fairies and the town thereon near the shores of the Bay of Faëry') was replaced by *Gwâr*, *Goros* '=Q. *Kôr* the town on the round hill'. This interpretation of the name *Kôr* clearly replaces that in QL, which belongs with the earliest layer of entries. See further under *korin*.

korin See *Kôr*. In QL there is a second root KORO (i.e. distinct from that which gave *Kôr*); this has the meaning 'be round, roll', and has such derivatives as *korima* 'round', *kornë* 'loaf', also *korin* 'a circular enclosure, especially on a hill-top'. At the same time as *Côr* was replaced by *Gwâr*, *Goros* in GL the word *gorin* (*gwarin*) 'circle of trees, =Q. *korin*' was entered, and all these forms derive from the same root (*gwas-* or *gor-* < *guor*=Q. *kor-*), which would seem to signify 'roundness'; so in the tale of *The Coming of the Elves* 'the Gods named that hill Kôr by reason of its roundness and its smoothness' (p. 122).

Koromas A separate and early entry in QL defines *Kormas* (the form in the text before emendation to *Koromas*, p. 22) thus: 'the new capital of the fairies after their retreat from the hostile world to Tol Eressëa, now Inwinórë. It was named in memory of Kôr and because of its great tower was called also *Kortirion*.' For *-mas* see *Eldamar*.

Kortirion   The word *tirion* 'a mighty tower, a city on a hill' is given in QL under root TIRI 'stick up', with *tinda* 'spike', *tirin* 'tall tower', *tirios* 'a town with walls and towers'. There is also another root TIRI, differing in the nature of the medial consonant, with meaning 'watch, guard, keep; look at, observe', whence *tiris* 'watch, vigil', etc. In GL are *tir-* 'look out for, await', *tirin* (poetic form *tirion*) 'watch-tower, turret', *Tirimbrithla* 'the Tower of Pearl' (see *Silmarilli*).

Kosomot   Son of Melko (see p. 93). With a different second element, *Kosomoko*, this name is found in QL under root MOKO 'hate' (*mokir* 'I hate'), and the corresponding Gnomish form is there said to be *Gothmog*. The first element is from root KOSO 'strive', in Gnomish *goth* 'war, strife', with many derivative words.

Kulullin   This name is not among the derivatives of KULU 'gold' in QL, nor does it appear with the Gnomish words (mostly names of the Sun) containing *culu* in GL. For the meaning of *culu* in Gnomish see *Ilsaluntë*.

Laisi   See *Tári-Laisi*.

Laurelin   QL has *laurë* 'gold (much the same as *kulu*)', *laurina* 'golden'. *laurë* is the final *l* of *tilkal* (p. 100, where it is said to be the 'magic' name of gold, as *ilsa* of silver). The Gnomish words are *glôr* 'gold', *glôrin*, *glôriol* 'golden', but GL gives no names of the Golden Tree. Cf. *Bráglorin*, *Glorvent*.

limpë   *limpë* 'drink of the fairies' is given in QL under root LIPI, with *lipte-* 'to drip', *liptë* 'a little drop', *lipil* 'little glass'. Corresponding forms in GL are *limp* or *limpelis* 'the drink of the fairies', *lib-* 'to drip', *lib* 'a drop', *libli* 'small glass'.

Lindeloksë   At one occurrence in the texts an emendation from *Lindeloktë* and itself emended to *Lindelos* (p. 22), at others an emendation from *Lindelótë* and itself allowed to stand (pp. 79, 131). See *Lindelos*.

Lindelos   *Linde-* is one of many derivatives from the root LIRI 'sing', as *lin* 'melody', *lindele* 'song, music', *lindelëa* 'melodious', *lirit* 'poem', *lirilla* 'lay, song' (cf. Rúmil's *tiripti lirilla*, p. 47), and the name of the Vala *Lirillo*. GL has *lir-* 'sing' and *glir* 'song, poem'. *Lindelos* is not given in QL, which has the name rejected in the text *Lindeloktë* (p. 22), here translated 'singing cluster, laburnum'.

Loktë 'blossom (of flowers in bunches or clusters)' is derived from a root LOHO, with *lokta-* 'sprout, put forth leaves or flowers'. This is said to be an extended form of root OLO 'tip', whence *olë* 'three', *olma* 'nine', *ólemë* 'elbow'. Another extended form of this root is LO'O, from which are derived *lótë* 'a flower' (and *-lot* 'the common form in compounds') and many other words; cf. *Lindelótë*, another rejected name of the Golden Tree (pp. 79, 131), *Wingilot*. For Gnomish words see *Gar Lossion*. No Gnomish name of the Golden Tree is found in GL, but it was in fact *Glingol* (which originally appeared in the text, see p. 22); GL has *glin* 'sound, voice, utterance' (also *lin* 'sound'), with the note that *-glin, -grin* is a suffix in the names of languages, as *Goldogrin* Gnomish.

Lirillo   (A name of Salmar-Noldorin, p. 144.) See *Lindelos*.

Lómëarni   (A name of the Dark Elves, p. 244 note 6.) See *Hisilómë*.

Lomendánar   'Days of Gloaming' (p. 69). See *Hisilómë, Danuin*.

Lórien   A derivative of the root LORO 'slumber', with *lor-* 'to slumber', *lorda* 'drowsy, slumbrous'; also *olor, olórë* 'dream', *olórëa* 'dreamy'. (For much later formulation of words from this root, including *Olórin* (Gandalf), see *Unfinished Tales* p. 396.) In GL are given *lûr* 'slumber', *Lúriel* changed to *Lúrin*=Qenya *Lórien*, and also *olm, oloth, olor* 'dream, apparition, vision', *oltha* 'appear as an apparition'. Cf. *Eriol, Olofantur, Olórë Mallë*.

Lúmin   (Rejected name for Aluin 'Time', p. 222.) GL has *lûm* 'time', *luin* 'gone, past', *lu* 'occasion, time', *lûtha* 'pass (of time), come to pass'. *Aluin* perhaps belongs here also.

Luvier   I have translated this word on the 'World-Ship' drawing as 'Clouds' (p. 85) on the basis of words in QL derived from the root LUVU: *luvu-* 'lower, brood', *lumbo* 'dark lowering cloud', *lúrë* 'dark weather', *lúrëa* 'dark, overcast'. GL has *lum* 'cloud', *lumbri* 'foul weather', *lumbrin, lumba* 'overcast', *lur-* 'hang, lower, of clouds'.

Makar   Given in QL ('God of battle') under root MAKA, with *mak-* 'slay', *makil* 'sword'. His Gnomish name is *Magron* or *Magorn*, with related words *mactha-* 'slay', *macha* 'slaughter, battle', *magli* 'a great sword'. See *Meássë*.

In the Valar name-list Makar is called also *Ramandor*. This was the original name of the King of the Eagles in *The Fall of Gondolin*, replaced by *Sorontur*. In QL under root RAMA (*rama-* 'to shout', *rambë* 'a shout', *ran* 'noise') *Ramandor* is translated 'the Shouter, =Makar'.

Mandos   This name is defined in QL as 'the halls of Vê and Fui (hell)', and a comparison made with *-mandu* in *Angamandu* 'Hells of Iron'. In GL is the following entry: '*Bandoth* [later changed to *Bannoth*] (cf. *Angband*)=Mandos (1) the region of the waiting souls of the dead (2) the God who judged the dead Elves and Gnomes (3) improperly used exclusively of his hall, properly called *Gwê* [changed to *Gwî*] or *Ingwi*'. For this distinction between the region *Mandos*, in which dwelt the death-gods, and their halls *Vê* and *Fui*, see pp. 76, 89-90.

Mánir   Not in QL; but GL has '*móna* or *móni*: the spirits of the air, children of Manweg'. Further relations are indicated in the following entry: '*manos* (plural *manossin*): a spirit that has gone to the Valar or to Erumáni (Edhofon). Cf. *móna*, Q. *mánë.*' See *Eruman* and pp. 91 ff. Other words are *mani* 'good (of men and character only), holy' (QL *manë* 'good (moral)'), *mandra* 'noble', and *Manweg* (Q. *Manwë*).

Manwë   See *Mánir.* The Gnomish names are *Man* and *Manweg* (for *-weg* see *Bronweg*).

Mar Vanwa Tyaliéva   For *Mar* see *Eldamar,* and for *Vanwa* see *Qalvanda. Tyalië* 'play, game' is an isolated entry in QL under root TYALA.

Meássë   A late, hasty entry in QL adds *Meássë* 'sister of Makar, Amazon with bloody arms' to the root MEHE 'ooze?', whence *mear* 'gore'. In GL she is *Mechos* and *Mechothli* (*mechor* 'gore'), and is also called *Magrintha* 'the red-handed' (*magru*=*macha* 'slaughter, battle', *magrusaig* 'bloodthirsty'). In the Valar name-list she is called *Rávë* or *Ravenni*; in QL the root RAVA has many derivatives, as *rauta-* 'to hunt', *raust* 'hunting, preying', *Raustar* a name of Oromë, *rau* (plural *rávi*) 'lion', *ravennë* 'she-lion', *Rávi* a name of Meássë. Very similar forms are given in GL: *rau* 'lion', *rausta* 'to hunt', *raust* 'hunt'.

Melko   The name is entered in QL but without etymological affinity. In GL the corresponding name is *Belca,* changed to *Belcha,* with a note referring to Qenya *velka* 'flame'. In the Valar name-list he is called *Yelur* (root DYELE, whence Qenya *yelwa* 'cold', *Yelin* 'winter'); the Gnomish form is *Geluim, Gieluim,* 'name of Belcha when exercising his opposite functions of extreme cold, Q. *Yeloimu*', cf. *Gilim* 'winter'. Melko is also called in the name-list *Ulban(d),* which is found in QL glossed 'monster', under the negative prefix UL-; his son Kosomot (Gothmog) was 'by Ulbandi' (p. 93). Other names for him in Gnomish are *Uduvrin* (see *Utumna*) and *Angainos* (see *Angaino*).

Meril-i-Turinqi   *Meril* is not in QL, but *turinqi* 'queen' is given with a great many other derivatives of the root TURU 'be strong', including *Turambar* (*Turumarto*), and *tur* 'king'. In GL are *tur-* 'can, have power to', *túr* 'king', *turwin* 'queen', *turm* 'authority, rule; strength', *turinthi* 'princess, especially title of Gwidhil'. Cf. *Sorontur, Valatúru, Tuor.*

There are also these later additions in GL: '*Gwidhil-i-Durinthi*= *Meril-i-Turinqi* Queen of Flowers'; *gwethra* 'bloom, flourish'; and the stem *gwedh-* is here compared to Qenya *mer-,* which is not in QL.

Minethlos   GL *min* 'one, single', *mindon* 'tower, properly an isolated turret or peak', *mineth* 'island', *Minethlos* 'Argent Isle (Moon)' – the same translation is given in the text, p. 192. Under root MĪ QL has *mir* 'one', *minqë* 'eleven'; and under root MINI *mindon* 'turret'. The second element of *Minethlos* must in fact be *lôs* 'flower' (see *Gar Lossion*).

Miruvor   QL *miruvórë* 'nectar, drink of the Valar' (see p. 161), with *miru* 'wine'; GL *mirofor* (or *gurmir*) 'drink of the Gods', *mîr*, *miros* 'wine'.

Moritarnon   'Door of Night' (see *Mornië*). GL gives *tarn* 'gate', *tarnon* 'porter'. Cf. *Tarn Fui*.

Mornië   Not in QL, but one of the many derivatives of root MORO, as *moru-* 'to hide', *mori* 'night', *morna*, *morqa* 'black', *morion* 'son of the dark'. (A curious item is *Morwen* 'daughter of the dark', Jupiter. In the original tale of Túrin his mother was not named Morwen.) The Gnomish name of the death-ship is *Mornir*, a later addition to original entries *morn* 'dark, black', *morth* 'darkness', *mortha* 'dim', with the note 'the black ship that plies between Mandos and Erumáni, Q. *Mornië* (Black Grief)'. The second element is therefore *nír* 'grief' (< *niër-*), to which Qenya *nyérë* is said to correspond. Cf. *Moritarnon*, *Móru*, *Morwinyon*.

Móru   GL in a later addition gives *Muru* 'a name of the Primeval Night personified as Gwerlum or Gungliont', hence my reading in the text *Móru* rather than *Morn* (p. 156). Among the original entries in GL is *múri* 'darkness, night'. See *Mornië*.

Morwinyon   This name of the star Arcturus is translated in the text (p. 182) as 'the glint at dusk', and QL, giving it under root MORO (see *Mornië*), renders it 'glint in the dark'. QL has a root GWINI with derivative word *wintil* 'a glint'.

   The Gnomish name is *Morwinthi*; presumably connected are *gwim*, *gwinc* 'spark, flash', *gwimla* 'wink, twinkle'.

Murmenalda   Translated in the text as 'Vale of Sleep', 'the Slumbrous Dale' (pp. 233, 235). QL under root MURU gives *muru-* 'to slumber', *murmë* 'slumber', *murmëa* 'slumbrous'. The second element is from a root NLDL, of which the derivatives in QL are *nal(lë)* 'dale, dell' and *nalda* 'valley' used as an adjective. In Gnomish occur *nal* 'dale, vale', *nal* 'down, downwards', *nalos* 'sinking, setting, slope', *Nalosaura* 'sunset', etc. Cf. *Murmuran*.

Murmuran   See *Murmenalda*. GL gives the Gnomish form corresponding to Qenya *Murmuran* as *Mormaurien* 'abode of Lúriel', but this seems to be of different etymology: cf. *Malmaurien=Olórë Mallë*, the Path of Dreams, *maur* 'dream, vision'.

Nandini   On an isolated paper that gives a list of the different clans of 'fays' the *Nandini* are 'fays of the valleys'. QL gives a root NARA with derivatives *nan(d)* 'woodland', *nandin* 'dryad'; GL has *nandir* 'fay of the country, Q. *nandin*', together with *nand* 'field, acre' (plural *nandin* 'country'), *nandor* 'farmer', etc.

Nauglath   GL gives the following words: *naug* and *naugli* 'dwarf', *naugla* 'of the dwarves', *nauglafel* 'dwarf-natured, i.e. mean, avaricious' (see p. 236). QL has nothing corresponding, but in GL the Qenya equivalent of *naug* is said to be *nauka*.

Neni Erúmëar (On the 'World-Ship' drawing, where I have translated it 'Outermost Waters', p. 85.) QL under root NENE 'flow' has *nen* 'river, water', and the same form occurs in Gnomish. *Erúmëa* 'outer, outermost' is given in QL as a derivative of ERE 'out', as in *Eruman*. Cf. *Koivië-néni*.

Nermir In the list of fays referred to under *Nandini* the *Nermir* are 'fays of the meads'. QL has an isolated entry *Nermi* 'a field-spirit', and GL has *Nermil* 'a fay that haunts meadows and river-banks'.

Nessa This name does not appear in the dictionaries. – In the Valar name-list she is called *Helinyetillë* and *Melesta*. In QL, among the very early entries, *helin* is the name of the violet or pansy, and *Helinyetillë* is glossed 'Eyes of Heartsease' (that being a name of the pansy); cf. *yéta* 'look at'. But in QL this is a name of Erinti. There was clearly much early shifting among the goddesses of Spring, the ascription of names and rôles (see *Erinti*). *Melesta* is doubtless from root MELE 'love' (*meles(së)* 'love', *melwa* 'lovely', etc.; Gnomish *mel-* 'to love', *meleth* 'love', *melon, meltha* 'beloved', etc.).

Nielíqui In QL this name (*Nieliqi*, also *Nielikki, Nyelikki*) is derived from the root NYEHE 'weep' (see *Nienna*). Where her tears fell snowdrops (*nieningë*, literally 'white tear') sprang. See the poem *Nieninqë* in J. R. R. Tolkien, *The Monsters and the Critics and Other Essays*, 1983, p. 215. For *ninqë* see *Taniquetil*.

The second element of *Nielíqui* is presumably from the root LIQI, whence *linqë* 'water', *liqin* 'wet', *liqis* 'transparence', etc. (see *Ulmo*).

Nielluin This name of the star Sirius is translated in the text (p. 182) as 'the Bee of Azure' (see *Ingil*). The first element is from the root NEHE, whence *nektë* 'honey', *nier* (< *neier* < *neχier*) 'honey-bee', *nierwes* 'hive'. The name of Sirius is given in QL as *Niellúnë* or *Nierninwa*; both *ninwa* and *lúnë* are Qenya words meaning 'blue'. In Gnomish the name of the star is *Niothluimi*, =Qenya *Nielluin*: *nio, nios* 'bee' and many related words, *luim* 'blue'.

Nienna In QL *Nyenna* the goddess is given under a root NYE(NE) 'bleat', whence *nyéni* 'she-goat', *nyéna-* 'lament', etc.; but there is a note 'or all to root NYEHE'. This means 'weep': *nië* 'tear' (cf. *Nieliqui*), *nyenyë* 'weeping'. In GL the forms of the name are *Nenni(r), Nenir, Ninir*, without etymological connections given, but cf. *nîn* 'tear'.

Noldoli The root NOL 'know' in QL has derivatives *Noldo* 'Gnome' and *Noldorinwa* adjective, *Noldomar* 'Gnomeland', and *Noldorin* 'who dwelt awhile in Noldomar and brought the Gnomes back to Inwenórë'. It seems that *Noldomar* means the Great Lands. But it is very curious that in these entries, which are among the earliest, 'Gnome' is an emendation of 'Goblin'; cf. the poem *Goblin Feet* (1915), and its Old English title *Cumaþ þá Nihtielfas* (p. 32).

In Gnomish 'Gnome' is *Golda* ('i.e. wise one'); *Goldothrim* 'the people of the Gnomes', *Goldogrin* their tongue, *Goldobar, Goldomar* 'Gnomeland'. The equivalent of *Noldorin* in GL is *Goldriel*, which was the form antecedent to *Golthadriel* in the text before both were struck out (p. 22). See *Nólemë*.

Noldorin   See *Noldoli*.

Nólemë   This is given in QL as a common noun, 'deep lore, wisdom' (see *Noldoli*). The Gnomish name of Finwë Nólemë, *Golfinweg* (p. 115), contains the same element, as must also the name *Fingolma* given to him in outlines for *Gilfanon's Tale* (pp. 238-9).

I Nori Landar   (On the 'World-Ship' drawing, probably meaning 'the Great Lands', pp. 84-5.) For *nori* see *Valinor*. Nothing similar to *landar* appears in QL; GL gives a word *land* (*lann*) 'broad'.

Nornorë   In QL this name has the form *Nornoros* 'herald of the Gods', and with the verb *nornoro-* 'run on, run smoothly' is derived from a root NORO 'run, ride, spin, etc.'. GL has similar words, *nor-* run', roll', *norn* 'wheel', *nûr* 'smooth, rolling free'. The name corresponding to Qenya *Nornorë* is here *Drondor* 'messenger of the Gods' (*drond* 'race, course, track' and *drô* 'wheel-track, rut'); *Drondor* was later changed to *Dronúrin* (< *Noronōr-*) and *drond* to *dronn*.

Númë   (On the 'World-Ship' drawing.) In QL *númë* 'West' is derived from root NUHU 'bow, bend down, stoop, sink'; other words are *núta-* 'stoop, sink', *númeta-*, *numenda-* 'get low (of the Sun)', *númëa* 'in the West'. Gnomish *num-* 'sink, descend', *númin* 'in the West', *Auranúmin* 'sunset', *numbros* 'incline, slope', *nunthi* 'downward'. Cf. *Falassë Númëa*, *Faskala-númen*, *Sirnúmen*.

Núri   Name of Fui Nienna: 'Núri who sighs', p. 66. This is given without translation in QL under root NURU, with *núru-* 'growl (of dogs), grumble', *nur* 'growl, complaint'. In Gnomish she is *Nurnil*, with associated words *nur-* 'growl, grumble', *nurn* 'lament', *nurna-* 'bewail, lament'.

Ô   (On the 'World-Ship' drawing: 'the Sea', pp. 84-5.) See *Ónen*.

Oarni   See *Ónen*.

Olofantur   See *Lórien*, *Fanturi*.

Olórë Mallë   For *Olórë* see *Lórien*. *mallë* 'street' appears in QL under root MALA 'crush' (see *Balrog*); the Gnomish form is *mal* 'paved way, road', and the equivalent of *Olórë Mallë* is *Malmaurien* (see *Murmuran*).

Ónen   The root 'o'o in QL has derivatives *Ô*, a poetic word, 'the sea', *oar* 'child of the sea, merchild', *oaris* (*-ts*), *oarwen* 'mermaid', and *Ossë*; the name *Ówen* (antecedent of *Ónen* in the text, pp. 61, 79) also appears, and evidently means the same as *oarwen* (for *-wen* see *Urwen*). The later form *Uinen* in the Tales is apparently Gnomish; GL *Únen* 'Lady of the Sea', changed later to *Uinen*. A form *Oinen* also occurs (p. 211).

In the Valar name-list *Ónen* is called also *Solórë* (see *Solosimpi*) and *Ui Oarista*. This latter appears in QL, with the definition 'Queen of the Mermaids', together with *Uin* 'the primeval whale'; but how these relate to the other names is obscure.

Orc QL *ork* (*orq-*) 'monster, demon'. GL *orc* 'goblin', plural *orcin*, *orchoth* (*hoth* 'folk, people', *hothri* 'army', *hothron* 'captain').

Oromë In QL *Oromë* 'son of Aulë' is placed under a root ORO that is distinct (apparently because of the nature of the consonant) from ORO (with meaning of 'steepness, rising') given under *Kalormë*; but these roots are said to be 'much confused'. This second root yields *órë* 'the dawn, Sunrise, East', *órëa* 'of the dawn, Eastern', *orontë*, *oronto* 'Sunrise', *osto* 'the gates of the Sun', and *Ostor* 'the East, the Sun when she issues from her white gates'. It is noted that *Oromë* should perhaps be placed under the other root, but there is no indication of the connections of the name. In *The Hiding of Valinor* (p. 214) Oromë has a particular knowledge of the East of the world. His name in Gnomish is *Orma*; and in the Valar name-list he is also called *Raustar*, for which see *Meássë*.

Oronto (On the 'World-Ship' drawing, 'East'.) See *Oromë*.

Orossi In the list of fays referred to under *Nandini* the *Orossi* are 'fays of the mountains', and this name is thus a derivative from the root ORO seen in *Kalormë*.

Ossë See *Ónen*. His Gnomish name is *Otha* or *Oth*.

Palisor See *Palúrien*.

Palúrien An early entry in QL gives *Palurin* 'the wide world' under a root PALA, whose derivatives have a common general sense of 'flatness', among them *palis* 'sward, lawn', whence no doubt *Palisor*. In GL the corresponding name is *Belaurin*, *B(a)laurin*; but she is also called *Bladorwen* 'the wide earth, the world and its plants and fruits, Mother Earth' (related words are *blant* 'flat, open, expansive, candid', *blath* 'floor', *bladwen* 'a plain'). See *Yavanna*.

Poldórëa Not in QL, but GL gives several corresponding forms: *Polodweg*=Tulcus (*polod* 'power, might, authority'); *polodrin* 'mighty', also in poetic form *Poldurin* or *Poldorin* which is especially used as epithet of Tulcus; Q. *Poldórëa*'.

Qalmë-Tári The root is QALA 'die', whence *qalmë* 'death', *qalin* 'dead', and other words of the same meaning. *Tári* is from TAHA: *tâ* 'high', *tára* 'lofty', *tári* 'queen', etc.; Gnomish *dâ* 'high', *dara* 'lofty', *daroth* 'summit, peak'. Cf. *Taniquetil*.

Qalvanda 'The Road of Death' (p. 213). See *Qalmë-Tári*. The second element is from root VAHA: whence *vâ* past tense 'went', *vand-* 'way, path', *vandl* 'staff', *vanwa* 'gone on the road, past, over, lost' (as in *Mar Vanwa Tyaliéva*). Cf. *Vansamírin*.

Qerkaringa The first element is obscure; for *-ringa* see *Ringil*.

Qorinómi See p. 227. The root is QORO/QOSO, whence *qoro-* 'choke, suffocate', *qorin* 'drowned, choked', etc.

Rána Not in QL, but GL has *Rân* 'the Moon (Q. *Rána*)' and *ranoth* 'month' (*Ranoth* was a rejected name preceding *Ranuin*, p. 222).

In the text (p. 192) it is said that the Gods named the Moon *Rána*.

Ranuin   See *Rána*.

Ringil   QL gives *ringa* 'damp, cold, chilly', *ringwë* 'rime, frost', *rin* 'dew'; GL *rî* 'coolness', *ring* 'cool, cold, a sudden breeze or cold breath', and (a later addition) *Ringli* 'the arctic colds, the North Pole (see the tale of the Coming of the Ainur)'. Cf. *Qerkaringa*.

Rúmil   This name is not found in either dictionary, but seems likely to be connected with words given in GL: *rû* and *rûm* 'secret, mystery', *ruim* 'secret, mysterious', *rui* 'whisper', *ruitha* 'to whisper'.

Salmar   This name must belong with derivatives of the root SALA: *salma* 'lyre', *salmë* 'harp-playing', etc.

Samírien   ('The Feast of Double Mirth', p. 143.) Presumably derived from the root MIRI 'smile'; *sa-* is referred to in QL as an 'intensive prefix'. Cf. *Vansamírin*.

Sári   Not in either dictionary, but in QL the root SAHA/SAHYA yields *sâ* 'fire', *saiwa* 'hot', *Sahóra* 'the South'; GL has *sâ* 'fire' (poetic form *sai*), *sairin* 'fiery', *saiwen* 'summer', and other words.

Sil   Under the root SILI QL gives a long list of words beginning with *Sil* 'Moon' and all with meanings of whiteness or white light, but neither *Silpion* nor *Silmaril* occurs in it. In GL *Sil* 'properly = "Rose of Silpion", see Tale of the Making of the Sun and Moon, but often used poetically = Whole Moon or Rân'. In this tale (p. 192) it is said that the fairies named the Moon 'Sil, the Rose' (earlier reading 'the silver rose').

Silindrin   The 'Moon-cauldron' does not appear in either dictionary; the nearest form is *Silindo* in QL, which is a name of Jupiter. See *Sil*.

Silmarilli   See *Sil*. In GL the equivalent of 'Q. *Silmaril*' is *silubrill-* (*silum(b)aril-*), plural *silubrilthin* (which occurs in the text, p. 128); a later addition compares *brithla* 'pearl', Qenya *marilla* (not in QL). The Tower of Pearl was named in Gnomish *Tirimbrithla*.

Silmo   See *Sil*. In QL *Silmo* is translated 'the Moon', and in GL *Silma* is given as the Gnomish equivalent of Qenya *Silmo*.

Silpion   See *Sil*. The Gnomish names are *Silpios* or *Piosil*, but no meaning is given.

Silubrilthin   See *Silmarilli*.

Sirion   QL root SIRI 'flow', with derivatives *sindi* 'river' (cf. *Kelusindi*), *sírë* 'stream', *sírima* 'liquid, flowing'. In GL are given *sîr* 'river', *siriol* 'flowing', and *Sirion* (poetic word) 'river, properly name of the famous magic river that flowed through Garlisgion and Nantathrin' (*Garlisgion* 'the Place of Reeds' survived in *Lisgardh* 'the land of reeds at the Mouths of Sirion', *Unfinished Tales* p. 34). Cf. *Sirnúmen*, and the name it replaced, *Numessir*.

Sirnúmen   See *Sirion, Númë*.

Solosimpi   QL gives *Solosimpë* 'the Shoreland Pipers', of which the first element is from root SOLO: *solmë* 'wave', *solor*, *solossë* 'surf, surge' (cf. *Solórë*, name of Ónen), and the second from SIPI 'whistle, pipe': *simpa*, *simpina* 'pipe, flute', *simpisë* 'piping', *simpetar* 'piper'. In GL the Gnomish name of the Solosimpi is *Thlossibin* or *Thlossibrim*, from *thloss* 'breaker', with a variant *Flossibrim*. The word *floss* is said to have been formed from *thloss* by influence of *flass* 'sea-marge, surf; margin, fringe'.

Sorontur Derived from a root SORO 'eagle': *sor*, *sornë* 'eagle', *sornion* 'eyrie', *Sorontur* 'King of Eagles'. For *-tur* see *Meril-i-Turinqi*. The Gnomish forms are *thorn* 'eagle', *thrond* '(eyrie), pinnacle', *Thorndor* and *Throndor* 'King of Eagles'.

Súlimo In QL under the three root-forms SUHYU, SUHU, SUFU 'air, breathe, exhale, puff' are given *sû* 'noise of wind', *súlimë* 'wind', and *Súlimi, -o* 'Vali of Wind = Manwë and Varda'. This probably means that Manwë was *Súlimo* and Varda *Súlimi*, since Varda is called *Súlimi* in the Valar name-list; but in GL it is said that Manwë and Varda were together called *i·Súlimi*. GL has *sû* 'noise of wind', *súltha* 'blow (of wind)', but Manwë's wind-name is *Saulmoth* (*saul* 'a great wind'), which is said to be an older form of later *Solmoth*; and this '= Q. *Súlimo*'.

In Gnomish he is also called *Gwanweg* (*gwâ* 'wind', *gwam* 'gust of wind'), often combined with *Man* (see *Manwë*) as *Man 'Wanweg* = Q. *Manwë Súlimo*. The root GWĀ appears in QL: *wâ* 'wind', *wanwa* 'great gale', *wanwavoitë* 'windy'; and in the Valar name-list Manwë and Varda are together called *Wanwavoisi*.

Súruli See *Súlimo*. *Súruli* is not in QL, but GL has *Sulus* (plurals *Sulussin* and *Suluthrim*) 'one of Manwë's two clans of air-spirits, Q. *Súru* plural *Súruli*'.

Talka Marda This title of Aulë, translated in the text (p. 180) as 'Smith of the World', is not found in QL, but GL gives '*Martaglos*, correctly *Maltagros*, title of Óla, Smith of the World' as the equivalent of Qenya *Talka Marwa*; also *tagros*, *taglos* 'smith'. He is also called *Óla Mar*; and in the Valar name-list *Aulë Mar*. (Long afterwards this title of Aulë reappeared. In a very late note he is given the name *mbartanō* 'world-artificer' > Quenya *Martamo*, Sindarin *Barthan*.)

Taniquetil Under the root TAHA (see *Qalmë-Tári*) *Taniqetil* is given in QL with the meaning 'lofty snowcap'. The second element is from root NIQI (*ninqë* 'white', *niqis* 'snow', *niqetil* 'snowcap'; cf. *nieninqë* 'white tear' (snowdrop) in entry *Nieliqui*).

The Gnomish form is *Danigwethil* (*dâ* 'high'), but the second element seems to be different, since GL gives a word *nigweth* 'storm (properly of snow, but that sense has evaporated)'.

Tanyasalpë Translated in the text 'the bowl of fire' (p. 187). *salpa* 'bowl' is given in QL under a root SLPL, with *sulp-* 'lick', *salpa* 'take a sup of', *sulpa* 'soup'. *Tanya* is not in QL; GL has *tan* 'firewood', *tantha*- 'kindle', *tang* 'flame, flash', and *Tanfa* 'the lowest of all airs, the hot air of the deep places'.

Tári-Laisi   For *Tári* see *Qalmë-Tári*. In QL the root LAYA 'be alive, flourish' has derivatives *lairë* 'meadow', *laiqa* 'green', *laito* and *laisi* both meaning 'youth, vigour, new life'. The Gnomish words are *laib* (also *glaib*) 'green', *laigos* 'greenness', =Q. *laiqassë*', *lair* (also *glair*) 'meadow'. The following note is of great interest: 'Note *Laigolas*=green-leaf [see *Gar Lossion*], becoming archaic because of final form becoming *laib*, gave *Legolast* i.e. keen-sight [*last* 'look, glance', *leg, lêg* 'keen, piercing']. But perhaps both were his names, as the Gnomes delighted to give two similar-sounding names of dissimilar meaning, as *Laigolas Legolast*, *Túrin Turambar*, etc. *Legolas* the ordinary form is a confusion of the two.' (Legolas Green-leaf appears in the tale of *The Fall of Gondolin*; he was an Elf of Gondolin, and being night-sighted he led the fugitives from the city over the plain in the dark. A note associated with the tale says that 'he liveth still in Tol Eressëa named by the Eldar there *Laiqalassë*'.)

Tarn Fui   See *Moritarnon, Fui*.

Tavari   In the list of fays referred to under *Nandini* the *Tavari* are 'fays of the woods'. In QL *tavar* (*tavarni*) 'dale-sprites' is derived from a root TAVA, whence also *tauno* 'forest', *taulë* 'great tree', *tavas* 'woodland'. GL has *tavor* 'a wood-fay', *taur, tavros* 'forest' (*Tavros* also a proper name, 'chief wood-fay, the Blue Spirit of the Woods'. Later, *Tavros* became a name of Oromë, leading through *Tauros* to the form *Tauron* in *The Silmarillion*).

Tavrobel   This is given in GL with the translation 'wood-home' (see *Tavari*). The element *pel* is said to be 'usual only in such place-names as *Tavrobel*', and means 'village, hamlet, -ham'. In a separate note elsewhere an additional Gnomish name *Tavrost* is given, and Qenya names *Tavaros(së)*, *Taurossë*. *Tavrost* evidently contains *rost* 'slope, hillside, ascent', with associated words *rosta* 'ascent' (*Rost'aura* 'Sunrise'), *ront* 'high, steep', ascribed to a stem *rō-, oro-*. These are etymological variants of words given under *Kalormë*.

Telelli   This term, which occurs once only in the Tales (p. 19), is obscure. In QL, in early entries, a complex of words is given all of which mean 'little elf': these include *Teler* and *Telellë*, and the adjectives *telerëa* and *telella*. There is no suggestion of any distinction between them. An isolated note states that young Elves of all clans who dwelt in Kôr to perfect their arts of singing and poetry were called *Telelli*; but in another place *Telellin*, a dialect, appears to be used instead of *Telerin*. See *Teleri*.

Teleri   See *Telelli*. In GL appears *Tilith* 'an elf, a member of the first of the three tribes of the fairies or Eldar; plural *Tilthin*'. The later meaning of *Teleri*, when it became the name of the Third Tribe, was already potentially present: QL gives a root TEL+U with derivatives *telu*- 'to finish, end', *telu* (noun), *telwa* 'last, late', with the suggestion that this was perhaps an extension of root TELE 'cover in' (see *Telimek-*

tar). In GL these meanings 'cover in – close – finish' are expressly assigned to the root TEL-: *telm* 'roof, sky', *teloth* 'roofing, canopy, shelter', *telu-* 'to close, end, finish', *telu* 'end'.

Telimektar   In QL *Telimektar*, *Telimbektar* is glossed 'Orion, literally Swordsman of Heaven', and is given under the root TELE 'cover in', together with *tel* 'roof', *telda* 'having a roof', *telimbo* 'canopy; sky', etc. *-mektar* probably derives from the root MAKA, see *Makar*. The Gnomish form is *Telumaithar*.

In the Valar name-list he is called also *Taimondo*. There are substantial notes on this name in both dictionaries, which appear to have been entered at the same time. In QL *Taimondo* and *Taimordo*, names of Telimektar, together with *Taimë*, *Taimië* 'the sky', were entered under the root TAHA (see *Qalmë-Tári*). The Gnomish equivalent is *Daimord* (*dai*, *daimoth* 'sky, heaven'), who appears also in the GL entry concerning Inwë's son Ingil (Gil, Sirius): he rose into the heavens in the likeness of a great bee and 'followed Daimord' (see *Ingil*). But the word *mordo* 'warrior, hero' in Qenya was actually a borrowing from Gnomish *mord*, and the true Quenya equivalent of *mord* was *mavar* 'shepherd' – this being the original meaning of the Gnomish word also, which developed that of 'man, warrior' through its use in poetry after it had become obsolete in prose and speech. Thus *Daimord* originally meant 'Shepherd of the Sky', as did the original Qenya name *Taimavar*, altered under the influence of the Gnomish name to *Taimondo*, *Taimordo*.

Telimpë   Not in QL under root TELPE, which has however *telempë*= *telpë* 'silver'. Gnomish words are *celeb* 'silver', *celebrin* 'of silver', *Celebron*, *Celioth* names of the Moon. See *Ilsaluntë*.

Tevildo   Given in QL under root TEFE (with derivatives *teve-* 'to hate', *tevin*, *tevië* 'hatred') and explained as 'the Lord of Cats' (see p. 47). The Gnomish form is *Tifil*, 'Prince of Cats'.

Tilkal   A name made up of the initial sounds of six names of metals (see p. 100 and footnote). For *tambë* 'copper' see *Aulë*, and for *ilsa* 'silver' see *Ilsaluntë*. *Latúken* 'tin' is given as a separate entry in QL, with *latukenda* 'of tin'; the Gnomish form is *ladog*. *Kanu* 'lead', *kanuva* 'leaden' are placed under a root KANA in QL. For *anga* 'iron' see *Angamandi*, and for *laurë* 'gold' see *Laurelin*.

Timpinen   The name stands in QL as the only derivative of a root TIFI, but under root TIPI are given *timpë* 'fine rain', *timpinë* 'spray', etc. See *Tinfang*.

Tinfang   The entry in GL is: '*Tinfing* or *Tinfang* the fluter (surnamed *Gwarbilin* or Birdward), a fay; cf. Q. *timpinen* a fluter (*Timpando*, *Varavilindo*)'. Other Gnomish words are *tif-* 'whistle', *timpa-* 'ring, jingle', *timpi* 'little bell', *timp* 'hoot, note of a flute', *tifin* 'small flute'. The first element in *Gwarbilin* is seen also in *Amon Gwareth* 'Hill of Watch', which occurs in the tale of *The Fall of Gondolin*; the second is *bilin*(*c*) 'sparrow, small bird'.

Tinwë Linto, Tinwelint ` GL has: '*Tinweg* (also *Lintinweg*) and more usually *Tinwelint*, =Q. *Tinwë Linto*; originally leader of the Solosimpi (after led by Ellu), but became King of the Lost Elves of Artanor'. The first element of the name is derived from TIN-, with such derivatives as *tim* 'spark, gleam, (star)', *tintiltha-* 'twinkle', *tinwithli* 'star-cluster, constellation'. The second element is possibly Gnomish *lint* 'quick, nimble, light' – which my father referred to in his essay 'A Secret Vice' (*The Monsters and the Critics and Other Essays*, 1983, p. 205) as a word he remembered from a very early stage of his linguistic constructions. The name is not in QL either in the earlier form (*Linwë Tinto*, p. 130) or the later, but under root TINI are *tinwë* 'star', *tint* '(silver) spark', etc., and also *lintitinwë* 'having many stars', the first element of this being a multiplicative prefix *li-*, *lin-*. Cf. *Tinwetári*.

Tinwetári 'Queen of Stars'. For the elements of this name see *Tinwë Linto*, *Qalmë-Tári*. The corresponding Gnomish name is *Tinturwin* with a different second element (see *Meril-i-Turinqi*). Varda is also called *Timbridhil*, *Timfiril*, with the same first element (*Bridhil* being the Gnomish name of Varda), and *Gailbridh(n)ir*, which contains *gail* 'star' (corresponding to Qenya *ilë* in *Ílivarda*, not found in QL).

Tol Eressëa Under root TOLO QL has derivatives *tol* 'island; any rise standing alone in water, plain of green, etc.', *tolmen* 'boss (of shield), isolated round hill, etc.', *tolos* 'knob, lump', *tólë* 'centre', and other words. GL gives *tol* 'an isle with high steep coasts'.

Eressëa is given in QL under root ERE (distinct from that seen in *Eruman*) 'remain alone': *er* 'only, but, still', *eressë* 'singly, only, alone', *eressëa* 'lonely', *erda* 'solitary, deserted', *erin* 'remains'. In Gnomish the Lonely Isle is *Tol Erethrin* (*er* 'one', *ereth* 'solitude', *erethrin* 'solitary, lonely', etc.)

Tolli Kuruvar (On the 'World-Ship' drawing, 'the Magic Isles', pp. 84–5.) For *Tolli* see *Tol Eressëa*. QL has a group *kuru* 'magic, wizardry', *kuruvar* 'wizard', *kuruni* 'witch', with a note: 'of the good magic'. GL has *curu* 'magic', *curug* 'wizard', *curus* 'witch'.

Tombo *Tombo* 'gong' is derived in QL from a root TUMU 'swell (with idea of hollowness)', together with *tumbë* 'trumpet', *tumbo* 'dark vale', *tumna* 'deep, profound, dark or hidden' (see *Utumna*). Words in Gnomish are *tûm* 'valley', *tum* 'hollow', *tumli* 'dale', *tumbol* 'valley-like, hollow', *tumla-* 'hollow out'.

Tuilérë QL root TUYU: *tuilë* 'Spring, literally a budding – also collectively: buds, new shoots, fresh green', *Tuilérë* 'Spring', and several other words, as *tuilindo* '(spring-singer), swallow'. Gnomish forms are *tuil*, *tuilir* 'Spring' (with the note that *Tuilir*=Vána); but Vána is also called *Hairen* 'Spring', presumably connected with *hair* 'punctual, timely', *hai* 'punctually', *haidri* 'forenoon'.

Tuivána See *Tuilérë*, *Vána*.

tulielto, &c.   *Tulielto* is translated 'they have come' (p. 114), and *I·Eldar tulier* 'the Eldar have come' (*ibid.*); *I·kal'antúlien* is translated 'Light hath returned' (p. 184). QL under root TULU 'fetch, bring, bear; move, come' has the verb *tulu-* of the same meaning, also *tulwë* 'pillar, standard, pole', *tulma* 'bier'. GL has *tul-* 'bring; come', *tultha-* 'lift, carry'.

Tulkas   QL gives the name under root TULUK, with *tulunka* 'steady, firm', *tulka-* 'fix, set up, establish'. The Gnomish form is *Tulcus* (*-os*), with related words *tulug* 'steady, firm', *tulga-* 'make firm, settle, steady, comfort'.

Tulkastor   The name does not appear in the dictionaries (nor the precedent forms, *Tulkassë*, *Turenbor*, p. 22); see *Tulkas*, *Meril-i-Turinqi*.

Tuor   *Tuor* is not given in the dictionaries, but it is probably derived (since the name is also written *Tûr*) from the root TURU 'be strong'; see *Meril-i-Turinqi*.

Turgon   Neither *Turondo* nor Gnomish *Turgon* are given in the dictionaries, and beyond the likelihood that the first element is from the root TURU (see *Meril-i-Turinqi*) these names cannot be explained.

Turuhalmë   'The Logdrawing' (p. 229). A second root TURU (TUSO) 'kindle' in QL (differing in the medial consonant from TURU 'be strong') has many derivatives: *turu-*, *tunda-* 'kindle', *turu* 'properly = firewood, but used of wood in general', *turúva* 'wooden', *tusturë* 'tinder', etc. In GL are *duru* 'wood: pole, beam, or log', *durog* 'wooden'.

The second element is in Gnomish *halm* 'drawing, draught (of fishes etc.)'. The name of the festival is *Duruchalmo(s) = Halm na-dhuruthon* (*Duruchalm* was written in the text and struck out, p. 244), translated 'Yule'; this was changed later to *Durufui* 'Yule (night), i.e. Log-night' (see *Fui*).

Uin   See *Ónen*. In GL *uin* is a common noun, 'whale', named after *Uin* 'Gulma's great whale' (*Gulma = Ulmo*); but apparently (though this entry is rather obscure) the original meaning of *uin*, preserved in poetry, was 'wave'. Another Gnomish word for 'whale' is *uimoth* 'sheep of the waves' (*moth* 'sheep', also '1000', probably originally 'flock'; *mothweg* 'shepherd').

Uinen   See *Ónen*.

Ulmo   *Ulmo* is given in QL under the root ULU 'pour, flow fast', together with *ulu-* and *ulto-* 'pour', in transitive and intransitive senses. His name in Gnomish is *Gulma*, with corresponding verbs *gul-* and *gulta-*. In the draft text of *The Music of the Ainur* he is also called *Linqil*: see *Nieliqui*. For other names see *Vailimo*.

Ulmonan   See *Ulmo*; the second element of this name is not explained.

Ungoliont   See *Ungwë Lianti*.

Ungwë Lianti, Ungweliant(ë)   Under a queried root GUNGU QL gives *ungwë* 'spider, especially *Ungwë* the Gloomweaver, usually *Ungwe-lianti*'. The second element is from root LI+*ya* 'entwine', with derivatives *lia* 'twine', *liantë* 'tendril', *liantassë* 'vine'. In GL the name as originally entered was *Gungliont*, as also first written in the text (p. 156); later this was changed to '*Ungweliont* or *Ungoliont*'. The second element is assigned to root *lī-* (*lind* 'twine').

Uolë Kúvion *Kúvion* was changed from *Mikúmi* (p. 198). The name is not in QL under the root KUVU 'bend, bow', which has derivatives *kú* 'crescent Moon', *kúnë* 'crescent, bow'. GL gives *cû* 'bow, crescent; the waxing or waning Moon', and also '*Cuvonweg: Ûl Cuvonweg* (=Q. *Ólë Kúmion*), the Moonking'. Under *Ûl* the Qenya equivalent is however *Uolë*, and here it is said that the name *Ûl* is usually in the phrase *Ûl·a·Rinthilios*; while *Rinthilios* is glossed 'the orbed Moon, name of the Moon-elf' (*rinc* 'circular', noun 'disc'; *rin-* 'revolve, return').

Ûr The root URU/USU in QL has derivatives *uru* 'fire', *úrin* 'blazing hot', *uruvoitë* 'fiery', *urúva* 'like fire', *urwa* 'on fire', *Ûr* 'the Sun' (with other forms *Úri*, *Úrinki*, *Urwen*), *Úrion* 'a name of Fionwë', *urna* 'oven', *usta-*, *urya-* 'burn' (transitive and intransitive). The Gnomish form is *Aur* (*aurost* 'dawn'), and also a poetic word *Uril*. See *Fionwë-Úrion*, *Urwen*.

Urwen, Urwendi In the earlier tales in this book the form is *Urwen*, becoming *Urwendi* in the *Tale of the Sun and Moon*. The original entry in GL was '*Urwendi* and *Urwin* (Q. *Urwen*) the maiden of the Sun-ship', but this was later changed to read '*Urwedhin* and *Urwin* (Q. *Urwendi*)'. In QL (see *Ûr*) *Urwen* appears as a name of the Sun. In the Valar name-list the Sun-maiden is also called *Úrinki*, and this also appears in QL as a name of the Sun.

The element *-wen* is given in QL under root GWENE: *wen* and *wendi* 'maid, girl', *-wen* feminine patronymic, like masculine *-ion*, *wendelë* 'maidenhood' (see *Wendelin*). In GL the forms were much changed and confused. The words given have stems in *gwin-*, *gwen-*, *gweth*, with meanings 'woman', 'girl', etc.; the root seems to have been changed from *gweni-* to *gwedhe-*, with reference both to Qenya *meril* (see *Meril-i-Turinqi*) and Qenya *wendi*.

Utumna In QL the root of *Utumna* ('lower regions of gloom and darkness in the North, Melko's first dwelling') is not given, but cf. the word *tumna* 'deep, profound, dark or hidden' cited under *Tombo*. In Gnomish the forms are *Udum* and *Uduvna*; Belcha (Melko) is called *Uduvrin*.

Úvanimor See *Vána*.

Vai The root VAYA 'enfold' in QL yields *Vai* 'the Outer Ocean', *Vaimo* or *Vailimo* 'Ulmo as Ruler of Vai', *vaima* 'robe', *vainë* 'sheath', *vainolë* 'quiver', *vaita-* 'to wrap', *Vaitya* 'the outermost airs beyond the world', etc. In Gnomish the form is *Bai*, with related words

Baithon 'the outer airs', *baith* 'garment', *baidha* 'to clothe', *bain* 'clad (Q. *vaina*)'.

Vailimo   See *Vai*. In Gnomish the form is *Belmoth* (< *Bailmoth*); there is also a poetic name *Bairos*. Ulmo is also called in Gnomish *i Chorweg a·Vai*, i.e. 'the old one of Vai' (*hôr* 'old, ancient (only of things still existing)', *hortha-* 'grow old', *horoth* 'old age', *Hôs* 'old age', a name of Fuil). For *-weg* see *Bronweg*.

Vaitya   See *Vai*.

Valahíru   (Marginal addition in the text against *Valatúru*, p. 180.) Not in the dictionaries, but probably to be associated with QL root HERE 'rule, have power': *heru-* 'to rule', *heru* 'lord', *heri* 'lady', *hérë* 'lordship'.

Valar   In QL '*Valar* or *Vali*' is derived from root VALA, with masc. singular *Valon* or *Valmo* and fem. singular *Valis* or *Valdë*; other words are *valin*, *valimo* 'happy', *vald-* 'blessedness, happiness'.

The Gnomish words are complicated and curious. As first written, there was *Ban* 'a god, one of the great Valar', plural *Banin*, and '*Dor'Vanion=Dor Banion=Gwalien* (or *Valinor*)'. All this was struck out. Elsewhere in GL is given the root GWAL 'fortune, happiness': *Gwala* 'one of the gods, including their divine folk and children, hence often used of one of the lesser folk as opposed to *Ban*'; *Gwalon* and *Gwalthi* corresponding to Qenya *Valon*, *Valsi*; *gwalt* 'good luck – any providential occurrence or thought: "the luck of the Valar", *i·walt ne Vanion* (Q. *valto*)'; and other abstract words, as *gwalweth* 'fortune, happiness'. Of the later interpretation of *Valar* there is thus no suggestion. See further under *Vána*.

Valatúru   See *Valar*, *Meril-i-Turinqi*.

Valinor   In QL two forms are given, *Valinor* and *Valinórë* (the latter also occurs in the text, p. 182), both glossed 'Asgard' (i.e. the City of the Gods in Norse mythology). For the Gnomish names (*Gwalien*, etc.) see *Valar*.

nórë is found in QL under the root NŌ 'become, be born', and is glossed 'native land, nation, family, country', also *-nor*, 'the form in compounds'. Other words are *nosta-* 'give birth', *nosta* 'birth, birthday', *nostalë* 'species, kind', *nossë* 'kin, people' (as in *Aulenossë*). The Gnomish form is *dôr*: see *Dor Faidwen*.

Valmar   See *Valar*, *Eldamar*.

Vána   A derivative of QL root VANA, together with *vanë* 'fair', *vanessë* 'beauty', *vanima* 'proper, right, fair', *úvanimo* 'monster' (*ú-*='not'), etc. Here also are given *Vanar* and *Vani=Valar*, *Vali*, with the note: 'cf. Gnomish *Ban-*'. See *Valar*.

Vána's name in Gnomish was *Gwân* or *Gwani* (changed later to *Gwann* or *Gwannuin*); *gwant*, *gwandra* 'beautiful', *gwanthi* 'beauty'.

Vána-Laisi   See Vána, Tári-Laisi.

Vansamírin   This name replaced *Samírien's road* in the text (p. 222). See *Qalvanda*, *Samírien*.

Varda   In QL the name is given with *vard-* 'rule, govern', *vardar* 'king', *varni* 'queen'. In Gnomish *Varda* was called *Bridhil* (and *Timbridhil*, see *Tinwetári*), which is cognate with Qenya *vard-*.

Vê   QL gives *Vê* 'name of Fantur' under root VEHE, but without meaning ascribed or other derivatives. The form in GL is *Gwê*, changed to *Gwî*: 'name of the hall of Bandoth, Q. *Vê*'. See *Mandos, Vefántur*.

Vefántur   In GL the Vala himself is called *Bandoth Gwê* (changed to *Bannoth Gwî*), *Gwefantur* (changed to *Gwifanthor*), and *Gwivannoth*.

Vene Kemen   See *Glorvent, Kémi*.

Vilna   In QL the root VILI (without meaning given) has derivatives *Vilna* (changed later to *Vilya*) '(lower) air', *Vilmar* 'dwelling of Manwë – the upper airs (but not *ilu*)', *vilin* 'airy, breezy', *vílë* 'gentle breeze'. The words 'but not *ilu*' refer to the definition of *ilu* in the sense of *ilwë*, the middle air among the stars (see *ilwë*). Manwë's dwelling *Vilmar* is not named elsewhere.

The Gnomish names for the lowest air were *Gwilfa* or *Fâ*; the latter is said to be of unknown etymology. The corresponding Qenya names are given in GL as *Fâ* and *Favilna*, and these appear in QL under a root FAGA without translation, merely as equivalents of *Vilna*. Other Gnomish words are *gwil-* 'sail, float, fly', *gwilith* 'breeze', *gwilbrin* 'butterfly': these correspond to words in QL under a root GWILI, *wili-* 'sail, float, fly', *wilin* 'bird', *wilwarin* 'butterfly'. Another name of Manweg as Lord of the Winds, *Famfir*, is given in GL.

Voronwë   See *Bronweg*.

Vorotemnar   For *voro* 'ever' see *Bronweg*. *Temnar* must be from root TEME 'tie', of which no derivative words are listed in QL.

Wendelin   This is not in QL, but GL gives *Gwendeling* (changed later to *Gwedhiling*) as the Gnomish name corresponding to Qenya *Wendelin*; 'Queen of the Woodland Elves, mother of Tinúviel' (the only occurrence of the name *Tinúviel* in the dictionaries). The name must be related to Qenya *wen* 'maid, girl' and the Gnomish forms given under *Urwen*.

Wingildi   See *Wingilot*.

Wingilot   Under the root GWINGI/GWIGI in QL are *wingë* 'foam, spindrift', *wingilot* 'foamflower, Eärendel's boat', and *wingild-* 'nymph' (cf. *Wingildi*). For the element *-lot* see *Lindelos*.

GL has the entry: '*Gwingalos* or *Gwingli*=*Lothwinga* or Foamflower, the name of Eärendel's (Ioringli's) boat'; also *lothwing* 'foamflower', *gwing* 'wavecrest, foam', and *gwingil* 'foam-maiden (mermaid, one of the attendants of Uinen)'.

Wirilómë   See *Gwerlum*.

Wiruin   See *Gwerlum*.

Yavanna   In QL this name is given under the root YAVA, together with *yavin* 'bears fruit', *yáva* 'fruit', *yávan* 'harvest, autumn'. The Gnomish form is *Ifon, Ivon*, 'especially in the combinations *Ivon Belaurin, Ivon Címir, Ivon i·Vladorwen*'; see *Kémi, Palúrien*.

SHORT GLOSSARY OF OBSOLETE, ARCHAIC, AND RARE WORDS

an   if, 64, 140, 149, 155, 165, 180, 182, 189, 197, 208

arrassed   covered with arras (rich figured tapestry), 17

astonied   stunned, astonished, 116, 185

bason   formerly a common spelling of *basin*, 164 etc.

bent   open place covered with grass, 34

brakes   thickets, 106

charger   large dish, 191

clamant   clamorous, noisy, 43

clomb   old past tense of *climb*, 122

constellate   formed into a constellation, 195

cools   coolnesses, 74

corbel   basket, 186

covetice   (inordinate) desire, 117; covetousness, 146–7

eld   old age, 59, 219, 228

fain   gladly, 45, 150; disposed, desirous, 195; **fain of** well-pleased with, 117, 208

fane   temple, 39, 43

fey   37. The old senses were 'fated, approaching death; presaging death'. It seems very unlikely that the later sense 'possessing or displaying magical, fairylike, or unearthly qualities' (O.E.D. Supplement) was intended.

flittermice   bats, 40

go   move, in the phrase *all the creatures that go* 219

houseleek   a fleshy plant that grows on the walls and roofs of houses, 95

inaureoled   surrounded with a halo, 204 (the word is only recorded in the O.E.D. in a poem by Francis Thompson, 1897).

jacinth   blue, 34

lampads   35. The word is only recorded in the O.E.D. (first used by Coleridge) of the seven lamps of fire burning before the throne of God in the Book of Revelation, iv.5.

lets upon   gives on to, opens on to, 210

lief   gladly, willingly, 163; **liever** more gladly, more willingly, rather, 105, 163

lustihead   vigour, 99

meed   requital, 105

minished   reduced, diminished, 150, 208

or . . . or   either . . . or, 127, 214

or yet   apparently means 'already', 166

ousel   blackbird, 47 (now spelt *ouzel*, in *Ring-ouzel* and other bird-names).

pleasance 'A pleasure-ground, usually attached to a mansion; sometimes a secluded part of a garden, but more often a separate enclosure laid out with shady walks, trees and shrubs . . .' (O.E.D.) This sense is present in *pleasa(u)nces* 74, 116, but in *rest and pleasance* 69 the sense is 'enjoyment, pleasure'; in *nor did he have lack of pleasance* 65 either meaning may be intended, but I think probably the former.

pled old past tense of *plead*, 167

plenilune the time of full moon, 205 (see *Letters* p. 310).

pricks (spurs his horse), rides fast, 114. *Oromë pricks over the plain* echoes the first line of *The Faerie Queene*, *A Gentle Knight was pricking on the plaine*.

recked troubled, cared, 179

rede counsel, advice, 141, 182, 217; plan, 180; **redes** counsels, 117

rondured (in **golden-rondured**) 35. *Rondure* 'circle, rounded form'; *rondured* is not recorded.

ruth matter of sorrow, calamity, 185; distress, grief, 191; remorse, 194; in *the greatest ruth was that to* [*the Valar*] *thereafter* 209 the sense is unclear: 'matter of sorrow or regret', or possibly 'harm, ill'.

saps deep diggings, 104

sate old past tense of *sit*, 58, 105, 153, 181, 190, 194

seamews seagulls, 124

selenites inhabitants of the Moon, 205

shallop 192. This word had precise applications to particular kinds of boat, but here apparently means 'open boat propelled by oars and sail'.

share 34, 38. *share*=ploughshare, but used here of the blade of a scythe.

sledge-blows blows as of a *sledge*, a large heavy hammer, 78

sprent past participle of the lost verb *sprenge* 'sprinkle, scatter', 192

sprite(s) spirit(s), 71, 74, 95, 115, 191

suaded persuaded, 69, 163

trillups 108, **trillaping** 109. This word is not recorded in any dictionary available to me.

umbraged (in **wide-umbraged**) 34, 38. *Umbraged* 'shaded, shadowed', but here in the sense 'shadowing', 'casting a shade'.

web(s) woven fabric, 58, 73, 95 (also used in senses 'webbed feet' 127, 'cobwebs' 77, etc.)

whickering 205 (*whickering sparks*). The verb *whicker* meant to laugh or titter, or of a horse to whinny, but the O.E.D. cites a line from Masefield *the wall-top grasses whickered in the breeze*, and the 1920 Supplement to the Dictionary gives a meaning 'to make a hurtling sound', with a single citation where the word is used of a thunderbolt *whickering* through the sky. In the 1962 version of *The Man in the Moon* the word *flickering* occurs in this verse.

whitethorn hawthorn, 76

wildered perplexed, bewildered, 163-4, 178, 231

wrack devastation, ruin, 177 (cf. (*w*)*rack and ruin*).

INDEX

This index provides (in intention) complete page-references to all entries with the exception of *Eldar/Elves*, *Gods/Valar*, and *Valinor*; the entries include the rejected name-forms given in the Notes, but the Appendix on Names is not covered.

Occasionally references are given to pages where a person or place is not actually named, as 'the door-ward' p. 46 under *Rúmil*. References are given to mentions of Tales that will appear in Part II, but not to mentions of those in this book. The explanatory statements are kept very brief, and names defined in the Index to *The Silmarillion* are not as a rule explained here.

Eönwë   Herald of Manwë. 63, 93

Ered Wethrin   The Mountains of Shadow. 112, 158, 242

Erinti   Daughter of Manwë and Varda. 58, 62, 202

Eriol   14–18, 20, 22–7, 32, 45–51, 63–5, 78, 94–8, 107, 112–13, 129, 140, 164, 166, 169, 174–5, 189, 195–7, 202–3, 225, 230, 234–5; *Eriollo* 24. For his name and history see especially 23–4; and see *Ælfwine*.

Ermon   One of the two first Men (with Elmir), 236–7, 239, 243, 245; *people, folk, sons, of Ermon* 237–8, 240

Eru   173

Eruman   Name interchangeable with *Arvalin*, q.v.; (originally) the region east of the Mountains of Valinor and south of Taniquetil (see especially 82–3, 91–3). 68, 70, 79, 82–3, 87, 91–3, 145, 151–2, 155, 157–8, 209; *Erumáni* 70, 79, 91, 125, 131, 149, 179, 188, 196, 200. (Earlier names of the region: *Habbanan, Harwalin, Harvalien, Harmalin.*)

Estë   88, 201

Evromord   Door-ward of Mar Vanwa Tyaliéva (apparently intended to replace Rúmil). 107

Faëry   129; *Faery Realms* 33, 36, 39. See *Bay of Faëry*.

Fairies   19, 22–3, 25–6, 32, 34–6, 51, 59, 110, 166, 175, 192, 196, 212, 228, 230, 232, 235, 237, 244; *lost fairies* 231, 235; *false-fairies*, see *Kaukareldar*; *fairy speech* 13, 51

Fairyland   110

Falas   134

Falassë Númëa   'Western Surf', on the shores of Tol Eressëa. 124

Falman-Ossë   See *Ossë*.

Falmarini   Spirits of the sea-foam. 66

Fangli   Earlier name of Fankil. 236–7. See *Fúkil*.

Fankil   Servant of Melko. 107, 237. (Replaced *Fangli/Fúkil*.)

Fantur   (Plural *Fánturi*.) The Valar Vefántur Mandos and Lórien Olofántur. 79, 89, 101; later form *Fëanturi* 79–80

Fanuin   'Year', child of Aluin 'Time'. 217–19, 222, 227. (Replaced *Lathos, Lathweg*.)

Faring Forth   17, 19, 25–7, 97–8

Faskala-númen   'Bath of the Setting Sun'. 187; *Faskalan* 187, 192, 215. See *Tanyasalpë*.

Fay(s)   94, 108, 120, 132, 215, 232, 234, 236–7, 239

Fëanor   128, 138, 141, 145–6, 149–51, 155–60, 162, 165, 168–9, 171, 173, 175, 181, 192, 198, 238, 240–3; *Sons of Fëanor* 192, 197, 238–43; Oath of Fëanor or of his sons 171, 238, 240, 243

Fëanorians   158, 173, 242–3

Fëanturi   See *Fantur*.

Feast of Reunion   240, 243. *Feast of Reuniting*, see *Mereth Aderthad*.

Finarfin   44, 171, 173, 223

Fingolfin   87, 132, 156, 173, 243

Fingolma   Name of Finwë Nólemë. 238–9

4/97

7-96

TOL

Tolkien, J. R. R.

The book of lost tales *part 1*

DATE			

© THE BAKER & TAYLOR CO.